"With this book, author Lynn Blackburn has moved from the status of an up-and-coming author to watch and cemented herself as an author to note. Her exceptional storytelling skills shine as she weaves an intricate plot, populated with characters we care deeply about. Another up-all-night-because-I-can't-put-down-the-book read."

—**Edie Melson**, award-winning author, blogger, and director of the Blue Ridge Mountains Christian Writers Conference

"*Beneath the Surface* is a swoon-worthy romantic suspense that packs a punch from page one. The nonstop action will keep you guessing until the end."

—**Rachel Dylan**, author of the Atlanta Justice series

"Just when you think you can relax, Blackburn brings you back to the edge of your seat in this riveting, high-tension suspense story."

—**Patricia Bradley**, author of *Justice Delayed*

BENEATH THE SURFACE

STIGATIONS

BENEATH THE SURFACE

LYNN H. BLACKBURN

Revell
a division of Baker Publishing Group
Grand Rapids, Michigan

Published by Revell
a division of Baker Publishing Group
PO Box 6287, Grand Rapids, MI 49516-6287
www.revellbooks.com

Printed in the United States of America

Library of Congress Cataloging-in-Publication Data
Names: Blackburn, Lynn Huggins, author.
Title: Beneath the surface / Lynn H. Blackburn.
Description: Grand Rapids, MI : Revell, a division of Baker Publishing Group, [2018] | Series: Dive team investigations ; 1
Identifiers: LCCN 2017044855 | ISBN 9780800729387 (softcover)
Subjects: LCSH: Serial murder investigation—Fiction. | GSAFD: Romantic suspense fiction. | Christian fiction. | Mystery fiction. | Love stories.
Classification: LCC PS3602.L325285 B46 2018 | DDC 813/.6—dc23
LC record available at https://lccn.loc.gov/2017044855

This book is a work of fiction. Names, characters, places, and incidents are the product of the author's imagination or are used fictitiously.

18 19 20 21 22 23 24 7 6 5 4 3 2 1

To James—my favorite brown-eyed boy. I'm cherishing every day I have with you. You're compassionate, conscientious, and loyal, and I adore you. You make me proud every day, and I'm so thankful I get to have a front-row seat to watch the story God has for you unfold. I love you!

Acknowledgments

Special thanks go to Jennifer Huggins Bayne—my sister and favorite nurse practitioner and the inspiration for Leigh in so many ways. Leigh has your name. Your compassion. Your fierce drive to protect and advocate for patients. Your strength. Your stubbornness. I hope she makes you proud. None of the medical scenes in this book would have been even close to accurate without your input and expertise. Thank you for replying to hundreds of texts about drugs and nurses and hospital procedures. I'm so lucky to have you as my sister and my friend.

Angel Glover—for sharing your experiences and helping me find a layer of complexity that Leigh was missing before your input.

Sergeant Chris Hammett—for your insights into the life of a homicide investigator. Thank you for the hours you spent explaining police procedures and giving me real-world examples of what it's like to do this day in and day out. Ryan, Gabe, and Anissa are each carrying parts of your story with them.

Mike Berry, Master Underwater Criminal Investigator (UCIDiver .com)—for answering my many questions about general dive team procedures and the specific approach the Carrington divers use in the first scene. Thank you for your willingness to share your personal experiences with recovering bodies—and their condition after being in the water. Any mistakes in diving and underwater criminal investigation procedures are mine.

Investigator Tim Martin—for explaining the world of white-collar criminal investigations to me and for helping me bring Adam to life in a realistic way.

Daniel Fetterolf—for being willing to help me find the sources I needed to make this story a reality.

Keith and Beth Beutler—for helping me understand the best way to sabotage someone's brakes. ☺

Josh Moulin, cybersecurity expert (https://JoshMoulin.com)—for helping me understand how unrealistic my original version of Sabrina was and for helping me turn her into a more credible character even though my personal knowledge of cybersecurity and computer forensics is minimal. All mistakes and misrepresentations of the field are on me.

My critique group—for helping me brainstorm this series. The storylines and characters are all richer because of you.

My sisters of The Light Brigade—you've been there for me from the beginning. Your prayers, love, and support are never more than a Facebook message away, and I am eternally grateful for you.

Lynette Eason—for believing in me and mentoring me on this journey. I can't imagine how I could do this without you!

Tamela Hancock Murray—the world's most patient and understanding agent. Thank you for your guidance, encouragement, and wisdom.

Andrea Doering—for giving me the chance to write this series.

Sandra Blackburn—for being the most supportive mother-in-law a girl could have and for being willing to do anything to help.

Ken and Susan Huggins—for being the kind of parents who taught me to work hard and love books and for still being there for me whenever I need you. Which is all the time!

Emma, James, and Drew—for being excited about every new book and for keeping my real world far more interesting than any I could make up.

Brian—without you there would be no stories with my name on them. My imagination never would have taken flight without your encouragement and your continual support and love.

My Savior—the Ultimate Storyteller—for allowing me to write stories for you.

> Let the words of my mouth and the meditation of my heart be acceptable in your sight, O Lord, my rock and my redeemer.
>
> ~ Psalm 19:14

1

Homicide investigator Ryan Parker flashed a thumbs-up to his dive buddy and fellow homicide investigator, Gabe Chavez.

Gabe responded in kind and they began a slow descent to the bottom of Lake Porter. He kept his breathing slow and steady. Unlike some people who experienced claustrophobia when diving, Ryan loved being surrounded by water. He paused to equalize the pressure in his ears and made sure Gabe did the same.

It had been too long since Ryan had been under. Too long since he'd been able to drown out the world and all its distractions. Beneath the surface, his focus was undivided. No phones rang. No sirens squawked. No tears dripped onto his shoulder from faces too small to be dealing with deserting, good-for-nothing . . .

No. He wouldn't go there.

Not today.

A fish darted past his arm. Then another.

Not everyone got to spend their day off floating around a real-life aquarium. Technically, he wasn't off work. He was on call until Monday morning, but he couldn't resist the chance to get a dive in. Most of the crazy stuff happened in the middle of the night anyway. This was about as relaxing as an on-call Saturday could get, even if they were on a training exercise.

"You guys are awfully quiet. You doing okay?" The voice of homicide investigator Anissa Bell interrupted his thoughts. Anissa took her role as Carrington County Sheriff's Office dive team captain seriously, and he appreciated the state-of-the-art equipment she'd managed to obtain, but he didn't love the chatter messing with his peaceful descent.

"We're good," he said.

"Just keeping it old school," Gabe said with a laugh.

Anissa didn't laugh at Gabe's joke. Those two needed to resolve their differences, but for now, not even Anissa's animosity toward Gabe could mar the perfection of being underwater.

"What's the visibility like?"

"Pretty bad," he said. "I can only see a few feet, and that's with the light."

"Perfect."

Only Anissa would be thrilled with less-than-optimal conditions. He could picture her hazel eyes flashing with delight. She might even smile. Or not.

"You must really hate me, Bell," Gabe said.

"We don't get to choose the conditions, Chavez," she said.

Ryan stayed out of their spat. She wasn't wrong. It certainly made the training more realistic, but at the same time he didn't blame Gabe for not liking it.

The dive team was made up of officers from multiple departments—all of them experienced divers who volunteered to be on call for water-related emergencies, underwater crime scene investigations, and evidence recovery. They trained at least once a month, and for today's training exercise they'd picked one of the deeper parts of the lake and scanned it with their side-scan sonar, looking for anything interesting to recover. They'd found a debris field of manmade objects—a rectangle and some round shapes that could be tires, along with a few other objects they couldn't identify. It was one of the more interesting debris fields they'd ever found on one of these exercises, so they'd marked it with a crab pot and suited up.

Ryan kept an eye on his depth as he followed the rope down. He didn't want to hit the bottom and stir up a lot of debris.

"We're almost there, Anissa," he said.

One never knew what a training exercise would bring. Ryan and his buddies often wagered what would be the find of the day. Old appliances usually won. Every now and then they'd come across random car parts. One time they'd found what must have been the contents of some girl's closet strewn over a large swath of the lake bottom. He wished he knew the story behind that one.

But most of the time they found a whole lot of nothing. He forced himself to concentrate and kept his light trained on the surface beneath him. Maybe this time they'd find a lost wedding band or a missing necklace they could return to the rightful owner. It would be nice to make someone smile for a change.

"Easy," Anissa said. She was watching everything on the cameras they had attached to their helmets.

Ryan glanced at his dive computer. Plenty of pressure. Plenty of air. Plenty of daylight left. He'd enjoy an easy ascent, and if the good citizens of Carrington County could avoid any unnecessary criminal activity, he might be able to dive again this afternoon for fun.

The other side of Lake Porter had a great area for recreational divers. A few caves, a couple of old boats, even parts of an old community that had been submerged when the land was flooded to form the lake eighty years ago. He'd have to see if Gabe wanted to jo—

What . . . ? An object materialized beneath him. He barely had time to stop himself from swimming into the mass hovering above the lake floor.

"I've got something here, Gabe," he said.

Gabe swam closer and directed his light in the same area as Ryan's. "Is that . . . ?"

Bile rose in Ryan's throat.

"Anissa, are you seeing this?"

Visibility was minimal, but he was able to make out weights and chains. More than enough to hold down the body they were wrapped around.

What was left of the body, anyway. Whoever dumped this person here had wanted to be sure no one ever found him or found out who he was.

Because from what little he could see, this body didn't have hands.

Or a head.

The sharp rap on the door shattered Leigh Weston's peaceful morning. She tried unsuccessfully to stifle the scream that flew from her mouth.

"Leigh, are you okay?"

She knew that voice. Relief and embarrassment collided in her nervous system. What was with her? She had nothing to be afraid of. Not anymore. She steadied herself against the kitchen counter for a moment.

"Leigh? If you don't open the door, I'm going to break it down."

"I'm fine, I'm fine," she called as she willed her legs to propel her forward and the flush to fade from her skin.

She opened the door. Ryan Parker stood a foot away, his body at an angle to her, hands twitching at his sides. She had no trouble believing he hadn't been joking about breaking down her door. She appreciated the protective response, but what was he doing standing on her front porch—in a wet suit—in the first place?

"What's going on?" she asked.

"Why did you scream?" he asked at the same time.

"You first," she said.

Concern-filled eyes held hers for a moment before he conceded. "Dive team training."

"Did you forget your clothes?"

A flicker of a smile. Then back to tall, dark, and brooding. "Going back later. Why did you scream?"

She wasn't going to get any more answers until she gave him at least one. "I wasn't expecting anyone. You startled me."

"Sounded more like terror than surprise."

"Are you an expert on screams now?"

"Something like that."

She refused to offer any more of an explanation. Her demons were her own. He didn't need to know—

"I'm sorry I *startled* you," he said. "We were doing a training exercise not far from here and came across something . . ."

She didn't miss the way he stumbled over the word. Whatever the something was, it must have been bad.

"We're going to need to spend some more time in this part of the lake and I was wondering if you'd mind if we use your dock."

"Of course not. You didn't even have to ask."

Now he grinned. The grin that had left more than one girl in a state of breathlessness, herself included. "I thought you'd say that." He looked over her shoulder. She turned and followed his gaze. Through the windows in the living room she could see at least four officers walking around on the dock and two boats tied on either side.

"Mind if we use your driveway too? Not everyone will be arriving by boat," Ryan said. "It shouldn't be more than a few days, but there might be more activity later on as evidence starts coming in."

Law enforcement officers would be surrounding her home? Excellent. Leigh struggled to keep her expression serene. "That won't be a problem. Always happy to come to the aid of Carrington's finest."

"I promise we'll clear out as soon as possible."

"No!" she said, nearly shouting. So much for cool, calm, and collected. "It's not an issue. Stay as long as you need to."

She didn't like the look Ryan was giving her. Had she given away more than she'd intended?

"I sure do appreciate it, ma'am," he said in an exaggerated Southern drawl, tipping an imaginary hat.

The unmistakable thumping of a helicopter reached her ears. "You aren't planning to land a chopper in the yard, are you?"

"No," he said with a frown. "My guess is that's the news." He walked out the door, down the steps, and onto the front lawn, shielding his eyes as he looked at the sky.

She couldn't resist following him. He was right. The local news station helicopter hovered far too low for comfort. She gestured toward it. "Are you going to tell me what you found in the lake, or do I have to wait for my house to appear in footage on the evening news?"

"I'm surprised it took them this long." Ryan's eyes were troubled when he looked at her. "We found a body."

Something about the way he said it made her shudder. "When you say 'we found,' you mean 'I found,' don't you?"

His quick nod confirmed her suspicions.

She couldn't imagine what that would be like. She'd spent more than her share of time around the dying, and the dead, but that didn't mean she ever wanted to swim into a body on the bottom of the lake. "How awful," she said. "I'm sorry."

"Not the most fun I've ever had on a dive, that's for sure," he said. "But don't feel too sorry for me. It's a good thing. We didn't know we had a problem before this morning. Now we know we have a killer out there. There've been no local reports of anyone missing that match the little bit of a description we have. My guess is this guy probably isn't from around here. I hate to think that there's a loved one out there somewhere who's wondering why he hasn't come home. At least we'll be able to give them some closure. No one deserves to die forgotten."

He moved toward the driveway and the path that led from there to the dock.

"Thank you, Ryan," she said.

He turned back toward her. "For what? Crashing your Saturday morning and invading your property?"

"No. For caring."

His eyes widened and he shifted from side to side. "It's no big thing. I gotta run."

This time he took off toward the dock without giving her a chance to respond.

Who would have thought a compliment would send Ryan Parker running for cover?

2

"She okay with us being here?" Anissa asked as soon as Ryan returned to the dock.

"Great with it. No problems."

"Good. How do you know her again?"

"She grew up here in this house. Her brother, Kirk, is one of my best friends. He and I were in the same class. She was a couple years behind me."

Ryan ignored Anissa's speculative look. Nothing romantic had ever happened between him and Leigh. He'd be willing to bet Leigh didn't know Kirk had made it clear to anyone and everyone that she was off-limits.

"She's a nurse, right? How can she afford a place like this?" Anissa turned in a circle on the dock. It was a beautiful home on a prime piece of lakefront real estate.

"Nurse practitioner. And she's not a suspect."

"I'm not saying she is. I'm simply asking a question."

It annoyed him that Anissa was so logical about this, but she didn't know Leigh and her question was valid. "Her dad was a lawyer and then a judge here in town. Both parents were in their late forties when they decided to adopt. Kirk from Bolivia. Leigh from China."

"Was?"

"Mr. Weston passed away five years ago. Heart attack. Mrs. Weston passed last year. Cancer."

"Leigh lives alone?"

"I assume so. I haven't heard anything about a roommate. She moved back to town around Christmas. Kirk called and asked me to keep an eye out for her." Leigh probably didn't know that either. Or that Kirk had told him about the stalker that had prompted her move back to Carrington.

Anissa nodded. "How well do you suppose she knows the security system here?"

Based on her motivation for moving home, he'd guess quite well. "Why?"

"Looks like there are a few security cameras pointing in this direction. Wondering if we could get some footage of a boat out on the lake."

"It's a long shot," he said.

"I know."

"What's with you? It's like you're looking for the most remote possibilities and we haven't even explored the most logical ones. Are you ticked Captain Mitchell gave me the case?"

He was on call, so the case should have been his anyway, but he'd caught the last couple of big cases and there'd been some speculation that the next big one would go to Anissa regardless.

"No. Not at all." Her quick denial seemed genuine. "I'll be happy to handle the underwater aspect of the investigation and leave the rest of it to you. It's just . . ."

"Just what?"

She sighed. "This one feels like it could go cold in a hurry."

He bristled at her remark. It was too soon to go there. They'd found the body only a few hours ago.

"We'll find the killer." He had to believe that.

Anissa didn't respond. Just checked her watch and turned her gaze to the lake.

"Who's under?" he asked.

"Adam and Lane. They should be coming up soon."

"Have they found anything else?" They'd already found weights, chains, and a piece of plywood, all stuff that could have been used in the dumping of the body.

Anissa's face darkened. "No."

The helicopter made several passes over the lake. Probably the news crew getting some B-roll for tonight's newscast. Or maybe they were live. He tried to ignore them as he waited for Adam and Lane to resurface.

It had taken a while to return the body to the surface. Recovering someone from that depth was something all of them had practiced but had never done with a real body. Their training and adherence to procedures had paid off. The recovery had gone smoothly and safely.

The body was missing not only his head and hands but also his feet. The depth and cold temperature of the lake water had slowed decomposition, but the medical examiner, Dr. Sharon Oliver, was going to have a forensic anthropologist come out on Monday to take a look at the body anyway.

The good news was Ryan liked the anthropologist. She was a brilliant woman who had a great working relationship with the sheriff's office. The bad news was that it meant he wouldn't have any sort of identification until Monday afternoon at the earliest.

Adam and Lane resurfaced, and the team assembled on the end of Leigh's dock.

"What do we have to do to make the chopper go away?" Gabe asked no one in particular. Ryan patted him on the shoulder. "Just keep your head down, man." Gabe had issues with having his picture taken. Working undercover would do that to a man.

"Fine." He stared at the dock. "I'm game to go back down, but I'm not sure we're going to find the rest of this guy. Why bother cutting off his extremities if you're going to dump them nearby?" Gabe said. "The murderer tossed them somewhere else."

"Or kept them," Adam said.

A collective groan rose from the group.

"What?" White-collar crimes investigator Adam Campbell refused to back down. "You may not want to say it out loud, and I know"—he held up a hand toward Anissa as she was about to interrupt him—"I know we don't have any evidence yet. But if someone goes to the trouble to cut everything off, then truss him up with that much weight and throw him overboard in one of the deepest parts of the lake? That takes planning. We can't ignore the possibility that the killer might be a collector."

No one argued the point.

Because no one could. It didn't take an FBI profiler to know whoever did this was seriously messed up.

But a collector? Could they have a serial killer running loose in central North Carolina?

"Could be a gang," Gabe said. "I can think of at least three that could be behind something like this. Although I didn't think they'd gotten a foothold in Carrington."

Vicious gangs or serial killers? Either way, something bad was going on in his town. Ryan reined in his thoughts. All of this was conjecture. They needed proof. "We'll start with the facts and follow them wherever they lead." He looked at each person on the team as he continued. "We'll explore every possibility. For now, let's finish searching the grids we laid out earlier. I don't want to find out later that there was a clue and we missed it."

The huddle disbanded, and Ryan and Gabe prepared to descend.

"How was Leigh?" Gabe asked.

"Fine." He checked the gauges on his tanks.

"I bet she was," Gabe said under his breath.

"Wait a minute. How do you know Leigh?"

"I've seen her around."

"Where?"

"Emergency department. Church. She's exquisite. Especially

if you like girls with long black hair who move with the kind of confidence and grace she does. She patched me up a few times. Her hands are quite delicate."

Ryan didn't respond.

"Your silence only makes me think that not only do you agree with me, but you don't like me talking about it."

"She's my best friend's little sister."

"She's Kirk's *younger* sister. She's an adult now, and I'm sure she's capable of making her own decisions. I bet he would love to have you as a brother-in-law."

Gabe chuckled at his own joke as he settled his mask over his face.

Ryan tried to keep his focus on his own pre-dive routine. Diving was fun, but it was also serious business. He couldn't be distracted by thoughts of Leigh's brown eyes and full lips . . .

No. No. No. He was not going there. Not with Kirk's little sister. Not with anyone. He was willing to face many different dangers—diving, solving crimes, babysitting his niece and nephew—all perilous and all worth the risks.

But not relationships. No way. Nohow.

That was a pain he intended to stay as far away from as possible.

He took a slow breath and descended into the lake. He didn't expect to find anything, but their dead body deserved his best efforts. Somewhere someone was wondering where that man was. The least they could do was try to find the rest of him.

Leigh balanced a tray of sandwiches in one hand and grabbed two bags of chips from the kitchen counter. A rather pitiful offering, but it was all she had. It wasn't like she'd been planning on feeding a bunch of police officers tonight. Hopefully the dessert would make up for the meager meal.

She wouldn't have had even this much food if she hadn't been planning to take a meal in for her coworkers. Most of them brown-bagged dinner for their twelve-hour night shifts in the emergency department, but sometimes it was nice to have something in the break room to grab as they ran from one room to another.

She took her time as she made her way down the grassy steps to the dock. She could walk this path with her eyes closed, but given her luck, tonight would be the one time she'd trip. She'd always been awkward around Ryan Parker and if this morning was any indication, that hadn't changed.

Why did guys have to get so much better looking as they aged? It wasn't fair. As a boy Ryan had been cute. The man? The man was . . . Her stomach clenched. It wasn't just his face or his physique, although neither were anything to complain about. But with Ryan, it had always been about his personality. His expressiveness. His laugh.

How many nights had she sat in the darkness, listening to him and Kirk cut up in the room next to hers? She knew way more about Ryan than he realized.

She pulled her mind back to the present. Memory lane was a lovely place to visit, but she lived in the real world. And in the real world, guys like Ryan Parker didn't make it to their thirties without getting married unless they had major commitment issues.

Not that it mattered. She wasn't looking for a relationship.

"Let me help you with that." A deep voice broke through her reverie.

In the split second it took for her mind to realize this was a friendly voice, another part of her brain scrambled to stop the scream that had become her knee-jerk reaction to being surprised. What came out was more of a strangled squeak than a scream.

Heat flooded her face and neck. She hadn't always been a screamer. Squeaker. Whatever. Her therapist had said it would pass with time. Liar.

Ryan grabbed the tray of sandwiches from her arm. "You okay?" he asked in a low voice.

She took a few calming breaths and nodded. "Great."

Then he spoke louder. "What have we here?"

She didn't know why he wasn't giving her the third degree the way he had earlier, but she was thankful he wasn't grilling her in front of his coworkers.

"It's not much. Just some sandwiches. Pimento cheese and chicken salad."

"You didn't have to do this."

"You've been here all day and I haven't seen any of you leave."

"We have a few snacks."

"Now you have a few sandwiches."

He laughed. "Where do you want these?"

Leigh pointed to the picnic table near the edge of the lake. "That okay?"

"Sure." He set the tray on the end of the table, then took the chips from her.

"Thanks." She turned to go back to the house.

"Where are you running off to?"

"I'm not running anywhere," she said. "I have more to bring down."

"I'll come with you."

She didn't argue. She probably should have, but she didn't make wandering around outside a habit. Especially as the day faded into twilight.

She used to. Sitting on the dock in the dark had been one of her favorite pastimes growing up. She'd listen to the sounds of the night—the water lapping on the shores of Lake Porter, chatter from the homes around them, the faint whir of boats. She'd spent hours out here, dreaming about the future, praying about the decisions she needed to make.

She'd felt closer to God on her dock than anywhere else. She wasn't sure what she'd done wrong, but somewhere along the line he'd stopped answering. Or maybe he'd stopped answering when she'd gotten too busy to talk?

Either way, the dock was no longer her sanctuary. When she wasn't at work, she spent her evenings inside. Doors locked. Security system on. Cameras running. Gun loaded.

This was the first time she'd ventured out this late since she'd moved back into the house in December. She'd forgotten how much she missed it.

One more thing her stalker had taken from her.

She pushed the melancholy memories as far away as she could. Maybe she could take advantage of the police presence to enjoy a few evenings on the dock. Although the whole "dead guy in the lake" thing didn't make that scenario likely.

"What are we going back to the house for?" Ryan asked.

"Lemonade. Tea. Dessert."

"Should I call for backup?"

"I think we'll be able to handle it."

"If you say so."

She smiled at his skepticism as they walked up the hill in silence. She scrambled to think of something to talk about. She didn't want him to have a chance to ask her any deep questions. "Did you come back to Carrington straight out of college?"

"Yep. Knew I would. Never wanted to be anywhere else."

She could understand that.

"Why did you stay in Durham?" he asked.

Oh boy. She chose her words with care. "I did an oncology rotation in nursing school and loved it more than I expected to. They offered me a job after graduation and I took it. It wasn't that I didn't want to be here. It was that the work I wanted to do was there. Then I decided to go back and get my master's, so I worked while I was in grad school and stayed on after I became a nurse practitioner."

"I get that. I guess. I'm not sure I could ever do that kind of work though. What was it about oncology that drew you to it? Most people would think it's a depressing field."

"It can't be any more depressing than your job," she said. "By the time you get to them, your victims are all dead. At least my patients had a chance. A lot of them went on to live long lives."

He threw back his head and laughed. She couldn't help but join him. "Point taken," he said as he held the door open for her and they entered the kitchen.

She pulled the lemonade and tea from the refrigerator.

"You still haven't answered my question about why you chose oncology. Don't get me wrong, I think it's important work. I'm just not sure how anyone could say they love it."

"It's complicated."

"I can probably follow along."

"You're annoying."

"I've been told that before."

Leigh leaned against the refrigerator door. "I think what drew me to it was the sense that it really mattered. That regardless of the outcome, I could make a difference in people's lives by either helping them live longer than they thought they would . . . or by holding their hand as they died."

She heard Ryan's whispered "wow" and the awe in his tone as he said it, but it was time to lighten the subject.

Leigh pulled the chilled cake from the fridge and set it on the counter in front of him.

Ryan's eyes widened. "Is that what I think it is?"

Her mom had called it "better than anything" cake, and Leigh hadn't forgotten that it had been Ryan's favorite.

"I can't believe you made this." He looked around the kitchen. "I spent a lot of happy days in this house."

"So did I," she said. "It was a great place to grow up." She wished she could figure out how to make it a great place to be an adult.

"I miss your mom," he said. "I'm really sorry."

Leigh swallowed. "Thanks. She was ready. Wanted to be with Dad and Jesus. Didn't want to go through any crazy treatments, and by the time we knew what we were dealing with, there wasn't anything to be done."

"Is that why you came back? To take care of her?"

"No. I did take some time off, but she passed away before I could even consider moving back." But he already knew that, didn't he?

"So . . ."

He wasn't going to let it go, was he?

"I needed a change. And we needed someone to live in the house during the summer. Neither Kirk nor I were ready to consider renting it out to tourists, but we also couldn't imagine it falling into disrepair."

"Makes sense," he said. His words said it made sense, but his expression remained speculative.

He took the beverages, she tucked the cake and paper products into a basket, and they headed back outside.

She paused to close the door and a soft chime accompanied the click as it closed.

"Anissa wanted me to ask you about your security system," Ryan said.

"What about it?"

"Do you have access to the cameras or is it all done off-site?"

"Both," she said. "The cameras keep about two weeks of footage. Some run all the time, some are motion activated. Why?"

"Do any of the cameras cover the lake area?"

"Not much of it," she said. "There are cameras at the dock and along the perimeter of our property line. During daylight hours you can see halfway across the lake at most."

"Would you be willing to let us look at what you have? And maybe see if we can avoid deleting anything that's currently available?"

"You think you might see something on my cameras that would help you with your dead body?"

"Honestly? I doubt it. But I've learned not to ignore any possibilities. Sometimes you find things you aren't looking for and they are the very things you need to break a case wide open."

"Okay. Do you need to see it tonight? I go in at eleven . . ."

Ryan jerked to a stop and she had to turn back to see him.

"You're working? Tonight?"

What was the big deal? "Yes. I do have a job."

"No." He shook his head. "That's not what I meant. I thought you worked twelve-hour shifts."

How would he know her schedule?

"I mean, I assumed. Most of the nurses I know do. Do you have different hours as a nurse practitioner?"

No way he was getting off the hook. "Kirk called you, didn't he?"

"Hmm?" Ryan took off down the hill at a quick pace.

"Don't run away from me, Ryan Parker."

Ryan stopped but didn't turn. When she caught up, she let him have it. "Did my brother call you? Tell you to keep an eye on me? Have you been watching me?"

"No! Yes! I mean, not like that."

She stomped past him. She should be mad. Furious. But if she was going to be honest with herself, she wasn't surprised. Even though it was unnecessary, it was exactly like Kirk. Always looking out for her. Or trying to, anyway.

"Oh, come on, Leigh." Ryan's hand closed around her elbow and she jumped. He released her like he'd received an electrical shock. Was she that repulsive? Or did he know?

"Sorry," he said.

He knew.

"What else did Kirk tell you?"

Ryan didn't back down. Or back away. He stepped closer. "He told me you'd been terrorized by a patient."

She clenched her teeth together. Great. Just great. Even from the grave that man was messing up her life. First he'd made her world a living haunted house for eight months and now he'd made her look like a victim in front of the one person she never wanted to appear vulnerable to.

Ryan had always treated her as a kid sister.

She'd never thought of him as a brother.

"Kirk said the patient is dead and you decided to move home to make a clean break. Makes perfect sense. I've put away a few stalkers who escalated too fast for anyone to stop them. I'm thankful he didn't get that far with you, Leigh. Truly thankful."

She didn't know how to respond.

"If you ever want to talk about it, I'll be happy to listen. But if you'd rather we never discuss it again, I'm good with that too."

Her throat worked a few moments before she could get any words out. "Thank you," she managed to whisper.

Ryan cleared his throat and pointed toward the lake. She followed his lead and they returned to the path. He didn't seem to be in any hurry to break the silence, and she took a few seconds to steady her nerves and her breathing before she spoke again.

"I usually work a twelve-hour shift," she said. "But I went in early two nights last weekend, so our lead nurse practitioner told me I could come in at eleven. I'll be happy to show you the security tapes before I go if you'd like to see them."

"Sounds great," he said as they put the cake and drinks on the picnic table. He called the rest of the team over as if nothing weird had just happened.

Maybe having him know wasn't such a disaster after all.

Maybe.

3

Ryan perched beside Leigh at the bar in her kitchen. Her laptop lay open in front of her. His third piece of cake sat in front of him. He took a bite. Chocolate, whipped cream, toffee, and caramel exploded across his taste buds. "I haven't had this stuff in years," he said as he prepped for another bite. "Yours is exactly the way I remember it."

He expected her to say something, but Leigh didn't reply right away. Man, he was a moron. Her mom had only been gone a year. Maybe it was too soon to talk this way.

"Mom always kept the ingredients on hand," Leigh said.

Her voice carried a heavy layer of nostalgia, with only a hint of melancholy. Whew.

"I guess she rubbed off on me. Hopefully in lots of other ways too."

He took another bite. "Your mom would have been proud of the spread you put out tonight," he said.

"Yeah," she said with a laugh. "I think she would have been."

Ryan let his gaze wander around the kitchen. "I like what you've done with the place."

She looked up from the screen and followed his gaze. "I told

Mom the fruit wallpaper had to go." Her laughter was contagious and he joined her. "Mom made me promise to update anything and everything after she was gone. It was one of her final gifts." Leigh smiled, but her eyes now shimmered with unshed tears. "She didn't want us to feel like making changes was an affront to her memory."

"Sounds like her," he said.

"She would have hated this security system though. She didn't like the idea of having cameras. She was convinced they could be hacked. But Kirk agreed with me that they were a necessity if I was going to live here alone."

He wished he could disagree with her, but he couldn't. "Your system seems pretty state of the art."

"It is, but I've never tried to pull up footage from days or weeks ago," she said as she typed in a password. "The cameras pointing toward the dock are motion sensitive and record for several minutes anytime they are activated. Now I need to figure out how to retrieve the videos."

"I appreciate your help," he said. "I know it's a long shot, but I want to be thorough. Oh, and I should tell you that I got a warrant for your security footage." He patted the piece of paper he'd placed on the counter. "I know you're willing for me to see it, but it's procedure. I don't want there to be anything a defense attorney could ever use to eliminate any evidence we might find."

She smiled. "My police knowledge is entirely based on TV shows, but that seems like a good move to me."

A few more keystrokes followed her words. "There they are. How far back do you want to search?"

The body hadn't been that decomposed because the way it was wrapped and the cold water from the lake had helped preserve it. They wouldn't have a firm time of death until the medical examiner finished her autopsy.

"Maybe two weeks?"

Leigh filled in a few spots on the page and hit the search button.

The screen filled with a list of video files.

"That's way more than I was expecting," Leigh said, her voice thick with apology.

He leaned closer to the screen as she scrolled down. There were several hundred clips. It would take hours to go through them all. He stifled a groan.

"Would it be safe to assume your bad guy dumped the body at night?" she asked.

"I never like to assume anything, but it's doubtful he would have tried to dump the body in broad daylight."

"Okay," she said. "Let's limit these search parameters a bit."

This time, the list was much shorter.

"What did you do?" he asked.

"I limited it to video clips between midnight and 5 a.m. I realize you'll need to look at all of them, but I thought these would be the best ones to start with."

"Great idea," he said.

She slid the computer to him and stood up. "As much as I'd love to see what sort of stuff goes on in the middle of the night, I need to get ready for work. Have fun."

"Thanks." He watched her disappear up the stairs. Interesting. The master bedroom was on the main level. Even with her mom's permission, she probably hadn't had the heart to move into it.

His phone buzzed. "Hey, Sis."

"Still at work?" Rebecca asked.

"Sort of." He clicked the video file from last night. The video showed the empty dock. Nothing else. "What's up?"

"I was wondering if you'll be at church in the morning."

"Hope to be," he said. Leigh's empty dock footage continued to play. "Need something?"

"Not really. Caleb was asking."

Caleb. He'd hate to disappoint him. "Tell him I'm going to try to be there, but I'm working on a big case and might not make it."

"I will. Thanks," she said.

"You okay?"

"Just tired."

"Maybe I could get Caleb one evening this week. Give you a break."

"I'm not holding my breath," she said with a laugh. "I saw the news, Ryan. You're working that body in the lake, aren't you?"

He'd have to get a copy of the newscast and see what the town saw tonight. "I am, but that doesn't mean I can't hang out with my favorite nephew. I have to eat supper like everyone else does."

"Let's play it by ear."

He heard the fatigue in her voice. "I'm serious. I'll find a way to make it happen."

"Okay. See you tomorrow."

He could tell she didn't believe him. Not that he could blame her.

He heard Leigh on the stairs. Her voice preceded her. "Find anything?"

"I gotta—"

"Who's that?" He could picture his sister's flashing eyes. "I thought you said you were working?"

"I am," he said into the phone. "Nothing yet," he said to Leigh.

Leigh paused at the entry to the kitchen. "Sorry," she mouthed.

"It's fine," he said. "Rebecca, I need to go."

"Who is that?"

He couldn't win. If he told her where he was, she'd jump to conclusions. If he told her he'd tell her later, she'd jump to conclusions. "I'm at Leigh Weston's looking at security footage," he said. "She's letting us use her dock."

"Leigh Weston?"

And there she went.

"Then I'll let you go." A low chuckle came through the line.

"Rebecca—"

"We'll talk tomorrow." With that ominous prediction, she hung up.

He stared at the phone.

"I'm sorry," Leigh said. "I didn't realize—"

"No apology needed," he said. "It was just my sister."

His sister, who was undoubtedly calling his mother right now.

"How's she doing?"

The question carried far too much nuance. "I guess you heard?"

She grimaced. "Hospital gossip can be fierce."

"What did you hear?"

Leigh looked like a trapped animal. "Maybe you could tell me the true version rather than me telling you the speculation?"

"How about if I tell you the truth, and then you tell me the speculation?"

She didn't look happy, but she nodded her assent.

"Clay left them for someone he met at his twenty-year high school reunion. They started chatting on social media, then in real life, and then he walked out of church on a Sunday morning and instead of going home to his wife and kids, he went to her."

"That's basically what I've heard," she said. "I'm sorry. I've always liked Rebecca."

"She likes you too."

"How's Caleb handling it?"

"Not good. He doesn't do well with changes in his routine." Caleb had been diagnosed with autism when he was two. How his own father could abandon him was beyond understanding.

The video on the screen stopped, and he clicked on the next file from 3:15 a.m. on Thursday.

"He doesn't understand why Clay doesn't come home. We think he misses him, but he melts down on the rare occasions Clay tries to visit." He stopped himself. Leigh didn't need to hear all their family drama. She had plenty of her own issues to deal with. "It's a mess."

Leigh shoved her hands into the pockets of her scrubs jacket. "I don't have much interaction with Dr. Fowler, um, Clay," she said. "But I know it shocked everyone at the hospital. The nurses who work with him the most don't have much nice to say about him. Not that it helps Rebecca, but in the court of public opinion, he's been convicted of being a wretched father and a sleazy man."

"Sleazy's pretty accurate," he said. Another nothing on the video clip. The next one was from ten minutes later. He hit play.

"Do you mind locking up when you leave?" Leigh asked.

He hit pause on the video. "I'm sorry. I can do this later."

"No, no. Go ahead and finish." She scribbled a number on a notepad. "Here's my number. Text me when you leave and I'll arm the security system from my phone."

"Are you sure?"

"Positive," she said. "Gotta run."

"Thanks."

She slipped out the door to the garage. He returned his attention to the screen as she left. The garage door had just closed when lights flashed across the screen.

He watched as the lights from a boat traversed across the screen and then disappeared from view.

He looked at the list. Nothing else had triggered the cameras the rest of that night. He made a note of the date and time of the video and eagerly watched the rest of the clips from the past two weeks. He saw a few deer on the edge of the lake. A couple of kids on jet skis. A boat moving so slowly along the shore it had to be someone doing some night fishing. But nothing else looked out of the ordinary for boat traffic on a lake in early spring.

Tomorrow he would ask other homeowners in this area if their security cameras picked up anything between 2:30 and 4:30 on Wednesday night/Thursday morning.

It might be nothing, but his gut told him it was significant.

Now to prove it.

Leigh walked out of the hospital at 7:35 a.m. She tried to work out some of the knots in her neck and shoulders as she walked to her car. Maybe she should schedule a massage. Or see a chiropractor. They'd have a field day with her. She knew she carried all her tension in her shoulders, but she couldn't blame it on her shift tonight. Work had been the least stressful part of the past twenty-four hours.

At least she'd scored a great parking space last night. No riding the shuttle to the other side of the sprawling hospital campus this morning. She climbed into her car and pulled away from the hospital a full ten minutes earlier than she usually did.

The forecast called for a sunny spring day, but the morning haze hadn't burned off yet. She turned on the defroster and seat warmers as she waited for the red light to allow her to turn left onto the highway.

She didn't always crash after a shift, but she planned to today. Ryan had assured her the dive team would be continuing their search of the lake bottom. She thought about the guy who had died and hated the idea that his family might be wondering where he was and what had happened to him. But she was looking forward to falling into a deep sleep. It might be the best sleep she'd had in a year. Although if she kept thinking about Ryan Parker, it might not be.

It was ridiculous how his presence calmed her. How his laughter made it easier for her to laugh. He'd changed some since high school, but her favorite things remained the same. He still laughed loud and long. He still took his responsibilities seriously. And he was still loyal to his family.

His barely contained hostility toward his brother-in-law hadn't surprised her in the least. She had no doubt it was taking every ounce of self-control he had not to pay Dr. Fowler a visit and leave him in far worse shape than he found him.

Dr. Fowler had been on call last night. He and Dr. Evans had stopped by the coffee station in the emergency department break area—everyone knew the ED had the best coffee in the hospital—and when she'd seen them, she'd turned and walked in the other direction. Maybe it was childish of her, but she had no use for a man who abandoned his children. She would be professional when necessary, but she wasn't interested in chatting with him in the hallway.

She turned off the exit ramp. She could drive this road in her sleep. Probably had a few times. Driving home was the worst part of working nights.

She crested a hill and her heart swelled as she took in the pastoral scene below. She did love this place. A few more miles of cow pastures and chicken farms and she'd be home. A quick shower, comfy clothes. Then blissful sleep.

She yawned and blinked hard as she approached the stop sign at the bottom of the hill.

She tapped her brake.

Tapped it again.

Stomped it.

Nothing.

Fatigue fled, replaced by adrenaline-spiking terror. What were you supposed to do if your brakes failed? Emergency brake? That sounded right. She stomped the parking break pedal. It slowed her a little, but not enough. The stop sign came closer and closer. A truck sat to her right. He had the right of way. Would he pull out?

The truck eased into the intersection.

She jerked her steering wheel to the left as she rolled through it.

The driver laid on the horn as she fought to get her car back into her lane, but no sounds of crunching metal reached her ears. That guy might be mad, but at least he was in one piece.

The road flattened out some, but not enough for her to come to a stop. It continued at a slight down angle for a half mile or so before it took a steep plunge into a valley. If no one pulled out in front of her before she got to the bottom of the hill—and if she were able to keep the car on the road—she'd be okay. There was no way her car would be able to coast up the hill on the other side. Once she slowed enough, she could pull off the road and call for help.

She pressed the brake again. Still nothing.

How was this even possible?

She could feel her heart racing in her ears as she scanned the area on either side.

Think, Leigh. Think.

Fences lined both sides of the road, but the shoulder on her right was full of pine trees and the ditch was steep. If she crossed the road and went down the left side, she should make it through the ditch, crash through the fence, and roll to a stop in the field. Fence posts were a lot more forgiving than trees and she could survive the crash.

She hoped.

She gripped the steering wheel tighter as the grade—and her speed—increased. She continued to press the brakes. If she pumped them, would that help? At this point, it couldn't hurt. But nothing slowed her descent into the foggy valley below.

Without warning, the bulky form of a farm tractor emerged through the haze.

Sunday morning was normally a good time to be on a rural road in your ginormous tractor, but not this morning.

Maybe she could pass—

Headlights burned in the opposite lane.

She continued to gain on the tractor and the car in the opposite lane came closer and closer. No way could she wedge between them.

She had no choice now.

She yanked the wheel to the left and held on as her car crossed the solid yellow lines, passed over the opposite lane, and careered down the shallow ditch. The angle of the ditch was sharper than she'd expected. The front of her car plowed into the ground with enough force to deploy her air bag, slamming her head back into her seat even as the back of her car flipped into the air and to the side.

She lost all sense of time and direction. When she was finally sure she was no longer moving, her left arm was pinned against the driver's side door. She tried to shift her position, but pain shot through her and left her gasping. The dashboard was much closer than it should have been and the steering wheel had smashed into her abdomen. Her left leg was pinned in the small space between the steering wheel, door, and dashboard.

Leigh pulled in a slow breath, then another. Then she began a self-assessment. Her head, neck, and right arm moved fine and with minimal discomfort. Nothing more than what she would expect to feel after her crash. She could move her torso and right leg. Everything ached, but as she concentrated on her body, she became aware of a creeping numbness in her left foot and leg.

She tried to run her hand along the part of her leg she could reach.

Uh-oh.

She couldn't see the painful lump on the inside of her thigh, but she didn't need to. She'd seen something like this before while doing a clinical in the vascular lab. The pain and the location made it highly unlikely that it was anything else.

The impact must have caused an injury to her femoral artery. Intense blunt force trauma could cause the femoral artery to almost shut down. Or she could have broken her leg and the fractured bone could have punctured the artery, but if that had happened, she would have expected the pain to be sharp.

Either way, she was in trouble. If she lost blood flow through the artery, she could lose her leg.

If it was punctured, she could bleed to death before paramedics could get her out of here.

4

Stay calm.

Leigh tried to think of any other explanation for her symptoms, but everything she came up with led her back to the same conclusion. She forced herself to take a slow breath in through her nose and then out through her mouth.

It didn't help. This wasn't good. At all.

She really didn't want to die. Not today.

Her heart pounded in her ears. Great. She was going to bleed to death even faster because she was afraid she was going to bleed to death. Good grief.

What would she tell a panicking patient? Take a deep breath.

She'd already tried that without any success.

What else?

Close your eyes. Concentrate on my voice.

Well, that wouldn't work either.

What other tricks did she have? She sang to children. Again, not helpful. She told funny stories about her coworkers to teenagers. She reassured mothers that their babies were okay and fathers that they would live to take their kids fishing. None of those coping mechanisms could help her now.

Leigh was alone.

And quite possibly dying.

Her mom had experienced such peace as she'd died. She'd welcomed it. Saw it as more of a transition than an ending. Her mom's final words had been a prayer.

But would God bother with Leigh now after she'd ignored him for much too long?

She kept as much pressure as she could on the lump on her leg.

At this point, what did she have to lose?

Um, Father? I, um, so we haven't talked much lately. I'm Leigh. I guess you know that already. But, um—

"Hey there! In the car. Can you hear me?"

Somehow she hadn't expected God to have a southern accent.

"I'm coming," the voice said.

So the voice wasn't God. Well, not God yelling at her. But maybe he was with her after all?

"I'm stuck," she said.

"That's okay," the man said. "I'm good at getting people unstuck. What's your name, hon?"

"Leigh. Leigh Weston. I'm a nurse at Carrington Memorial."

"Leigh Weston? Not Judge Weston's baby girl?"

"That would be me," she said.

"Aw, kiddo. I'm sorry. Your dad was a friend of mine. Miss him a ton. You probably don't remember me. Name's Floyd Cook."

An image appeared in her mind. A man her father's age, old jeans and a flannel shirt, sitting on the bleachers beside her dad. Her dad still had on a tie. He'd come straight from court to watch Kirk's basketball game.

"Your grandson played ball with Kirk," she said. Part of her brain recognized that Mr. Cook was using her own tactics on her.

He was trying to develop a rapport and keep her mind off the seriousness of the situation she was in.

"He did," he said. She could hear him moving around her car. "How'd you wind up in this ditch?"

She told him. Or tried to. The words kept getting jumbled.

"No brakes, huh? Sounds like you made the best decision you could make at the time. Good girl."

She tried to answer. It was important that she tell him about her leg. He needed to know how serious this was.

"My leg," she said. "I think I have a pseudoaneurysm of the femoral artery."

"Those are some big words. Care to give me the nonmedical version?"

"I think my femoral artery is bleeding internally."

"Okay, hon. I've got a whole team headed our way. We're gonna get you out of there. Don't you worry. Stay with me."

She tried.

She really tried.

Ryan hit snooze three times before he dragged himself to the kitchen for coffee. He had forty minutes to get ready for church if he wanted to be on time for the early service. He'd already told the dive team he'd be on Leigh's dock at eleven with coffees for everyone, and if they wanted to start before he got there they should feel free. He'd missed the last three weeks of Sunday services and didn't want to let Rebecca down.

Normally he'd be working every angle of their John Doe homicide. Most homicides left him several days of work to do before he ran out of options. Not this one. He would be interviewing residents all along the lakeshore this morning but would wait until after church since the sheriff tended to frown on knocking on the doors of his constituents before 10 a.m. on Sunday.

He'd be out of church by 9:30, and this investigation wasn't going to go anywhere before then anyway. Working homicide could make a man bitter and cynical. His mentor in the department had stressed to him the importance of making the time to worship. To refocus on the One who was beautiful and true in a world of darkness and lies.

And he wanted to see his niece and nephew. Zoe was eleven months old, and her smiles could take away almost every worry he had. Caleb wouldn't have much to say, but he would know Ryan was there.

That was all he could do these days. Try to be a stable, constant presence in Caleb's life.

He pulled into the parking lot with ten minutes to spare and parked beside Rebecca's minivan just in time to help her with the kids. He slid his phone into his jacket pocket and reached for Zoe. She squealed with delight as he spun her around before settling her in his arms. Caleb gave him a grunt and a muffled "Hi" without being prompted. A victory.

They got the kids into their classes and found seats near the back as the music began.

Ten minutes later, his phone buzzed. Rebecca cut her eyes at him as he glanced at the text message. She did not approve of checking text messages during church, but it could be about a case.

It was from Kirk.

Leigh in car wreck. Brakes failed. She's at the hospital.

He read it once.

Twice.

He leaned over to whisper in Rebecca's ear. "I have to go."

She gave him her most disapproving look until he showed her the text.

"Go. I'm praying," she said. She squeezed his hand as he rose from his seat. He tried to keep his pace normal until he was outside, then he broke into a run.

He called Kirk. Voicemail.

He forced himself to drive with care through the parking lot. As soon as he hit the highway, he turned on his lights and floored it.

The drive to the hospital should have taken fifteen minutes. Ryan made it in eight. The spaces reserved for law enforcement were full, he refused to park in a handicapped space, and the circular drive was packed. Any other day he'd have been able to slide into a space right in front of the entrance, but today it took longer to find a parking space than it had to get there. He had managed to call Anissa and let her know he would be late to the dive. He had also called his buddy in the forensics department, Dante, and had given him a heads-up on the car coming in. Dante was good, and he'd get back to him as soon as he had any sort of news.

Ryan had so many questions. Why hadn't Kirk called him back? What were the odds of her brakes failing? She drove a decent car, and he'd never heard of anyone's brakes failing, unless . . . His mind jumped into negative mode. Could someone have done this intentionally? Surely not. She didn't have enemies. Well, not anymore. Her stalker was dead.

How many more enemies could she have?

Ryan walked into the emergency department and straight into his soon-to-be ex-brother-in-law.

They stared each other down. This must be what it had felt like to be a cowboy in a standoff. Except at the moment he was the only one with a weapon. Not that he would use it on the no-good piece of trash in front of him. He wasn't worth a bullet.

"You heard about Leigh," Clay said.

Ryan didn't want to think about why it bugged him so much that Clay already knew why he was there. "Yes," he said. "Where is she?"

"Surgery. That's all I can say."

"Whatever." Saying she was in surgery told him nothing other than she needed surgery. It could be a broken bone or massive internal hemorrhaging, but Dr. Self-Righteous couldn't even give him a clue about what he was walking in to.

Jerk.

Ryan continued to hold his position and stare at Clay. He wanted to say so many things. Every one of them true, but not any one of them kind. Or professional. As much as he despised the man standing in front of him, he wouldn't be part of a brawl in the middle of the emergency department. Even if the image of his hand flying out and making contact with Clay's jaw did bring a smile to his face.

Clay stood there another ten seconds before he turned and walked back in the direction he'd come from. He paused for a moment and without turning around said, "If you flash that badge of yours at the front desk, you may get some more information."

Ryan didn't acknowledge him. He'd already planned to do that. And he knew something Clay didn't.

He showed his badge at the front desk and security waved him through. Then he approached the nurses station and waited until the harried woman behind it glanced at him before returning to the stack of files she was digging through. Miss Edna was a fixture in the Carrington ED. She ran a tight ship and didn't suffer fools. "I'm here about Leigh Weston," he said.

"Are you next of kin?"

"No, but—"

"I can't release any information—"

"Yes, ma'am," he said. He hated to interrupt her, but he'd heard her give this speech before and it wasn't a short one. "But I believe if you check her records, you'll see I'm listed as an emergency contact and as someone with whom you can share medical information."

Her hands stilled. "Excuse me? Who are you?"

"Miss Edna, you know me. I'm Investigator Ryan Parker."

She pulled off her glasses and studied him. "Parker. Yes. I've seen you before. What are you doing on this girl's paperwork? I know Leigh. Work with her all the time. Never heard her mention you."

"Yes, ma'am. I understand that, but if you'll check, you'll see I'm telling you the truth."

Miss Edna eyed him with deep suspicion but put the stack of files on the counter and turned to her keyboard. It took thirty seconds of pecking away before her eyebrows lifted in surprise. "Well, well, well. So you are," she said.

She picked up the phone and punched a couple of keys. "I've got Investigator Ryan Parker headed to the waiting room," she said. "He's listed as Leigh's emergency contact and you can share medical information with him."

A long pause was broken by an indelicate snort. "That girl's been keeping secrets for sure. We'll get to the bottom of it. Don't you worry about that."

Great. Now the hospital gossip mill would be running overtime as people speculated over something that was nothing. Kirk had asked him if Leigh could list him as an emergency contact for exactly this type of situation. He'd agreed, but he hadn't anticipated this would ever happen.

Miss Edna hung up the phone and handed him a slip of paper. "Follow these directions. Ask for Carol when you get there. She'll fill you in."

"Thank you, Miss Edna."

Miss Edna's only reply was to return to her files.

He wound around to the surgical waiting area and found Carol expecting him. Her smile was quite unlike Miss Edna's. "Investigator Parker. How can I help you?"

"I'm here about Leigh Weston."

"Right." She gave him a sly grin. "We had no idea y'all were so close."

What was he supposed to say? He didn't mind people assuming

they were an item, but Leigh might not appreciate it. "Can you give me an update, please?"

"Oh, sure," she said. "She came in with a hematoma on the femoral artery. They've been in surgery forty-five minutes."

Femoral artery. His mouth went dry. He wasn't a medical expert, but femoral arteries weren't the kinds of things you wanted to mess with. She could have bled to death.

"Thank you," he said. His phone buzzed. "I'm going to step out into the hall and take this."

"You may need to go down to the end by the windows," Carol said. "Reception is terrible in here."

"Thank you."

He accepted the call as soon as he stepped into the hall. "Parker."

Garbled speech cut in and out.

"Hang on." He jogged to the end of the corridor and found a door to a small garden area. He stepped outside.

"Yo. Parker. You there, man?"

"Sorry, Dante. I'm at the hospital. Couldn't get a signal. Had to step outside."

"Oh sure. I got that," Dante said. "How's Leigh?"

"In surgery."

"That stinks. When she wakes up, tell her I said hi. I never would have made it through American Lit without her."

"Will do. What's up?"

"We have a problem," Dante said.

"What do you mean?"

"Her brakes didn't fail. They were cut."

"How do you even have the car?"

"Old Mr. Cook is the one who found her. He tried to keep her talking, and she told him what happened before she passed out. The car was lying on its side. He was able to see the cut brake line plain as day. Took a few pictures. Sent them to me and rushed the guys to get me the car."

Sounded like Mr. Cook. People underestimated him. Saw his flannel and heard his drawl and assumed he was clueless. Nothing could be further from the truth.

"This was intentional and whoever did it didn't try very hard to cover their tracks. There are other ways to mess with a car that aren't quite so obvious."

"You're sure it wasn't an accident? Wear and tear? Poor quality brake line? Or maybe she ran over something sharp?"

"No way," Dante said. He sounded convinced. "The front line is cut, but not all the way. It's a smallish hole. If they'd sliced it all the way through, she wouldn't have had brakes from the get-go. A cut like this would have let her get out of the parking lot and onto the road, probably several miles, before all the brake fluid would be gone and she'd lose her brakes completely."

A knock on the glass grabbed Ryan's attention. Carol stood on the other side of the wall waving at him. He held up one finger and she motioned for him to come back inside before she walked away.

"Listen, Dante. That's great work, man. I think Leigh may be coming out of surgery. I gotta go. I want to see this, but it may be a little while before I can get over there."

"Not a problem. I can send you some pictures in the meantime."

"Thanks."

Ryan hung up the phone and walked back into the hospital. He found Carol, who had him take a seat in a small room off the main waiting area. It felt like an hour before the door opened and the doctor walked in.

"Ryan, how are you, son?"

"Dr. Price?" He stood and shook the older man's hand. He'd grown up with Dr. Price's kids. "You operated on Leigh? How is she? What happened?"

Dr. Price took a seat in one of the chairs and Ryan followed his lead. "I have a few questions for you, young man, but I'll answer yours first. Leigh is fine. Her femoral artery did receive a small puncture in the accident, but the combination of the pressure from the entrapment and her own efforts were enough to prevent significant blood loss. We were able to reestablish blood flow in plenty of time, so we're not worried about her losing the leg."

"They told me she'd passed out . . ."

"Hmm . . . I'm not sure about that. She was fully alert in the ambulance and when she arrived. No signs of a concussion. I think it's very possible she dozed off a few times. She'd worked all night and it was her third night on. I think the fatigue combined with the adrenaline spike wearing off knocked her out."

That was a new one.

"Regardless, the repair wasn't a problem. She's going to be stiff for a while, but I expect her to make a full and speedy recovery. I want her to spend the night, but I may be willing to send her home tomorrow."

Ryan released the breath he'd been holding. "Thank you, God," he whispered.

"Indeed," Dr. Price said. "From what I hear, she definitely had some serious protection over her today. Now how about you tell me how your name came to be on her emergency contact list. I didn't realize you were a couple."

5

Leigh opened her eyes and took inventory. She could feel her arms and legs. She could move her neck and torso. Her leg was bandaged.

She had an IV in one arm. A pulse oximeter on her finger. She could hear the monitor to her left recording her heartbeat.

The last things she remembered crashed through her mind. The terror. The adrenaline. The disorientation. The stillness.

Then the pain.

Mr. Cook had been there. She'd talked to him. Hadn't she? Or had she dreamed that? No. He'd definitely been there.

But she couldn't remember how she got out of the car or how she got to the hospital. Wait. The ambulance. The emergency department. Yes.

At least she was still in Carrington. That was a good sign. If she'd been in critical condition, then they might have sent her to one of the trauma hospitals.

A nurse she didn't know sat at a computer to her right.

"Hi," the nurse said. "I'm Wren. You're doing great."

Leigh tried to sit up.

"Hold on," Wren said. "There's no hurry. You've only been out of surgery about thirty minutes. You're a nurse. You know how this works. Relax."

Something on the edge of Leigh's consciousness wouldn't leave her alone. She tried to grab it, but it floated away. Something was wrong. Very wrong.

What couldn't she remember?

"You're okay," Wren said again, no doubt responding to the increased frequency of beeps from the monitor. Leigh took a slow breath. The uncertainty, the fear, the vulnerability—these were things she avoided at all costs.

"How did they get me out?" she asked. She needed answers. She needed to feel some sort of control over her situation.

"I'm sorry, Leigh. I don't know," Wren said. "I can try to find out for you."

"Yes. Please."

Leigh closed her eyes. She needed to think. She needed a car. She needed to call Kirk and tell him what was going on. Or maybe not. He was in Germany. He and his wife, Simone, had moved six months earlier. It was a great opportunity for him. International experience was crucial to advancement with his firm.

And they'd been happy to get away from Simone's family for a while. Her decision three years earlier to convert from Islam to Christianity and then marry the man who'd told her about Jesus had caused a horrific split in her family. Most of them refused to acknowledge her existence. The few who did continually tried to get her to recant.

She'd seen the opportunity to put an ocean between her and her family as a blessed relief.

But Leigh knew Kirk didn't trust Simone's family, even from an ocean away, and he wasn't inclined to leave Simone alone. But if he knew she was in the hospital, he'd want to come home. Which was ridiculous.

She could take care of herself. Although she didn't know how she would get home from the hospital.

Wait a minute. She could get home just fine. She'd get a ride with a friend. Or call a taxi. She could figure this out. It was just the anesthesia making her anxious over nothing.

Voices on the other side of the curtain pulled her back to full consciousness. "I'm this young woman's surgeon," a gruff voice said. "And I have known her since she was born. You keep up the good work, young man."

"Yes, sir."

The curtains parted as Dr. Price entered her recovery area and she caught a glimpse of a police officer standing on the other side.

Something about that didn't make sense. Had Dr. Price been talking to the police officer?

"I always love chatting with you, Leigh," Dr. Price said as he approached her bed, "but I prefer you come see me conscious and on your feet. You scared me this morning."

"Sorry, Dr. Price." She'd been good friends with Dr. Price's youngest daughter, and he was one of her favorite doctors in the entire hospital. Everyone loved him.

His daughter had died from a rare form of leukemia when she was a sophomore in college and more than once Leigh had caught a wistfulness in Dr. Price's expression when he looked at her. She had a funny feeling he was thinking of his daughter whenever that happened.

"Tell me everything," she said.

"I can't tell you everything, but I can fill in a few gaps for you. They brought you in by ambulance this morning. Your little off-roading adventure resulted in a nicked femoral artery, but you did a great job of applying pressure while you waited to be freed from that metal trap you wound up in. We got the blood flowing again with no problem and the nick was no worse than what could happen in a heart catheterization. Easy to repair. Minimal recovery time. I want to keep you overnight for observation because you did flip your car today, but there's a chance I'll let you out of here tomorrow. Assuming you behave yourself, that is."

"I'll try," she said.

Dr. Price ran through some of the usual post-operative questions. He asked about her pain level, if she was nauseated, if she had any other questions. He seemed satisfied with her answers.

He glanced at the nurse who sat in the corner before turning back to her. He lowered his voice. "There's a young officer who would like to see you. Ryan Parker?"

Heat flooded her face.

"You did list him as your emergency contact, did you not?"

She was going to strangle her brother. "It was Kirk's idea."

"It was a good one."

"I guess."

"Can he come in? He's worried about you."

What could she say? No, I don't want him to see me like this? That would be awkward since she shouldn't care one way or the other how Ryan Parker saw her. And it wasn't like Ryan thought of her as anything other than Kirk's little sister. He wouldn't have been worried if it weren't for Kirk.

"Sure," she said.

"Wren, I'm going to allow Investigator Parker in here for a brief visit. Then when she's ready, let's get Leigh settled into a room for the rest of the day. I believe you'll see a note about that." He pointed toward the ginormous monitor in front of Wren.

"Yes, Dr. Price. I'll make sure she's well taken care of."

"I've got a few other folks who couldn't wait for normal office hours to utilize my services, so I'll be in surgery most of the day, but I'll be back by to check on you before I leave for the night. If you need anything, you holler. Got it?"

"Yes, sir. Thank you."

Dr. Price left and the police officer was still out there. The anesthesia was clearing from her mind. Something was not right. Dr. Price's comment about there being a note in the computer about her room? Where were they taking her?

"Wren?"

"Yes? Would you like something to drink?" Wren picked up a can from the desk. "Maybe try some ginger ale?"

"Sure, but—"

"Knock, knock." Ryan's voice came through the curtain. "Dr. Price said it was okay . . . ?"

"Come on in, Investigator Parker," Wren said.

"Thanks," Ryan said with a nod. Then he turned his attention to Leigh. "You scared me to death," he said.

He seemed to mean it.

"I got a text this morning saying you were in a car wreck. That you didn't have brakes. I got here as fast as I could, but you were already in surgery. How are you feeling?"

"I'm okay," she said. "I hate that you came over here. It's not a big deal."

Ryan's brow creased.

"Ryan?"

Where was Ryan's smile? His crazy laugh? Why wasn't he joking with her?

"Why do I get the feeling I'm missing something?"

"We need to talk."

Those were not words she had ever wanted to hear from Ryan Parker.

"Let's wait until you're settled into a room and feeling better," he said.

"Let's not."

"Leigh, please." Ryan glanced at Wren, then toward the curtains all around them. "Later," he mouthed.

This was bad. This was very, very bad.

"Please," he whispered.

"Fine," she mouthed. "Wren," she said, raising her voice to a normal volume. "What do I need to do to get out of here?"

Wren laughed as she handed her a cup with a bendy straw. "Not much more than you already have. I'm waiting on your room to be ready and we'll get you settled."

"Thanks."

She took a sip of ginger ale. She didn't even like ginger ale. But she really didn't want to throw up in front of Ryan, and the combination of anesthesia and fear had her stomach heaving.

"Investigator Parker?"

The police officer from the hallway poked his head in. "Sorry to bother you, sir. A word?"

Ryan gave Leigh a small smile. "I'll be right back," he said, and then he disappeared to the other side of the curtain.

Was that supposed to make her feel better or worse?

"He's so cute," Wren said with a conspiratorial whisper. "Are you dating?"

"Oh goodness, no," Leigh said. "He's just a friend."

Wren didn't look convinced.

"I've known him since I was little. He's my brother's best friend."

Wren nodded as she typed something into the computer. "Whatever you say," she said. "Ready to get a room with real doors?"

"I'm ready to go home," Leigh said.

"First things first," Wren said.

Another noise outside her room captured her attention and a friendly face poked through the curtain.

"Hey, girl. If you didn't want to work tonight, you could have said so."

She smiled at the sight of her coworker's mischievous grin. Keri Marshall had been the one to teach her the ropes in the emergency department and was one of the finest registered nurses she'd ever had the privilege to work with. "What are you doing here?" she asked.

"Checking on you. You look good."

"Liar."

Keri chuckled as she approached the bed. "I brought you a present."

A present?

Keri dropped a small duffle bag on her bed. A quick glance through the bag explained everything. New pajamas, underclothes, and some basic toiletries.

Her eyes burned. "You didn't have to do that."

"Ain't no big thang," Keri said with a shrug. "If I was in here with a bunch of coworkers, I'd want to be able to cover up all of the essentials, you know?"

Leigh's thoughts flashed to Ryan. Yeah. She knew. "Thank you," she said.

Keri patted her arm. "I'm on tonight. If it slows down for a second, I'll come check on you. Try to keep it on the road next time. Got it?" Keri blew her a kiss as she disappeared.

"Got it," Leigh whispered to no one.

Wren bustled around the bed, adjusting IV cords and preparing her for transport. Leigh didn't pay her much attention. Too many questions were begging for answers. How could her brakes have given out that way? She'd had the car serviced a week ago. Wasn't that something they would have checked? And what could Ryan want to talk to her about? Why couldn't they talk in front of Wren?

Did the police think she'd fallen asleep at the wheel? It wouldn't be the first time someone working nights had nodded off on the way home. She'd seen more than one of them after they had crashed their cars. But they never could quite remember what had happened.

That wasn't the case for her. She'd never forget the acid that filled her mouth when her brakes went all the way to the floor. Or the adrenaline surge as she careened across the road and into the ditch.

The appearance of the transporter and the uniformed police officer pulled her back to the present.

"Ready to go, Leigh?" The smiling face of the transporter stood in sharp contrast to the fierce expression on the police officer's face. Was she in some sort of trouble? Is that what Ryan wanted to talk to her about? Had she done something wrong? She'd run her car off the road because she was trying to protect the people in the car and the man on the tractor. Were they going to arrest her for something?

The police officer barely acknowledged her, even as they were wheeled into a service elevator and whisked to the fourth floor. When they arrived at her room, he went in first and checked out the room, but as soon as the bed was secured, he went back outside.

"You're all set," the transporter said. "Your nurse is on her way."

"Thank you."

For a brief, blissful moment, Leigh was alone. She didn't have to pretend to be okay. Didn't have to keep her face passive or try not to let anyone see how frightened she was.

Then the nurse bustled in. "I'm going to be your nurse today," she said. "I'm Megyn. That's spelled m-e-g-y-n because that's the only proper way to spell Megyn."

Leigh nodded in agreement. "Of course."

"Excellent. I'm glad we agree. I think we'll get along fine."

Megyn was efficient and moved quickly as she helped Leigh settle. She gave her some grief about her wanting to change into the pajamas Keri had brought but relented with a dramatic sigh.

"I shouldn't let you do this, you know," she said.

"I know," Leigh said. "Thank you."

At least she'd be able to talk to Ryan without the distraction of a stupid hospital gown. Megyn left with a promise to return soon. The door didn't close behind her. A strong hand caught it. A soft tap.

"May I come in?"

Ryan.

"Get in here," she said.

His eyes widened as he approached her bed. "Are you okay? Is something wrong? Do I need to get the nurse?"

Had he lost his mind? "No, everything is not okay. Yes, something is wrong. Don't you dare go get a nurse. You tell me what is happening and you tell me right now."

The relief that filled Ryan's face at her outburst made no sense at all. Especially when it faded to speculation and concern.

"Leigh . . ." He paced around her small room before coming to a stop at the foot of her bed. "I'll try to explain what I know, but it's okay if you don't want to talk about it right now."

Why wouldn't she want to talk about it now? "Okay."

"Your brakes failed today."

"Yeah. I kinda noticed when I was hurtling down a hill at seventy miles an hour and they didn't work."

He should have smiled at that. He didn't.

"Leigh, someone cut your brake line."

Of all the things he could have said, that was the last thing she'd expected.

"What?"

"Your brake line—it had a small cut. It was intentional."

She tried to process his words. "I had it worked on last week. Surely they would have noticed—"

"It was done last night. While you were at work."

"How could you possibly know that?"

"Because if it had been done any earlier, your brakes would have failed before you got to the hospital."

This couldn't be happening. Why would—? Who—?

The familiar terror crept up her spine. No. No. It couldn't be. He was gone. Dead. Buried. Literally.

"I'm sorry about this," Ryan said. "But when you're ready, I'm going to need you to tell me everything you can about your stalker."

The color drained from Leigh's face. The volume on the monitor had been turned down, but Ryan could see how her heart rate accelerated as he spoke.

"Leigh," he said. "It's going to be okay. I won't let anything happen to you. We'll figure this out."

"He's dead," she whispered. "It wasn't even his fault. The cancer messed up his brain. Barry never would have done the things he did if he hadn't had a tumor wreaking havoc on his mind."

He could tell she believed that. He'd have to check the police reports and talk to the officers in Durham to see if they agreed. He admired her ability to see the guy as a victim rather than a monster.

But he'd met a lot of monsters.

Most of them didn't deserve any sympathy.

Oh, sure, they'd had hard lives, caught some tough breaks. But no one had the right to take another life. No one had the right to abuse and terrorize another human being.

He waited to see if Leigh would say anything else. He hated talking to her like this. Now. Right out of surgery. He'd had his appendix out a few years ago and couldn't remember anything that happened for a solid twenty-four hours after the surgery. Would she recall their conversation? Or resent him for it?

"He started calling the hospital," she said in a faraway voice. "He'd ask to speak to me, refused to speak with anyone else. We all knew about the tumor. Everyone humored him."

She looked out the shaded window to her left. "I didn't think anything of it at first. Sometimes it annoyed me. Most of the time I felt sorry for him. I helped him with all his symptom management, pain management. I'd even go check on him when he came in for chemo."

She closed her eyes. "Then he showed up at the door of my house one night."

Ryan could imagine the scenario.

"I wasn't overly alarmed at first." She looked at him now, her eyes pleading for understanding. "He was sick. Dying. I tried to be nice. I didn't let him come inside or anything. I've thought about it a million times, but I can't think of anything I did to encourage him."

"Leigh—"

"I know." She cut him off. "I know it's not my fault. But you can't help but wonder if there wasn't something you could have done differently. Something that would have kept it from being such a mess later."

He didn't try to argue with her. He could imagine how her compassion had kept her from seeing the danger at the time—and still made it difficult for her to blame the man entirely for his actions.

"I called his daughter. She came and picked him up. So apologetic. But then he was back at two in the morning. Scared me to death when my doorbell rang. When I saw it was him, I didn't even open the door. Told him he needed to go home. Called his daughter. Again."

She took a sip of a pale beverage and wrinkled her nose.

"Want me to get you a fresh drink? What would you like?"

"A Coke," she said without hesitation.

"Consider it done."

He opened the door. The officer stationed outside glanced in his direction. "We're okay in here," he said. "Just do me a favor. Catch the nurse the next time you see her and get Leigh a Coke."

"Will do," the officer said.

Ryan walked back to Leigh's side. She was smirking at him.

"What?"

"There's this handy little thing on the bed." She pointed to the glowing lights on the rail. "It calls the nurse. You don't need a cop to get a Coke."

She was almost smiling.

"You're a real smart aleck, aren't you?"

"Can be."

"I remember."

They sat in silence for a moment. "I take it he didn't go quietly?"

"Oh no. He yelled at me through the door while I waited for his daughter. Yelled at his poor daughter when she came to get him. I thought that would be the end of it. Didn't hear anything else from him for a few weeks, and then weird things started happening. Flowers delivered to the hospital. To the house. Notes saying I would be his forever. That he loved me and couldn't live without me. Some of them would have been sweet if they hadn't been so out of left field, but some of them were graphic and disturbing."

Megyn came in with a can of Coke and a cup with fresh ice. "Here you go. I've ordered a meal tray for you. Should be here soon."

"Thanks," Leigh said.

As soon as Megyn left, she groaned.

"Are you hurting?"

"No." She opened the Coke and poured some over the ice. "Have you seen the stuff we give people after surgery? Bleh. Gelatin and unsalted broth. You have to get me out of here or I'll starve."

As soon as he was done talking to Leigh, he'd ask Dr. Price if he could get her something more palatable. He'd get her anything she wanted, but he didn't want to make her sick. Of course, she was the nurse. She should know what she could and couldn't handle.

Leigh took a sip and blew out a breath. "Anyway, it went from bad to worse to bizarre. He showed up at my church and caused a nasty scene in the middle of a service. He showed up at a friend's birthday party. I never did find out how he knew where I was, unless he'd been following me."

"He was still driving?" Surely the guy should have had his license revoked.

"Not legally," she said. "Finances were tight. The family was doing the best they could, but they hadn't taken the step of getting a full-time caregiver yet. And they couldn't afford a nursing home."

She traced the edge of her cup with her finger.

He didn't rush her.

"Then one morning he was in the parking garage at the hospital. With a gun. Told me I was coming with him."

She looked at Ryan. "You have to understand, he wasn't much of a physical threat. By this point, he probably only weighed a hundred pounds. He was frail and weak. I could have outrun him easily. But I really was afraid he was going to shoot me that day."

"How did it end?"

She shrugged. "Oh, it was a big mess. It was shift change. The garage was full of people. Didn't take long before the security guards were on-site, the police were on their way, and there were about fifty doctors and nurses standing around us, many of whom knew the situation. I was able to talk him into giving the gun to one of the residents he knew. Then the security guards grabbed him. They held him until the police came. That was the last time I saw him."

She blew out a long breath. "He died a couple of months ago. And he was completely bedridden for at least a month before that. He hasn't been a threat to me in a long time. He didn't do this."

Her points seemed valid. It did seem unlikely that her stalker was responsible for the current situation. Not that he didn't intend to pull death records and confirm all this for himself.

But if it wasn't Leigh's stalker, then who did it?

"Can you think of anyone else who would even consider harming you? Any patients you've treated in the ED who might have an axe to grind?"

She leaned her head back on the pillow and closed her eyes. "I can't think of anyone," she said, weariness lacing her words. "I work nights. We get everything from babies with croup to grown men who need stitches from a bar fight. We get overdoses and car accidents and domestic violence cases. But that's part of why I chose emergency medicine when I moved home. I wanted a break from being so involved in my patients' lives. They come in. They leave. I'm the one they see when the baby has a high fever and the mom panics or when the elderly dad has trouble breathing during the night and the kids bring him in. I don't do a lot of trauma unless we get swamped. Other than the frequent flyers, I never see them again."

Ryan tried not to let his frustration show.

How could he find out who did this with no clues and no motive?

And how could he have two cases in the space of twenty-four hours with absolutely nothing to go on?

While he'd been waiting for Leigh to get out of recovery, he'd spent some time in the ED. Everyone he'd talked to said the same thing. "Leigh Weston is a dream to work with. She's fabulous with her patients. Gets along great with the doctors. All the nurses want her to be on their shift. She's good with kids, the elderly, and everyone in between."

How could someone who everyone liked have someone so determined to kill her? And what were the odds that it would happen twice in one year?

"I need to ask you one more question," he said. "Then I promise I'll leave you alone." For a little while. "Were the police one hundred percent certain the flowers and cards and notes were from the patient you treated?"

Leigh's face crinkled in confusion. "I'm not following you."

"You had physical encounters with your patient in Durham. He showed up at your door. He called. He confronted you in public places. Those were obviously him. But what about the other stuff? The gifts and flowers and notes. Did anyone ever confirm he sent them?"

"Who else would have sent them?"

"Did he deny sending them?"

"Yes, but he also denied coming to my house at two in the morning. He wasn't mentally stable at that point."

Ryan jotted a quick note in his phone.

"Do you think there was someone else?"

"I don't have any idea. But I'd like to see some proof that this guy was the one who sent the stuff. Some credit card receipts, security footage of him delivering them, something. Because without that, and in light of this recent development, I have to wonder if it's possible you had not one stalker, but two. One of whom is still very much alive."

6

Is that why you put a cop outside my door? You think someone's after me?" Fuzzy pieces of her memory started to fall into place. The police officer in the recovery room wasn't there to arrest her. He was there to protect her. But from whom?

Ryan's skin flushed. "I didn't order it. The sheriff ordered it. Right after he got the call from Mr. Cook."

"Mr. Cook?" He'd kept her company after the accident. His voice hadn't given away that he was worried about anything other than her.

"He noticed the brake line was cut while he was talking to you. I've already been assigned your case, and you will have an increased police presence around you until we get to the bottom of this."

She owed Mr. Cook a plate of cookies. And a long hug. But why would Ryan be assigned to something like this? She couldn't pull him away from the murder he was already working.

"You work homicide, Ryan. Seems like this wouldn't fall to you. Besides, you're in the middle of a big case."

He dropped his head and his voice was low but steady. "I work attempted homicides too."

The weight of his words forced the air out of her lungs.

Attempted homicide. Is that what the police were calling this?

Really, God? Are you determined that I die some horrible death? Barry didn't get me, so you've found someone else to torment me?

Ryan paced the room. "If you want me to have someone else assigned, I can try to do that."

What was he talking about? Why was his face all red?

"But I am the investigator on call," he said, "so it would have fallen to me regardless. And the captain thought it would be easier for you. Since we know each other."

Leigh gave up trying to make sense of his rambling. "Did I miss something?"

"What?"

"I'm not following you. Did I say something to make you think I don't want you to work the case?" It was possible. Between the anesthesia and pain medicine, her eyelids were begging to close.

"You said that thing about me working the other homicide. I thought you meant I wouldn't have time to work this case too."

Leigh still didn't get it. "I did. I mean, aren't you super busy on that? Seems like that would be more important than getting stuck babysitting me and stalker number two."

Ryan stopped pacing. "Wait a minute. You don't mind me working the case?"

Was he going to make her say it again? "Ryan, I can't think of anyone else I would rather have on my side, but I assumed the dead body in the lake was more important. I don't want to be the annoying little sister you're having to put up with as she tags along while you do your real job."

Memories of their trip to Six Flags flashed into her mind. Her parents had been older when they'd adopted her and they had a bit of an overprotective streak. The morning the youth group left in the church buses, Leigh's parents made Kirk and Ryan promise to stay close to her and her friend Shelly. Kirk had been so mad. Although now that she thought about it, Ryan hadn't seemed to mind.

He put his hands on the low footboard of her bed. “Leigh Weston. You have never been an annoying little sister.”

Whoa. Not the response she’d been expecting.

She stared at him. He stared back.

Wait. Did he mean what she thought he meant?

His phone buzzed. He closed his eyes slowly and pulled in a deep breath through his nose. When he opened his eyes, he gave her a forced smile. “I need to take this.”

“Sure,” she said. She tried to sound nonchalant, but the word came out hoarse and rough.

“Parker,” he said as he stepped into the hall.

Then she was alone.

What had just happened?

Had he—? No. That couldn’t have been it. He must have meant she hadn’t been annoying. She was reading way more into it than she should. She needed to get a grip. She could probably blame it all on the accident. Too bad they said she didn’t have a concussion.

The door opened and she plastered on a cheery smile . . . for a tall, middle-aged woman and a big baby-faced cop who looked like he’d be right at home in a football uniform.

The officer nodded at her and stayed near the door. The woman had her hands full.

“Here’s your tray.”

Leigh studied her. She looked familiar, but her name tag was flipped around and Leigh couldn’t see it.

She put the tray on the bedside table and then positioned the table across the bed. “I can’t say much for the broth, but the gelatin is actually pretty tasty.” Her face was full of sympathy.

“Will you rat me out if I order a pizza?” Leigh asked, only half joking.

“Only if you don’t share it with me,” she said with a wink. “But don’t worry, you’ve got a great nurse tonight. She won’t give you any grief.”

"Good to know. Any particular nurse I need to look out for?" Leigh asked.

"Oh yeah," she said. "If you get Tiffany, you're in for it. She's going through a nasty divorce and thinks every patient is a drug-seeking addict as opposed to a postoperative patient who just might actually be in pain. But everyone else is okay."

"Thanks for the heads-up," Leigh said.

"You're welcome. Enjoy your meal," she said as she left. The officer nodded again and followed the woman out.

Leigh looked at the pitiful offerings on the tray. A cup of tea she knew would be sweet enough to attract every honeybee in the state. A mug of broth. A plastic container of neon yellow gelatin.

Nope. She couldn't do it. She shoved the tray aside.

Her stomach growled in reaction. Maybe she could get Ryan to run over to the Pancake Hut and get her some scrambled eggs and toast.

Ryan.

Her stomach reacted in a completely different way at the thought of him. She rested her head on the pillow and closed her eyes. She had problems. Real problems. Worrying about him was a waste of time and energy.

She tried to shove him from her thoughts.

But it was his image that floated before her closed eyes as she drifted off to sleep.

It was his voice—rough and whispering that pulled her back to consciousness.

"I won't. I won't," he said. "I know."

She lay still and kept her eyes closed.

"I'll see you later . . . yeah . . . okay . . . I love you too."

The words pierced her. Wow, she was an idiot. Of course he had someone in his life. Why wouldn't he?

She was the only one who couldn't have that.

She made a show of stretching.

"Hey," he said. "I hope I didn't wake you up."

"Hmm?" she said. Was it lying if she didn't actually answer? Probably.

He was standing so close. "You didn't touch the food on your tray."

She didn't see any need to justify that comment with a response.

"Yeah, I don't blame you. But you need to eat." He waved his phone in the air. "Rebecca is convinced I'll starve to death at some point. I promised her I'd eat. Is there anything I can get for you?"

His sister?

Somehow everything in the room looked brighter. Why was she relieved? Must be because she was hungry. And she did want something decent to eat.

"I talked to Dr. Price," he said. "Told him you didn't want this stuff. He said you could eat whatever you felt you could handle. He suggested soup. Or eggs. Or egg drop soup. Or rice. I don't know." His face crinkled in frustration. "He wasn't super helpful."

"Getting his permission is helpful enough. I think I'd like to start with some crackers. Then maybe some scrambled eggs and toast. There's a Pancake Hut around the corner—"

"I love that place," he said.

"Me too."

"I get the Kitchen Sink every time."

"Seriously?" The Kitchen Sink was three pancakes, two eggs, bacon, and grits. The pancakes were the size of a small flying saucer.

"Of course. What else would I order? What do you get? Please tell me it isn't an egg white omelet. Or oatmeal. Please, not oatmeal."

She tried to stifle her laughter at his tragic expression. "What do you have against oatmeal?"

"Nothing," he said. "But you don't go to the Pancake Hut for oatmeal. You can eat oatmeal at home. If you tell me you usually order oatmeal, I don't know if I'll be able to handle it."

She grinned. "Well, when I'm not ordering the oatmeal . . ."

Ryan's face registered mock despair.

"I order the Produce Drawer."

Ryan threw back his head and laughed. *That* was the laugh she remembered.

"The Produce Drawer. Nice."

The Produce Drawer was a massive omelet filled with every imaginable vegetable and served with a pancake on the side. He regarded her with obvious approval. "I'll make you a deal. I'll get you some scrambled eggs, grits, and toast for tonight. As soon as you feel up to it, I'll take you to get a Produce Drawer."

Had he—? No. He was just being nice. She needed to remember he was looking out for her like a brother. "You make it sound chivalrous, but somehow I think you're just offering so you can get a Kitchen Sink." She held up two fingers. "Twice."

He hung his head. "Busted. You would make a great cop."

"Ha," she said. "I can assure you, that is not the case. I would make a lousy cop. I'm too much of a wimp." Sadly, that part was completely true. One patient literally loses his mind and she falls apart. Can't handle it. Has to leave town and start over.

No. She would make a horrible cop.

"Earth to Leigh." Ryan stood at the foot of her bed, waving a hand in her direction. Had she fallen asleep? Or zoned out?

"Sorry," she said.

"No worries. I asked if you wanted anything to drink besides this sugar water they brought you." He pointed at her tray.

"Another Coke."

"Coke it is. Be right back."

"Wait," she said. "I, um—" Where was her stuff? Her purse, her wallet?

"What's wrong?" He rushed back to her bed, worry lining his features.

"I don't have any money," she said, heat flushing her skin.

He quirked one eyebrow. "You can pay me back later. In cake."

There was an awful lot of "later" in his conversation today. "Fine."

He winked at her and headed for the door.

She rested her head again. Closed her eyes. This day. What was going on? Someone had cut her brakes? Why? She could have been killed. Or could have killed someone else, which would have been so much worse.

It didn't make sense. None of it. At least with Barry, as bizarre as the situation was, it did make sense. She'd been the nurse practitioner he saw almost every time he came in the office. She'd been the one to talk to him and his daughter about treatments and pain medicines and where to sign up for services offered by their incredible cancer society. She'd been there when they got the scans back. She'd shed more than a few tears with the oncologist as they reviewed the results, and then more tears with Barry as he processed the news.

They had a connection, and when his brain betrayed him it was understandable she would be someone it focused on.

But now? There was no one. Her patients came and went. They had a few regulars in the ED, but no one who would do something like this. She didn't have enemies.

She barely had any friends.

That wasn't true. She had friends. Good ones. Great ones. In-between ones. But she'd kept a pretty solid wall up for months. Very few had been able to breach it.

All she had to do was shoot out a message on social media or send a text or two and her social calendar would be full.

But she didn't want to.

And now? Now she didn't dare do that. Anyone who was with her could be at risk. Could Ryan be right? Could she have had a second stalker the whole time?

But why would he have backed off for so long?

One reason popped into her mind.

Jail.

He could have been in jail and now he was out.

Awesome. A criminal was stalking her.

Stop it. This train of thought wasn't going to get her anywhere but worked up and agitated. She took a few deep breaths. Tried to use some of the calming techniques her therapist had taught her. They worked reasonably well.

They'd worked better when she didn't think anyone wanted to kill her.

But that wasn't true anymore.

Somewhere, probably nearby, there was someone who hated her so much they were willing to end her life and possibly a few more.

Why?

Ryan stalked the halls of the hospital in search of a spot that would provide decent phone reception. When he found one, he planted himself against the glass wall and dialed.

His first call was to the Pancake Hut.

His second was to the dispatcher at the sheriff's office. It wasn't precisely protocol, but he found an officer in the vicinity of the Pancake Hut willing to pick up his order.

His third was to Kirk. It rang twice and Kirk picked up. "Ryan. What's going on?"

"Where have you been, man?"

"Working."

"It's ten o'clock at night there."

"I know that. It was a meeting with my boss. My stupid phone only works about half the time. When I left the office, I got all your messages at once. How's Leigh?"

"She's fine," Ryan said. He filled Kirk in on the surgery and the situation with the brake line.

"Someone tried to kill her?" He could hear Kirk's frustration from forty-three hundred miles away.

"Yes."

"But . . . why?"

Ryan shared the stalker theory.

"You don't sound like you really think that's what's going on," Kirk said.

"You can tell?" He thought he'd done a good job of hiding that.

"Dude, I've known you my whole life. What aren't you telling me?"

"It doesn't make sense. None of it. And I don't like things that don't make sense. It's possible there's another stalker out there who has been laying low for the past few months, but this is a weird way of coming back on the scene. I would have expected more flowers, more weird messages, more creepy notes. Not a cut brake line. That's escalating way beyond anything normal. It might be different if there was a new man in her life, but she isn't dating anyone."

"True."

Ryan released the breath he hadn't realized he'd been holding.

"What can I do?" Kirk asked.

"Just be there for her."

"You think we need to come home? I can't leave Simone over here by herself. I wouldn't put it past those uncles of hers to kidnap her."

"I don't mean physically be there for her. I mean emotionally. Encourage her to talk to me and keep me in the loop if she even thinks she sees something suspicious. Help me keep her talking."

"You got her talking?"

"Yeah."

"Impressive. You're good. Thanks for taking care of her."

Ryan wasn't sure what to say to that. If Kirk had any idea how much he was enjoying taking care of her, he'd probably reach through the phone and strangle him. "No problem," he finally mumbled.

Ryan disconnected the call after promising to call him with any updates. And after promising to continue to keep an eye on Leigh.

The updates might be hard.

Keeping an eye on Leigh wouldn't be.

Ryan called the dispatcher again and located Leigh's personal belongings from her car. Then he called Gabe.

"You missed a fun one today, Parker," Gabe said as he answered. "Anissa is extra mean to me when you aren't around."

"What'd she do?"

"She made me do all the no-visibility work."

"That's because besides her, you're the best diver on the team. She wasn't being mean. She was doing her job."

And doing it well.

"I guess." Gabe's tone gave away how hard it was for him to agree. "She's letting me cut out early to come check on you in a little bit. And she wants me to give her an update."

"See, she's not so bad. If you'd give her a chance . . ."

"Whatever. What do you need?"

"A favor."

When he finished with Gabe, he walked down to the main entrance. Five minutes later, a car pulled up.

"Thanks," Ryan said to the young officer as he handed him a plastic bag.

The aroma of pancakes and bacon wafted through the halls as he hurried back to Leigh. He knew she was going to give him grief about the Kitchen Sink, but he hadn't eaten in hours. And he wanted her to have some warm food. No one wanted to eat cold grits.

The officer outside Leigh's room nodded toward the door. "Nurse is in there, Investigator Parker."

"Thanks. What's your name?"

"Peter Stanfield. Most people call me Pete."

"Thanks, Pete. Anyone else been around?"

"No one but the woman that delivered the food tray and the one that shows up every hour to take vitals. Oh, and the one that came by a few minutes ago to get her tray. If anyone goes in there except for the nurse, Megyn, I go with them."

"Thanks."

"Happy to do it. I hadn't met her before today, but she's super nice." He glanced around the hall. "You really think someone might try to pull something on her in here?"

"I think it's highly likely," he said. "Someone familiar with the hospital and grounds was able to puncture her brake line sometime between eleven last night and seven this morning. There's a good chance they're an employee."

Pete's face hardened. "I'm on it."

Megyn emerged from Leigh's room. She glanced at the bag in Ryan's hand. He braced himself for a tongue-lashing.

She glared at him for a long moment before snorting in laughter. "She's a big girl. But if she throws up everywhere, I'm coming after you."

"Yes, ma'am," he said as he tapped on the door.

Leigh was on the phone as he entered.

"I know. I will. Okay. Yeah. He's right here. Won't go away. What did you say to him?"

The words might have hurt if she hadn't winked at him as she said them.

Leigh winked at him? Interesting. He'd almost blown it earlier. She was a victim—as much as he hated to use that word, it was accurate under the circumstances—in an active investigation. One he was in charge of.

And Kirk would kill him.

Might be worth it though.

Still, this was neither the time nor the place. Her emotions had to be at a breaking point. This would have been a frightening enough situation if she hadn't been traumatized in the past few months. Adding a stalker to the mix meant she was in a fragile state at the moment.

Not that he thought she was weak. Far from it. She was one of the toughest people he'd ever known. But even the most imposing tower could be weakened after taking a blow to a support structure. And her support structures had taken a beating.

He pulled a bottle of Coke from the bag and presented it to her like a sommelier presenting a bottle of wine. Still talking to Kirk, she twisted the cap off and took an approving sniff.

He couldn't keep himself from laughing.

He pulled Styrofoam boxes from the bag, then plastic packets of butter, tiny bottles of syrup, and forks and knives as Leigh wrapped up her call with Kirk.

He heard her sigh as she placed the phone on the bedside table.

"Everything okay?" he asked.

"Kirk's upset. Wants to come home. I told him not to. Not that he could anyway. He can't leave Simone, and she can't get off work. He'd probably lose his job too. The case he's working on is important."

"You're important too."

A soft smile lit her face. "That's what he said. But I think I've convinced him to sit tight for now." Her expression grew pensive, but he couldn't bring himself to ask her what she was thinking about.

He arranged the eggs, grits, toast, butter, and jelly on the tray and rolled it so it was across her bed.

She smiled her thanks.

"Mind if I ask the blessing?" he asked.

"Please do."

"Father, we thank you for the food. We thank you for your protection of Leigh today, and we ask that you will give us wisdom and discernment as we investigate and help us to find out what's going on. We ask for your continued protection over Leigh, and we thank you that we can come to you boldly and know you hear us. In Jesus's name, amen."

"Amen." She lifted her head and pointed to the food. "Thank you."

He poured a healthy serving of syrup over his pancakes. "No, thank *you*," he said. "Always happy to have an excuse to eat the Kitchen Sink."

They chatted easily. They talked about Kirk's case and Simone's family. He told her about Zoe's antics and Caleb's mad LEGO skills.

He tried to pace himself, but it took him no time at all to inhale his food while she picked at hers. A few bites of egg. A few bites of toast. Then a pause before she attempted the grits.

"You aren't going to throw up, are you?" he asked. "'Cause that nurse is gonna beat me up if you do."

She snorted. "Megyn wouldn't hurt a fly. I think you're safe."

"That's a relief, but you didn't answer my question."

"I feel okay. Just trying to be sure it stays that way. It all tastes great, but I'll never be able to finish it. Will you take some of it?"

"What?"

"Based on the way you polished off those pancakes, I'm guessing you haven't eaten all day. And you haven't had the advantage of being under anesthesia."

"I'd hardly call that an advantage."

She smiled as she pushed the grits in his direction. "Want some?"

He shouldn't.

"Oh, okay," he said. He took the bowl of grits and tipped it over his plate.

A loud crashing sound came from the hallway. The grits missed the plate and hit the floor as he jumped to his feet. He reached for his weapon and stood between Leigh and the door.

The door flew open and Megyn stood there, her face ashen. "I'm sorry to bother you, but something is very wrong with this officer."

"What?" Leigh's question followed Ryan to the door. He didn't dare race into the hallway. It could be a trap.

"What's going on?" Relief flooded through him at the sound of Gabe's voice.

"Pete," Gabe said. "What happened, man?"

Ryan still hesitated. Gabe could take care of himself, but opening the door could put Leigh in danger.

Then Gabe called out, "Parker? Everything okay in there? I could use a hand here."

Ryan poked his head out the door. Megyn was on the floor beside Pete, who was struggling to stand.

"You're trying to kill me, aren't you?" Pete slurred his words and it took Ryan a second to figure out what he'd said.

Ryan looked from Pete to Megyn to Gabe. Megyn was horrified. Gabe was . . . not.

"Yo, Pete, my man," Gabe said as he approached him with measured steps. He made eye contact with Ryan and then dropped his eyes to the weapon at Pete's waist.

"Get away from me," Pete mumbled. He continued to try to stand, but he couldn't seem to get his legs underneath him. "I'm too young to die."

What was going on? Pete was acting like he was on some sort of weird acid trip.

Oh.

Gabe had reached Pete. "Pete, nobody's gonna hurt you, man. Let's sit here for a second and you tell me what's going on."

Pete flailed against the wall. He cried something about seeing through a hole, but by now his words were so slurred, Ryan couldn't make any sense out of them.

Gabe never took his eyes from Pete. Ryan had no idea what he was up to, but he trusted his friend. Gabe knelt over Pete and in a flash had him flipped over onto his stomach and handcuffed.

Pete continued to thrash about as Ryan removed his service weapon.

"Sorry to do that to you, Pete," Gabe said soothingly. "I promise you're safe. Just trying to protect the ladies."

"Ryan, call for backup."

Ryan didn't wait for an explanation. He dialed the dispatcher and called it in as Pete moaned from the floor.

"Ma'am," Gabe said to Megyn, his voice soothing and calm.

"Yes?" Her voice quavered, but she approached with caution. "I believe this officer has been drugged. He's going to need medical attention."

She nodded.

"Now," Gabe said with a bit more urgency. Megyn darted to a phone. He heard her say something that echoed through the hallway speakers. Hopefully that was her calling in the cavalry.

"What happened?"

Leigh's voice came from much closer than it should have. Ryan turned and she stood beside him, IV tubing dangled from her arm.

"What are you doing? You need to get back in bed. You just had surgery."

She ignored him and knelt by Pete. It must have hurt because she let out a small grunt as her knee hit the floor. "Pete? Hey, Pete?"

She checked his eyes and then her eyes widened. "A K-hole?" She directed the question to Gabe.

"Maybe. He's tripping on something."

"We need to get him sitting up. Now," she said. More like ordered.

Ryan jumped to help Gabe position Pete against the wall, while keeping an eye on the hallway.

"You could take the handcuffs off, Gabe," Leigh said.

So they were on a first name basis, were they?

"He's not a danger to anyone."

Ryan wasn't sure she was right, but Gabe was the drug expert. He helped keep Pete propped up as Gabe removed the cuffs.

"Thank you. That's going to make it much easier on the team," Leigh said.

Every time they tried to let go of Pete, he slid down the wall or crumpled to one side or the other. His eyes were unfocused and they couldn't get any response from him.

Leigh kept one hand on his wrist. "His heart rate is skyrocketing," she said.

Ryan and Gabe both jumped back as Pete vomited all over himself. Some of it got on Leigh. She never flinched.

That must have been why she wanted him sitting up. He could have choked. "You might want to try to collect some of this for evidence," she said. If she was grossed out, she didn't show it. "Megyn, could you get us some basins?"

A commotion drew Ryan's attention to the elevators. Doctors and nurses were converging on their location.

"Leigh, we need to get you back in your room," Ryan said.

"In a minute," she said. "I need to report."

"Leigh Weston." The doctor who reached them first did not look happy. "What are you doing out of bed?"

"Dr. Sloan, this officer has been guarding my room all afternoon," she said. "I have no idea how it could have happened, but he's presenting with signs of a Special K overdose."

The doctor didn't seem upset anymore. "How long?"

"Less than five minutes since Megyn noticed erratic behavior. He hit the hole, vomited, and went catatonic."

"That's awfully fast," Gabe said under his breath.

The doctor began yelling orders, and then they had Pete on a stretcher and were racing him down the hall in under a minute. As they turned the corner, the doctor looked back.

"Get back in the bed, young lady," he said.

"Yes, sir."

"Are you okay?" Ryan asked Leigh.

Her expression could melt steel. "I'm fine." She swallowed hard.

Two officers stepped off the elevator and Ryan pointed at them and then to the right and left. "Take each end of this hall," he told them.

Ryan looked at Gabe. "I have a bad feeling about this."

"Me too." Gabe retrieved a small box from the floor and handed it to him.

Megyn leaned against the wall. She pushed her hair back from her face with a shaking hand. "This is why I don't work in the ED. He started jabbering. Making no sense at all. And then it was like his legs gave out. He dropped. Right in front of me. He's so young. What could have happened to him?"

Gabe walked over to where Megyn stood and leaned against the wall beside her. "I'm not sure," he said. "But I need to ask you a couple of questions. I'm sorry to do it, but it might help us find out."

She swallowed hard and her face took on a determined expression. "No. Don't apologize. I'm tougher than I look. I'll answer all your questions if you can ask them while I'm helping my patient get back in her bed."

Thank goodness.

Gabe gave her an encouraging smile as they entered Leigh's room. "Have you seen anyone today you weren't expecting?" he asked Megyn.

Ryan appreciated the way she took her time responding.

She bit down on her lip and shook her head. "I don't know. We're crazy busy. They've got people from all over the hospital working in places they don't usually work today. The nursing assistants are overworked. The food service folks are understaffed. I honestly don't know if there was anyone here that shouldn't have been."

Leigh leaned against the bed. "Oh no." Her voice was rough.

"What is it? Are you hurting? You need to get off your feet." Ryan took her arm, but she refused to budge.

"No. The food."

The food? Who cared about the food?

"My food. It was supposed to be me," she said in horror.

"What are you talking about?"

"I gave Pete my gelatin."

"What?"

"My gelatin, from my tray. I didn't want it. When the girl came to get the tray, he came in the room with her. He made a comment about me not eating anything. I told him I thought about the gelatin but I couldn't get motivated to eat it, and he said he'd always had a soft spot for it. I told him to take it."

She dropped her head. "He did."

"What flavor was it?" Gabe asked.

"Lemon. Strong enough to hide the taste of Special K," she said.

Ryan wasn't an expert on drugs, but he was pretty sure they weren't talking about breakfast cereal. "What's Special K?"

Gabe answered. "It's the street name for ketamine. It's used in veterinary clinics and sometimes by anesthesiologists as a pre-anesthetic drug. But people take it to enter a dissociative state. It can cause hallucinations. It's common for them to see something they call a K-hole. It's when it looks to them like there's a hole about the size of a tennis ball and that's all they can see through. Everything else goes dark. Special K is used recreationally in clubs, that kind of thing, but in a high enough dose, it can kill."

Leigh continued to stare at the floor.

"It was meant for me."

7

Leigh didn't want to look at anyone. She wanted to crawl into a hole and disappear.

Pete had been drugged.

And as fast as he'd reacted, it must have been a huge dose. Enough to kill her, and maybe enough to kill a big guy like Pete.

"Gentlemen." Megyn's voice broke through her thoughts. "I don't think we're going to solve this in the next two minutes, and I need to get my patient into some clean clothes and off her feet."

"Of course," Ryan said. "How can we help?"

"Stay out of the room for a few minutes."

Heat flooded his face. "Yes, ma'am."

Leigh tried to focus on the positive. The doctors knew what was going on. Dr. Sloan was awesome. Pete was getting the best possible care right now.

But would it be enough? Special K caused hallucinations and paralysis, and in high enough doses it could stop lung function. If enough oxygen didn't get to the brain, a person could have permanent brain damage.

If she'd eaten that gelatin while in her room alone, she could have died before anyone knew she was in trouble.

Why?

As Megyn grabbed some towels, Leigh closed her eyes and prayed silently as she hadn't prayed in months. She might not be able to generate much enthusiasm for praying for herself, but surely God couldn't want Pete to die. Whatever his beef was, it was with her, not poor Pete.

"You okay?" Megyn asked as she helped her pull the vomit-covered shirt off. Thank goodness Keri had brought her pajamas that buttoned—or it would have been extra gross.

"No," Leigh said.

"You shouldn't have gotten out of the bed," Megyn said in a chiding voice.

"I couldn't just lie here."

"Most would have."

Leigh didn't believe that.

Megyn smiled at her, her eyes full of compassion. "I don't know what's going on, but I'll be praying for you. And I'll be sure you get a great nurse tonight. But you need to promise me you'll take it easy. You'll regret it if you don't. There's no point in slowing your recovery. The best way to get back to one hundred percent is to be sure you don't overdo it."

"Yes, ma'am," Leigh said. Megyn was right. She knew it. But taking it easy hadn't ever been her strong suit.

Getting into clean pajamas and settling into the bed took fifteen minutes.

When Megyn left, it was with the promise that she'd be back to check on her soon.

The door never closed on her. Ryan poked his head into her room. "Can we come in?"

"Sure," she said. He could bring in an army if he wanted to. She was terrified to be alone, but at the same time, her pounding head and throbbing leg begged for her to close her eyes and be still. When Megyn came back, she'd have to ask for some pain medicine or she'd never get through the night.

Gabe followed Ryan in. "Hey there," he said.

"Hey yourself. Haven't seen you around here lately."

He dropped his head and shrugged. "Yeah."

That was all the answer she got. There was a story there, but either he didn't want to share it, or he couldn't. She'd patched him up a few times in the ED the first month she'd been on the job. Once because he'd "missed the curb" and somehow split open the back of his head. The other time he'd "cut himself with scissors"—on his forearm.

Dr. Sloan had taken care of him both times, very quickly and quietly, and then Gabe had slipped away. When Leigh questioned it, she'd been told it would be in everyone's best interest if she forgot she'd ever seen him.

But Gabe wasn't the kind of guy you forgot. Not only because he turned the heads of every female in the place. But more because he was funny and intense.

He was similar to Ryan in some ways and completely different in others. They seemed at ease with each other. Like they'd been friends for a while. Or maybe they'd become friends fast because of what they'd been through together.

Gabe's face had been splashed all over the news two months ago when the sheriff's office busted a drug ring and the whole thing was broadcast live by a reporter in the local news helicopter. As soon as Leigh saw his face on her television, all the pieces fell into place. He'd been working undercover. But he couldn't work undercover anymore. At least not in Carrington.

Ryan handed her a small box. "Gabe brought this from the station," he said.

Leigh opened it. Her phone, purse, sunglasses, hospital ID, and headphones stared back at her.

Her eyes burned and she blinked hard and fast before looking up. "Thank you," she said, first to Ryan, then Gabe. "I really appreciate this."

"You're welcome," Gabe said. "It was Ryan's idea."

She set the box to the side.

Ryan shifted from one foot to the other. Gabe cleared his throat. These two had something to say but neither one seemed to want to be the first to speak.

"What's on your mind, gentlemen?"

Ryan took a deep breath.

"Is it that bad?" she asked.

Ryan pulled out a small, clear bag from his pocket.

Leigh stared at the wretched gelatin container. "Where'd you find that?"

"Trash can two feet from your door," Ryan said.

He'd dug through the trash?

"You think it's the one from my tray?"

"There's no way to know for sure until we test it. It was lemon flavored. It was by your door. There was no other food in the trash can. Odds are good."

He handed it to Gabe. "Gabe's gonna get the forensics guys to check it for drugs. We'll compare it to the vomit. If we get a match, we'll know for sure. This could be a solid piece of evidence."

Evidence. In an attempted homicide.

Maybe a successful one if Pete died. Had she killed Pete?

She tried to reach for the phone on the bedside table, but the IV Megyn had insisted on reattaching snagged on her pillowcase.

"Whoa," Ryan said as he jumped to help her. "What do you need?"

"I want to check on Pete," she said. "Does he have family? A wife? Kids?"

Ryan handed her the phone. "I don't know. He's fairly new. I've seen him in the halls, but we haven't worked together." He looked to Gabe, but Gabe didn't have more to offer. "I'll find out."

Leigh called the ED desk. Miss Edna answered. "Miss Edna, this is Leigh Weston," she said.

Gabe paused at the door. He and Ryan probably wanted to hear what Miss Edna had to say too.

"Leigh Weston, what are you doing calling me? You should be resting. I already heard you hopped out of your bed and got puked on. Don't make me come up there and hog-tie you. Because I can and I will."

Miss Edna's love language was bossiness.

"Yes, ma'am. I'm in the bed and I'm not going anywhere."

"Good," Miss Edna said with a *humph*.

"Can you tell me how the officer is doing?"

Father, please, please let him be okay. Please.

"Oh, child," Miss Edna said.

The compassion in her words did not bode well for what would come next.

"He's not too good. There's about a hundred cops in here right now. Not sure who's out there keeping Carrington safe at the moment, since they all seem to be converging in my department."

Miss Edna didn't care for converging.

"Dr. Sloan's still in there. They'll be taking him to ICU in a few minutes. Got him on a vent. His lungs quit working. They're trying to get as much of that mess out of his system as they can. I heard them say they think if they can keep the oxygen going that he'll be all right. We just have to wait and see."

Leigh had to pull the phone away from her ear as Miss Edna yelled at someone. She'd hate to be working right now. This was going to have Miss Edna on the warpath for the rest of the shift and possibly the rest of the week.

"Leigh, hon, I need to go. You call me back whenever you want to, okay?"

"Yes, ma'am. I will. Thank you."

She handed the phone to Ryan and he returned it to the side table. "It's not good," she said. She filled them in on Pete's condition.

"I'd better get this to the lab and then see what I can do," Gabe said. "I'll call you when I find out more about Pete," he said to Ryan. "You behave," he said to her.

When the door closed behind him, Ryan leaned against the wall. She didn't miss that he'd positioned himself between her and the door. Again.

"I need to get out of here," she said.

"You need to recover."

"How many more people are going to get hurt because of me?"

"First of all, no one has been hurt because of you," Ryan said. "And in the case of Pete, we don't actually know that you were the intended target."

It took every ounce of willpower she possessed not to throw something at him.

"Ryan Parker. You don't honestly expect me to believe that, do you?"

He offered a weak smile. "It was worth a shot."

She could not believe this was happening. "I can't even eat here," she said. "And I *am* a nurse. I can take care of myself well enough at home."

"We can make sure you have plenty of food. We'll get it from outside the hospital—and we won't advertise where it's coming from. And I'll talk to Dr. Price about getting you out of here as soon as it's completely safe for your health."

"Being *here* isn't safe for my health."

"It will be tonight. I made a few phone calls while you were getting cleaned up, and I think you'll like your nurse tonight. You can take some high-powered pain medicine and get some sleep."

Like she could sleep now. "I'll stick with ibuprofen if it's all the same to you."

"Well, it isn't all the same to me," Keri said from the door. "I don't know what kind of pull you have, Parker, but I get here a bit early and find out I've been asked to babysit a very difficult patient up here for the night. This is not in keeping with standard hospital procedure."

Ryan looked unrepentant.

"You're my nurse for tonight?" she asked Keri.

"I am. And you're going to regret it. I'm going to insist on pain medicine. And something other than Coke to drink." Keri glared at the Coke bottle tucked at her side.

"I like it."

"That stuff can kill you."

"It's going to have to get in line."

Keri and Ryan both reacted to that. Keri frowned. Ryan looked like he was considering punching a wall.

"Not tonight," Keri said.

"We will figure this out," Ryan said.

The silence filled the room like a weighted blanket.

"I need you to live long enough to take care of my cats while I'm on vacation," Keri said in an obvious attempt to lighten the mood.

"You don't take vacations," Leigh said.

"That's because I'm saving for a big one. I'm going to Ireland for a month."

"When?"

Keri ignored her question. "Investigator Parker, unless you have further questions for my patient, shouldn't you be out investigating?"

She couldn't help but notice the intentional change of subject, but Keri had a point.

"She's right, isn't she? Don't you need to work on your other case?"

Ryan groaned.

Had she said the wrong thing? Maybe she shouldn't have mentioned it in front of Keri.

"Sorry. Am I not supposed to talk about that?"

"Oh no. It's not that. I'm frustrated because the case is currently in limbo. We're waiting on the autopsy, and due to the intensity of this situation, the medical examiner wanted a buddy of hers from Raleigh to help out. Water exposure has a drastic effect on the decomposition process. I won't get anything back until tomorrow at the earliest."

"I would think the water would mess up a lot of things," Leigh said.

"It does," Ryan said. "There's a good chance we won't get anything back on any sort of tox screens. And all the tox screens and DNA analysis take a lot longer than they do on TV anyway. We're talking weeks on the tox screens and months on the DNA."

"This homicide investigating thing doesn't sound nearly as exciting as it is on TV," Keri said.

"Not usually. But on the other hand, I'm okay with not getting shot at every week." Ryan gave them a small smile. "In reality, it's a lot of long days and late nights. Right now I have a new investigator poring through missing persons cases in ever-widening circles from here, trying to find something to go on. The problem is all we know is we have a male. The ME is guessing he was around six feet tall and could have been in his fifties, but until she gets him opened up, she won't know more."

"That doesn't narrow things down much," Leigh said.

"Doesn't narrow things down at all," Keri said.

"The guy doesn't have any tattoos or obvious birthmarks. Unless someone reports a missing person that in some way matches our body, we've got a whole lot of nothing."

Ryan's frustration was palpable, and Leigh found herself wishing Keri would go away so she could try to encourage him without an audience. As it was, she couldn't think of anything helpful to say.

Keri didn't have that problem. "That stinks," she said.

"Yeah," Ryan said. "But while I'm waiting, I'm happy to help find you something tasty to eat for supper. If your dietary guardian will allow it."

"Dietary guardian." Keri rolled the words around. "I like it."

"I don't need anything right now, but at some point I'd like another Coke," Leigh said. "And some crackers from the store, not from here, obviously. Saltines."

Keri smacked her hands together. "I've got it," she said. "Let's order from Soup's On. They have a great chicken soup that wouldn't be too hard on your stomach. It's only ten minutes from here."

Ryan nodded. "On it."

He looked like he wanted to say something else but changed his mind. He shifted his weight from one foot to the other, cleared his throat, and pulled his phone from his pocket. "Text me when you place your order and I'll get it. I'll plan to be back around seven." With that, he walked out the door.

That was weird.

"Oh, Leigh," Keri said. "I think you've been keeping secrets. Very handsome secrets."

An hour later, Ryan stared at the monitor on his desk. He'd forced himself to come back to the office. All he wanted to do was hang out with Leigh at the hospital, but when he'd delivered the soup, she'd been sleeping. Keri said she was exhausted and might even sleep through the night. He'd left her a note and told her he'd be back to check on her Monday morning.

He'd also told her not to leave the hospital without checking with him first. Visions of some nut job posing as a police officer and then abducting Leigh haunted him.

He shoved them aside. She was smart and not oblivious to the danger. She wasn't going to do anything stupid. Right now she was asleep and well protected.

And as much as he didn't want to admit it to Leigh, he had a ton of work to do.

He spent several hours managing the paperwork already flooding in from the John Doe. Reports from every member of the dive team and the officers who'd set up the perimeter, as well as statements from the homeowners they'd interviewed, all had to be filed. The paperwork on a case like this was a beast he had to stay in control of or it would devour him.

Investigators had had a surprisingly difficult time retrieving footage from the security systems on the lake. Not because they couldn't get the warrant they needed on a weekend or because the homeowners were uncooperative. The problem was that many of the homeowners weren't home. They'd only managed to review footage from five other houses. Two of them had camera angles that showed a boat had driven by during the time period they were interested in, but none of them were close enough for them to identify the boat.

He had several investigators who had volunteered to go door-to-door and now were calling each homeowner in an attempt to get the footage they needed. The process was taking forever. He'd had no idea half the lake population took vacations in April, but at the rate they were going, it would be a couple of weeks before they would get through all the footage.

Maybe tomorrow would be better.

He placed the John Doe file to the side. It was thin now. By the time this case went to trial, it would be a foot thick. At least. And it would go to trial. They'd find who did this. There was no way they could rest until the person responsible was behind bars.

Gabe came through the door and tossed a takeout box on Ryan's desk. The scent of garlic permeated the room. "Are these what I think they are?" He eased the lid back. Garlic knots the size of baseballs lay in a tub of butter and spices. His mouth watered. "You went to Luigi's without me?"

"You went to Pancake Hut without me."

"It was a mission of mercy."

"Whatever," Gabe said. "I also brought you some ziti if you want it."

"Thanks," he said. "I owe you."

He owed him for more than the ziti and garlic knots. Gabe

wasn't even on call. He didn't have to be here, but he'd been hard at work all afternoon and had pulled hospital personnel records, security camera footage, and highway cameras showing Leigh's trip to and from the hospital.

He looked at the gigantic board they'd started for their John Doe. Lots of questions, but no answers.

Then he looked at the new board beside it. The one for Leigh. Lots of questions, but no answers.

This was not how he liked to work.

There was always a reason for a murder. Always. And there was no such thing as a perfect murder. There were clues. They just hadn't asked the right questions yet. Or maybe the answers weren't available yet.

Sometimes the hardest part of a homicide investigation was asking all the questions you thought would matter, only to stumble onto the ones that really did matter. And as his mentor had told him a million times, there were no shortcuts. You never get to the right question without asking a lot of the wrong ones.

Time to get asking.

Gabe flopped down at the desk across from him. "You sure you want this case?"

"What?"

"Leigh. You sure you want it? You're awfully close—"

"That's why I want it."

Gabe's eyebrows bounced up. "You're too close."

"I don't buy that line of reasoning."

Gabe didn't argue with him, but Ryan could tell he didn't agree either. Gabe was too good of a friend to be a jerk about it. Too good of a cop to let it go without saying something.

"Look," Ryan said. "I need something to do while we wait on forensics from the John Doe case."

"Whatever."

The "Don't say I didn't warn you" was implied.

8

Monday morning came way too early. Ryan pulled into the hospital parking lot running on three hours of sleep, a large coffee, and a chicken biscuit.

His first stop wasn't Leigh's room.

His first stop was a waiting room on the third floor. He'd called on his way in for an update. Pete was off the ventilator and had been moved to a room.

Two officers stood outside the door. A chaplain and several of Pete's friends spoke in hushed tones from some chairs in the corner. Pete's folks had just arrived after driving nonstop from their home in Iowa. His girlfriend was with her sister on a cruise in the Caribbean. She still didn't know.

Ryan's stomach churned as he approached Pete's parents. "Mr. and Mrs. Stanfield, I'm Ryan Parker."

"You're the one who was with him when it happened," Mrs. Stanfield said.

"Yes, ma'am."

She nodded toward the chaplain and dropped her voice. "He told us he was guarding someone?"

"Yes, ma'am. I'm afraid it's an open investigation and not something I can talk about, but he was injured in the line of duty and we're doing everything we can to find out who did this."

Mr. Stanfield's deep voice shook when he spoke. "Can you tell us if he was guarding a prisoner or . . ."

Oh. Now he understood.

"No, sir. He was protecting an innocent individual who'd been attacked earlier in the day."

Somehow that seemed to ease Mr. Stanfield's mind. Not that it changed what had happened to Pete, but maybe it made the reality a tiny bit easier to swallow.

"I just wanted to check in on you this morning before I go to the office," Ryan told them. He nodded toward the chaplain. "If you need to reach me, Chaplain Sullivan has all my information."

They nodded and said thank you.

He wasn't sure what they could possibly be thanking him for. He still had no idea what had happened or why. But maybe it helped them to put a face and name to the man who was searching for the person responsible.

Ryan took the stairs to the fourth floor and down the twisting hallways to Leigh's room. He pulled up short. An officer should have been stationed outside her room. He placed one hand on his weapon and took measured steps toward her door.

The door opened and two officers emerged.

"Oh, hey, Parker," Carlos said. "I introduced Charlie to Leigh. I'm headed out. Everything was quiet here."

Way to overreact, Parker.

Ryan hoped his laughter sounded natural. "Great," he said. "I'm assuming she's awake?"

"Yeah."

Ryan knocked on the door and found Leigh sitting in a chair. Eyes bright.

"Did you bring me a biscuit?" she asked.

He handed over a paper bag. "As requested," he said. Leigh wasted no time unwrapping the biscuit.

"Thank heaven," Keri muttered from the corner. "She's not very nice when she's hungry."

"I am so," Leigh said through a mouthful of food.

Keri didn't attempt to hide her obvious disagreement. She looked at Ryan with an expression that said, "See what I've had to put up with all night?"

Leigh threw a wadded napkin at Keri and they all laughed. She seemed more herself this morning.

"So when are you going to let me out of here?" Leigh asked.

"I could ask the same," Keri chimed in.

"As soon as the doctor releases you," Ryan said. "I have to get in to the office, but he's promised to give me a call once you're free to go."

Keri smirked. "I'll have you know I am not the patient here. Once Megyn returns, I'll be finding my way to my nice, warm bed."

It had taken Ryan about three seconds to figure out that Keri was worried sick about Leigh. She'd caught him outside the recovery room and the way she lit into him, demanding to know what had happened, he had to wonder if she somehow thought he was the one who'd cut Leigh's brake line. But then her voice had cracked. All the sauciness she threw around was a shield, probably one she raised regularly to protect herself. But even when she tried, she couldn't mask her genuine affection for Leigh.

And Leigh must have known that herself, because the look she gave Keri was full of feigned outrage. "Fine," she said with an exaggerated huff. "Leave me in here. Go sleep. I'll be fine."

Keri folded her hands in front of her and whispered, "Dear Lord, give me patience with this patient."

"I'll be back," Ryan said. Their laughter followed him into the hallway. At least Keri was keeping Leigh entertained. And if she was entertained, then he could hope she wasn't spiraling into fear.

With everything she'd been through, anything that kept her mind occupied in the present had to be good medicine.

Thirty minutes in heavy morning traffic and he finally made it to his office in downtown Carrington. Today was going to be brutal.

Ten hours later he came up for air.

One of his dive team buddies, Adam Campbell, had been the one to escort Leigh home. He reported back that she was in good spirits when he left. The sheriff had approved an around-the-clock security detail, and there was no shortage of volunteers.

Every member of the law enforcement community—the local city police departments and the sheriff's office—felt the weight of what had happened to Pete.

Whoever was behind this had unwittingly made it easier for investigators to catch them. Leigh's case would have been taken seriously and the criminal behind it would have been hunted down. But with the addition of one of their own spending the night in the ICU and at least one more day in the hospital, the sheriff's office had been deluged with offers of aid.

And the sheriff wasn't too proud to accept them. He'd even received a call from a professor from the local university's computer forensics/cybersecurity department who was willing to volunteer her team to comb through the video footage. Adam knew her well and was going to help coordinate with her office.

While Leigh was being released from the hospital, Ryan had spent most of the day juggling paperwork, coordinating the volunteers and offers of assistance, setting up protective details for both Leigh and Pete, and of course, there were the two hours he'd spent at the autopsy of his John Doe.

He took a sip of stale coffee as he looked over the report again. Both the ME and the anthropologist had gone over everything but had given him almost nothing to go on.

Their John Doe was a white male. Probably between the ages of fifty-five and sixty. He'd been in decent physical condition. He'd broken his right arm and his left femur, probably in his teens, and he'd had surgery on both knees. They estimated his height to be six-one to six-three.

Ryan had no idea how they'd come to that conclusion given that the guy was missing some key parts, but they were the experts.

The water exposure had messed up almost every other thing they would normally be able to tell about a body. Tox screens would be useless. They would need the bones for the DNA analysis and those tests took months to get back—and that assumed the guy was in a database of some kind, which almost never happened.

Given the way this case had gone, he wasn't holding his breath.

But the case had some other unique aspects. The killer hadn't undressed the body. Whoever this guy was, he'd lopped off his head, hands, and feet but hadn't bothered to remove the guy's clothes. They were in pretty bad shape because it appeared the killer had doused the body in some sort of acid before wrapping it like a mummy and dropping it into the lake. The clothing was eaten away, as was some of the skin, but not all of it.

This case got weirder every time someone gave him a new piece of information.

The ME was hopeful some forensics buddies of hers could pull something off the clothing. Maybe a brand or something about the chemicals used.

Another thing Ryan wasn't going to hold his breath for.

He glanced at his watch. Six-thirty. Hardly a late night this soon into a homicide investigation, but he was, once again, at a dead end.

It was temporary. By tomorrow there would be more missing persons cases to review, more security footage to watch, more homeowners who'd come back from vacation for him to visit.

Normally a delay like this would make him crazy, but not tonight.

He dialed Leigh's number.

"Shouldn't you be working?" Leigh had answered his calls that way all day. Not that he'd called often. Six times wasn't often. Right?

"As a matter of fact, I'm leaving the office and wanted to see if you'd had dinner yet," he said.

"You're leaving the office?" Skepticism laced her words.

"Yes, ma'am." He waited for her to reply. He hadn't expected it to take but a second, but as the silence stretched it became awkward.

"Leigh?"

"Yeah, I'm here," she said. "I don't want to bother you."

"What's wrong?"

"Nothing," she said. "Other than the obvious, of course."

"Of course," he said. "Then what is it?"

Her sigh floated through his headset. "You have to be tired. I'm sure you'd rather go home . . ."

She thought he didn't want to come over? Wow. He must be hiding his mixed-up emotions better than he'd thought. Or maybe the anesthesia had dulled her senses enough that she didn't remember their tense conversation in her room yesterday.

Keep it professional. Keep it friendly. Keep it in the realm where Kirk won't kill you and the sheriff won't fire you. "I need to eat. You need to eat. If I go home, I'll eat a frozen pizza. If I bring you a meal, I can probably get the sheriff to pay for it. Trust me, you're doing me a favor."

Her silence made him wonder if she'd bought his argument. "Fine," she said. "But I'm not picking the food. Surprise me."

Awesome.

"See you in a few."

He would have texted Kirk, but with the time difference, Kirk was asleep by now. So he did the next best thing. He pulled up her profiles on social media. She liked coffee. She liked college football. She liked the lake.

And she liked barbecue.

Leigh Weston might be the perfect woman.

Whoa. Slow that train down, Parker. You couldn't base a relationship off of a shared interest in smoked pork. Leigh was fine and sensitive, and she didn't need someone like him—with a job like his—messing up her world.

But that didn't mean he couldn't enjoy her company for the time being.

That was perfectly acceptable.

Leigh paced the living room, straightening an already straight stack of books, fluffing an already fluffed pillow. Everything hurt, but the more she kept moving the faster her recovery would be.

Her breathing spiked when her phone chimed, but as she read the message every cell in her body relaxed.

Ryan was here.

Get yourself together, girl. It's not a date.

The doorbell rang and she started to skip to the door, but her throbbing leg brought that to an immediate halt. She kept her pace measured as she limped the rest of the way to the door. She didn't open it at once. "Who is it?"

"Ryan."

She checked the peephole to be sure, then disarmed the security system and threw back the locks.

He carried in two plastic bags and set them on the counter with a triumphant smile. "Dinner is served."

The hint of smokiness in the air could only mean one thing. "You brought barbecue? I could kiss you!"

His eyes widened in surprise.

If only there was a way to call back those last four words. She could apologize or try to explain herself, but that would make it worse. No. Better to carry on like nothing weird had happened. It was just an expression. It wasn't like she was actually going to kiss him.

He cleared his throat. "I wasn't sure what you liked or what that tender tummy of yours would be up for. I got a little of everything." He pulled out round containers, square containers, tiny plastic containers of sauce, and one giant tub that had to be slaw.

"This is perfect," she said. She grabbed plates, forks, and spoons, and they served themselves from the minibuffet he'd provided. She took a small portion of everything—beans, slaw, macaroni and cheese, pulled pork, and hush puppies.

When they'd fixed their plates, they settled in at the kitchen bar much as they'd done two nights earlier. Ryan blessed the food and they dug in.

"Have you eaten at all today?" she asked as he piled a second bun high with pork, slaw, and barbecue sauce.

"Some," he said. "More than I usually get to eat in the middle of a case."

"Any leads on the John Doe from the lake?"

Ryan held up one finger as he chewed. Maybe she could have timed her question a little better. She took a bite of her hush puppy while she waited. The food was amazing, but she forced herself to chew each bite, swallow, and pause.

Ryan took a sip of his tea before he answered her question. "Not much. But enough to keep things moving. Under the circumstances, it's more than I would have expected to have at this point."

She took another bite. So did he. She guessed that was all the information she was going to get on the subject of the John Doe. There were probably confidentiality laws or something at work.

But why hadn't he told her anything about her case? "Any leads on who messed up my brakes?"

Ryan's entire body tensed. His fork froze in the air. She regretted the question. She should have waited. At least until after they had finished supper.

He put it down and turned to her. "Sorry. I shouldn't have made you ask. That was quite insensitive."

"No, it's fine," she said.

"Gabe and I have been going over security footage from the hospital."

"Found anything?"

"No," he said. "But we will."

By the end of the week, they'd fallen into a pattern of sorts. Ryan called every morning on his way to work. Random officers and friends bought groceries and delivered meals from restaurants. Ryan came for dinner every night. They'd had Thai, Mexican, and Cuban food, chef salads, and pizza.

Leigh hadn't stepped an inch outside her door.

And she was about to lose her mind.

Sure, she was all safe and sound tucked away in the house, but this was no way to live. This was existing. This was hiding.

It had been a week since Ryan and Gabe had discovered the John Doe, and as far as she could tell, they weren't having much luck finding out anything about him, much less who had put him in the lake.

Today was a beautiful spring Saturday. She could see trees blossoming. Boat traffic had picked up on the lake as families got out to enjoy a day on the water.

But she couldn't even open her windows to let in some fresh air.

It had been six days since her brakes had been cut and they weren't any closer to figuring out who'd done that either. Ryan was trying to be optimistic. At least in front of her.

She understood why he wouldn't want to admit things had stalled out. Especially to her. She didn't want to make him feel bad. She was confident he had been and was continuing to do everything he could possibly do.

But she was done sitting around waiting for something to happen.

She picked up the phone and called Dr. Price.

She'd just hung up when her phone buzzed again.

Ryan.

"I've been in the neighborhood this morning," he said. "Thought I might stop by before I head back to the office. Do you mind?"

"Of course not," she said.

"Good. Could you open your door?"

He was already here? She glanced around the house. One advantage to being cooped inside was she had no trouble keeping everything nice and neat.

And having her house surrounded by police officers ensured that she got up and got dressed every morning. There was no lounging around all day in her pajamas when total strangers were standing guard on her deck.

She opened the door and Ryan entered with a bouquet of flowers in one hand and a bouquet of balloons in the other.

"You have a lot of admirers," he said as he placed the flowers beside the four others on the kitchen counter.

"Not really," she said. "I suspect Keri has something to do with this."

"What do you mean?"

She checked the card. "Today's bouquet is from my friends in post-op."

"So . . ."

"I don't have many friends in post-op." She pointed, one by one, to the other bouquets that had been delivered throughout the week. "I also don't have many friends in the PACU or pediatrics." She pointed to the last one. "I do know most of the radiology folks, but my guess is Keri arranged for a different bouquet to come each day. Who are the balloons from?" She looked for a card and couldn't find one.

"They came with the flowers. Where do you want them?"

They had come tied to a cute little pot as a weight. "I guess over on the dining room table," she said.

Ryan carried them to the spot she'd indicated. He took a few extra seconds to center them on the table.

"You know, if this homicide investigating thing doesn't work out, I think you could find some success in the floral delivery arena."

He tipped his head back and laughed.

This was the Ryan she remembered. Quick to laugh. Fun. Teasing.

Not stressed out and worried.

"I have to head back to the office," he said.

"Okay." It was time to tell him. She took a deep breath. Somehow she had a feeling the stressed out and worried Ryan was about to be back in full force.

"I was going to tell you," she said. "I've been cleared to go back to work."

"What?"

"I need to go back to work," she said. "Tomorrow."

9

"You cannot be serious." Ryan came very close to shouting the words.

This wasn't a side of Ryan Parker she was used to seeing. She hadn't expected him to be thrilled with her plan, but she hadn't been expecting this either.

Who did he think he was? He wasn't her boss, her father, or even her brother. She was an adult. An intelligent, independent woman who was not going to be trapped in her home one day longer.

Although . . .

There was something in his eyes. Something in his tone. She'd almost missed it in her knee-jerk reaction to his words.

He was scared.

For her?

Ryan paced to the massive windows overlooking Lake Porter. He ran both hands through his hair. It was just long enough that the curl was showing. He'd get it cut soon.

Too bad.

She remembered the way it was in high school when he let it grow longer. Black waves of hair all the girls loved and all the boys were jealous of.

He whipped around and the intensity of his movements shoved all other thoughts away.

"Leigh, please. Don't. The hospital is where you're most at risk. I can't protect you there."

"You can't stay with me twenty-four seven. Nothing has happened in the past week."

"That we know of."

"I know what I need to do. Take different routes to work. Bring my own food. Keep the doors closed and locked. Stay away from windows. Don't go to movies. Don't go anywhere at night. Stay in crowded places." She rattled the list off. "I've been down this road before, Ryan."

"Yeah, and you still wound up on the wrong side of a gun."

His words knocked the breath out of her. She'd think of a crushing reply soon, but in this moment, she couldn't think of a single thing to say.

"Leigh," Ryan whispered. He reached for her arm. She jerked out of his grasp.

"It wasn't my fault." Wasn't that what everyone had told her? That it wasn't *her* fault Barry had come after her? Bunch of liars.

"No," he said. "It wasn't. And neither is this. But that doesn't mean you need to take unnecessary risks."

"Going to work—"

"Is an unnecessary risk."

"I'm not independently wealthy, Ryan," she said. "How long do you expect me to stay barricaded behind my own door? Another week? Two? I appreciate your skills as an investigator, but you have no idea who did this or why. Neither do I. I can't stay in hiding for the rest of my life."

"You could be killed."

"I could be killed here too. The longer I stay here, what's to keep some maniac from blowing up my house? Huh? Thought of that one?"

Why was he smirking at her? No way.

"You've thought of that one?"

"No one gets anywhere near your house without going through a police barricade, Leigh."

"That's not sustainable. I'm costing the taxpayers thousands of dollars."

"Hardly. We've caught so many speeders, we're making money on the deal. No one realizes what's happening. They think it's a speed trap. And a good one at that."

"You have an answer for everything, don't you?"

That wiped the smirk away. "No," he said. The heaviness in that one word pierced her. "I don't. I'm about to lose my mind, if you want to know the truth. I don't know why any of this happened to you. I don't know why there was a dead guy in the lake. I don't know why my brother-in-law left my sister. I don't know why your mom died of cancer. And I don't know why my nephew is autistic."

He caught a breath and plunged on. "And you know what? I do not like it when I don't know why things are happening. So no, I don't have an answer. But I'm doing the best I can with the knowledge I have and you going to work is going to make that much harder."

His argument, his vulnerability, his honesty. It shook her resolve.

But didn't destroy it.

"I get that. I do."

"But you don't care."

"I do care." He had no idea how much she cared. "But this"—she waved her hand around her living room—"is not a long-term solution. I need to work. I'll agree to stay home when I'm not at work. For now. But my patients aren't dangerous." Most of the time.

She didn't give him a chance to argue with her on that point. "My coworkers aren't dangerous. You can't even get into the department without scanning a badge. There are security guards present at all times. I'll agree to having an escort to and from work if you want, but you cannot keep me from going to work. Dr. Price has cleared me. He said there was no medical reason I couldn't return to work."

Ryan narrowed his eyes. "What if you put your coworkers in danger?"

Way to hit her where it hurt. Pete had given them all a scare, but once they got all the drugs out of his system he'd improved fast. He'd gone home on Monday and was already back at work. But if he hadn't been in the hospital when he consumed that high dose of ketamine, he would be dead. Could she risk anyone else's life that way?

She'd thought about it most of the morning and had come to the conclusion that the risks were minimal. Her coworkers would be in no more danger than what they faced every day in the emergency department. Going to work would free officers to work on the investigation and, ultimately, fewer of them would be at risk.

"Again, it's a secure department."

He turned his back to her and stalked back to the window. "I don't like it."

She didn't have an answer for him.

"When do you want to go back?"

"Tomorrow night."

"It's risky," he said with resignation.

"I won't leave the department without an escort. I'll even wait for you to come pick me up if you want."

If this craziness kept up, she was going to forget how to drive. But she had multiple reasons for wanting Ryan to agree with her. Sure, she could do whatever she wanted, but as soon as she did, he would call Kirk and Kirk would make her life miserable. He might even insist on coming home.

And as much as Ryan's worrywart attitude rankled, the reality was no one else was as determined as him to keep her safe. She didn't want to think about what the last week would have been like if Ryan hadn't been around.

"I'll set up a protective detail. Please promise me you'll listen if they tell you they need you to leave."

She could do that. "I will."

"I need to make some calls," he said. He walked out onto the deck. She could see him pacing back and forth as he talked. Could even hear his voice every now and then.

She made a phone call of her own, assuring the lead nurse practitioner she'd be in at seven on Sunday night.

Then she headed to the kitchen. Cookies seemed like a good idea right now.

She pulled out her mom's baking pans and fitted the beater on the stand mixer. Anytime she baked, memories of her mom filled the room along with the aroma of whatever was in the oven.

Her mom had been a firecracker. Her dad had always said she was the perfect complement to him. As a judge, he got used to people doing what he told them to do, but she kept him grounded. Whenever he said that, her mom would roll her eyes at him or give him a gentle slug to the shoulder.

The truth was her mom wasn't one to keep her opinions to herself, and she wasn't afraid to rock the boat. But even when they disagreed, such a strong undercurrent of love and genuine respect flowed between them that Leigh had never experienced a moment of worry that their relationship was in danger. If anything, the way they disagreed and reached consensus had taught her it was okay to have a contrary opinion—just because she didn't agree with someone didn't mean they couldn't be friends. Or more.

It also taught her that true, meaningful, long-lasting relationships were built more on the way a couple handled conflict and adversity than on romantic dinners and moonlit strolls.

Not that her parents didn't share plenty of those.

She added the chocolate chips and a cup full of toffee chips and gave the cookies a final whir in the mixer. She grabbed a spoon and tasted the dough.

Perfect.

"You really like to live dangerously, don't you?" Ryan asked from the other side of the counter.

She hadn't heard him come in and didn't turn around as she spooned the dough onto the baking sheets.

"Don't tell me you're afraid of a little raw egg."

He laughed. "No. But it would be dangerous for you not to share some of that cookie dough with me."

She grabbed another spoon and scooped out a heaping helping. When she handed it to him, he took it, but then squeezed her hand.

"I'm sorry I was being so bossy," he said before he tasted the cookie dough.

"It's okay," she said. "I do appreciate your concern."

He took another bite. "This is really good."

"Yes, it is," she said. "And I'm sorry I'm being so difficult."

"You are difficult," he said, but this time the teasing words carried no sting. "These are my favorite cookies."

"I know."

He stared at her long enough that she finally broke eye contact. She didn't know what she was doing. And she needed to stop doing it. Now.

Ryan's phone rang and he stepped outside to answer it.

Whew.

She needed to get a grip. She didn't flirt. She'd never been that kind of girl. And Ryan wasn't the kind of guy—

No. That was the problem. Ryan was exactly the kind of guy she'd consider spending a lifetime with.

Maybe the only one.

Yeah.

That was a big problem.

"Parker. Where are you?"

He had no idea why the captain would want to know where he was on a Saturday afternoon. He wasn't on call. Any homicides today would go to Anissa. But something in the captain's tone made him think there was a problem.

"I'm at Leigh Weston's house, sir."

"I need you over at the Cooks' farm."

"Sir?"

"I don't want to talk about it right now. Get over here."

"Is Mr. Cook okay?"

"Parker."

Wow. It must be bad. He'd pushed the captain as far as he dared. "I'll be there in ten minutes."

"Make it five."

Ryan ran back into the house and explained what was going on. He grabbed his coat and jogged to the door.

Leigh stood there with a paper plate heavy with cookies. "Take it with you. You never know . . ."

"You're amazing," he said as he took the plate. He planted a quick peck on her cheek. Her breath faltered as their eyes met. Oh man. Her mouth had the gravitational pull of a supernova.

The oven timer buzzed and broke through the force pulling them together. He stepped back and so did she, the space between them filling with unspoken energy.

"Thank you," he said, his voice rougher than he'd expected it to be.

"Be safe," she said, her eyes wide.

He yanked open the door and jogged to his car. He placed the cookies and his coat on the passenger seat and floored it.

Why was he out of breath?

What had he done?

What would have happened if he'd kissed her? Really kissed her.

There was so much tension, so much wondering, so much maybe, so much what if, it left his mind spinning.

One thing was certain. If that stupid oven timer hadn't gone off, he wouldn't be wondering. And he would have been very late getting to Mr. Cook's.

He came to a police barricade six minutes later.

What was going on?

He showed his badge and was waved in. Mr. Cook owned two hundred acres on the edge of the county. Some of it was lakefront property he'd never developed. Said he never would let anyone develop it. Most of it was wooded, and the driveway meandered into the heart of it, where he lived in the old farmhouse he'd been born in. A couple of chicken houses stretched to one side. A pasture with twenty head of cattle sat on the other side. Behind the house were several acres of soybeans.

Ryan relaxed a little when he saw Mr. Cook standing on the wide front porch talking to the captain. At least the older gentleman was unharmed. As soon as the captain saw Ryan approaching, he waved him over.

"Captain, Mr. Cook," Ryan said. "Everything okay?"

"Not even a little bit," Mr. Cook said. "Come on."

Mr. Cook took off at a brisk pace and Ryan rushed to follow him. The captain joined them.

This was weird.

"Got out here this morning, walking the property. I don't do it often, but I've got a lot of land out here and every now and then I find a spot where kids have been hanging out, that kind of thing," Mr. Cook said as he led them deep into the wooded property. "Had Ole Blue with me. We was just meandering. Walking and praying. It's what we do."

Mr. Cook's prayer walks were legendary. Some people said if you got Mr. Cook to pray about your situation while he was on one of his walks, you could be sure the Lord had heard about it. Whenever Mr. Cook heard that, he'd shush the speaker and remind them God heard the prayers of all his children and nothing was special about his prayers.

No one believed him.

If Mr. Cook decided to pray for you, you could be sure the Almighty was going to get involved.

"Ole Blue wanders through the woods. Sometimes he catches a rabbit or squirrel. Usually he just chases 'em. This morning he got all bothered about something out here, so I left my trail to investigate."

Sounds that didn't match the tranquility of their surroundings filtered through the trees. As they rounded a bend and left the trail, Ryan caught a few flashes of yellow police tape. Then he heard Anissa calling out crisp orders. It took another couple of minutes to push through the thick undergrowth. Thorny branches slapped at his hands and arms, and he was thankful he'd put his jacket on when he got out of the car.

Mr. Cook paused. "Still can't believe it," he said. He pointed them in the direction of Anissa's voice and after another hundred feet of maneuvering through the branches, Ryan came to the scene.

A shallow grave. A body. Or what was left of it. Anissa covered in dirt. Forensics techs with evidence markers and the medical examiner preparing the body bag.

Ryan tried to process what he was seeing. He didn't want to speak too soon and make himself look like an idiot in front of his boss and one of the most influential men in the county.

"Parker," Anissa called to him. "Glad you're here."

She was? He liked Anissa well enough, but ever since they'd both made homicide investigator two years ago and become the youngest homicide investigators in the county's history, he'd always suspected she was determined not to let anyone ever accuse her of not knowing what she was doing. She rarely requested assistance. He didn't take it personally. The truth was she rarely needed assistance.

He made his way to her. "What's going on?" he asked in a low voice.

"Didn't they tell you?" She kept her voice low as well.

"No. Just dragged me out here."

"Sorry," she said. "I'm afraid I insisted."

Okay. This was very weird.

She pointed to the body. "You need to see this."

He approached the medical examiner. "May I?"

"Oh, hey, Ryan." Sharon Oliver gave him a grim smile. "I'm getting tired of this stuff." She pointed to the body. Now that he was closer, Ryan studied the skeletal remains.

Or what was left of them.

"Where's the skull?"

Sharon shrugged. "Your guess is as good as mine. We're looking for it."

Ryan knelt beside the bones. This could not be happening. "I don't suppose there's any chance the hands and feet got carried off by animals?"

"We'll have to get the anthropologist back out here," she said. "But no. The hands, feet, and head were severed from the body. I don't want to speculate, but I won't be surprised if the method is the same as your John Doe from the lake."

Ryan looked around the area. Getting a body in here would have required patience. The grave wasn't deep. Barely deep enough to be sure no wildlife dug it up. "Any idea on timing?"

"A year, maybe a little less," she said. "I'll be able to firm up the timing after we examine the remains."

He walked back to where Anissa stood lost in thought. "You okay?" he asked.

"Yeah."

"Two bodies."

"Ticks me off. Adam will be insufferable."

Anissa was rattled. And Anissa was never rattled. "No he won't. No one wants to be right about something like this."

Her only response was a quick huff. She still hadn't made eye contact.

"Thanks for calling me out here," he said.

"Welcome. Captain wants to try to keep it close to the vest."

He could understand that. No one wanted the county in an uproar over a possible serial killer who cuts off hands and heads.

"Do you want the case?"

Wow. Anissa offering to give up a high-profile case? That was not normal behavior.

"I'll take it if you want me to, but I don't want it."

She finally looked at him. "Why not?"

"I'm working the lake John Doe, and Leigh's stalker, and I have four other open files moving closer and closer to court dates."

"So you're too busy?"

"No. I'm not. I can take it, but I think it makes more sense for you to work this scene and this case while I work the John Doe from the lake until we are certain we're dealing with the same killer. And then I think we should work it together. There are going to be so many moving parts to this one. I think an extra set of eyes will be invaluable."

She nodded. "Thanks, Parker."

"You sure you're okay?"

Her mouth formed a thin line. "I'm fine."

She wasn't. But he wasn't going to get any more from her. Not now at least.

"Okay. I'll leave you to it," he said. "Let's plan to talk later tonight or tomorrow and compare notes."

"Sounds good," she said.

He walked back to where the captain and Mr. Cook stood. "Ole Blue found the body?"

"Sort of," Mr. Cook said. "He went crazy over here, so I followed him in. He dug up a bone and I pulled him off and called the captain."

"Have you been on a vacation recently, Mr. Cook?"

"Huh?"

"In the last year or so, have you gone on a trip? Been away from home for a while?"

"Boy, I don't take vacations. Why are you asking?"

"I'm wondering how someone could have gotten the body in here and buried without you hearing or noticing."

"Are you accusing me of murder?"

"Absolutely not, sir."

"Are you even going to consider me as a suspect?"

"Absolutely, sir."

Mr. Cook slapped the captain on the back and howled with laughter. "You've got a good one here, Mitchell."

The captain looked like he'd swallowed an ice cube.

"Parker, I will look back over my calendar for the past couple of years, see if I can find a space where I was gone for more than a day. Can't think of anything off the top of my head, but that doesn't mean much these days."

He shook his head. "Can't believe that kind of evil came so close," he said. "Makes me sick. Glad Mrs. Cook didn't live to see this." He turned to the captain. "I've already told Anissa this, but you can have whatever you need from me. Traipse all over this property. Bring in more dogs. Do whatever you need to do. I won't complain. Don't hold back because you're trying to be polite. You hear me?"

"Yes, sir," the captain said.

"This has to stop. I'll be praying."

Ryan followed Mr. Cook and the captain back through the woods, to the trail, and eventually back to the house. Mr. Cook didn't speak the entire time.

He had probably already started praying.

Ryan said goodbye and headed for his car, but before he pulled away, Mr. Cook waved at him. He rolled down the window. "You need something, Mr. Cook?"

Mr. Cook walked over to him. "How's Leigh Weston doing?"

How on earth would Mr. Cook know he . . . ?

There was no sense in fighting it. The man knew everything and everybody.

"She's doing fine, sir. Going back to work tomorrow."

"Good. Good. Glad to hear it. Captain says you're working on her case."

"Yes, sir."

"Any leads?"

Ryan imagined whatever it was Mr. Cook liked about him going up in a puff of smoke, but he couldn't lie to the man. It would be like lying to a preacher. "No, sir. Not really."

Mr. Cook nodded. "I'll be praying on that too then."

10

8:58 P.M.

Leigh glared at the digits glowing from the wall oven.

He wasn't coming.

Which was fine. It wasn't like they had a date or anything.

But he'd come over every night this week. And with the way things were when he left . . .

She unlocked her phone. No missed calls. No texts. He could have called.

She grabbed a bottle of water from the fridge and flopped onto the sofa. It was almost comical. Almost, but not quite. She'd pined after Ryan most of her high school years. She'd skipped sleepovers with her girlfriends if he was coming over to her house. She'd gotten up early on Saturday mornings to fix her hair and put on her makeup because she couldn't risk him seeing her in her pajamas when he came down for breakfast. Of course, he and Kirk usually stayed up so late they'd sleep until noon, so she'd tiptoe around the house trying to avoid waking them while secretly wishing they would get up.

Eighteen years later, and she was lying on this couch, fighting tears because he hadn't come to say good night. Had she misunderstood?

Heat flooded every inch of her body. That was it. He hadn't missed the supercharged emotions she was tossing around, and he'd been too kind to tell her he wasn't interested. Then this morning . . .

But it hadn't seemed like she was the only one interested.

Ugh.

She grabbed a throw pillow and pulled it over her head. She wanted to scream. She wanted to rage against everything that had happened. She wanted to yell and shake her fist at . . .

No. Not at God. She knew better than that.

But . . .

How could he do it? How could he let it all happen? He was God. He was in control. He had the power to stop it. Didn't he? She knew he did. So if he did have the power, then why wouldn't he use it on her behalf?

Didn't he care?

She didn't have answers. Her parents would have said of course he cared. That he was working out everything for her good and his glory. But it certainly didn't feel that way.

It felt like she'd been abandoned. Again.

She didn't remember the orphanage in China. But she remembered being terrified, even into her early teens, that her parents would leave her. That she would do something and they would send her away.

As an adult, she understood her issues with abandonment. She also understood how deeply and completely her parents had loved her. How much Kirk loved her. Their bond forged not by blood but by shared experiences.

She could call Kirk. He would understand.

But he would understand too well. He would be worried, even more worried than he already was, and he would come home.

An image flickered through her mind. She could see it against her eyelids. Mom and Dad, hands entwined, heads bowed.

Praying.

They had believed. When they couldn't have biological children, they chose to adopt. Mom never shied away from the truth that barrenness had broken her, and yet she always said she wouldn't have had it any other way. That she'd never ask God to change it because she got Kirk, and Leigh, and a relationship with her heavenly Father that could only have been forged through struggle.

"You can let it drive you away from him or you can let it drive you to him, Leigh," she would say. "I let it drive me to him. And he was faithful."

Faithful?

He didn't feel faithful. He felt far, far away.

"I will never leave you, nor forsake you." The words learned long ago in Sunday school wormed their way into her mind.

Really? You haven't left? So you were hanging around when Barry lost his mind? You were there when I got in a car with cut brake lines? You watched as Pete ate poisoned gelatin meant for me?

Her heart pounded in her chest at the audacity of her thoughts. Her breath sounded loud in her ears.

She was alive.

Very much alive.

When she should be dead. Barry could have killed her several times. She should have died Sunday. Twice.

But she was still here.

Was that what God was trying to get her to see? That he'd been protecting her all along?

Her phone buzzed and she ignored it, choosing to allow this concept to percolate a few moments longer. If God had protected her, that was awesome. But why allow any of it? Was this some sort of effort to drive her toward him and not away from him?

Maybe.

Her heart rate slowed. Her breath came easier. She still wasn't sure about everything or about why God would keep her safe but not Pete. Why he'd protect her from Barry but still allow the tumor that killed him.

But somehow, just being still and asking the questions—wait. Was this praying? It certainly wasn't what she thought of as praying. But maybe this wrestling about hard things was what her mom had been talking about.

A fresh ache pierced her. If her mom were still here, she would be able to explain it all. Why hadn't she asked her to tell her everything while she had the chance?

The pounding on the door scattered her thoughts in a million directions. She jumped from the sofa, still clutching the throw pillow.

"Leigh! You okay in there? Open the door."

Ryan. He had some nerve.

"Coming," she said. She took her time letting him in.

"You scared me," he said once she opened the door. "Why didn't you answer your phone?"

"I was busy."

"Busy? Seriously? I've been going out of my mind. I . . . you . . ."

"Don't you dare fuss at me. I don't owe you an explanation for anything."

His head jerked back like she'd slapped him. She stared him down. She would not apologize. He'd kept her waiting all evening and then yelled at her because she didn't answer her phone?

The tension between them tonight bore no resemblance to the electricity from this morning.

Ryan took a step back. "I'm sorry to bother you, Ms. Weston. I'll leave you to your evening. Good night."

He walked out.

She stared at the door. He'd come back.

But he didn't.

At 11:13 p.m. Gabe's car pulled up beside Ryan's. Ryan rolled down the window. "What are you doing here?"

"I called for a status update and heard you were pulling the night shift in the car. What'd you do to get banned from the house?"

Awesome.

"I wasn't going to spend the night inside the house anyway," he said. "Might as well sit here."

"'Cause she kicked you out?"

"She did not."

"I heard you pounded on the door, demanded she open up, and then stayed inside less than two minutes before you came out and got in your car to start pouting."

"I am not pouting."

Gabe lifted his eyes heavenward. "Okay. Sulking? Moping? Wait, have you been crying?"

"Shut up."

Gabe laughed at his own joke for a good thirty seconds before he regained some composure. "Seriously, man. What happened? I thought you were making progress."

"Progress on what, exactly? You know as well as I do that we have nothing to go on with this case. Nothing. If that computer forensics professor Adam knows doesn't find something, we're dead in the water."

"Adam says she's awesome," Gabe said. "I'm sure she'll find something. But that isn't what I was talking about and you know it."

Ryan crossed his arms. No way he was talking to Gabe about this. Whatever *this* was. Or wasn't. Since he'd apparently misread every cue he thought she'd been sending.

"Wow," Gabe said. "You've got it bad."

Ryan wanted to argue with him, but that wouldn't do any good. Gabe loved to argue. He'd pick a contrary side for the fun of it.

His best bet was to change the subject. "You drove all the way out here to mess with me?"

"Pretty much."

Great.

"You could have apologized."

"For what? For being worried about her?"

"I heard you yelled at her for not answering your call."

"Oh, good grief. I did not yell."

Gabe made a show of looking at everything but him as he drummed his fingers on the steering wheel. "Not sure how the officer outside the house could have heard it if you weren't yelling."

"I was—"

"Yes?"

"I was concerned something might have happened. No one had talked to her in hours. She could have been in there dead for all I knew. And she knows we have people watching out for her. The least she could do is answer the phone."

Gabe pursed his lips. "Ever occur to you that maybe she couldn't answer the phone?"

"That's exactly what occurred to me, you moron. That's why I was worried." What was confusing about this? Why was he the bad guy for being scared half to death that something had happened to Leigh?

Gabe gave him the kind of look he'd give a five-year-old who didn't understand why he couldn't have more candy.

"You're the moron. Maybe she was in the bathroom. Maybe she was brushing her teeth and didn't hear it. Who knows what women do when we aren't around. I certainly don't. The bottom line is, you could have given her the courtesy of assuming that if she could have answered, she would have."

"I'm not sure she would have."

"Did you have a fight this morning?"

Ah. This morning. The softness of her cheek. The way her breath had caught when his lips had touched her. The way he'd literally had to run away to keep from pulling her into his arms.

Gabe waved a hand at him. "I'm going to take your vacant, dreamy expression as a no. Did you kiss her this morning?"

Not the way Gabe meant. Not that he hadn't wanted to.

"You did?"

"No. I mean. Yes. No. I kissed her cheek."

"I'm confused," Gabe said.

"You and me both, bro."

They sat in silence for a few minutes.

"I still think you should apologize. Or at least ask her if you could talk to her. Fix it."

"It's probably best that I don't."

"You know, if you keep on this way, my eyes are going to roll right out of my head," Gabe said. "You cannot be serious."

"She was completely irrational."

"Someone tried to kill her twice a week ago and she's been cooped up in her house ever since. I give her a gold star for maintaining even a loose grip on her sanity."

"You don't have a high bar."

"On the contrary," Gabe said. "I set a bar so high it's impossible for any woman to ever measure up to. I set it that way on purpose. I'm not marriage material, and I won't date a woman just to have someone to hang out with and kiss good night."

"Your point?"

"You, on the other hand, *are* marriage material. You want the wife and the kids and the house. Maybe a house on the lake with the boat and the skis and the diving and the whole domestic bliss package."

Ryan snorted.

"Why are you fighting it, man?"

"I've seen what it does to people."

"You talking about Rebecca?"

"Of course I'm talking about Rebecca. She loved that idiot. Still does, I think. And he had all of us fooled. Now what does she have?"

"She has two beautiful children and a life that isn't what she was planning but isn't as awful as you're making it out to be," Gabe said.

"Her life is hard."

"It was going to be hard regardless."

"What sort of bizzaro philosophy is this? Something you cooked up on all those nights undercover?"

Gabe didn't rise to the bait. "Life is hard, Parker. Everyone has tough stuff. There's no perfect relationship or perfect job or perfect house that will somehow make your life easy. What throws us for a loop is when life is hard in ways we weren't prepared for. Divorce. Illness. Disability. Money problems. Rebellious kids. Reporters who blow undercover ops. Friends who don't have the good sense to see they are messing up something really good that has fallen in their lap and they'd better fix it before it's too late."

Leave it to Gabe to drop some deep truth and then end it with a jab.

"Fine. I'll call her in the morning."

"Text her."

"Now? She's asleep."

"I doubt it."

Ryan grabbed his phone off the console.

Can we talk?

"There." He showed the phone to Gabe.

Gabe smirked. "I was right," he said.

Ryan looked at the screen. Three little dots blinked back at him. She was texting him back.

His entire body tensed. The dots continued blinking. Was she writing a book? How long did it take to say yes or no?

The dots disappeared. Was she not going to respond at all?

The dots continued to appear and then disappear.

His frustration grew with each passing second.

Gabe's chuckling didn't help.

Of course.

Really? Two minutes of typing for two words. He showed the phone to Gabe. Gabe shook with laughter. "You are in big trouble, buddy. But I think you'll survive."

Now?

I guess so. Why, are you awake?

I'm sitting outside your house.

No dots this time. Three seconds later the front door opened. "Seriously?" Leigh did not sound pleased to see him.

Gabe slid down in his seat. "I can see you, Gabriel Chavez," Leigh called.

"Good luck," Gabe said.

Ryan rolled up his windows and got out. "Thanks a lot," he said to Gabe before walking toward the house.

"I'm here for you, man," Gabe called after him.

Leigh leaned against the side of the house. "You wanted to talk," she said.

Yikes. She was still mad. Not good.

"Yes. But not out here."

She huffed but reentered the house and didn't slam the door in his face as he followed her. Maybe that was a good sign. "I was wondering if we could go over how our days went from the time I left this morning until the time we saw each other again tonight, because I'm thinking I missed something along the way."

"I have no idea what you did all day," she said. "I was here. All day. Like I've been for the past week."

He was definitely missing something, but what? "Okay. When I left here I went out to Mr. Cook's because this morning he and Ole Blue found a body. Same M.O. as our John Doe from the lake."

"Oh no." Leigh's face filled with sorrow.

"Yes," he said, thankful the hostility had fallen from her tone.

"Are you working that case too?"

"No. Anissa will work it, but if it turns out we have the same killer, then we'll work together."

"Are you okay with that?"

"Sure. She's a good investigator. I spent most of the afternoon working on your case and then we had a homeowner from across the lake call. He'd been out of town for two weeks and he'd just gotten home. Adam and I went over there and looked at his security footage. I called as soon as we finished. I'm sorry I didn't call earlier. Every time I got ready to call you, the phone would ring."

She swallowed hard. "Oh, that's not a problem at all. You have work to do. I get that."

She shifted her weight from one foot to the other as she spoke, looking away. She was lying.

Well, maybe not lying now.

But—

"Were you upset I hadn't called all day?" He took a risk and stepped closer to her. She didn't move away.

"No." She laughed like that was the most ridiculous idea in the world. Which made him think he was on to something.

"Leigh, you do know I interrogate people, right?"

She didn't respond.

"I'm thinking maybe you were a little upset, and I'm sorry. I wanted to call you. I've been thinking about you all day."

"Really?" She barely spoke the word. In fact, based on the way she pulled back when she said it, he would be willing to bet she hadn't meant to say it out loud.

He stepped closer. "Really."

She nodded a couple of times. "I didn't ignore your call, exactly," she said. "If you must know, I was kind of praying. Sort of. It's hard to explain. And when I heard the phone buzz, I didn't even look at it. I didn't know you'd tried to call until you told me. After you left, I saw you had texted and that I had missed a call. I had no idea you were worried."

This was probably not the time to go for tough and macho. "I was terrified," he said.

"I guess I overreacted."

"I guess I did too."

"Sorry." They said the word at the same time. She didn't seem to know where to look. Her eyes bounced from the floor to the ceiling. Everywhere but to him. Eventually they landed on the door.

"Why were you and Gabe sitting outside my house?"

"I didn't want to leave," he said. "Gabe came to say hi."

"At midnight?"

"He's a good friend."

"I didn't know you were going to be here all night," she said.

"I wasn't planning on telling you." Might as well be up front about it.

Another long pause. Filled with some sort of weird vibe. They'd had their first real fight and lived to tell about it. But it wasn't like they could kiss and make up when they hadn't kissed in the first place, and he wasn't sure he wanted their first kiss to be like this.

"I'd better get back out there," he said. "Gabe won't leave until I fill him in."

"Okay," she said. "Good night."

She followed him to the door. If he turned around now . . . no. Not now. He kept moving until he heard her close the door behind him. He leaned against the porch rail for a moment. No sense standing out here like a lovesick puppy. He jogged to the car.

Gabe leaned out his window. "Well?"

A boom. A scream. A flash.

Ryan raced back to the house, Gabe on his heels. He didn't bother to knock. He used the key Leigh had given him earlier in the week. He braced himself for what he would find when he went inside.

Father, please, please let her be okay.

11

Leigh had no idea why her dining room table had spontaneously combusted. She picked herself up from where she'd landed when she dove behind the sofa and raced for the fire extinguisher as orange flames danced across the dining room chairs.

She stood a few feet away. Pull. Aim. Squeeze. Sweep.

One chair out.

She had to stand much closer than she wanted to get the job done. Sweat poured from her face and burned her eyes as she attacked the flaming chair to her left.

"Leigh!" Ryan appeared beside her. "Get out!"

"No!" The fire department was only a mile away, but if they let it burn, the house would be destroyed before the firefighters could get here. There was only one chair not burning and it was near the curtains. If it went up in flames . . .

She couldn't lose this house. She'd lost so much.

The second chair was out.

Gabe joined the fray. Where had he found two more fire extinguishers? He gave one to Ryan and the three of them put out the last two chairs as the sirens from the fire trucks screamed closer. "I called it in. They said they'll be here in two minutes."

The three of them stood at the ready, fire extinguishers pointed toward the smoldering heap that had been a one-hundred-year-old pine table.

What had happened? She had no idea how long they stood there before two first responders raced into the room. One of them reached for the fire extinguisher she was still holding. "Ma'am, I'll take that."

She had to force each finger to release. Why did it weigh so much more than it had a few moments ago? Or maybe it was her arms that weighed more than usual. The adrenaline rush had passed and a deep fatigue flooded in to take its place.

Leigh stumbled against the kitchen counter as her home filled with firefighters.

Ryan leaned against the counter beside her. "Thank you," she said. The words did not come close to conveying the depth of emotion swirling in her heart and mind. The relief she'd experienced when she knew she wasn't alone. The gratitude for Ryan and Gabe's efforts to put out the fire. But if she tried to express any of that in words, she'd fall apart.

Ryan stood there with her for several minutes without saying anything. "What happened when you came inside?" he asked.

Thank goodness. A question she could answer. "The table blew up," she said. "I don't know what else to tell you. I closed the door and walked into the living room to grab a book and it . . . exploded."

Ryan put his arm around her. She leaned against him and made no protest as his other arm wrapped around her and he squeezed her close. She couldn't stop her entire body from trembling. Was it a reaction to his touch or the stress of the last few moments? Or both?

She had no complaints as he rubbed her back. "It's okay. You're okay."

His lips pressed into her hair and she didn't even care that ten men in full turnout gear were roaming through her home.

A throat cleared. "Excuse me," a deep voice rumbled from

behind Ryan. He pressed her a fraction closer before releasing her. Well, most of her. He kept one arm around her as they turned to the voice.

"Ms. Weston." The man stuck out his large hand to offer a handshake. His grip was firm, his eyes kind. "We'd like to bring in a couple of dogs to check for any other flammable items."

"Sure," she said. "Whatever you need to do."

He nodded and waved at another firefighter at the door. That man nodded and disappeared.

"The fire was contained to the dining room," he said. "Although I cannot condone you staying inside a house with a fire, I must say that you did a great job of putting it out before we got here. There's no evidence of any sort of structural damage, but you might want to stay somewhere else for the night. We need to do a thorough check of the house."

Leigh couldn't believe this. A few hours ago, all she wanted to do was get out of this house. Now? All she wanted to do was stay.

A fireman yelled from the dining room. "What was on this table, ma'am?"

The table? She tried to picture it.

"Was it the balloon bouquet I brought in this morning?" Ryan asked.

"Yes," she said.

"Balloons?" Three firemen spoke at once.

"Explains a lot," one of them said.

"It's too soon to say that," the older man said.

"Not too soon to say that something detonated on this table." Another fireman held up a charred object in his hands.

"There was a small decorative pot with a small green plant," Ryan said. "The balloons were tied to the handle."

"Looks like your plant blew up and ignited the balloons. Gave you a nice little fireball, and I'm guessing this table was pretty flammable."

"The plant blew up?" Leigh asked.

"Don't quote me on it, but that'd be my guess. Where did you get it?"

"Friends from the hospital sent it," she said. Which group was it today? The post-op people? Yeah. That's who it was. No one in post-op would do this.

"Balloons don't explode," Ryan said. "Helium is an inert gas. It wouldn't catch fire like that."

"We may never be able to prove it, but my guess is the balloons were filled with hydrogen. Not helium," the fireman said.

"That would do it," Gabe said.

Leigh racked her brain. Hydrogen was extremely flammable. No one in their right mind would fill a balloon with it. Unless . . .

Someone had tried to kill her with a flower arrangement.

The next hour was a blur. Firefighters. Forensics teams. Investigators. Someone made coffee. She sat on the end of her sofa and sipped the bitter brew. Who had made this stuff? It was awful.

Someone came in with some dogs. Another hour passed. The firefighters declared her house clear. All the flower arrangements had been checked for explosives. They were all clear. Her bedroom. Her garage. Her parents' room. Everything.

But she wasn't safe anywhere.

The Lord is a strong tower. The righteous run into it and are saved.

She hadn't thought of that verse in a long time.

She stood in the darkness of her dad's old office, looking out over the lake. Her dad had made it a point to teach her as many verses as he could find about the safety and security that were hers as a child of God. All in an effort to help her handle the fear and anxiety that had chased her all the way from China. Her dad had always wanted her to live bravely. To tackle anything. To know she was secure, both in his love and in God's.

She'd lived in fear for too long.

She was done. She wasn't going to be chased away from her home. She wasn't going to be forced to hide inside it. This person would either succeed in killing her or make a mistake so Ryan could catch them.

She would live or she would die.

She wouldn't live afraid of dying.

Not that she had a death wish. There were so many beautiful things to live for.

"Leigh?" Ryan's voice floated into the darkness. "Can I come in?"

"Sure," she said. "What do they need?"

"Nothing. They're packing up."

"Great." She should go downstairs and tell them thank you.

She could hear Ryan approaching her. His pace measured. He stopped behind her. "What do you need, Leigh? What can I do?"

She didn't know how to answer.

His hands rested on her shoulders, and without making a conscious decision, her body melted against his. His arms came around her. His chin rested on her head.

"I'll catch him, Leigh."

She knew he would try.

The phone in his pocket buzzed. He kept one arm around her as he answered it. "It's Kirk. I called him earlier and had to leave a message."

She could hear her brother's frantic voice. Ryan explained the events of the night.

"She's right here. She's fine."

"Here," he said, handing her the phone. "He wants to talk to you."

"Kirk."

Ten minutes later she returned his phone. He'd kept his arms around her the entire time. Except for the moment when he'd started playing with her hair.

"Leigh," he said, his voice rough. "I need to tell you something."

She had a bad feeling she wasn't going to like this.

"Years ago, when you were still in middle school, Kirk made it very clear that you were off-limits."

"What?"

"To his friends. He made it clear that trying to date you was unacceptable."

She was going to kill her brother.

"I respected his wishes, but I've always wondered if you would have ever considered—"

"Yo! Parker! Where are you, man?" She could hear Gabe walking up the stairs.

"Unbelievable," Ryan muttered. He released her and stepped away. "We're in the office," he said.

Gabe approached the door with his usual bouncy step but paused when he hit the darkened room. "Um, sorry. I, um, hope I wasn't interrupting anything. Wait. That's not true. I hope I *was* interrupting, because if I wasn't, then you're an idiot."

Leigh could feel her cheeks burning. Ryan didn't acknowledge Gabe's insinuations. "What do you need, Gabe?"

"I was coming to see if Leigh wanted me to find a hotel room for her or if she wanted to stay here."

"A hotel," Ryan said.

"I'll stay here," Leigh said at the same time.

"What?" they both said.

"Okay, then," Gabe said, stepping backward into the hall. "I'll take that as an undecided. When you work it out, let me know. I'll be in the hall."

He made a show of leaning against the wall, still in sight of the door.

"Leigh," Ryan said.

"No. I will not go."

"Please."

"Do you really think I'd be any safer in some random hotel?"

"I think you'd be safer where no one knows where you are."

"I'm not hiding."

Ryan ran his hands through his hair. He still hadn't cut it. What would it be like to run her hands . . .

She didn't realize she'd stepped closer to him until her hands rested on his chest. He stilled at her touch. "I'm not hiding."

He dropped his head until his forehead rested on hers. "I don't know how to protect you." It sounded like the words had been wrenched from the deepest parts of him.

"I don't think it's up to you."

Not up to him?

Who did she think was going to protect her from this madman?

"You can't keep me alive," she said.

"I'll die trying."

"I know." He heard the warmth in her voice. "And I appreciate that you are doing everything you can to save me, but there's only One who can do that, Ryan. I've been wrestling with it, and I'm still not okay with everything going on in my life, but I do know this. He's in control. Like it or not."

He wanted to argue with her. She was saying all the things his heart kept telling him. All the stuff he kept trying to ignore.

"You can't make yourself crazy over whether or not someone sneaks a bomb in a flower arrangement."

"I should have thought of that," he said.

"Now you'll know. The next time someone's being stalked by a homicidal maniac, you'll refuse to allow their friends to send them flowers."

Was she trying to be funny?

"There's nothing amusing about this."

"I'm not laughing. Or kidding."

"You could have been killed."

"So could you. You carried it in the door. What if it had blown up in your hands? Did you think of that?"

He hadn't.

"What if it wasn't meant for me at all?"

He did not like the way her mind was working on this one. "That is an interesting theory, but it would have been hard to know I would be the one carrying it in. I'm not convinced you weren't the target."

"We need to find out if the post-op group really sent flowers," Leigh said. "For that matter, we probably need to see if anyone at the hospital has sent any this week."

How could she be so calm and logical?

"I'll take care of it," he said.

"I can ask arou—"

"No," he said. The last thing he needed was Leigh doing her own investigating.

"Why not?" She pulled away from him and looked into his face. "What's wrong with asking a few questions?"

"Because you could tip off the person responsible. I'm not going to walk around the hospital flashing my badge. I'm going to call the flower shop. I'm going to ask a few discreet questions. I have a plan. Please." He reached for her face. He shouldn't. She was a victim. A witness. She was under police protection. His protection. He'd allowed far too much physical contact between them today. He shouldn't be touching her.

He closed his eyes and willed himself to drop his hand and step back.

When he opened his eyes, hers were on him. They were filled with confusion. Maybe even hurt.

"Leigh, when this is over . . ." He took a deep breath. "Look, I don't want to take advantage of you. Of this situation. When it's over, if you'll let me, I'd love to hang around with you. All the time."

"Are you concerned that I'm emotionally fragile?" She stepped closer. He took another step back.

"I wouldn't put it that way, but I do think emotions run high in near-death situations, and I wouldn't want—"

"You're afraid when this is all over my feelings will change? Or are you afraid yours will change?"

There was no chance his would change.

"Or are you afraid of Kirk finding out? Or your boss?"

"Yes."

"Which?"

"Both."

She took another step. "Guess what?"

The back of his legs bumped against her dad's desk.

"I'm not afraid of either of them."

She leaned into him, her hands on his forearms. Somehow his hands wound up on her hips. Her lips brushed his cheek. If he turned his head an inch . . .

"Thank you for being such a gentleman," she said.

He clenched his jaw.

"And I promise I won't ask questions at the hospital when I go to work tonight."

This woman would be the death of him.

"And don't worry about Kirk. I'll protect you from him." She slid from his arms and walked out the door. When she reached the hallway, she paused. "I'm going to get some sleep. You two are welcome to stay. Let me know what you decide."

He reached the hallway in time to see her disappear into her room.

Gabe shoved himself off the wall. "You're in trouble," he said in a singsong voice. Ryan followed him down the stairs.

What had just happened? Had she—? Was she saying she was as interested as he was? Or was she saying she appreciated that he wasn't pushing her into something she wasn't sure she wanted?

He rubbed his eyes. When had he slept last? Sleep would probably help a lot.

"I vote we crash on the couches," Gabe said.

"The downstairs smells like smoke," Ryan said. "We'll have headaches."

"We have two guest bedrooms in the basement," Leigh said from the end of the hall.

Ryan paused on the stairs. She leaned over the bannister toward them. "If you aren't going home, you could shower and sleep down there. I'm assuming you both have a change of clothes?"

Gabe shrugged like it was fine with him.

"Thanks. That's where we'll be if you need us," Ryan said.

Leigh disappeared again.

"She's like a ninja," Gabe said in a quiet voice. "Fearless and kind of terrifying."

Pretty accurate description.

They walked outside to grab their bags from their cars. "What did you two talk about?" Gabe asked. "I did my best to eavesdrop, but you kept your voices too low."

"We didn't talk about anything of interest to you."

"I doubt that very much."

"There was one thing . . ."

"Yes?"

"She mentioned the possibility that the flowers were supposed to blow up while I was holding them."

"That would have been unfortunate."

Indeed. "I don't think there's anything to that, but—"

"We need to keep it in mind."

"Exactly."

"Anything else?"

"Yes," Ryan said. He dropped his voice even lower in case Leigh had a window open or something. "We need to find out everything we can about everyone who works in the emergency department.

How long have they worked there? Has Leigh ever worked with any of them anywhere else?"

"You think her stalker is someone she works with?"

"We aren't even sure she has a stalker, remember? This behavior isn't textbook stalker. This is . . ."

"Crazy," Gabe said.

"And it doesn't fit any profile that makes sense."

"Maybe she has a new stalker. She does seem to have the ability to make grown men lose their ever-loving minds in the space of a few days." Gabe punched his shoulder.

"I haven't lost my mind," Ryan said.

"What makes you think I was talking about you?"

"Who else would you be talking about?"

"No one. I find it interesting you claimed it so quickly, that's all."

"Go to bed, Gabe," Ryan said. "I'm going to check with the guys out here keeping watch tonight before I come in."

Gabe was laughing as he walked back into the house. Ryan had always liked Gabe, but ever since he quit working undercover, he'd lost his filter. If he thought it, it popped out of his mouth. It was almost like he'd spent so many years keeping everything bottled up and now he just exploded everywhere.

In some ways the honesty was refreshing. You always knew where you stood with Gabe. But in other ways, like tonight, it was intrusive and embarrassing.

Ryan made sure the officers on the night watch had his information. He locked the doors and set the security system before making his way down the stairs. He showered quickly and fell into the bed. It wouldn't be much, but maybe a couple of hours of sleep would help him make some sense out of what was going on.

Because there was only one thing he was sure of right now.

He was missing something.

Something big.

And if he didn't figure it out soon, someone was going to die.

12

Leigh slept until ten Sunday morning.

She reached for her phone even before she opened her eyes. She had three texts.

One from Keri.

One from Gabe.

One from Ryan.

Keri's text was full of exclamation marks and emojis and expressed her relief that Leigh hadn't been harmed and her joy in hearing that Leigh would be back at work.

Gabe's text was surprising. Just a few words.

He's got it bad.

Who had what bad? There was only one possible answer to that question, and the thought of it made her skin flush. Had Ryan confided something in Gabe? What would he have said? Did he really like her? He said he did. Sort of. If "I want to hang out with you all the time" meant that he liked her.

Ryan's text was longer.

Hope you slept well. Thanks for letting us crash in the basement. We left everything clean and neat. I'm going to church with my sister and her kids and then we're going to get brunch. I would love for you to join us when this is all over. Anyway, I'm going to be running down some leads today, but if it's okay with you, I'd like to drive you to work and see how the security is set up. Let me know.

Three little dots started scrolling on her screen. She waited to see what else he had to say.

If you're up for it, Adam Campbell is going to come over this afternoon to chat with you. I want to get a fresh set of eyes on things. Let me know.

She texted back that all of that was fine and she wanted to leave her house around six.

Three hours later, Adam Campbell knocked on her door. She'd known Adam forever. He'd been two years behind her in school, and back then he'd been a bit gangly and awkward. But the confident man standing outside her door—slim but athletic with light brown hair and green eyes—looked every bit like the middle son of the powerful Campbell family that he was. The Campbells owned half of Carrington. Adam could have done anything, but he studied criminal justice in college, went through the police academy, and then started in the Uniform Patrol Division like everybody else. White-collar crime made sense for him. That was a world he probably understood better than most.

Still, what could he possibly add to the investigation? What leads was Ryan working on? Why was he texting her rather than calling?

Her face grew warm as she thought about last night. The darkened office, the moonlight on the lake. She'd been so forward with him, she'd surprised herself. Pretty sure she'd surprised him too.

She was going to strangle Kirk. When he called later, he was going to get a piece of her mind. A large one. How dare he? Had Adam been part of the prohibition? How wide a net had Kirk cast in his efforts to protect his baby sister?

When he showed up, Adam looked like a man out for a Sunday afternoon cruise on the lake. Shorts. Boat shoes. Polo shirt. Sunglasses on his head. The badge and the gun kind of ruined his casual look, but maybe this was as casual as he got.

"Adam." She stuck out her hand. "Come on in. How can I help you?"

They took a seat in the living room. "I won't take much of your time. I'm helping Ryan with a few aspects of a couple of the investigations he's working on. I was wondering if you'd be willing to give me access to your security system?"

"Sure, but why?"

"I want to go through it more closely than we've looked before. I want to look at every camera angle and see if anything unusual pops up. It's a long shot, but you'd be surprised how many investigations hinge on things like this."

"What do you need?"

"Honestly, I'd just like your permission. We'll get a warrant and be able to work directly with the security company, but your permission will help speed things along."

"You've got it. What else?"

Adam shifted in his seat. "I'm sorry to do this, but I need to ask you about your boyfriends. Past, present, good, bad, that kind of thing."

So many pieces fell into place. Ryan staying away. Sending in Adam. Of course he could have asked her himself, but that would have been awkward.

Not like this wasn't.

"There's not much to tell."

Adam raised one eyebrow at her.

"There isn't. I dated a couple of guys in college—"

"Names?"

"They aren't responsible for this."

"How do you know?"

"One of them is married and lives in Virginia. I was in his wedding. His wife is now a very good friend. The other is on the mission field in Brazil."

"I still need their names."

She spent the next thirty minutes giving him the names of every guy she'd ever gone out with, even once. Then he wanted the names of every guy who'd ever asked her out. That list was a bit longer.

Then he wanted to know why she had turned them down.

"I'm picky," she said.

"Anyone ever make you uncomfortable?"

"No more than it ever makes me to have to tell them no when they've put themselves out there and risked rejection by asking. It's flattering to be asked, but I don't date doctors, I don't date coworkers, and I don't date guys who haven't grown up yet."

Adam tapped his pen on the notebook he'd been writing in. "Given that many people find their spouse in their workplace, I would imagine that would narrow the field considerably."

"You could say that."

"So what is it about Ryan—"

"Okay, we're done here." She couldn't believe he'd done that. Adam Campbell had a teasing side. Interesting.

Adam laughed. "Yes, we're done. Thank you for your time, Leigh. I'll be back tomorrow with that warrant and we'll look through your files. How late do you sleep?"

Wow. That was quite considerate. "Normally I sleep until three or four. I doubt that will happen tomorrow."

"Why don't you call me when you wake up."

"Sounds great."

When Adam left, Leigh packed her lunch, changed into her scrubs, and thought back over the list of names she'd given Adam.

None of them could have done this.

Could they?

The ride to the hospital with Ryan was . . . weird.

She probably should have expected it to be, after everything that had happened between them last night. Unresolved feelings did not make for easy conversations.

He seemed determined to avoid talking about anything related to her case, or to the John Doe case. He asked her how she had slept. Mentioned the weather—the forecast called for severe thunderstorms tonight. Asked her how she was feeling and what time she got off work in the morning.

She answered all his questions and bit her tongue to keep from asking him everything she wanted to know.

What was with the relationship quiz from Adam?

What was the status of the body they found at Mr. Cook's place?

What was happening with the John Doe from the lake?

What had he been doing all day?

Did he want to hang out with her because he wanted to be with her? Or did he think hanging out with her was the best way to protect her?

When he pulled into the emergency department parking lot, Leigh reached for her bag. The thing weighed a ton tonight. But since she'd promised not to eat or drink anything she hadn't personally prepared, she'd had to pack coffee and snacks. And chocolate.

"Leigh, wait." Ryan grabbed her arm. Had he seen something suspicious? Should she duck?

"What is it?" She could hear the alarm in her voice.

Confusion clouded his features for a moment, then awareness. "Sorry. I didn't mean to scare you. I . . ."

He stared at the steering wheel for a moment. "Just be careful tonight, okay?"

"Of course," she said with forced cheerfulness. "Nothing to worry about."

She wished she believed her own bravado.

Ryan didn't answer her as they got out of the car, but she didn't think he believed her either.

He walked close by her side as they approached the hospital entrance. She scanned them in and paused. "I need to put my stuff away and report," she said.

"I'm going to snoop around," he said.

"You'd better check in with Miss Edna before you do any snooping."

"Good point."

"See ya."

She could feel Ryan's eyes on her as she walked away.

As soon as she set her bag down behind the nurses station, she was enveloped in a hug. "Leigh!" Keri's joy was infectious. And loud. Over the next few minutes she was hugged and squeezed and waved at. There's no way any of these people had been trying to kill her.

For tonight, here, she'd be safe.

The news of a five-car wreck rippled through the department ten minutes after she took report. For the next four hours, she moved from one crisis to the next. One patient to the next. Two patients were children who needed to be checked out, but thanks to their car seats were physically fine. Two patients came in with lacerations and possible concussions. Painful and traumatic in their own way, but nothing that would take their lives.

One patient died before they got him out of the ambulance. The combination of head trauma and blood loss had been too severe for him to survive.

His wife was in hysterics. Leigh had heard her crying down the hall as she and Dr. Sloan worked on a twenty-five-year-old woman who'd been in the passenger seat of a compact car. The first responders had needed the Jaws of Life to get her out. She was in shock. It had taken a while to clean her wounds and stitch her up.

"I'm still not sure what happened," she said under her breath.

"I know." Leigh tried to comfort her. "I was in an accident a week ago. It's so disorienting."

The young woman nodded but didn't say anything else.

Her boyfriend arrived in a panic. He burst into tears when he saw her. "I thought I'd lost you," he said over and over again.

Dr. Sloan banished him from the room after a few minutes. Thank goodness. She didn't know how much more of that gushiness she could handle.

When they left the patient's room, she paused to regroup.

Dr. Price strode down the hall toward her. "You okay, Leigh?"

"I'm fine," she said. "Taking a second to catch my breath. What are you doing here?"

"Checking on my favorite patient," he said. "Are you sure you're okay?"

"She was amazing," Dr. Sloan said with a smile. "Glad to have you back, Leigh."

"Thank you."

"Oh, Leigh, there you are." Barb waved at her from down the hall. Barb was one of the nursing assistants who worked nights. "I have a note for you. From that cop you came in with tonight."

Ryan. When had he left? She'd been so busy, she hadn't even noticed.

"You came in with a cop?" Dr. Price eyed her with speculation. "I don't suppose that would be Ryan Parker, now would it?"

"Yes," Barb said with a giggle. "How did you meet him?"

This could not be happening.

"Ryan Parker?" Dr. Sloan said. "I know him. Homicide investigator, right?"

"Yes, that's right." Leigh was trying to be polite, but what she wanted was for everyone to leave so she could read the note.

"He's the one who gave me the third degree yesterday about the security setup in here. Now I know why."

"Sorry," she said.

"Don't apologize. He asked some good questions. The ED should be the safest place in the hospital. And everyone working here should be able to come to work without worrying about anyone being around who shouldn't be here. I rather enjoyed the conversation," he said. Then he winked at her. "I'll enjoy hassling him about it even more now that I understand the motivation behind it."

Awesome.

Dr. Price took pity on her. "Come now," he said to the others. "Let's leave Ms. Weston alone so she can read her love note, shall we?"

So much for the pity. She clenched her jaw to keep herself from sticking her tongue out at him.

Then she opened the note.

> *I'll see you at seven. Stay in the department. Trust your instincts. If anything seems off, grab the officers at the desk or call me. R.*

Hardly a love note. Although she could almost see his intensity, even feel his worry, bleeding through the words.

She put the note in her pocket. Now that she'd had time to catch her breath, she was paying more attention to the hunger pains. She went to the break room and pulled out her supper from the locked cooler Ryan had insisted she use. How goofy was that?

Regardless, she nibbled on chicken salad and sipped her canned sparkling water. No one would succeed in poisoning her. At least not tonight.

Dr. Fowler came into the break room and fixed himself a cup of coffee. She didn't make eye contact. She had no use for the man. He was a great radiologist. Didn't make him a great person.

"Glad you're doing okay, Leigh," he said.

"Thank you." She took another bite. Maybe he would get the point that she didn't want to talk.

He sat down in one of the chairs and sipped the coffee. Couldn't he drink his coffee in another room? Like in his own office, maybe? Or the doctors' lounge? This was what they got for having the best coffee in the hospital. Couldn't keep anyone out.

A few nurses came in, and their chatter eased the tension in the room.

She finished off her chicken salad and eyed the mandarin oranges she had packed. Maybe she'd save them for later.

"Dr. Fowler? Dr. Fowler, are you okay?" she heard one of the nurses ask.

Dr. Fowler was bent over, his arms tight around his stomach. He jumped to his feet, stumbled to the trash can, and vomited.

Great.

The nurses excused themselves. Chickens.

Leigh walked to the sink and ran water over a couple of paper towels. She handed them to Dr. Fowler. He reached for them, but then began heaving so violently she was afraid he was going to fall over.

"Dr. Fowler? Were you feeling ill tonight?"

"No," he gasped.

"Have you had anything to eat?"

"Just—" He pointed to the coffee cup on the chair.

"Okay. Would you like to sit?"

He shook his head no and proceeded to heave for the next minute.

Leigh went for more paper towels.

The door burst open and Keri ran in. "Oh, hey," she said as she reached for a duffel bag. "Claire is puking her guts out. Didn't make it to the bathroom. It's a mess."

"Dr. Fowler is puking his guts out right here," Leigh said with a gesture toward the trash can.

Keri frowned. "That's weird."

"Is anyone else sick?"

"Not that I know of."

One of her favorite transporters, Glen, stumbled into the room. "I don't feel so hot," he said. "Mind if I sit for a minute?"

"This might not be the best place—"

"Too late," Keri huffed as Glen lost it.

"I hate vomit," she said. "Blood. Protruding bones. No problem. But vomit?" She shuddered.

Leigh pulled a chair over to the trash can and helped Dr. Fowler into it. She handed him the damp paper towels. "Sit here."

What a night. She turned to Keri. "Take the clothes to Claire, but make a pit stop at the nurses station and get housekeeping and one of the officers to come in here. Okay?"

She didn't wait for Keri to answer. She grabbed another trash can and took it to Glen.

"You're a saint," Keri said as she ran out the door.

Leigh looked from Dr. Fowler to Glen. Every nerve ending was tingling. Something wasn't right about this. Maybe it was because she was alone in this room with two men? No. She couldn't possibly be in any danger from either of them. They could barely hold their heads up.

The officer arrived first. "Leigh? You okay?"

"I am," she said. "But I need you to find out if anyone else has been violently throwing up tonight."

"What?"

"At least three people are puking right now. Doesn't that seem odd to you?"

The officer shrugged. "I guess?"

"Please ask around."

"Yes, ma'am."

She looked at her watch. One in the morning. If she called Ryan, she'd wake him. And he hadn't gotten much sleep last night.

She was probably overreacting. Seeing danger in nothing more than a nasty stomach bug.

That hit three people within ten minutes of each other?

But if she called Ryan, he'd be convinced she wasn't safe in the ED. Except none of these people worked in the ED. Claire worked in the lab, Glen took patients all over the hospital, and Dr. Fowler worked in radiology.

"We got another one," Keri called from the door.

Seriously? "Who is it now?"

"Dr. Price."

Oh no. "Where is he?"

"In the OR."

That did it. Leigh reached for her phone.

Ryan strode through the emergency department. He tried to tell himself his sense of urgency was due to his concern about the ones who'd gotten sick tonight. But he knew the truth. Right now all he cared about was Leigh.

He scanned the area.

"She's in room three," Keri said.

"Is she all right?"

"She's with a patient."

Right.

"What are you doing here?" Keri asked.

Interesting. Leigh must not have told anyone she'd called him. "Just checking on things here."

"It's been a doozy. I won't be sorry to go home and crawl into bed. After I take a very hot shower." She pointed to a row of rooms numbered from one to ten. "Room three."

"Thanks." He walked down the hall. No one gave him any grief about being there, but then his badge and weapon were in clear view. He waited outside the room. Five minutes. Ten minutes.

Twelve minutes later, Leigh emerged, giving orders to the nurse who was with her. Something about starting an IV and some pain medicine. The patient called out from the room and Leigh and the nurse shared an exasperated look.

"Go on," Leigh told the nurse. "I'll see what he needs."

The nurse hurried down the hall, but Leigh came close enough that he could smell her shampoo. She squeezed his forearm. "Give me five minutes."

He grabbed her hand as she walked away. She turned back to him and he saw surprise but no fear in her eyes. He tugged and she stepped back to him. "Are you okay?" he asked.

"Completely fine," she said with a soft smile that eased the raging creature inside him that was prepared to destroy anyone or anything that caused her pain. "Promise."

This time he let her go.

She returned to her patient and, true to her word, was back at his side five minutes later. She led him to a small break room.

"I'm sorry to wake you over something like this."

"I told you to trust your instincts."

"You may not feel that way after tonight."

"Try me. How many have gotten sick?"

"It was four originally."

"And now?"

"Since I called you, we've checked with the other departments. Three in post-op. Two in pediatrics."

"Where are they?"

"Everyone is in a room down here right now," she said.

"No, I mean where is pediatrics?"

"That's what's crazy. Post-op is on the second floor. Pediatrics is on the fifth. None of the people who got sick in pediatrics or post-op left their department all night. At first I thought it might be something specific to the ED, but now I don't know."

Ryan couldn't keep the smile from his face. "And you said you would make a lousy cop."

"And I was right." She put her hands on her waist. "I would make a lousy cop because my investigating has come up with a big fat nothing."

"Welcome to my world."

She huffed in frustration. It was adorable.

"Do you have any idea what caused it?"

"Maybe."

"Care to share?"

"It might be the coffee."

"The coffee was bad?"

"More like tampered with. There are quite a few drugs in a hospital that can be used to induce vomiting. And most of the coffee around here is so bad, you might not even notice it. We have great coffee down here, but all the people who drank it used flavored creamers. It could have been in the creamer or in the coffee. Either way, it might have been enough to disguise the taste."

She shifted her weight from one foot to the other. "It's probably none of those things, but that was all I could come up with. Unfortunately, by the time I made the connection, all the departments where someone got sick had made fresh pots of coffee."

"Even down here?"

"Things got crazy for a few minutes when they brought a nurse and one of the nursing assistants from pediatrics down. One of the secretaries came in and saw the pot was almost empty and figured there'd be a run on the coffee later. She dumped it out and made a fresh pot."

She pointed to herself. "Like I said. Lousy cop material."

He pulled her hand away. "Not a chance," he said. "You've given me a lot to work with. And I'm glad you're okay." He squeezed her fingers.

On the job, Ryan. No time for this right now.

He released her and pulled out his notebook. "Give me the timeline of events."

She grimaced.

"Is something wrong?"

"No?" She said it like a question.

"I'm going to assume there is a problem, but for some reason you're hesitant to share it with me."

Why did that bother him so much? Was he already so far gone that the thought of her keeping any secret from him was physically painful? Man, he was in big trouble.

"It's not a problem, exactly."

He waited.

"While I was eating, Dr. . . . Dr. Fowler came in and got a cup of coffee. He sat in the chair and was surfing on his phone. He said he was glad I was doing better. I said thank you. That was the extent of our conversation until he doubled over and then started vomiting."

"Dr. Fowler. You mean Clay Fowler?" He should not feel this way. Should not. But if anyone had to get dosed with some sort of vomiting drug, the fact that it was Clay made him ridiculously happy.

"Yes," she said. "I'm sorry."

"Why are you sorry?"

"Because you're going to have to go talk to him."

Oh. That. "It's okay. Part of the job. We've had a few conversations over the past couple of months. All of them unpleasant. I'm sure this one won't be any different."

"It might be."

"Why is that?"

She looked at her shoes. Then the wall. She chewed the inside of her lip.

"Leigh? What's going on?"

She leaned closer to him and spoke quietly. "She's here." The emphasis was on the *she*.

There could only be one she who would generate this response. The girlfriend.

"You're kidding."

Leigh wouldn't joke about something like that. He knew it. She knew it.

"Okay. Give me the rest of it."

Leigh filled him in on the events from her perspective. Then she went back to work and he interviewed everyone he could think of before he quit stalling and went to Clay's room.

Keri found him standing outside Clay's room. "I'm on my way in. Mind if I hang around while you grill him?"

Ryan couldn't keep himself from laughing. "I don't care."

"Awesome," Keri said with a mischievous grin. "Follow me."

He followed her into the room. Clay lay in the bed. Ashen. Eyes red. A beautiful woman sat in the chair beside him. Ryan knew who she was. He knew where she'd gone to school. Knew what hospital in Raleigh she worked in. Probably knew more about her than Clay did. But he never referred to her by name, even in his own mind. To him, she was the girlfriend. The home wrecker. Or a few other names that weren't as kind.

"Dr. Fowler," Keri said with more volume than was necessary, "Investigator Parker needs to ask you a few questions about the events of the evening."

Clay's only response was a slight dip of his head.

"Can you tell me what happened tonight?" Ryan asked.

"I threw up."

Keri snorted. Ryan glared at her. If she couldn't be professional, then she was going to have to leave. But he had to admit he rather enjoyed the way she didn't try to cover up her thoughts.

She gave him an apologetic shrug and then made quite a show of checking Clay's IV.

"I heard that part. I mean before. What were you doing down here?"

Clay swallowed. The action seemed to cause him some discomfort. He winced and the girlfriend rubbed his hand.

Ugh. If he had to watch much more of this he might be the one vomiting soon.

"I was on call tonight. Came down to grab some coffee. Decided to sit in the break room a few minutes. It was quiet. Leigh was the only one in there and she's not a big talker."

Keri rolled her eyes in spectacular fashion. They both knew why Leigh didn't talk to Clay. She didn't like him. She was too professional to be rude, but she didn't make any effort to be nice either.

"After a few minutes, I started to feel queasy. Then dizzy. I was afraid if I got up, I might fall over. Cold sweats. Stomach cramps. Then it hit. I have no idea how long I threw up. I've never experienced anything like it."

Ryan tried to keep his face impassive. There was sweet justice here. He'd be willing to bet his next paycheck that Clay had no idea that when Rebecca found out what he'd done, she'd thrown up.

"Anything unusual about this evening before that point?"

Clay's head moved back and forth on the pillow. "No. We had that bad wreck. I had a heavier load of emergency cases all at once, but that's part of being on call. I wouldn't say that is unusual."

"Okay. If you think of anything else, give me a call."

They both knew that would never happen.

Ryan refused to allow himself to run from the room, even though he wanted to. Just being in there, watching that hussy fawn all over Clay. Had she no shame?

Keri followed him out of the room and muttered several words Ryan wanted to say.

"How long will he be here?"

"Not long," she said. "The vomiting has stopped, so once he gets the rest of that bag of fluid in, he'll probably be released. He's a doctor. She's a nurse. If they can't figure out how to handle this at home, they need to find different professions."

Leave it to Keri to call it like she saw it.

"Thanks."

He leaned against the wall. Keri called over her shoulder, "She's in eight."

Ryan gave her a small salute and made his way to where Leigh was.

He only had to wait a couple of minutes before she came out.

"How did it go?" she asked.

"I survived."

"Did he?"

"Sadly, yes."

"You don't mean that."

"Sometimes I do."

She led the way to a small sitting area with more privacy than the hallway. "What happens next?"

"This won't be my case by lunchtime," he said. "I don't technically have jurisdiction in town. I'll hand it off to someone in the police department. They'll look through all the security footage. I'll tell them specifically to look for the movements of our victims—and anything that ties them to each other. I'll give them your tip about the coffee. We'll see if anything comes up."

"I'm sorry I woke you for this," she said. "You said to trust my instincts."

"I'm glad you did."

"But my instincts were off."

"I'm not sure about that," he said. "Something weird happened tonight. We'll make a note of it. We won't forget it. We'll look for patterns. Who knows where they might lead."

"Yeah, but someone else could have taken care of it. I could have called the police department and let you sleep."

"You most certainly should not have. If I'd gotten up in the morning and heard about this . . ." He stopped himself. She wasn't a child. He wasn't her boss. He could tell her that the thought of anything happening to her made him wake at night in a near panic or that the thought of another man even thinking about her in a romantic way made him want to run away with her to a deserted island where no one could ever find them.

But that might not be the best plan either.

She could have forced the issue, but she didn't. "I'd better get back to work," she said.

"I'll be back for you at seven."

"You don't have to do that. I can catch a ride with Keri. You need to rest."

The worry in her voice did funny things to his insides.

"I'll be here."

13

Ryan held the car door for Leigh and raced over to the driver's side.

"This is ridiculous," Leigh said. "You should be catching up on some sleep. Keri could have given me a ride. She volunteered."

"So did I," he said.

She didn't respond. When he glanced over, her eyes were closed. She had to be exhausted.

He certainly was.

"All the sick nurses and doctors and nursing assistants have gone home," she said. "I can't help but think there's something significant about this."

He didn't disagree.

"Maybe I'll be able to make some sense of it when I wake up," she said.

"Let me know if you come up with anything," he said. "Sometimes a good night's—or I guess in this case, day's—sleep is exactly what's needed."

"Hmm."

They rode in silence the rest of the way to Leigh's. He wasn't sure if she was asleep or not, but he didn't want to risk waking her if she was. He waved at the officer who had been on guard duty during the night. The officer gave him a thumbs-up. So things had been quiet here. Thank goodness for small mercies.

She stirred when he put the car in park. "Thanks for the ride," she said.

"My pleasure."

She stared at her house. Something was bothering her. Her entire body was tense, and she kept squeezing the armrest and releasing it.

Was she frightened? That would be completely understandable. But he didn't want to plant the idea. "Would you mind if I walk through the house before you come in? For my peace of mind?"

The relief on her face pulled at every protective instinct he had. He'd been right, but it frustrated him to no end. She shouldn't be afraid to come home.

"Stay in the car," he said. "I'll be back in two minutes."

He started in the basement and worked his way upstairs. He hesitated at the door to Leigh's room. He didn't want to invade her privacy, but if she had a stalker, her room was a logical place for them to violate.

Her room was as neat as he'd been expecting. Bed made. Bible on the arm of a chair by the window. He opened the blinds. She had lovely views of the lake from here. The houses across the lake wouldn't be visible after all the leaves came back, but for now he had a clear view of two houses. He made a note in his notebook to find out who lived in those houses. High-powered binoculars would give them a view into Leigh's room.

The thought made him cringe.

He turned back to look at the rest of Leigh's room. Trophies from her gymnastics years sat in one corner, mixed in with moments from her childhood, but the rest of the room spoke of a more mature woman.

The color palette, the arrangement of the furniture, the photographs on the mirror—everything reflected Leigh's touch. One photograph caught his eye and he stepped closer to examine it.

He remembered that night—his and Kirk's high school graduation. Mrs. Weston had been taking pictures of Kirk and Leigh, and he'd jumped in beside her at the last second.

In the picture, he had his arm around Leigh and they were all laughing. Why would she have this on her mirror?

The possibilities intrigued him, but he didn't have time to linger with them. He finished walking through the house and returned outside to Leigh. "All clear."

She smiled her thanks. "Are you in a hurry to get to work?"

The question startled him. The real answer was yes. "Um, no. I don't guess so. Why?"

"Have you had breakfast?"

"No." Where was she going with this?

"Me neither. And my dinner was interrupted last night. Let me fix us some breakfast before you go to work. It will only take a few minutes. It isn't the Pancake Hut, but I make a mean omelet."

"If you twist my arm . . ."

He followed her inside and didn't argue when she refused to let him help. She was a whiz in the kitchen. And she wasn't wrong about the omelet. It was fabulous. Bacon, tomatoes, some sautéed onions, goat cheese, and spinach. He was stuffed. He sipped a cup of coffee and took a final bite.

"That was fabulous," he said.

"I hope I haven't made you late for work." Leigh nibbled at her omelet. For someone who'd been starving, she hadn't eaten much.

"I cannot begin to tell you how much I do not care about that."

Her laughter warmed him all the way through. She was stunning all the time, but when she laughed, she radiated joy. He couldn't look away. She caught him staring at her and he held her gaze.

When she bit down on her lip he almost came out of his seat. At this rate, he would never make it through this case without doing something he shouldn't. Did she feel this? Was she as drawn to him as he was to her?

His phone buzzed and the moment shattered. The regretful smile she gave him tempted him to ignore the phone.

"You'd better get that," she said.

"Yeah."

He forced himself to walk away from her. He glanced at the phone. Gabe. He'd texted him earlier and told him where he was. This had better be important.

"Parker," Ryan said as he stepped onto Leigh's deck. He'd always loved this view. Would love it more if it was safe for Leigh to sit out here with him and enjoy it. "Tell me you've got something."

"Maybe," Gabe said. "When I called the hospital this morning to give them a heads-up about the warrant we're going to get for their footage from last night, they remembered they had some footage we'd requested from the cameras in the employee parking garages."

"Glad they remembered," Ryan said.

"Yeah. I'm not super impressed with the security guy we've been dealing with. Adam said the guy in charge is in Hawaii on his twenty-five-year wedding anniversary trip. He'll be back later this week. When he gets back, we're going to need to talk to him. In the meantime, I thought you'd want to take a look at this stuff for yourself."

"Okay," Ryan said. "Did it require a phone call in the middle of my breakfast?"

Gabe's chuckle spoke volumes.

"Just for that, I'm not bringing you any cookies."

"She made cookies?"

"Yep. She had cookie dough in the fridge and she's sending more in. But I'm going to conveniently forget them on the counter."

He disconnected the call in the middle of Gabe's apology. He helped Leigh clean the kitchen and an hour later—armed with two dozen cookies—Ryan found Gabe at his desk.

"Cookies. Sweet." Gabe grabbed one and stuffed it into his mouth. "Yo, Parker's got grub," he called out in a loud voice.

Ryan grabbed one before the vultures descended. Leigh had intended for him to share them, but he never promised to share all of them.

He settled in at his desk and pulled up a video file. More hospital security footage rolled on the screen. The team had been staring at hours of this stuff for days, looking for any sign of Leigh's attacker.

"I'm not seeing anything yet," Gabe said. "Still got a lot to go through though."

This could prove to be another dead end. Or it could be the break they'd been waiting for. There was never a way to know until you put in the work.

Thirty minutes later, shadowy movement on the edge of the parking structure caught his eye.

"Check this out," he said. Gabe stood behind Ryan's seat. "Am I imagining things? Do you see that?" He pointed to the shadow on the edge of the screen. It moved along the wall and then disappeared.

"Play it again," Gabe said.

He did.

"That's weird. It's too big to be a critter. But too far along the wall for it to be someone walking through. There's no reason to be against that wall unless you're staggering drunk or trying to avoid the cameras."

"The time stamp works. We don't have any footage of anyone at Leigh's car, but we know it's in there during this time."

He continued to watch the footage. Fifteen cars came out of the garage over the next several hours. Then the shift change hit and the cars poured in and out of the garage.

"Let's get this over to the forensics guys and see if they can enhance it. Maybe we can get a better view."

"I wouldn't hold your breath," Gabe said. "Whoever this is, they are out of the camera view."

"I don't disagree, but we still need to try. We might get more info on build, clothing, something we could use to match them to other camera views."

"Sounds good, but there's one big problem. Forensics is backed up two weeks at least."

"We might not have two weeks."

Ryan poked his head out of the homicide office and scanned the desks in the main office. "Adam. Could you come here a minute?"

Adam held up one finger. After a few keystrokes, he grabbed his ever-present tablet and maneuvered through the maze of desks. He stuck out his hand. "Parker. How's it going? You get my notes about my interview with Leigh?"

"Yeah. I did. Thanks for doing that."

"No problem."

"You got a minute?"

"Anything for the homicide division."

Ryan led him into the office he shared with Gabe, Anissa, and the rest of the homicide investigators.

Gabe hopped up from his desk when he saw Adam. "Campbell. What's up, man?"

"No idea," Adam said as he took the chair Ryan pulled out for him.

"We need a favor," Ryan said.

"We?" Gabe protested. "Don't be using up my favors, man. This one's on you."

Adam laughed. It was a long-running joke. His parents had not been happy with his decision to join the sheriff's office, especially when they realized he'd be spending at least two years in the Uniform Patrol Division. Without his knowledge, they'd tried to call in a bunch of favors in an attempt to get him moved into an investigative division early.

At the time, Ryan was a property crimes investigator and had gotten to know Adam when he joined the dive team. At first he wasn't too sure about a guy he'd assumed would be a spoiled brat playing cop, but he'd been impressed with his intensity during training and they became friends.

Ryan had been the one to tell Adam what his family was doing. Adam blew his top and put a stop to it. He'd handled it as well as could be expected, but from then on Ryan had teased him about calling in favors.

The crazy thing was, Adam's connections had been invaluable to more than one investigation. But this time Ryan wasn't interested in capitalizing on the Campbell family name. This time he needed a different kind of connection.

"How well do you know that forensics professor at the university?"

"Do you mean Dr. Fleming?"

"Yeah."

"Well enough. Why?"

"Tell me about her."

Adam gave him a questioning look, but answered. "Her PhD is in computer forensics and cybersecurity. Not many people have PhDs in that field. She's the one we call if we have a computer our forensic techs can't get into or if we are trying to get information off a hard drive someone dropped in their bathtub to keep us from being able to use it as evidence. When we need someone to analyze computer files in a hurry, she's been quick to help. But she's also an all-around computer genius, and she has access to top of the line equipment in her labs. She and some of the other professors in the department do a lot of volunteer work with groups that hunt down cyber predators, and they are working on more efficient ways to analyze video surveillance with the hope of sharing the technology with law enforcement agencies all over the country."

Wow. Brains and a big heart. Ryan could see why Adam was impressed by the professor. "She sounds great, but I have to ask this. How much does she charge?"

"Why?"

"I'm wondering if she'd be willing to help us out with more video surveillance stuff. We have the video feeds we need analyzed, but the forensics guys are at least a couple of weeks behind and I don't want to wait that long."

"I thought she was already on board to look at the lake stuff," Adam said.

"Yeah, but this is about Leigh Weston's brakes."

"Oh. Then you'll have to get it approved first, but Sabrina's not trying to get rich off the sheriff's department," he said. "Her department consults with law enforcement agencies all over the country, but she gives us priority. Says if she can't help keep her own community safe, then she doesn't have any business helping anyone else."

"Is she pretty?" Gabe asked.

Adam's eyes flashed. "She is," he said. "And not your type."

"Oh, I see how it is," Gabe said. "I want to meet her."

"She doesn't usually come to the office," Adam said. "Sorry."

Gabe didn't attempt to hide his amusement.

For his part, Ryan didn't care if Adam had a crush on the professor. What he cared about was whether or not she could review their video.

"If the captain approves it, will you introduce me to her? I'd like to get her to take a look at some files."

"Sure thing. I'll give her a call and see what her schedule looks like."

"Thanks."

After Adam left, Gabe leaned back in his chair. "I don't think Adam wants me to meet the lovely Dr. Fleming."

"I agree, but I don't care."

An hour later, he'd gotten easy approval from the captain to have Dr. Fleming look at the video, and Adam had sent her the files.

He started hunting down the cars that had come out of the garage and matching them to their owners. His next step was to get a list of every car that had come out during the shift change. If this guy was smart enough to stay out of sight of the cameras, he would have been smart enough to wait on the shift change to leave. Anyone coming out of the garage could be Leigh's attacker. Or none of them could be.

People thought being a homicide investigator was glamorous. But staring at security footage until your eyes crossed was anything but glamorous.

Two hours later, Ryan leaned back in his seat when someone knocked on the office door.

Adam poked his head in. "You got a minute?"

"Sure. What's up?"

Adam pulled open the door further and ushered in a woman—her dark-rimmed glasses gave her a studious air, her superhero T-shirt made him think she'd fit right in at a Comic-Con.

But her eyes told him she'd come here with something to say.

"Dr. Fleming, I presume?" He stood and reached for her hand. Her grip was firm and businesslike.

"You must be Investigator Parker."

"It's Ryan, but yes."

She had a lovely smile. "And it's Sabrina."

Gabe bounded around the desks, hand outstretched. "Gabe Chavez," he said, his teeth flashing white against his dark brown skin.

Standing behind Sabrina, Adam skewered Gabe with a look that said, "What are you doing?" and "Back off" at the same time.

It took all Ryan's willpower not to laugh. "Sabrina," he said as he steered her away from Gabe, "what brings you to the sheriff's office this fine Monday afternoon?"

"I was in the area and thought I would come in and introduce myself. Also, I don't have much yet, but I was able to take a look at your video footage earlier and I have something that might be useful for you."

"Don't keep us in suspense, Doc," Gabe said.

She grinned at Gabe. Adam glared. "You won't be able to ID anybody off this, but it might help you rule out some people. Your shadow is between five foot eight and five foot eleven."

Seriously?

"That is . . ." He really wanted to say "useless," but that wouldn't earn him any brownie points. And she was supposed to be the best.

"Check your email," she said. "I sent you the enhanced file."

Sabrina waited at his shoulder as he opened the file. "May I?" She gestured to the mouse on the desk.

"Be my guest."

She had the section she wanted pulled up in seconds. "Look here." Ryan watched the shadow. It was definitely a person and not an animal.

"Is he wearing a hat?"

"This individual is wearing a hat. Can't make out what's on it, but it's similar to a baseball cap."

The forensics folks were always very careful not to say anything definite, but that was their job. It looked like a baseball cap to him.

"This person is either heavyset or wearing some heavy clothing. Hard to say for sure."

He could see that. Looked like a jacket of some sort, but that could be intentional to disguise a smaller build.

"But here's the spot I want you to see. I spoke with a colleague of mine and we ran a few calculations, looking at the lighting, comparing things we could measure. Shadows are tricky because someone can appear tall or short depending on the angle of the light. But I'd be surprised if this person is over five-eleven. I think they are closer to five-ten but definitely not over five-eleven or shorter than five-eight."

Five-ten?

"What if they are hunched over?"

"I took that into account," she said. "Looking at the shape of the shadow and the angle of the hat and then the legs, there's not much room for hunching."

"Thank you," Ryan said. "I appreciate this."

"No problem. We have a team working on an experimental program to improve video enhancements, and they were thrilled to test it out. They are going to see if they can get it cleaned up further. If they do, you'll be the first to know." She looked at Adam. "I hate to run," she said, "but I'm due in class in twenty minutes."

"I'll walk you down," Adam said.

"She is even prettier than I was expecting," Gabe said after the two had walked away. "Did you see Adam's response? He was about ready to climb over this desk." Gabe rubbed his hands together. "I am going to have so much fun with this."

"You shouldn't flirt with her like that," Ryan said.

"Like what? I was just talking to her."

There was no point in arguing. Gabe flirted without realizing it. But to be fair, he was always respectful toward women. And he didn't date a lot, even though he could. Most women seemed to find him very attractive.

"Adam can't keep me from talking to her," Gabe said. "And I have a case that could use her expertise . . ."

"Why don't we get back to the case in front of us," Ryan said.

"Fine." Gabe returned to his seat. "She said shorter than five-eleven? Taller than five-eight? That eliminates a lot of people."

"It definitely gives us a way to rank our suspects," Ryan said. "Not that I don't trust her, but I don't want to make any assumptions that will come back to bite us later."

"So we're looking for a guy between five-eight and five-eleven?"

"No," Ryan said. "We're looking at anyone in that range. Male or female."

"You think a girl cut Leigh's brake lines?"

"Are you saying a girl couldn't?"

"No. Of course not. But you have to admit the MO does make a male more likely."

"I don't disagree. But I want to be sure we don't rule anything out until we have evidence to back up the decision."

"Okay. We'll rank our suspects by height and focus on the men and women taller than five-eight and shorter than five-eleven, with special mentions for those coming in at five-ten."

"Right."

Gabe groaned. "That narrows things down." The sarcasm was thick.

Ryan couldn't disagree. This was going to take forever.

For the next several hours, he cross-referenced driving records and personnel records and looked at faces and watched people go in and out of the hospital.

And it could all be for nothing.

They were literally chasing a shadow.

Leigh's phone rang at twenty after five. Ryan was on his way.

She sprinkled fresh parsley over a pot of chicken and dumplings. Her mom had made this dish at least twice a month. It was the very definition of comfort food.

After the past few days, she needed some comfort. She'd slept until two this afternoon and then gotten up and cleaned up the mess in the dining room. The table had been a total loss and the firefighters had been kind enough to remove it from the house. But everything still smelled like smoke—even though she'd thrown caution to the wind and opened all the windows and gotten a nice breeze through the house for most of the afternoon.

Still, she couldn't complain. The ceiling would need to be repainted, and probably the walls, but the house hadn't burned down and no one had died.

Funny how the things she was thankful for had shifted in the past week. Everything had taken on new levels of intensity.

She glanced over her shoulder into the now empty room. She'd been thinking about painting it a new color anyway. Maybe she'd even experiment and paint the ceiling something other than white—assuming she lived long enough to do it.

That was the other funny thing. Somehow over the past week, she'd realized how much she wanted to live. Not that she hadn't wanted to before. She'd never been suicidal, not even in the darkest times when Barry was coming after her. But it hadn't felt like she had much to live for.

But now?

The sharp rap on the door sent butterflies skittering through her stomach.

Yes, she had a few new things to live for. Things she wanted to at least explore and see where they led.

She opened the door and smiled at Ryan. "Come in."

"Thank you."

"Are you hungry? I fixed supper," she said.

"In case you haven't noticed, I'm always hungry," he said.

She'd noticed.

He followed her into the kitchen, all the way to the stove. "You didn't," he said with a hand pressed to his heart. "Chicken and dumplings?"

"You like them, right?"

"Love them," he said. "Rebecca makes them every now and then. She even tried to teach me how once. It was a disaster."

"Oh, come on, it couldn't have been that bad."

"Trust me," Ryan said. "I don't know how it happened, but the pot bubbled over and the whole thing got scorched. We had to order takeout. She hasn't offered to let me try again."

Leigh couldn't stop herself from laughing at his bewildered expression. "I'll be sure to remember that," she said. "Although I have to wonder if it wasn't a ploy to avoid having to learn how to do it yourself."

He widened his eyes at her in feigned innocence. "Me? Never."

She loaded two deep bowls with the chicken and dumplings and poured two glasses of tea. They sat at the kitchen island as they had almost every night for the past week.

Ryan asked the blessing on their meal and they dove in, chatting about the weather, the flood of tourists that would soon descend on Lake Porter, the boat she had in storage and wanted to get in the water, Kirk's latest update from Germany, and the cute things Ryan's niece and nephew had done recently.

Their conversation was so normal she was surprised to find herself blinking back a few tears. This was what life was supposed to be like. Good food shared with good people, talking about kids and boats and the happenings around town.

This was wonderful, but she couldn't help but think the entire conversation was all a big cover-up for the real things they should be talking about.

Like the attempts on her life.

Three of them if you counted the exploding balloons—which she did. But she wasn't ready to bring up any of that yet. She tried to stay in the moment and enjoy Ryan's company.

But the real world couldn't be pushed away forever. They finished their meal and she packed a thermos with the still-hot leftovers. "Have you checked on Pete? Is he still recovering okay?"

"Apparently he's like you. Doesn't have the good sense to stay home when he can. He's back at work and pestering the captain to get off desk duty this week."

Leigh sighed. “I want to do something nice for him, but I don’t want to be anywhere near him. I’d hate to put him at risk again.”

Ryan leaned against the kitchen counter. “Don’t take this the wrong way, but I’m more worried about you wandering around town than about you putting Pete at risk. I can pass along your best wishes, and I’ll include the fact that we’ve recommended you stay away from him for right now.”

“This is getting ridiculous,” Leigh said.

“We got a possible lead on something today,” he said. “It isn’t much, but we work with a professor from the forensics department at the university from time to time, and she found a suspicious shadow on some parking garage footage.”

Leigh turned to him. “The parking garage?”

“We’ve been thinking whoever did this has to have a solid understanding of how the hospital system works and might be an employee—or at the very least a frequent visitor. We were checking some of the security camera footage, but as you can imagine, there are a lot of cameras at the hospital and it took a while.”

This was all very interesting, but she didn’t care too much about the methods he used. “What did you find?”

“The professor thinks we are looking for someone between five-eight and five-eleven.”

This was a lead? Leigh put the now empty pot in the sink. What had she been expecting? Maybe something like gender, ethnicity, eye color, what they were wearing?

And what did they have? A three-inch height range?

“I know,” Ryan said from right behind her. She didn’t dare turn around or she’d be staring straight into his chest. “It doesn’t seem like much, but it could be huge. That range eliminates a lot of people, and every time we can eliminate someone from the suspect pool, it helps us get closer to finding the culprit.”

She couldn’t let him see how terrified she was.

A week had passed and all they had was a shadow on a security camera and a height range?

She'd be dead by summer.

"Leigh."

Had he stepped even closer?

"I promise I'm doing everything I can. The professor—she's amazing. Really talented. She's got a team running the video footage through some new software. If she finds anything, she'll let us know."

"That sounds great," she said. The words came out too high and too fast to be believable.

The warmth of his hand on her elbow confirmed that she hadn't fooled him.

"I, uh, I need to get ready for work." She left the pot soaking in the sink and slid past him. He made no effort to stop her. Thank goodness. She ran up the stairs to her room and closed the door.

She leaned against it and fought to catch her breath. Her stomach roiled and she ran into her bathroom and leaned over the sink. Every inhale came in short, rough gasps as she fought to regain her composure and keep her dinner down.

It took several minutes before she was fairly certain she wouldn't be sick. She pulled her scrubs on and slid into her favorite shoes. Every muscle in her body twitched from the tension. She sat on the edge of her bed for a few moments.

Lord, are you there? Are you listening? Am I going to die? Now? Now that Ryan Parker is interested? Now that I've found a new direction for my career that I might love? Now that things are starting to fall into place?

She had no idea if the Lord was listening, but even if he heard her, he didn't seem to feel like answering. She returned to her bathroom and brushed her hair with a trembling hand.

Get a grip. She had work to do. Patients who needed her. Coworkers who counted on her.

She checked her reflection. Stared into her own eyes. She couldn't see the fear that had overwhelmed her earlier. She was as ready as she was going to be.

She opened the door and found Ryan standing a few feet away, his eyes full of an emotion she couldn't identify.

"Are you okay?"

She tried to give him a genuine smile. "No. Not really, but I'm okay enough for tonight."

14

At 2 a.m., Leigh adjusted her ponytail and rolled her head in slow circles. Wow, her neck was tight. Tomorrow she was making time to get through her favorite yoga routine. She'd missed her usual yoga class while she was recovering, and now she didn't dare go. She liked the women who came to her class, and she'd never be able to live with herself if any of them were hurt on her account.

She laced her fingers behind her back and stretched her shoulders and chest.

"You okay?" Keri asked from a station a few doors down.

"Yeah. I'm good."

"Liar."

"I'm not lying."

"Oh? You're going with that? The 'no one has tried to kill me in the past twenty-four hours equals a good day' approach to life?"

"It's as good as any."

"No, it isn't," Keri muttered. "Your investigator have any leads yet?"

She couldn't say why, but she had a strong sensation that she shouldn't share what Ryan had told her, even if it made him look bad for now. She resisted the urge to defend him to her friend and instead gave a noncommittal shrug. "They're working on it."

Keri cut her eyes over in her direction. "Working on it? Wow. That's . . . encouraging."

Leigh ignored the snide remark. When this was over she'd explain to Keri, but not now. Who knew who might be listening? Or who might overhear Keri talking about it with someone else. Better for Keri to have the wrong idea about things. She'd forgive her later.

If there was a later.

"Hey, did you see I put your jacket with your bag?" Keri asked.

"What jacket?"

"The one I borrowed last night when I got cold."

Typical Keri. "Okay. I hadn't noticed," Leigh said.

"Yeah, you don't seem to notice much of anything when Ryan Parker shows up." Keri pretended to swoon.

"Whatever," Leigh said with a chuckle.

"Are you officially dating him or not?"

A flurry of activity distracted Keri and ended her interrogation. "Looks like we've got one on the way in," Keri said. "You okay to take it? I need to check this little guy's vitals again. I'm hoping he'll get to go home soon."

Keri's patient was an adorable boy who'd had a rough night and had to come in for a breathing treatment. They'd all been smitten by his dimples and curls. The cuteness made it even harder to hear him gasping for air.

"Yes," Leigh said. "Get him out of here."

She walked down the hall and joined the others waiting for the ambulance. Zeke, a registered nurse, and Bill, one of her favorite security guards. "What do we have?"

"Drunk and disorderly is what they said. Probably needs some stitches and a chance to dry out," Bill said.

She smiled at him. No matter how crazy things got, he kept his cool.

Zeke yawned. "How long you been doing this, Bill?"

"Longer than you young whippersnappers have been alive," Bill said with a wink.

Ten minutes later, Bill's prediction proved half accurate. The young man from the ambulance needed stitches, but if he was drunk, she couldn't smell any alcohol on his breath. Maybe he'd been on some sort of high when he got in the fight that resulted in the stab wound?

She tried to talk to him as she and Zeke worked. His blood would be checked for drugs and alcohol, but it would be much easier if he would tell them what he'd been doing. "Mr. Smith." She had serious doubts that this man's name was John Smith, but it was what he'd told them. "Do you know who did this to you?"

He looked at the wall.

"Have you been drinking tonight?"

He looked at the floor.

"Doing drugs?"

He kept looking at the floor.

"Okay," she said. "I'm not the police. I don't care what you've been doing, but it helps us to know so we can treat you accurately."

Still nothing.

"All right, then. We'll get you stitched up in a few minutes."

Behind Mr. Smith's head, Zeke pointed to himself and gave her a quizzical look. One she interpreted to mean, "Maybe he'll talk to you but not with me in here."

He might be right. Sometimes male patients were more willing to open up when there weren't other men around. It was worth a shot. "Zeke, can you see if Dr. Sloan is ready? I'll keep pressure on this."

"Sure thing," Zeke said.

She looked at the patient and lowered her voice. "Mr. Smith, are you sure there isn't something you'd like to tell me about your activities tonight?"

He made eye contact with her for the first time. "Your name is Leigh?"

That wasn't the question she'd been anticipating, but she'd run with it. "Yes, it is. And yours is John?"

He took a deep breath. Good. Maybe he was ready to get something off his che—

Before she could process what was happening, John Smith put both his hands around her neck.

And squeezed.

What was happening? She couldn't get any air. He was crushing her trachea. She kicked and thrashed, but his grip didn't slacken.

Part of her brain—a big part—screamed for oxygen. But another part recognized she wouldn't be able to physically get away from this guy. But people were in the halls. If she could scream . . .

Which she couldn't.

She continued to thrash. He didn't let go, but she did manage to make him shift his position. She didn't have long before she would pass out, but she saw an opportunity. Instead of kicking him, she kicked the tray of instruments she'd set out for the doctor to do the stitches.

Metal clanged and clashed.

Then everything went black.

"Leigh! Leigh Weston! You wake up right now, young lady. I will not tolerate this nonsense." The deep voice of Dr. Sloan pulled her from wherever she'd been.

What happened?

Where was she?

Why were bright lights burning her eyes?

She blinked a few times.

"There she is," Zeke said.

Zeke. She'd been with Zeke.

No, Zeke had gone to get Dr. Sloan.

So why was she lying on a bed?

"Wha—" Okay, that was weird. What was on her face? Why did her throat hurt?

Her eyes flew open as the memory of beefy hands wrapped around her throat flooded her mind.

She jerked into a sitting position, but more large hands restrained her. She tried to pull away.

"Whoa," Zeke said. "Leigh, it's okay. You're fine. He's gone. You're okay. We're here to help."

The hands moved to her back and rubbed in circles. "Leigh." Zeke said her name in the same tone you would use with a skittish animal. "Look at me, Leigh."

She looked at him and the room came into focus. She took a deep breath, but the air moving across her throat burned. She tried to remove the mask from her face, but Dr. Sloan, with tenderness she'd never known him to possess, pulled her arm down.

"Don't try to talk," he said. "We're going to get some X-rays."

She held her hands out to her sides and lifted her shoulders in the universal sign for "What on earth?"

"Do you remember what happened?" Dr. Sloan asked.

She put her hands back to her throat. This time around them.

"Yes," he said. "Your patient was choking you. Zeke pulled him away."

She signed "Thank you" to Zeke, who was now fighting back tears. "You scared me, girl," he said in a choked-up voice.

"Bill grabbed one of the police officers," Dr. Sloan said. "John Smith—if that's his real name—is now in custody."

Dr. Sloan leaned closer. "Leigh, did he do anything else to you? Are you injured in any other way?"

She shook her head no.

"Okay. Zeke?"

Zeke placed a wheelchair by the bed. "Your chariot, m'lady," he said, still blinking back tears.

She put her hand on his arm and squeezed. He wrapped his arms around her in a bear hug. "I've never, ever been that scared," he said in a whisper. He released her and helped her into the wheelchair. Then he grinned in a way much more in line with his usual personality. "Let's go get that pretty throat of yours checked out so you can tell me how heroic I am."

The next hour was a blur of oxygen, a bronchoscope, X-rays, and consultations. When the pulmonologist, Dr. Julia Stallings, gave her permission to speak, nothing came out.

"Try to say your name," Dr. Stallings said. "You're doing great."

"Leigh Weston." That voice did not belong to her, did it?

"Good. That's good." Dr. Stallings seemed pleased.

"How long?"

"It may take a week or so for your trachea to heal. But I don't see anything that concerns me about any sort of permanent damage. Try to keep the talking to a minimum for the next day or two."

Dr. Stallings left the room and for a brief moment, Leigh was alone.

She put her head in her hands and tried to forget the pressure of his hands on her throat. Tried not to think about the way her body begged for oxygen.

So of course that's all she *could* think about.

The tap at the door made her lift her head. "Leigh?" Keri asked. "Can Ryan come in?"

She nodded. Keri backed up and Ryan entered. Keri closed the door behind him. He stared at her a moment and then dropped to his knees beside her chair. "Oh, Leigh," he said.

She reached for his hands and squeezed them. "I'm okay," she said.

The roughness of her voice didn't exactly prove her point.

"They told me what happened," he said.

"I should have seen it coming," she whispered. "Should have let Zeke stay with him. You never know what a person will do when they are drunk or high."

Ryan shook his head. "Leigh, he wasn't."

Wasn't?

"He was stone cold sober."

What? Sober? Everything she'd been thinking and feeling toward John Smith twisted on its axis. He had done this intentionally? He wasn't some poor soul who wouldn't hurt a fly when he was clean but a man who waited for his chance and then . . .

"This is a Carrington Police case. The officer is a good guy. I told him about the previous attempts on your life. He's promised to keep me in the loop. If we confirm they are connected, the case will be transferred to me."

"He tried to kill me on purpose?"

Ryan looked at the floor. "Looks that way."

"Why did he do it, Ryan? Why would anyone want to kill me?"

"I don't know. But so help me, we are going to find out."

Ryan sat with Leigh in her house until she fell asleep on the couch. She didn't come right out and say it, but he got the distinct impression that she didn't want to be alone.

He didn't blame her.

He didn't want to let her out of his sight.

Between the crazy hours she worked and the bizarre events of her life, she had to be past the exhaustion point. He watched her sleep for several minutes, but he needed to burn off some energy or he was going to punch a hole in a wall.

He slipped through the French doors and paced the deck, back and forth, always keeping Leigh's slumbering form in view.

The captain hadn't had a problem with him working from the lake today. He had plenty of work he could do from his computer, and he needed to visit three homes within a mile of here this afternoon. He'd been tracking down the residents of this part of the lake for the past week.

He'd had no problem obtaining warrants for all the security footage from the area, but it was nice when the community was cooperative and he didn't have to get too official with them. All the homeowners were more than happy to share their security footage from the night Ryan suspected John Doe's body had been dumped.

Some of them seemed more worried about their property values than the fact that a man had met a horrible end, but as long as they turned over the security footage, he really didn't care.

The problem hadn't been with getting permission to see the footage. The problem had been in locating the residents. The three he was going to see today had all been wintering in Florida. They'd just come home for the summer.

Hopefully they'd have something that could help him.

His phone rang and he glanced at the screen. City of Carrington Police Department. This should be interesting.

"Parker."

"Hey. This is Steve, the arresting officer from this morning."

"Sure. How's it going?"

"I guess it depends on how you feel about knowing that when we told Mr. Smith we were charging him with attempted murder, he asked for a plea deal."

A plea?

"He's claiming he was blackmailed into it."

"What?"

"Says someone sent him pictures of his mom, who is in a nursing home in Winston-Salem. Told him if he wanted her to live, he'd have to kill Leigh Weston. Apparently the note suggested the emergency department was the best place to access her."

Ryan swallowed the bile that rose in his throat. Someone had put out a hit on Leigh? How many more could there be?

He ended the call and stared at the lake.

Lord, what am I going to do? How can I protect her?

He was missing something. What was it? What possible reason would anyone have for harming Leigh?

Unless . . .

No. It couldn't be.

Could it?

His phone rang again. This time he recognized the number. "What's up, Adam?"

"Nothing. Wanted to see how Leigh's doing."

Wow. That was nice. "She's doing okay. Pretty shook up. Sore throat. Bruises that are going to get way worse before they get better."

Adam called the creep a few choice names. "Sorry," he said. "I'm trying not to talk that way anymore. Sometimes it pops out."

Adam was a new believer, and Ryan had enjoyed watching the changes in his life. He hadn't been a bad guy before, but there was no question that he was a new creation.

"I understand. I can't deny I haven't thought the same." He was glad the police had gotten that piece of filth out of the emergency department before he got there. If they hadn't, he wasn't sure how he would have reacted. He was sure it would have involved a lot more than a few derogatory descriptors.

"The other reason I called was to tell you that Sabrina has been reviewing some of the footage. I called her this morning to tell her what happened, and she wanted me to tell you she's clearing her schedule for the rest of the week. Anything you need. No charge."

"That's awesome, but why would she care so much?"

"I don't know," Adam said. Was there a hint of regret in his voice? "Every now and then she says something that makes me think there might be some tough stuff in her past. For all I know, even in her present."

Interesting.

"Please tell her how much I appreciate it," Ryan said. "And tell her I don't have anything specific at the moment, but by this evening I'm going to have three new batches of security footage I might need some help with."

The footage wasn't specifically related to Leigh's case. Although if his hunch was right, it might be more connected than he'd originally thought.

"I'll pass it along."

There was a brief pause.

"And Ryan?"

"Yeah."

"I know there's not much I can do from my end to help, but I'll do anything you need."

"Thanks, man. I appreciate it."

After he hung up with Adam, Ryan sent Gabe and Anissa a text asking them to come meet with him at Leigh's house.

They both said yes within the minute. He slid his phone back into his pocket.

Maybe he was crazy. Maybe he'd finally cracked under the pressure. Maybe Gabe and Anissa would laugh at his theory. It was barely an idea, much less a full-blown theory. But if he was right . . .

Gabe and Anissa arrived, separately, thirty minutes later. He considered hassling them about wasting government resources by not carpooling, but he needed them to be civil to each other for the rest of the afternoon.

When Ryan answered the door, Gabe held up a bag of sub sandwiches. "I have the food," he said.

"Thanks," Ryan said. "And thanks for coming. Do you mind if we sit outside? Leigh's asleep on the couch."

"And you don't want her to hear this," Gabe said under his breath.

Anissa gave Ryan a quizzical look. "Is he right?"

Busted.

"She has every right to know what's going on," Anissa said.

He could almost see the head of steam Anissa was building. Best to end this one as fast as possible. He raised his hands in surrender. "I couldn't agree more, Anissa. But she's been through so much. I may be way off base . . ."

He ran his hands through his hair. "It wouldn't be fair to get her mind going in this direction if I'm wrong."

The fight went out of Anissa with his explanation. "I can respect that. And support that," she said. "But if this theory of yours is right, you have to tell her immediately. Withholding information won't help her in the long run."

"It won't help your relationship either," Gabe said with a grim smile.

"Are you dating her?" Anissa asked.

"No."

"Not because he doesn't want to," Gabe said.

Anissa actually smiled at Gabe's remark. That had to be a first. "She's a lovely person," she said. "I could see you as a couple. You should definitely ask her out. When this is over, of course."

Of course. Ryan's stomach flipped at the thought of asking her out. Then it flipped again when he remembered why Gabe and Anissa were here. "I appreciate the relationship advice from both of you," he said. "But do you think we could get back to discussing the case?"

They both smiled and agreed. He led them through the living room and out to a table on the deck. He'd brought his laptop and notebook. A pitcher of water and a few cups waited beside them. The case file—already a behemoth—sat on one of the chairs. The three of them took the remaining seats.

Gabe poured himself a glass of water.

Anissa rested her elbows on the table and leaned toward Ryan. "What's this theory and why did you want us to hear it first?"

Here goes nothing. "I think the killer for both of our John Doe cases and Leigh's stalker might be the same person."

15

Gabe spit water across the table.

Anissa jerked back in her chair.

Both of them stared at him like he'd sprouted a third eye in the middle of his forehead.

"I told you it was just a theory."

Gabe emptied out the subs onto the table and grabbed a napkin. "You've got some serious explaining to do." He wiped water from his mouth and shirt.

Anissa cocked her head at him the way she did when she was considering something. He'd seen that look at crime scenes. Anissa had a keen mind, but she was a ponderer. Not a rapid-fire reactor.

He waited.

She blinked a few times. She looked from him to the lake, her glance skittering past Gabe to the spot where they'd pulled the John Doe from the water.

"The attacks started immediately after we found the body," she said.

Ryan blew out the breath he hadn't realized he was holding. Anissa was already tracking with him. That didn't mean he was right, but at least it meant he hadn't gone bonkers.

Gabe paused in the middle of unwrapping his sub. "It was the choppers," he said. "I hate news choppers."

Ryan's initial relief was quickly being replaced by apprehension. If they were both seeing what he was seeing, they might not be able to poke holes in the theory.

"Yes, the choppers. But let's start at the beginning and re-create the timeline."

"Agreed." Anissa unwrapped her sub. She glanced at the house. "We didn't order anything for Leigh," she said, concern furrowing her brow.

"I know," he said. "The doctor said she should probably stick with a soft diet today. Soups, milk shakes, stuff like that."

"Subs are soft." Gabe took a huge bite.

"Not when you have a sore throat." Anissa spoke with authority. "I had my tonsils out a few years ago. Worst pain of my life. Even the tiniest piece of bread felt like trying to swallow rocks. You should get her a smoothie when she wakes up. And then something warm, but not too hot, for dinner. Egg drop soup would work. Plenty of protein. Slides down easy."

"Thanks," he said. "Those are great ideas."

They all chewed in silence for a few bites. Ryan didn't rush to start the conversation again. He knew them both well enough to know they were processing his theory. Trying to find the holes. Searching for the inconsistencies.

No one spoke until they'd finished eating. As they gathered the trash and wiped their faces and hands, he could sense the tension mounting.

"Ready?" Ryan asked.

They both nodded.

"Then let's start with Gabe and me finding the John Doe in the lake."

Anissa pulled out a notepad. "You found the body at 10:37 a.m.

We called it in around 10:45 a.m. The body was out of the water around 12:45 p.m. The ME arrived around 2:00 p.m."

"The choppers were out way before then," Gabe said. "They were flying around when you went to ask Leigh if we could use the dock."

"We find the body," Ryan said. "The news picks it up. Without any of us realizing it, Leigh's drawn into the whole business when we start using her dock."

"We need to get copies of the newscast," Gabe said. "Not just the part they ran but also any sort of promos they aired during the afternoon or any of those breaking news segments. See if Leigh's face is visible, even for a moment."

"Or if you can tell we are at her house," Anissa said.

"I'll take that," Gabe said.

Ryan didn't try to hide his surprise. Neither did Anissa.

"What?" Gabe asked. "I'm a grown-up. I can handle the news media."

"More like you'd like to harass the news media," Anissa said under her breath.

She was on to something there. Gabe would love a chance to stick it to a few reporters. Particularly the one who'd blown his cover.

"Moving on," Gabe said.

"Right." Ryan looked at his own notes. "Let's say by the end of the day last Saturday, anyone who was paying close attention could have made the connection that Leigh was aware of the John Doe and that the body had been located near her home."

"Agreed," Gabe said.

Anissa nodded.

"They would have had to act quickly to plan something like cutting her brake line," he said. "She didn't go to work until after ten and they had to act during the middle of the night. So we're dealing with someone who was either watching Leigh . . ."

Gabe finished the sentence for him. "Or who already knew her well enough to know her routine and schedule."

Gabe and Anissa looked at each other.

"See, that's the part that makes me think my theory is useless. What are the odds the same person who killed our John Doe knows Leigh?"

Anissa stared out over the lake. Gabe studied his hands.

"I'm not sure that's a hole in your theory," Anissa said. "Mr. Cook got back to me this morning about his absences from home over the past two years."

Ryan had no idea where she was going with this.

"The only time he's been gone for more than a night was eleven months ago. Which, incidentally, fits the timeline the anthropologist and medical examiner gave us for when our second John Doe was killed and buried on Mr. Cook's property."

She took a sip of her water. "He was gone for three nights, and everybody knew it."

Mr. Cook wasn't the type to advertise his whereabouts.

"Where was he?" Gabe asked.

"In the hospital."

For a long moment, none of them spoke. He wasn't sure if any of them took a breath.

"If the killer is an employee at the hospital . . ." Ryan said.

"They could have known Mr. Cook wasn't home and his property was unguarded," Anissa said. "Perfect time to dump a body."

"And," Gabe said, "they would know the layout and schedules well enough to cut Leigh's brake line without anyone noticing."

"And they might know the food service system well enough to poison the gelatin," Anissa said.

"And they could have heard about the flowers the different departments were sending to Leigh," Gabe added.

"And they would possibly be able to get to the coffeepots in different areas," Anissa added. "Oh, and access her work schedule, and maybe even make sure she wound up in a room alone with a killer."

Another long silence.

"But," Ryan said, "why not just grab her?"

"She's been pretty hard to grab for the past week, man," Gabe said with a wave toward the uniformed officers who kept making laps around the house.

"I don't know," Anissa said. "That first night, she would have been easy to grab . . ."

Ryan disagreed. "Not without a plan. Leigh's no cupcake. She's been through a lot with that stalker of hers. She's quite aware of her surroundings. She doesn't take unnecessary risks. She parked in a place with plenty of visibility for her to walk in at an off time. She would have walked out with coworkers."

"A spur of the moment decision?" Anissa asked.

"That didn't work," Gabe said.

"Came close," Ryan said.

"But now she's on her guard. She's being protected."

Ryan rolled his head in a slow circle. "But it's still nothing more than a theory," he said. "The only things we have tying our John Doe's killer to Leigh are that the attacks started the night after we found the John Doe in the lake and that the second body may have been dumped while Mr. Cook was in the hospital where she works. And keep in mind, we don't even know for sure that the second John Doe was killed by the same person who killed the first John Doe."

"We know that all the attacks relate, in some way, to the hospital," Gabe said.

"So what are we dealing with here?" Ryan couldn't sit still any longer. He slid his chair back, trying not to scrape it along the deck floor. "We've got a possible serial killer who chops off heads and dumps the bodies where he thinks no one can find them, and he suddenly switches up his M.O. to go after Leigh because we used her dock?"

When he said it out loud, it sounded very thin. But neither Gabe nor Anissa seemed inclined to throw it out.

"It's a theory. A weak one. But one we still keep in play?" he asked.

"Definitely." Anissa slid her chair back. "Although I don't think it's as weak as you want to believe."

"I agree," Gabe said.

Ryan noticed how Gabe and Anissa made eye contact after their rare moment of cooperation. Maybe they could learn to work together after all.

"My two cents?" Gabe stood as he spoke. "We keep moving forward with the investigations concurrently. If they intersect, we won't be surprised."

"And Leigh stays away from the hospital," Anissa added.

Ryan nodded. "Agreed."

The door opening behind Ryan caught him off guard. Leigh joined them on the deck. "Why, exactly, do I need to stay away from the hospital?"

She'd intended for that question to sound more demanding and forceful. But her voice wouldn't cooperate. The words had come out weak and, as much as she hated to even think the word, pitiful.

Or she thought they had.

But Ryan immediately moved toward her, his eyes full of something she couldn't understand. Anissa dropped her gaze to the ground, but not before Leigh caught the worry in her expression. Gabe widened his eyes and pursed his lips as he studied a piece of paper on the table.

"Did we wake you?" Ryan held her gaze. If he was trying to distract her, it was working. She needed to focus. And she needed to be able to project her voice. She cleared her throat even though the action was excruciating.

"No. I woke up and saw you guys out here, and then I heard you say I needed to stay away from the hospital. Apparently you've been talking about me and planning my life for me, so maybe you should fill me in?"

She wanted to scream, but screaming would be too painful to be worth the release. Speaking those few sentences had hurt far more than she'd expected.

"Leigh, why don't we all sit down and talk," Anissa said.

Anissa wanted to talk to her? She'd expected more female solidarity from Anissa. Surely she didn't agree with this plan to run her life?

Gabe clapped his hands together. "Excellent suggestion." He came toward her, arm bent, and bowed slightly. "M'lady. May I escort you inside?"

Gabe certainly knew how to turn on the charm. Not that it was working on her, but if they went inside, she could sit in her favorite chair and talk some sense into them.

She accepted his arm and he walked with her. "Where would you like to sit?"

"What is this, a wedding?" She pointed to the recliner in the corner of the seating arrangement.

Gabe laughed and leaned closer, pressing her arm against him. "That gravelly voice is awesome. You sound mean. The problem is I know you're one of the nicest people on the planet, so you can't quite pull it off. But it's fun to imagine you as a grouchy lady who's waiting to bite people's heads off if they cross you."

"I wouldn't be so sure that isn't what she's planning," Anissa said from behind them. She took a seat across from Leigh and winked. "If you decide to take him out, I'll help you."

That was more of what she was expecting from Anissa. Maybe she wouldn't be alone in this after all.

Ryan closed the doors to the deck and joined them. He dropped a mammoth file on the coffee table before sitting beside Anissa on the love seat.

Gabe took the sofa for himself.

They all stared at each other.

"What's going on?" she asked again. They all looked at one another, and something about their expressions sent a cold wave of terror crashing over her. "What don't I know?"

She listened in mute horror as Ryan shared his theory. Anissa and Gabe interjected from time to time—clarifying, not contradicting.

When Ryan finished, she leaned back in the recliner. "You think the same person who killed the John Doe in the lake also killed the John Doe at Mr. Cook's house, and you think they are the same person who is trying to kill me?"

Ryan shifted in his seat. "I don't know, Leigh. I honestly don't. But something weird is going on, and it's one theory we have to give serious consideration to."

"But that would mean I know this person. I don't know anyone capable of this kind of horror."

The three of them did that thing where they looked at one another again. It was annoying. She wasn't sure if they were using secret signals or what, but they must have decided it was Anissa's turn to talk, because she responded.

"The truth is you never know what someone is capable of," she said. "People are capable of extraordinary good. They are also capable of indescribable evil. Sometimes the same person can pull off both in the same day. And serial killers, if that's what we're dealing with, are known to be gifted at hiding the darkness they walk in."

"But why me?"

Gabe leaned toward her. It must have been his turn to talk. "Why is a great question to ask, Leigh, but it isn't the one that's going to solve our problems. Right now we need to know who is behind this. When we find them, we'll ask them what they were thinking."

"And we probably won't get a rational response," Anissa said. "Serial killers operate from a very twisted view of the world. What makes perfect sense to them would be completely ridiculous to someone with a normal psychological status."

"So I've got a sociopath on my trail. No one knows why. And you think they may work at the hospital."

None of them contradicted her.

She swallowed again. Ow.

"The bottom line is we don't know," Ryan said. "But there is ample evidence to suggest that whether or not your attacker is the serial killer we're hunting, they have access to you at the hospital and you are in extreme danger when you are there. That's why we're recommending you take a leave of absence."

She didn't miss the way he said "we" and not "I."

"Even if you believe the risk is worth taking," Anissa said, "you have to think about the others. The coworkers who could be killed in an attempt on your life. The patients. The police officers and security guards who are trying to protect you. Given the credible threat we see, it would be irresponsible for you to return to work at this time."

When she put it that way . . .

"I guess I don't have a choice," she said.

"We're all working on it," Gabe said. "In fact, Ryan and I are headed out in a few minutes to collect more security footage similar to what you gave us. The people who live two houses down finally came home. We're hoping for a solid lead."

Leigh looked at Ryan. He nodded in confirmation. So she would be here alone. Well, not alone. The police officers were patrolling the place, but it wasn't the same.

"Actually," Anissa said, "I was hoping you wouldn't mind if I hang out here while they run down the footage? I promise I'll be quiet. You can sleep. I need to go over all my notes in light of this news, and it's a lot nicer here than the office. The captain gave us the green light to work from here, and I hate to pass up the view."

Leigh wasn't fooled. She knew Anissa had picked up on her fear. But she didn't care. It was a great idea as far as she was concerned.

Gabe and Anissa excused themselves and went back to the deck, leaving her alone with Ryan.

He moved to the coffee table and sat on the edge of it, his knees touching hers. "I am sorry," he said.

He probably expected her to say something, but she was at a loss. What could she say? She wasn't fine. Nothing about this situation was fine.

"It feels . . . it feels like I'm on a roller coaster and someone is shooting at me. I'm trapped, flying at top speed, flipping and twisting in the air, and I can't get off. There's nothing I can do except hold on and pray I don't get hit. But I don't want the ride to end either, because if they are smart, they'll be waiting for me to pull into the station, and right when I think it's finally over, they'll get me."

Ryan reached for her hands.

"We're going to get them before they get you. Things are starting to pull together. The hospital angle gives us a whole new investigative direction—"

"But what if it's the wrong one? You said it's a theory. I agree with the validity of your theory, but what if we're missing something obvious? What if the psycho trying to kill me doesn't have anything to do with the psycho who killed the two John Does?"

Ryan didn't come back with a quick answer. She appreciated that he was taking her question as seriously as she meant it.

"First of all, we won't ignore any angle," he said. "This doesn't mean we aren't trying to learn the identities of the John Does, and who knows how things will go when we have that information. We'll run down each and every lead we have, regardless of whether it fits this theory or not."

"Okay, what's second?"

He rubbed circles on the back of her hand with his thumb. "The second reason is more a matter of odds," he said. "We have our own share of craziness in Carrington, but the true psychos don't usually show up in pairs. I'm not saying it couldn't happen, but most of our violent crimes have very different motives. Domestic violence, greed, drugs, alcohol, that kind of thing."

"You don't know who I might have ticked off," she said. "What if it's a patient? Or the family of a patient who died and they blame me?"

"We're looking into that," he said.

"I could help," she said. "Try to think back to any crazy incidents, that kind of thing."

"That would be great," he said.

Gabe tapped on the glass and touched his watch. "I guess you need to go." She looked at Ryan.

Ryan squeezed her hands once more, then released them as he stood. "I'll be back. We can talk about your crazy cases tonight, but for now, please try to rest."

Ten minutes later, she draped herself in a blanket and closed her eyes. In her dreams, she was back in the emergency department, running to a room where the monitors were going crazy. It took her several moments to realize it wasn't the beeping of an IV pump but the sound of sirens breaking into her dreams. When she opened her eyes, Anissa was standing two feet away. Gun in hand. Body tensed. She made eye contact with Leigh and put one finger to her lips.

16

Ryan didn't bother to knock. He ran into Leigh's house. His knees threatened to buckle under the relief of seeing Leigh wide awake and Anissa in full bodyguard mode.

"What's going on?" Anissa's voice drowned out Leigh's, but he heard them both ask it at the same time.

"I have no idea," he said. "Heard the sirens and came straight here. The detail that's supposed to be outside—isn't."

His phone rang. "Parker."

He gave Anissa and Leigh an all clear sign. "Got it. Let me know when you're back."

He put the phone back in his pocket. "False alarm. Well, not really. False alarm for us."

"What happened?" Leigh's hoarse voice cracked.

"Two doors down. Possible heart attack. The man's young. Probably in his forties. His teenage son panicked. Knew there were police officers nearby. Came out of the house screaming for help. They kept an eye on the perimeter but went to assist."

"They shouldn't have left," Anissa said in a tone that could freeze lava.

He understood her anger. "They knew you were inside," Ryan

said. "I agree they should have checked with you first, but they maintained a watchful presence while providing aid to a terrified boy."

"It could have been a trap." Anissa wasn't ready to drop it.

"It wasn't."

"How's the man?" Of course Leigh would be worried about the man, not the potential danger the officers had put her in by helping. He tried to focus on her face, but the bruises snaking around her neck fought for his attention.

"Ambulance is on the scene."

Leigh's eyes burned with compassion. "The paramedics are better equipped to handle something like this than I am," she said. "I hope he'll be okay. Those folks moved in a few weeks ago. I don't even know their names."

"I don't like it," Anissa said. "You need to find out more about them. And follow up on this supposed heart attack. It might have been a ploy. We may have gotten very lucky."

She wasn't wrong.

"And you need to talk to the officers outside. Tell them this is just the kind of thing that could be done to get to Leigh."

Leigh dropped her head.

What was he going to have to do to get Anissa to shut up? "Thank you, Investigator Bell," he said. "I know how to do my job."

"I wasn't implying you didn't." Anissa's retort was cool. "Just thinking out loud."

"He's trying to protect me," Leigh said. "He's not mad at you for what you said. You're right. He's frustrated that you won't quit saying it in front of me."

Anissa cocked her head to the side and looked at Ryan with a mischievous grin. "Well, Investigator Parker?"

He wasn't sure what annoyed him more—that Leigh was right or that Anissa found it amusing.

"I don't need to be kept in the dark," Leigh said. "I can take it.

You're going to have to keep me in the loop whether you want to or not. In fact, you probably need to start talking about the case with me. If your theory is right, if there is a connection between me and the John Doe killer . . ." She raised her hands in exasperation. "I can't imagine what it could be, but the more you include me, the more likely it is that I will figure out what this connection is."

He didn't like it. At all. It was not the way things were usually done. Sure, he made it a point to keep the interested parties informed in an investigation. It was the least he could do. But to include them in a brainstorming session? To discuss tactics? No.

But . . . the sheriff had made it clear that he wanted this case solved no matter what. He'd told them to do whatever it took to find the killer and keep Leigh safe.

And nothing was usual about this case. Hadn't been from day one. It kept getting crazier by the day. Maybe she was right.

Anissa's phone buzzed. Her face lit up in anticipation. "Excuse me."

He expected her to step outside, but she didn't. "Dr. Oliver. Do you have some good news for me?"

So it was safe to assume Anissa agreed with Leigh's suggestion.

He mouthed the words "medical examiner" to Leigh. She nodded in understanding.

Anissa's mouth formed a small O and she scrambled for a piece of paper. "Okay. Got it. Yes, email it please. This is fantastic. Thank you."

She put her phone on the table and looked at him and Leigh in triumph. "We have a name."

His mind raced at the implications of her words. A name could change everything. "How?"

"Knee replacement. Dr. Oliver has been tracking down the serial number. Our John Doe is Calvin Staton from Cleveland."

"Cleveland?" Leigh asked in a gruff voice. Her question mirrored his own.

"That's all I know. The knee was replaced five years ago." She glanced between him and Leigh. "I need to get to the office."

"Go," he said. "Keep me informed."

"How about I bring pizza around seven?" she asked. "We'll compare notes."

He didn't know what notes he would have to share, but it sounded like a good plan.

Gabe burst through the door. His eyes darted from Leigh resting on the sofa, lingered for a second on her neck, then flashed to Anissa gathering her things, and then to Ryan. "Everyone okay over here?"

"Better than okay," Anissa said. "Parker can fill you in. See you guys around seven." She paused at the door. "Chavez, make sure we have some ice cream. Leigh's going to need a milk shake."

Gabe looked from Ryan to Leigh. "What did I miss?"

"Anissa's got a name on the John Doe found at Mr. Cook's place," Ryan said. "She's bringing pizza at seven. Here. And apparently you're bringing ice cream."

"Oh, I'm bringing more than that." Gabe winked at Leigh. "We have a consultant on your case who has volunteered to take a look at the security footage from all the area homes."

Where was Gabe going with this?

"She's outside," he said. "She has some information for us. Do you mind if she comes in?"

Leigh swung her legs to the floor.

"Don't get up," Ryan said.

Of course she would ignore him.

"If it's a problem . . ." Gabe's voice trailed off.

"It's not a problem," Leigh said. "I'm not an invalid, but based on the way you two keep looking at my neck, I'm guessing I look pretty rough. I'm going to get a different shirt."

Gabe shook his head in apology. Ryan moved to intercept her. "You're beautiful," he whispered.

"Thank you," she said. "But I know how hard it can be to have a conversation with someone when they have such an obvious physical distraction. You aren't being rude. It's a natural response and eventually you won't notice it, but I don't want to have to deal with it all night." She smiled at Gabe. "Of course she's welcome."

"Adam's here too."

Of course he was.

"That's fine."

Leigh slipped up the stairs.

"You should go with her," Gabe said.

"Why?"

"Because she's not going to like what she sees when she looks in the mirror."

Was he right? Would she let him provide some measure of comfort? Was there anything he could say that would help?

Leigh couldn't get away from their pitying looks fast enough.

She wasn't offended. At all.

But if she didn't get a few minutes of silence and solitude, she was going to scream.

Or she would try to. It would probably sound like a cat trying to cough up a hairball, which wouldn't be nearly as dramatic as what she was attempting.

She rummaged in her closet for a shirt with a collar. Something other than the V-neck T-shirt she had on. There. She pulled the shirt from the hanger and held it to her face.

It was one of her dad's casual shirts. For Judge Weston, casual still meant a button-down, but the tie was optional. Her dad had been a tall, thin man, and after he'd passed away, she'd claimed some of his favorite shirts for her own wardrobe.

This was the shirt he'd had on the day she was accepted into the nurse practitioner program at Duke. She'd come home to tell him.

He'd hugged her, told her he wasn't surprised and how proud he was. He'd held her face in his hands and said, "Baby, I've known from the day we first saw you that you were going to do amazing things. I'm so thankful God allowed me to be your dad."

Her eyes filled with tears at the memory. It was one of those moments that was etched into her brain. The hug. The sense that all was right in the world. The hope for the future. All of it had been there that day.

Two weeks later he had a heart attack.

And nothing had been quite right since.

Every holiday highlighted his absence. Every big moment shone a spotlight on the fact that he wasn't there to share it. She'd adored her mom, but her dad had been her rock. Her stability.

With him gone . . .

She slid her arms through the sleeves.

Why did you take him? I wanted more time.

Was that when it all started? The slow drift away from a God who, in her mind at least, had let her down? Did she quit talking to him when he didn't save her dad?

She hadn't done it on purpose, but as she buttoned the long row of buttons, she knew. She'd been mad at God for a long time.

Is that why you're trying to kill me?

She arrested the thought. She knew better than that. God wasn't trying to kill her. Get her attention? Maybe. But kill her?

No.

More memories surrounded her as she shoved the too-long sleeves up her arms. Her dad's rich baritone singing "Great Is Thy Faithfulness." Her mom's alto joining in perfect harmony. Their lives hadn't been easy. Years of barrenness. Years of begging God to give them a child. The long road to accepting that God's choice for them was to complete their family with a little boy from Bolivia and a little girl from China.

Getting there had nearly destroyed their faith and their marriage.

Leigh knew the story, but she'd never personalized it to her situation. God didn't give them what they wanted. Or what they thought they wanted. Both of her parents always said if they'd had any idea what it was like to live out adoption, they would have done it earlier. But then they might not have found her, so they knew God's timing was perfect.

Was his timing in all this perfect too? Was he working for her good even though it looked like he was dropping the ball?

Instead of seeing the bruises on her neck as evidence that he didn't care, should she instead see that he did care? That he had protected her from an unknown enemy yet again?

Could she trust him to keep her alive? Or trust him if that wasn't his plan at all?

Snatches of long-lost memory verses meshed with random things her mom and dad would say and joined in with sermons heard and songs sung.

The tug in her spirit, the one she mostly chose to ignore, refused to be shoved to the side.

The walls she'd worked so hard to erect shook. And why wouldn't they? They rested on a shaky foundation of fear and lies.

She knew the truth. She'd known it all along.

But believing God truly loved her, truly had her best interests at heart even when it didn't look like it? She didn't know if she could muster that kind of faith.

The best she could do was whisper a humble "Help me."

Somehow she knew that would be enough for now. That he heard her. That he wasn't waiting for her with a long list of grievances. That he was running toward her, longing to hold her close if she'd let him.

"Help me," she whispered again as she opened her door.

Ryan all but fell into her room. "Sorry," he said as he caught his balance. "I came to see if you were okay."

Was she okay? No. But she was better than she'd been thirty minutes ago.

"Leigh?" Ryan glanced around the room, then back at her. "Is there anything I need to know?"

She could see the worry in his eyes. Hear the desire to protect her in his voice. But how could she explain what had happened over the last few minutes when she wasn't even sure herself?

"I've . . . I've been praying. Sort of."

She tried not to laugh at the expression on his face.

"Good," he said. "Although I'm not sure how you sort of pray."

"Me neither," she said. "It's been a while since I made praying a priority. I guess I've kind of lost my way over the years. Or maybe I quit believing God would listen to anything I had to say. Or that my prayers could make any difference."

"And now?"

"Honestly? I'm still not sure. I mean, I know the Sunday school answer. God hears and answers our prayers. But where does that get you when your dad dies? Or your mom dies? Or you think you're going crazy and it turns out you have a patient stalking you? Or now, when someone is quite literally trying to kill you? Why hasn't he stopped it?"

She took a breath. Talking that much at once was extremely painful, and her voice was so rough and low she wasn't sure if Ryan had been able to understand a word she had said.

"I get it," he said with a grim nod. "Why does he let your nephew have autism? Or how do you deal with it when your sister, who scrimped and saved and sacrificed to get your worthless brother-in-law through medical school, has to deal with him when he cheats on her and leaves her and his two kids? What's up with that?"

Wow. So she wasn't the only one who'd asked these kinds of questions. And not the only one who didn't have solid answers for them.

"Sorry," he said. "I realize those things aren't the same as loved ones dying or having a maniac try to strangle you."

"No," she said. "They're all different kinds of deaths. Deaths of loved ones. Deaths of dreams. Deaths of relationships."

"And so death entered the world," Ryan said under his breath.

"What?"

"What you said, about the deaths, it made me think of that verse where it says that when sin entered the world, so did death. I guess I've always seen it as physical and spiritual death, and of course it is, but all those other deaths are also the result of sin."

"I guess so," she said. "I don't have any answers, Ryan. I'm starting to talk to him again. I think he's listening, but sometimes I'm not sure what to say."

"I don't think he cares so much about what we say. I think he mostly just wants us to talk to him."

"For now he's going to have to deal with me whispering," she said.

Ryan chuckled. "I'm ready to rip someone to pieces and you're making jokes."

"It's a coping mechanism," she said. "And not the most healthy one, I might add."

"What, the jokes or the desire to dismember someone?"

"Neither."

He sighed dramatically. "I guess you're right."

They stood for a few moments in silence. It wasn't strained. Was he praying? Should she?

Lord? She reached out in her mind. *I don't know what's happening. Please help me. Help me process it. Help me trust.*

"Ryan? Leigh? Could you come down?" Gabe called up the stairway. His voice carried a sense of urgency but not fear.

"Think he's got something?" Leigh asked.

"Let's find out."

She pulled the neck of the shirt a bit closer as they descended the stairs.

"You're fine," Ryan whispered.

He was lying, but she appreciated the gesture.

When she entered her kitchen, she barely recognized the place. Adam and Gabe both sat at the kitchen table with laptops, tablets, and notepads. Computers and cords stretched all over the island and there was even one propped on the stovetop. That didn't seem like the best idea, but the young woman in the middle of it all didn't seem perturbed by it.

She stretched out a hand. "Sabrina," she said. "You must be Leigh."

"I am. It's nice to meet you."

This was the brilliant computer forensics professor they'd brought in? She looked like she was twelve.

But then she started typing some sort of code. Her fingers flew. Her eyes flashed.

"We have something you need to see," she said.

17

Ryan had no idea how Sabrina Fleming did the things she did. In minutes, she'd taken the footage from multiple houses and somehow spliced them all together.

"We've scanned hours of footage, and of course there are hundreds of hours more we could look through, but with what we were able to obtain today, I think we have enough to show the boat came from the east, stopped, turned around, and then returned in the direction it came from."

With a few keystrokes, the video came to life. Sabrina narrated the video footage, her glasses in one hand, the other pointing to the screen. "As you can see, based on the video surveillance we've been able to obtain, we have proof a boat was in the water at 3:08 a.m. I ran a few calculations and determined it wasn't going particularly fast. Maybe five miles per hour."

She chewed on the end of her glasses. "Hazarding a guess, I'd say either the driver didn't know where they were going, which is not my first choice of theory by the way, or they were being careful to keep the boat noise to a minimum. At five miles per hour, it's unlikely people sleeping in these houses," she said, pointing to the houses on either side of the lake, "would have been disturbed."

The screen went blank. "The boat falls off the radar, so to speak, for four minutes, fifty-three seconds before it reappears for a few seconds in this neighbor's footage, and then we get several seconds from your video feed." She nodded toward Leigh. Blips of light flickered on and off the screen for another few minutes, then the video stopped.

"We've received a few bits of video footage from several houses further down the lake that don't have any sign of the boat. That doesn't necessarily mean it wasn't there though. The lake widens considerably, and if the driver kept the boat in the middle of the lake, nothing would show up. However, I recommend checking with the owners of the houses at Two, Six, Eight, and Ten Porter Trail."

Ryan glanced at his notes. "We have video footage from Two, Four, Six, and Ten."

"Yes, but I want you to check their boats."

"Their boats?" Oh. "You think someone stole a boat?"

"I don't know," Sabrina said. "I think we have to consider it. Certainly there's a chance the boat came from any number of places. It's even possible they put the boat in the water at a boat ramp, drove it over here, dumped the body, and then meandered around the lake and pulled it back out of the water. They could have done it anywhere."

"Why those houses?"

"Because that's where we lose the lights."

"You're thinking our killer could have stolen a boat, eased it into the middle of the lake, and hit the lights sometime after they got to number Twelve Porter Trail?"

"I'd like to check to be sure," Sabrina said.

"If someone took their boats, it would have shown up on their video footage. Eight's the only one we're missing, but they don't have any cameras on their property."

"None? That's unusual." Leigh's brow furrowed.

Ryan flipped through his notes. "It is, but they are an older couple who've lived there forever and still operate under the blissful delusion that Carrington is as safe as it was fifty years ago. The husband is in the hospital, but his wife has been very cooperative."

When he said the words out loud, Gabe's and Leigh's heads swiveled away from Sabrina and to him.

Leigh's face registered the greatest level of concern.

"Leigh, is something bothering you?" Sabrina's quiet question hushed the room.

"Yes," Leigh said.

"I'm not a law enforcement officer," Sabrina said with an encouraging smile, "but my experience is there's nothing too small to mention. Did you see something that doesn't make sense? Is there a hole in my theory?"

Adam chuckled, but Sabrina cut him off with a dark look. "I do make mistakes, Adam," she said. "And even if I didn't, if there's something unclear to Leigh, I'd like to hear it. I may find myself presenting this information to a jury at some point. I need to see the flaws in it now, not then."

"It isn't anything you said," Leigh said. "It's the people at Eight Porter Trail."

"What about them?"

"Why is he in the hospital?" Leigh directed her question to Ryan.

"Mr. Gordon had a stroke."

"When?"

"About three weeks ago," Ryan said.

"Any family around?"

"Mrs. Gordon has refused to leave his side. They have grown children, but I didn't meet them. They live in the area."

"Where are you going with this, Leigh?" Sabrina asked.

"When he had his stroke, did he go to the Carrington emergency department?"

Ryan looked at Gabe and Adam. "I don't know. Either of you?"

They both shook their heads.

"Why are you wondering that, specifically?" Sabrina was watching Leigh like she was the most fascinating creature on the planet. Which, she was.

Leigh made eye contact with Sabrina. "They"—she pointed first to Ryan, then to Gabe—"have a theory that the killer may be connected to the hospital."

Ryan noticed she didn't mention the part of their theory that the killer was after her. Maybe she didn't want to think about it. Maybe she didn't believe it. Either way, probably best not to mention it at this point.

"If someone at the hospital is responsible for this, they would have known eleven months ago that Mr. Cook was in the hospital and his property was untended, giving them time to drag and bury a body there without anyone knowing."

"Yes!" Sabrina's face lit up with understanding. "And they might also have known that the couple from Eight Porter Trail was at the hospital and wasn't leaving anytime soon."

"We need to pay Eight Porter Trail a visit," Ryan said. He pulled his phone from his pocket. It was three o'clock. "I need to get into the office and see if we can get a warrant."

"I'll come with you," Gabe said. "Let me grab my stuff."

"Go," Adam said. "Sabrina and I are here for the rest of the day." He looked at Leigh. "Assuming that's okay with you. We just got everything set up." He pointed to all the computers and devices.

"It's fine," Leigh said.

Ryan hated to leave Leigh like this, but she was surrounded by officers, and Adam was no slouch. She'd be fine.

But the pull to stay was strong.

He forced himself to walk to the door. Leigh followed him.

"I'll be back," he said.

"I'll be here."

Her eyes held so much—strength mingled with fear, confidence mingled with confusion—and still she smiled. She'd make a great cop's wife.

Where had *that* come from? He wasn't in the market for a wife . . . but the idea refused to release its hold.

"Ready?" Gabe slapped him on the back and back to reality.

"Yeah." He stepped back from Leigh. "I'll call you with an update."

He was making that call far sooner than he'd expected.

Gabe had gone straight to Carrington Memorial Hospital to talk to the family and explain the situation. Mrs. Gordon had been surprised but more than willing to give her consent for them to search the house, dock, and boat.

Judge Jarvis had been all too happy to sign the search warrant as he walked out the door. The news of the body found on Mr. Cook's property had started to spread. It wouldn't be long before some nosy reporter put two and two together, and then they wouldn't be able to go anywhere without a gaggle of cameras following them.

When Leigh answered the phone, he could hear voices in the background.

"Hey," she said. "That didn't take long."

"I'm afraid I'm not calling to tell you I'm on my way back. I'm on my way to the Gordons' house. We've got consent and a warrant. Gabe's meeting me there with the keys."

"What do you think you'll find?"

"No idea. Tonight we're going to see if there's anything obvious. Forensics will come out tomorrow. I've already called Anissa. She's still planning on bringing pizza, but it may be more like nine than seven."

"We won't starve," Leigh said. "Be careful."

"Always."

He parked his car in the driveway. Gabe pulled in right behind him. The officers they'd requested to join them arrived moments later. He wasn't going to take any chances. If they happened to find something, he wanted to have plenty of backup and a solid chain of evidence.

He and Gabe pulled on gloves as they walked around the Gordons' house. The yard had the look of a place that had once been immaculate and now needed a bit of attention. The split-level house was small for this part of the lake. They walked to the back. The house might be small, but the view was spectacular. The lake spread wide in front of them and on both sides.

"Didn't realize this place was on a point," Gabe said.

"Me neither. Look at the dock," Ryan said. "It would be easy to back the boat out. If the wind was right, you could almost float to open water before you'd need to crank the engine. And the security cameras from the lots on either side wouldn't pick up anything."

He glanced back at the house. A large deck came off the top floor and shaded the spacious patio below.

"Sliding glass door," Gabe said with a disgusted shake of his head. "I guess it gives them a good view, but let's encourage them to replace it with a nice set of French doors with a double-keyed lock."

"How much you want to bet they don't have a broom handle in that thing," Ryan said. It would be all too easy to open an old sliding glass door like that.

"Let's go find out."

"I want to look at the dock first," Ryan said.

"Fine by me."

They stepped onto the wooden planks. He loved docks. Loved the feeling of being on the water, the familiar way the dock swayed. The Gordons owned a nice double-decker dock, similar to Leigh's. The bottom level was U-shaped with the boat resting in the middle. A set of stairs led to the top level. It would be a fabulous place to relax on a spring evening or drink coffee on a fall morning.

During the summer, they didn't need to keep the boat covered, but Mr. Gordon probably kept the pontoon covered during the winter.

He and Gabe inspected the cover.

"Does this look weird to you?" Ryan asked.

"What do you mean?"

"The cover. I think it's been removed recently."

Gabe tilted his head and studied the cover. "What makes you say that?"

"The dents are in the wrong place."

"You are not making any sense."

"Look." Ryan pointed out places where the cover had, at one time, been stretched over seats, but now those places didn't match. "Someone has put the cover on backward," he said.

"I think you might be right."

Gabe let out an appreciative whistle as they pulled the cover off the boat. "Wow."

"Double wow," Ryan said as he walked around the U-shaped dock. The Gordons might not have spent much money on the upkeep of the house, but they hadn't skimped on the maintenance of the boat. The pontoon boat was one of the nicest he'd ever seen. It wouldn't keep pace with a ski boat, but you could easily take twelve people out for a day on the lake with a boat like this. Everything about it showed how much Mr. Gordon—or one of his kids—loved this boat.

"I don't think we should mess with anything until we get forensics to go over everything on the boat," Ryan said.

"Agreed," Gabe said. "Let's check out the house."

Ryan asked two officers to cordon off the dock with crime scene tape. Once he was comfortable the area was secure, they headed to the house. As they stepped off the dock, Ryan's foot slipped into a rut in the grass.

He stopped and studied the area. He wasn't a skilled tracker, not by a long shot, but he didn't need to be.

"Gabe."

"Yo."

He pointed to the track that wound its way up the hill. He followed it, careful not to step on it again. The trail ended at the shed. Gabe produced a set of keys, but Ryan stopped him.

"I don't think our killer would have needed to jimmy the lock."

On the side of the shed, in plain sight, was a small key. Sure enough, it opened the door.

And once inside, they found a wheelbarrow.

"There's no way Mr. or Mrs. Gordon has used the wheelbarrow lately," Gabe said.

"I agree. Could be one of their kids used it."

Not that he believed it. His Spidey-sense was tingling. This meant something. He wasn't 100 percent sure what it was yet, but this could be the break they'd been looking for.

"Ryan."

He turned and found Gabe pointing to a small row of hooks on the wall of the shed. Keys hung from every hook.

Including the keys to the boat.

Leigh had been hiding in her room for the past hour.

Adam was nice enough. She'd always liked him. But he was working on a case and was on the phone a lot.

Her phone rang. Rebecca Fowler? Why would she be calling? "Hello?" Leigh said, her throat still raw.

"Leigh. How's it going? I heard what happened at the hospital. I'm sure you aren't supposed to be talking much, but I wanted to let you know I'm praying for you and if there's anything I can do, let me know."

Leigh couldn't believe it. As if Rebecca Fowler didn't have enough to keep her hands full and her mind occupied. She didn't need to be worried about her.

"Did Ryan tell you?"

"No. I haven't talked to him today. Keri told me."

Leave it to Keri to share the good news. That girl could not keep a secret. Not that it was a secret. The whole hospital knew about it. "When did you see Keri?"

"Ran into her at the store," she said. "And she told me you aren't supposed to talk a lot, so I'm not going to keep you. I realize this may seem strange, but I felt compelled to call you and remind you that you aren't alone. And no matter how it feels, God hasn't lost sight of you, Leigh Weston."

"You really believe that?"

"Yes."

Rebecca didn't need to elaborate. If she could hold on to her faith despite everything going on in her world . . .

"Thanks," Leigh said.

"Tell that brother of mine to call me later, okay?"

"I will."

The phone disconnected and Leigh tossed it on her dresser. She pulled out the legal pad she'd been scribbling on for the past hour. She'd listed every person she worked with in the emergency department, how often she worked with them, and how often their schedules coincided.

She still couldn't see a pattern.

She was missing something. Someone.

Who is it, Lord? Help me see it, before it's too late. Before they kill me—or someone else.

A flurry of activity downstairs drew her from her self-imposed isolation. She grabbed a scarf and wound it loosely around her neck. Maybe it would help keep everyone's eyes off her bruises.

The buzz of easy conversation greeted her before she turned the corner at the bottom of the stairs. Ryan, Gabe, Anissa, Adam, and Sabrina filled her kitchen. Stacked pizza boxes wobbled precariously on the counter. In front of the refrigerator, Sabrina busied herself by filling cups with ice and then handed them off to Anissa, who placed them on the island. She caught Ryan scavenging through her pantry, and while she stood watching, he pulled out paper plates and napkins. On the other side of the kitchen, Gabe filled a blender with ice cream, chocolate syrup, and milk.

"Holler your preference one at a time. Supreme or pepperoni," Adam said.

"There she is," Sabrina said with a cheery smile. "Did we wake you up?"

"No," she said. "Not that anyone could sleep with all this going on." She tried to infuse her words with humor and the overflow of gratitude she felt toward all of them. They didn't have to be here. They could be doing all this work in their office. It would probably be a lot easier for them to do it there.

But instead they were here, making a party out of it. The warmth and affection in their laughter and chatter soothed her knotted nerves.

She probably should have gone to help Sabrina and Anissa, but as if some sort of tractor beam were pulling her toward him, she found herself drawn to Ryan's side. "Hey," he said in a whisper. "You okay?"

She nodded. He squeezed her elbow. Something about the way his eyes lingered on her lips did funny things to her insides.

They settled in the den. Plastic cups and napkins and pizza—it almost made her feel like a teenager again. Her mom would have loved this scene.

"Who's gonna bless this food?" Sabrina asked.

"Anissa," Ryan, Gabe, and Adam said in unison. Everyone laughed.

She rolled her eyes at them. But then she said, "Let's pray," and bowed her head. Everyone followed suit.

"Abba, it's been a crazy day. One filled with insights and leads and possible answers to some of our questions. But there are still some big ones lingering. We ask that you guide our thoughts. Direct us to the answers only you have. Protect us as we seek justice. Father, we especially ask that you comfort the families of the victims. Those who are finding out even tonight that their father, husband, and friend has passed away. And we also ask that you comfort Leigh. Help her to know you are with her and for her. That none of this has caught you off guard and you are working things for her good. We confess that in this moment, we can't see the good, but we trust you and ask you to give us eyes to see what you're up to."

Anissa paused as if she expected God to answer her on the spot.

"We thank you for the food, the friendship, and the faith we share around this table, and we ask that our conversation be pleasing to you. We love you. You're the best. Amen."

A chorus of amens filled the room. When Leigh opened her eyes, she caught the look on Sabrina's face. Did hers look the same? A mixture of confusion and awe? No one else seemed surprised by the intimacy and sincerity of Anissa's prayer. That must be why they'd all voted for her to ask the blessing.

The words Anissa had spoken had been lifted to God, but they'd also been soothing to Leigh's tender soul. *What she said, Lord. That's what I want.*

Leigh alternated between sips of the chocolate milk shake Gabe had made her and tiny bites of a slice of supreme pizza. Each swallow hurt, but not as much as she'd expected it to. And it was worth it. She was starving. She had nibbled her way through half a slice when Adam—who had inhaled four slices and at least half a bag of chips—stood.

"As fun as this is, it's already nine-thirty. Some of us have been up for a very long time"—his gaze flickered to her—"and some of us have to get up super early for court." His eyes lingered on Sabrina.

"And some of us," Gabe said as he picked up plates and napkins and carried them to the trash can, "want to know what everybody found."

Ryan gave Leigh a quick wink. "I agree. We have a lot of moving parts and things are only going to pick up speed from here. At least I hope that's where we are in these investigations. We need to coordinate and share all the info we have."

"Agreed," Anissa said.

Leigh slid her legs to the floor. "Whoa." Sabrina held an arm out in her direction. "What do you need? I can get it for you."

What was with this girl? She didn't know her. Why did she even care?

"I appreciate the gesture, but it's not necessary. My legs work fine." Leigh hoped her smile would make it clear to Sabrina that she wasn't trying to be a jerk about it.

"Of course they do, but you've had a tough time over the past week, and it makes the rest of us feel better if we can make things easier on you. We haven't been able to solve your case yet, so getting you a refill eases our consciences. Not much, but a little."

Adam choked on his tea.

Anissa froze with a stack of plates in one hand and a wad of dirty napkins in the other.

Gabe stared at Sabrina like she had said the sky was tangerine.

Ryan's brows were drawn so tightly together that a deep crease formed between his eyes.

"What?" Sabrina asked. "It's true, is it not?"

Leigh couldn't decide what was funnier. The horrified expressions on the faces of all four law enforcement officers or the innocent bewilderment on Sabrina's. A chuckle bubbled up and there was no stopping it. Once it popped out, she couldn't keep from laughing. Soon tears prickled her eyes.

Ryan's laughter joined hers, then Gabe's. Anissa followed. Adam never lost it completely, but even he had a grin on his face.

Sabrina threw her hands in the air. "What did I say? I'm not wrong."

Adam schooled his features. "You aren't," he said. "It's just not something we would have said out loud."

"Why not?"

Leigh tried to swallow her laughter. "Don't worry about it," she said. "You busted all of them. It was fabulous."

Sabrina frowned and Leigh adored her for it. This girl—well, woman—didn't seem to feel the need to try to impress anyone. She didn't care if she said the "right" thing. Her honesty was refreshing.

Leigh grabbed her cup and stretched it toward Sabrina. "I would love a refill, if you're headed to the kitchen."

The relief on her face was priceless. "Yes. Coke, right?" Adam followed Sabrina into the kitchen.

Leigh turned to the others. "You shouldn't laugh at her."

"You started it," Ryan said, still chuckling.

"I wasn't laughing at her. I was laughing at all of you. Your faces." She had to bite down on her lip to keep from losing it again. "I'm not a fragile flower. I don't need to be babied. And I don't hold any one of you responsible for what has happened or is happening or will happen. You're amazing. You're doing the best you can with the information you have. You're going to figure this out. And hopefully I'll live long enough for us to all tell our children about that time there was a serial killer in Carrington. Quit tiptoeing around me and let's get to the bottom of this."

"Yes, ma'am." Gabe gave her a quick salute.

"Hear, hear." Anissa tipped her cup in her direction.

"What did we miss?" Adam asked as he and Sabrina reentered the den.

"Oh, nothing much," Ryan said. "Just Leigh putting us all in our place."

"Excellent," Adam said. "Now, where we?"

"We were comparing notes on what we've learned today." Sabrina handed Leigh her now full cup and then grabbed her laptop. “And I want to go first, because I have news I think may impact all three cases.”

She pointed to Leigh, then Ryan, then Anissa in turn.

“I say all three, but to be honest, I’m pretty sure it’s really all one.”

18

Ryan sat straighter on the sofa and put his arm around Leigh's shoulders. "One? That's an interesting theory, Dr. Fleming," he said.

Anissa caught his eye and shook her head. She hadn't said anything to Adam. Gabe widened his eyes at him in a look that clearly said "It wasn't me."

"I think you should hear her out," Adam said. There was no mistaking the protectiveness in Adam's tone.

Gabe raised his eyes to the ceiling. Anissa dropped her gaze to her hands. Leigh choked back a giggle. Adam and Sabrina must have been the only two people left on the planet who didn't realize there was something going on between them.

But Dr. Sabrina Fleming didn't need Adam to defend her. "Thank you, Adam. But I understand their skepticism. They haven't heard the facts presented the way you have."

"By all means," Ryan said. "Please share."

Sabrina turned on Leigh's television. "Hope you don't mind. I thought it would be easier for us all to see it this way."

After a few taps on her keyboard, the screen of Sabrina's laptop was mirrored on the sixty-inch flat screen in front of them.

"Let's start with the timeline."

Gabe started. "We found the first John Doe a week ago Saturday—"

"Excuse me, Gabe, but not that timeline."

The TV screen filled with a few words.

> Calvin Staton murdered–eleven months ago.
>
> Body buried on Mr. Cook's property while he was hospitalized.

Then the screen filled with a wide-open space before another set of facts appeared.

> John Doe murdered–ten days to two weeks ago.
>
> Body dumped in Lake Porter.
>
> Possibility the Gordons' boat was used to transport the body–92%.
>
> Mr. Gordon was in the hospital at the time.

Sabrina glanced around the room. "Everyone good with this so far?"

Nods all around.

> John Doe found in Lake Porter. News reports show Leigh Weston's property and image–ten days ago.
>
> Leigh Weston's brake line cut–nine days ago.
>
> Officer Peter Stanfield drugged with gelatin meant for Leigh–nine days ago.

Balloons blow up in Leigh's home—three days ago.

Possible coffee tampering—two days ago.

Patient tries to strangle Leigh—earlier today.

Sabrina turned her gaze to Leigh. "I'm very sorry about this, Leigh. But this timeline, this level of escalation, it doesn't speak to a stalker who has been silent prior to this point. I'm not a profiler, but I chatted with a friend at the FBI who is and she agrees that this points to a significant event happening sometime in the days prior to your brake line being cut that precipitated action."

She turned to the group. "Leigh lives a relatively quiet life. She works nights, sleeps days. She's quick to take overtime or fill in for coworkers. That, combined with her fantastic medical skills, has endeared her to them."

Leigh gave Ryan a look he interpreted to mean that she didn't understand where Sabrina was going with this. He squeezed her shoulder. He wanted to let Sabrina get through her explanation. If they had reached the same conclusion from different angles, that would be quite significant.

Sabrina continued. "She has a handful of close friends. She doesn't have any bad habits."

"That you know about," Leigh said.

Everyone laughed, even Sabrina, but she didn't break her stride. "She doesn't party. She doesn't drink or do any sort of drugs. She doesn't even do a lot of shopping. She reads a lot. Does yoga. Studies for her PhD."

Her PhD? All the eyes in the room turned to Leigh, whose skin flushed scarlet. "How did you find out about that?" she asked.

Sabrina had the decency to look chagrined. "I'm sorry, Leigh. I do this all the time and I forget how many things people think are private are really quite easily accessible if you know where to look. I wasn't trying to be intrusive. I'm just trying to figure out why someone would target you."

Leigh blew out a breath. "It's okay."

Sabrina's smile for Leigh was full of hopefulness. For a split second, Ryan wondered how many friends the nerdy professor had. Probably not too many. Maybe she saw potential with Leigh?

"You're freakishly intelligent," she said to Leigh. "And kind in a way few people think to be. Your patients in Durham raved about you. Your coworkers at Carrington adore you. I've been unable to find anyone who doesn't think you are a wonderful person. I had to ask myself how you could have someone this determined to come after you. Based on this timeline, only one major event makes sense."

She touched a button on the laptop. A Venn diagram with its overlapping circles appeared. Circles with church and friends appeared, but the only two that had any space in common were the circles that said "hospital" and "John Doe."

"I've been reviewing the security footage of the night your brakes were cut. I ran it through some experimental software some of my colleagues are testing. The algorithms are pretty complex, but it returned a very interesting statistic. If, and admittedly this is a big if, but if the shadow we've found on the security footage is the person who cut Leigh's brake lines, then there's a seventy-two percent chance our killer is a woman."

A woman?

"Serial killers are almost always men," Sabrina continued. "And it would take some strength to mutilate the bodies and bury them or dump them. But it's not beyond the realm of possibility that a woman could do it. And, if we are dealing with a serial for our two bodies, which is increasingly possible, then the targeting of Leigh also makes sense."

Anissa raised her hand. Ryan didn't blame her. Sabrina's

presentation had the feel of a classroom lecture. "How does it make sense? Both victims are males. Estimated age for our John Doe found in Lake Porter is late fifties. And our other victim was confirmed to be fifty-nine. He was from Cleveland, and there's a good chance our John Doe wasn't from around here either. So why would a serial killer, male or female, who targets men from out of town decide to kill Leigh? And in ways that bear no resemblance to his or her preferred methods?"

"Excellent question. The answer is, I cannot say conclusively."

"That's not an answer," Gabe said under his breath.

"I operate in a world of facts and statistics and verifiable analysis," Sabrina said. There was no rancor in her voice. "I cannot say for certain. However, I can hazard an educated guess, and I would think each and every one of you could do the same."

"The killer thinks I can identify them," Leigh said.

Sabrina acknowledged her with a small thumbs-up.

"But I don't know who it is."

"Or you don't know you know," Sabrina said.

"What does that mean?" Gabe frowned at all of them.

"It means," Adam said, "there's an excellent chance Leigh does, in fact, know the killer. And while she may not realize she knows the killer, there are facts currently available to her that, when spliced together, will identify both the killer of our John Does and the person attempting to kill her."

"Look out, Adam, that Ivy League education of yours just popped out." Gabe laughed at his own joke. The others chuckled. Adam didn't.

As usual, Gabe plowed forward. "But I get what you're saying. You think Leigh knows the killer, and if the right set of events or facts were placed in front of her, she may be the one person who could make sense of them."

"And that makes her very dangerous to the killer," Adam said. "So the killer breaks out of their usual M.O. and targets Leigh."

"Possibly," Sabrina said. "It's a theory."

Ryan waited for Anissa to make eye contact with him. Her grim nod gave him the go-ahead. "It's a fascinating theory, Dr. Fleming. Particularly because, minus the part about the killer being female, it's the same one we came up with this afternoon."

Leigh liked Sabrina. A lot. She was such a nerd—and didn't appear to care what anyone thought about her. She kept her brilliance reined in when talking with mere mortals, except for every now and then when it popped out by accident.

She spoke to all of them like a professor giving a lecture, but as soon as she took a seat beside Adam, she retreated into her shell. Leigh had the distinct impression that spending time in a group was hard on the professor. She'd probably go back to her lab and stay there for a week when this was over.

Sabrina looked up from the tablet she'd been tapping away on and Leigh smiled at her. The smile was returned with a small shrug.

Around her, the room buzzed. Adam and Gabe were in the middle of one conversation. Ryan and Anissa were talking about something Anissa was showing him on her laptop. Leigh tried to follow both discussions, but it was impossible. Especially when Gabe slipped into Spanish and Adam followed him.

Leigh raised her hand and the room quieted. "I think it might be more beneficial for all of us if we don't try to talk over each other. I'd like to hear what Anissa has learned about her John Doe. And I think we're going to need to talk about everyone I've ever worked with at the hospital."

"Agreed," Anissa said. "Here's what we know."

She turned her laptop around so everyone could see the screen and Sabrina jumped into action. "Allow me." It took less than a minute for Anissa's laptop to be mirrored on the TV screen. Leigh caught a flash of tropical water before the screen was flooded with pictures. "This is Calvin Staton," Anissa said. "Fifty-nine. Owned a trucking business out of Cleveland."

A few more images popped up on the screen. A massive home. A sports car. Another home on a lakefront. "Mr. Staton lived large."

Another photo flashed onto the screen. A Christmas card. So much loss. Such devastation for the family. "Mr. Staton's wife, Shelly, and their three children." The woman looked like a typical woman in her mid-fifties, except—

"Look at that diamond." Gabe whistled.

"Yes. Mr. Staton was quite generous with his wife. Unfortunately"—another series of photos appeared—"he was also quite generous with his girlfriend."

Leigh struggled to find the feelings of sympathy she'd had toward Mr. Staton moments earlier.

"Did the wife know?"

"Still not sure she does."

"How did you find out?"

"Given the nature of the case, I wanted to fly out to Cleveland and interview all the parties, but when I called to talk to our counterparts in Cleveland, I discovered the missing persons case had not left the desk of one of their investigators. He's been working the case hard. He found the girlfriend through some interviews he did with some of Mr. Staton's employees. But he says the wife and the girlfriend are both clean. Airtight alibis. The girlfriend knows about the wife but swears the wife doesn't know about her."

"The wife always knows," Gabe muttered.

"No. She doesn't." Ryan glared at Gabe.

"Sorry," Gabe said.

Ryan didn't reply.

"Regardless," Anissa said with no attempt to hide her efforts to steer things off such a touchy topic, "the thing that makes no sense at all is how Calvin Staton wound up in the ground at Mr. Cook's place. Neither the wife nor the girlfriend could account for his absence."

"Another girlfriend?" Adam asked.

"The detective couldn't rule it out but said Calvin's schedule, his secretary, his wife, his girlfriend, his friends, and his employees all believed he was attending a conference in Richmond, Virginia."

"That's not far from here."

"No, it isn't. And when the detective tried to construct a timeline, he discovered the conference was real and Mr. Staton was registered for it, but he never checked in."

"That's weird."

Gabe pointed to Adam. "I'm liking the second girlfriend."

"Maybe. But if there's another one, I'm not sure how he would have had time for her. Between the wife and the girlfriend in Cleveland, Mr. Staton was a very busy man. The girlfriend believed he would leave the wife when the kids were out of the house."

Leigh groaned. "Those kids look like they are about ten to twelve. She was planning to wait that long? For Calvin?"

Everyone laughed, except Sabrina. "What do you mean, for Calvin?"

"I'm sorry, but he's not much of a catch."

Gabe, Adam, and Ryan roared with laughter.

"You laugh now," Leigh said. "You're all three drop-dead gorgeous and you know it. Someday you'll be pushing sixty and your cheeks will have jowls and your eyes will have dark circles and you will look in the mirror and wonder what happened."

Leigh didn't miss the way Sabrina's cheeks turned pink at her words or the way Anissa looked from Gabe to Adam and then to Ryan as though she were seeing them for the first time.

"Oh, come on. Back me up here, ladies. All three of them could be in a law enforcement calendar and you know it."

Anissa gave an unwilling shrug. "I guess they're all right."

"All right?" Gabe gasped in mock horror. "I'm hurt, Bell. That was cold."

"Leigh's point is valid, if not one I probably would have considered," Sabrina said from her spot in the corner of the sofa. "This girlfriend is much younger and quite attractive. Why go for a guy like that?"

Anissa pulled up a new set of photos. The girlfriend and Mr. Staton on a yacht. On a sandy beach. In Paris. In Rome.

Sabrina dropped her head. "I get it. He's got money. That's all she cares about."

"To be fair," Anissa said, "the detective said she seemed genuinely distraught. She may have cared for him. But interestingly enough, she had expressed concern that she had been afraid he might leave her for—get this—a younger woman."

"Oh, good grief," Gabe muttered.

"Look, we can dissect this guy's motives and poor life choices all night. None of this explains how he wound up decapitated in the woods in central North Carolina," Ryan said.

His comment silenced the room.

Leigh expected Anissa to give them some sort of answer, but she didn't.

"Do we think this killer, male or female, killed this guy in Cleveland and brought him here to bury him? Because that's sick."

Adam looked a little green. He didn't typically work homicides and Ryan had told her he had no interest in it. Maybe he didn't have the stomach for it. Not that that was a weakness. She didn't blame him.

"It's also a jurisdictional nightmare," Ryan said.

"What do you mean?" Leigh asked.

"If we've got a serial killer committing crimes in multiple states? Ugh. It would get messy. No pun intended."

"I don't think your killer did this far from here," Sabrina said. "If the key to the location of the dump sites is the Carrington hospital, then the person must work there or be someone who regularly goes to the hospital. Maybe a florist—which would tie in to your balloon explosion—or maybe someone who does those food deliveries."

She tapped her glasses against her lips a few times. "But I still think you're looking for someone who works in the hospital. They know the routines, the parking lots, and no one notices them if they are in random parts of the hospital. They can blend in. And if your serial killer is female, that also fits the profile. Female serials are rare, but they are statistically more likely to work in a caregiving profession. Either medical or with children."

"That's terrifying," Gabe said.

"I'm with you all the way, brother," Adam said.

"So what do we do now?" Leigh was afraid to hear the answer to her question, but she had to know.

"Tonight?" Ryan looked around the room. "Tonight we sleep."

"You cannot be serious," Leigh said.

"Oh, yes I can. You're tired. I'm tired. We're all exhausted. We have to be back out at the Gordons' first thing tomorrow while forensics goes over everything inside and outside the house. I'm going to run a different kind of search on the missing persons stuff, looking specifically for very wealthy men. See if it narrows down the possibilities any."

"I could work on that," Sabrina said. "I'd be happy to help."

"I appreciate that. I do. But it's not the best use of your skills." And he wasn't sure the sheriff would approve of him hiring her for something they could do themselves.

She smiled. "I'm volunteering my services here. No charge."

"Why?" Leigh couldn't help herself from asking.

Sabrina shrugged. "I live here. I have a unique skill set that I like to use to help my community when I can. I can take a few hours to run through some missing persons reports and see if anything grabs me."

Leigh still wasn't convinced. There was more to Sabrina's interest in helping than she seemed willing to share.

"But more than that," Sabrina said, "there's an evil to this that scares me. This person needs to be caught. Before they strike again."

"I'm not one to turn down the offer of free help," Ryan said. "You understand the parameters I'm looking for. Let's start by checking for any missing person who has a similar profile to Mr. Staton and see where it gets us."

"I'm on it," Sabrina said.

"Thank you," Ryan said.

"I've already asked Adam to help me by running some of the financial records the Cleveland Sheriff's Office sent over," Anissa said. "We'll look for anything that doesn't make sense. They've already looked, but they weren't looking for charges specific to this area. Maybe we can find something that ties him to Carrington."

"That all sounds good," Ryan said. "And I'm not trying to tell you how to run your investigation"—he looked at Anissa—"but now that we have a face, I think we need to get the airport security footage from Richmond and look specifically for Calvin Staton."

"Good idea," Anissa said.

They all had things to do. Big, important, meaningful things to do. And Leigh would be sitting here alone going crazy.

"I have a job for you." Ryan turned to her.

If he suggested she bake a cake, she would throw something at him. "What?"

"I need you to make a list of everyone you have ever worked with."

"I've been working on a list of all my coworkers—"

"Not just your coworkers. I want everyone. Here, in Durham. Even in nursing school or grad school. If you can think of them, write them down. We will be able to eliminate ninety-nine percent of them, but I'm convinced someone on that list is going to be our man." He glanced at Sabrina. "Or woman."

"I can do that, but it's still hard for me to believe anyone I know could be this evil."

"Serial killers rarely present as evil," Sabrina said. "They are often charming and compassionate. Something in them is broken, but they understand enough of social constructs to know they have to put on a show of civility. In fact, in most cases, they are genuinely kind to those who aren't in their target population."

"That's what's scary about this," Leigh said. "How could I possibly know who it is?"

"You couldn't," Sabrina said. "The problem is, they think you do."

19

Ryan couldn't shake the sensation that the answers to their questions were floating all around them. Somehow, with this group of diverse talents, surely they would be able to find them.

"I want to thank all of you," he said as they packed up laptops and files and power cords. "This case is going to take all of us, and I appreciate you being in here with me."

A chorus of "yes" and "agreed" and even one "hooah" echoed through the den. Leigh smiled and nodded and accepted gentle hugs from Adam and Gabe. Sabrina stuck out her hand, but Leigh grabbed it and pulled her in for a hug. The shock on Sabrina's face was priceless, but after the hug was over she looked pleased.

So did Adam. Ryan needed to talk to that boy. If he was going to wear his heart on his sleeve, he might as well do something about it.

Anissa kissed Leigh's cheek and said something to her he couldn't hear. Whatever it was, Leigh's eyes were shimmering as she closed the door. Their voices faded away as she turned back to him.

"You okay?" he asked her.

"Yeah."

She adjusted the scarf at her throat again.

"Why don't you take that off?"

"It's fine."

"You've messed with it all night."

She puffed out her cheeks and blew out a long breath. "It isn't itchy. I don't know how to explain it. Let's say I'm not sure if I'll ever be able to wear a turtleneck again."

Of course. He walked over to her and unwound the scarf from her neck and placed it on the counter. He looked into her eyes as he reached one hand toward her neck and brushed the bruises with the back of his fingers. "I am sorry, Leigh," he said. His voice was rough with the emotion he'd been holding in all day. All week. Oh, who was he kidding? More like for the last fifteen years.

She reached up and took his hand, lacing her fingers through his. "It wasn't your fault. None of this is."

He should walk away. He should slide his hand away and tell her good night.

But she pulled him toward her with the slightest pressure and all his thoughts of leaving fled. His arms wrapped around her, and when she leaned against him, it was like a concussive force went off inside him. Not subtle like a tremor. More like an earthquake.

The tectonic plates of his heart had shifted and the rearrangement wasn't something he would ever recover from. He held her and breathed in the fragrance of her and knew he would never feel this way about anyone but her. Ever.

He needed to be careful not to push her into something she wasn't ready for. When this was over, would she still want him around? Would she always associate him with this dark time? Or would she be able to see him as the silver lining around the clouds?

"I'm scared," she whispered into his chest.

"So am I." He doubted her fear was the same as his. She was afraid for her life. And she should be. He was afraid of losing her before he'd ever had a chance to explore what life could be like with her.

She pulled back and looked into his eyes. "I'm not talking about dying."

She wasn't? Was she—? "I'm not either. I'm in uncharted territory here. I don't want to hurt you. Or push you." Her hands moved to his shoulders. What was she doing? "Or rush you . . ."

She pulled him closer. "I don't feel rushed," she whispered, her lips tantalizingly near his own.

He closed the distance. Her lips were so soft. Her body so warm. How could this be possible? He kissed her with all the tenderness he could, still afraid of hurting her. He pulled away and she leaned back, her eyes no longer full of fear but of something else that scared him more than anything he'd ever seen before.

Longing. Desire. Trust.

If he hurt her, or failed her, he would never be able to live with himself.

Three quick raps on the door shattered the sacredness of the moment. Leigh stepped away, her hand running down his arm until it reached his hand. She squeezed it before releasing it and turning for the stairs. "Good night, Ryan."

"Good night."

Twelve hours later Gabe was still apologizing. "Man, I had no idea," he said for the fiftieth time.

"I told you to drop it," Ryan said.

"But she kissed you. Like, a real kiss. Not an accidental—"

"How does someone kiss somebody accidentally?"

"It could happen."

Ryan walked back around the Gordons' house. The forensics teams would be done soon. At least he hoped they would be. They'd photographed and dusted the house, the boat, and the toolshed. There wasn't much else to see. No blood. No remains. But strong evidence, albeit circumstantial, that someone had wheeled a heavy object down to the boat. They'd taken the boat out for a little while, returned it and the wheelbarrow, and if it wasn't for the keen eyes of a certain professor, they might never have been the wiser.

His phone rang and his stomach dropped. Not Leigh.

"Dr. Fleming. How can I be of assistance this morning?"

"I have a name you need to follow up on," she said in her usual crisp tone.

"Seriously?"

"Yes. He's been reported missing from the Chicago area. But, and here's the kicker, another man with the same description has also been reported missing in the Atlanta area. Different first name. Same last name."

"No way."

"I've sent over all the information to your email," she said. "I'm going to keep digging, but this is the only name that jumps out and screams to be investigated further. If you could get something with DNA from the family, you could compare it to your John Doe. It's something to consider."

"This is great, Sabrina. I'll be back in the office later this morning and I'll get right on it. Thank you. You're awesome."

"Who's awesome?" Gabe asked.

Ryan hung up the phone and filled Gabe in on Sabrina's news.

"You get the feeling things are spinning toward a resolution?"

"Yeah. I hope they don't spin out of control first."

"We aren't that lucky, man."

No. No they weren't.

The officer patrolling Leigh's deck caught her eye.

Again.

She looked back at the list on her laptop. Columns of names spoke to her from their cells on her spreadsheet.

All of them proclaimed their innocence.

She'd listed every coworker she could think of—nurses, doctors, surgical techs, secretaries, security guards, transporters, and even the radiology techs with whom she had incidental contact.

The list was ridiculous. Hundreds of people, their faces floating before her eyes as she scanned the sheet. This was wrong. How could she ever set the police loose on any of them?

But . . .

What if they were right? What if, somehow, she was the key to solving these murders?

Father, this is beyond me. If the name is here, you're going to have to point it out. A shiny arrow appearing on the screen would be great. Or maybe you could highlight it in red?

She stared at the page. Nothing happened.

It had been worth a shot. And somehow, throwing out the questions, regardless of how ridiculous they were, heightened her sense that she wasn't alone. That God was here. With her. That he knew what she was working on.

He might have even found her joke funny.

She didn't have any answers, but the tightness in her chest had eased over the past twenty-four hours. Which made no sense at all, given everything she'd learned.

Still . . . she kept scanning the pages. Considering and rejecting name after name. After three hours, she'd narrowed down the list to fifty names. None of them were people she knew well—just men and women whose paths crossed hers on a semiregular basis.

Was the killer here? On this list?

The phone rang. Rebecca Fowler's number popped up on the screen. Had Ryan told her? Her skin warmed at the thought of last night. Her boldness. Where had that even come from?

Not that she was sorry.

The taste of him, the strength of his embrace, the gentleness of his kiss. She understood his tentativeness. But he didn't know she'd had a crush on him for a couple of decades. This wasn't some new emotion borne out of intense circumstances.

Heightened by them? Sure. But there was no way she'd ever get over them.

"Hey, Rebecca."

"Hey. I just have a second and I know you aren't supposed to be talking a lot. But I'm in the car and didn't want to text. Your voice sounds a little better."

"Thanks. I'm good. Throat's still sore. And the bruises look much worse today than they did yesterday. I could audition for a horror movie and they wouldn't need to use any makeup on me."

Rebecca laughed. "It can't be that bad."

"I'd send you a picture, but I don't want to give you nightmares."

"This is a nightmare that will be over soon. I have faith."

How Rebecca had any faith at all remained a mystery, but she wouldn't complain. "Thanks. I'm trying to believe."

"You try too hard," Rebecca said. "Trust me on this. God's got you whether you are trying to be gotten or not. He's working something awesome out of all of this. I don't know what it is. But I know—"

A crash and a child's wail in the background came through the phone. "Sorry, Leigh. I have to go."

"Everyone okay?"

"Everyone except the block tower Caleb had been building. We're good. Tell my brother to call me tonight, okay?"

The phone disconnected before Leigh could respond. Rebecca hadn't been fishing for anything, so Ryan must not have talked to her.

Maybe no one knew.

What if . . . what if he didn't want anyone to know?

The rap on the door drew her to her feet. No one could have gotten by the officer outside. Could they?

"Yo, Leigh, open up." Gabe's merry tone calmed her nerves.

She opened the door and Gabe bounced inside. Was he ever in a bad mood? Or was it all an act? She hadn't decided yet.

"First, I bring greetings from Parker. He's at the office running down a lead, but he says he'll call you as soon as he comes up for air. I was commissioned to obtain dinner instructions for the evening."

Before she could respond, he continued. "Second, I wanted to apologize for my interruption last night." He wagged his eyebrows at her. "I promise, if I'd had any idea, I would have sat outside for an hour or two."

Ryan had told him?

He must have read the surprise on her face. "Don't get me wrong. Ryan's not one to kiss and tell. But he was so aggravated when he opened the door, it was pretty obvious. I badgered him into a full confession."

She had no idea what she was supposed to say to that. Not that Gabe was going to give her a chance to say anything. "I think it's awesome, although you know your brother is going to kill him. You'll need to be prepared for that."

"That doesn't worry me in the slightest."

"Great. Let me know when you tell him. I want to be there to hear it all go down. Should be entertaining."

Gabe shifted from one foot to the other. Was he stalling? Was all this some sort of cover-up?

"What's going on, Gabe?"

His eyes dropped to the floor. How had he ever survived a decade of undercover work? He was a horrible—

Unless he wasn't. Unless all of it was intentional. "Is there something you want to tell me but you aren't supposed to tell me?"

He looked up with a grin and winked.

"Something about the case?"

His eyes darted away. He looked everywhere but at her. What did he know?

"Gabe Chavez, I'm in no mood for games. If there's something going on that involves me, you'd better tell me and tell me now." She was trying to be demanding, but her battered larynx betrayed her and the words came out whispery.

Gabe grinned. "Since you forced it out of me . . . we have a solid lead on our John Doe. We might even have a name by tonight."

"That's great."

"Yeah, but dinner may be late. Everyone's planning to meet here tonight to discuss. Will that be okay with you? Because I have to tell you, hanging out here is way more comfortable than being in the office."

"That's awesome with me. I don't care what we eat. Order whatever everyone wants. I'll be good with anything. I'll bake a—"

"Whoa." Gabe held up his hands. "You're supposed to be resting."

She didn't argue with him. She'd whip up something after he left.

"You're going to bake anyway, aren't you?" he asked.

She didn't respond.

He laughed. "I did what I could. See you tonight."

She locked the door behind him and checked the clock. It would probably be at least seven before they all arrived. She had four hours. Maybe if she baked and prayed and thought about her list, something would come to her. Some missing piece would fall into place.

She emailed the list to Sabrina, then pulled out flour and sugar and cocoa.

Five hours later, her kitchen counters were covered with empty takeout containers and half the cupcakes she had baked were devoured. She listened to the updates.

"Anything new on your end, Bell?"

"No." Anissa growled the word. "I cannot figure out how Calvin got here. He definitely arrived in Richmond. And then he . . . disappeared. No car rental. No bus ticket. It's like he got off the plane and vanished."

Ryan's phone buzzed. "Excuse me a moment." He stepped onto the porch and the conversation resumed.

"Have you found any footage of him in Richmond?" Sabrina chewed on her straw while she waited for Anissa to respond.

"Yes. I've got footage of him at the airport and one brief glimpse of him on a camera as he left the airport. It looks like he was walking toward the economy parking area. And then . . . nothing."

"Someone picked him up?"

"Maybe."

The door burst open. "We have a name! John Doe #1 is Harold Claussen." Ryan's excitement brought everyone to their feet.

"What? How?"

"We will still have to confirm with DNA, but the anthropologist is ninety-eight percent sure. She had told me our John Doe had broken his left leg and his right arm probably in his teens. When we got this name to check out from Sabrina"—Ryan pointed to Sabrina and she dipped her head in acknowledgment—"I called the responsible officer in Chicago. She followed up with his wife and told her she was still working on the case and needed to get a more detailed medical questionnaire filled out. In the process, she asked her if he'd ever broken any bones. His wife volunteered the information. A bad skiing accident in his teens. He broke his right forearm, his left femur, and apparently did some serious damage to his left foot. But obviously that doesn't help us any."

Leigh couldn't stop the shudder that rippled through her. She tried not to dwell on it, but the idea that some maniac out there could kill her and then chop off her head, hands, and feet . . .

When had the room gone quiet? She looked up and found five pairs of sympathetic eyes on her. Ryan's face filled with horror. "I'm sorry," he said in an anguished whisper. "We shouldn't be doing this here. It's not fair to you."

"No, I'd rather hear it. I don't want to end up buried in an unmarked grave or dumped in the lake—or whatever else this person might be planning for me. But I also don't want anyone else to wind up that way. If you're right and I can somehow help figure out who the killer is, then I need to stay engaged."

Ryan's head shook back and forth in obvious indecision. Anissa cleared her throat. "This is why we don't typically involve the affected parties in our discussions," she said. "But I agree with Leigh. We've got a twisted soul out there. Possibly someone who we know. Someone we would never expect. This situation with Leigh has forced them out of their usual patterns and we have a chance we wouldn't have had otherwise to find them and stop them once and for all."

"I agree," Sabrina said. "Leigh's tough enough. We need to be respectful of how difficult this is for her and appreciative of her willingness to sacrifice so we can get to the bottom of this. But that doesn't mean we have to shut her out of these conversations. She needs to hear them."

Leigh smiled at both women. It was nice to be understood.

"Of course, she'll probably need therapy when it's over." Sabrina's matter-of-fact statement shocked the room. Everyone froze, their eyes wide, mouths open in stunned disbelief.

The thing was, Sabrina wasn't wrong. But she was the only one who would say it out loud.

No one would make eye contact with Leigh, but as the silence draped over the room, the absurdity of all of it flooded over her. What started as a snicker blossomed into a chuckle. She cleared her throat and pinched her lips together, but another snicker escaped. She could not do this again. She blinked hard several times, but then Gabe lost it and broke into laughter. Then Anissa. Even Adam. Sabrina looked confused. Ryan looked like he might cry.

The laughter hurt Leigh's throat and neck, but it was also cathartic. She wiped her eyes and walked over to Ryan, who was watching her intently. "I promise I'm okay."

"It isn't funny," he said.

"Believe me, I know it isn't."

"It's like laughing in church," Anissa said. "You know you shouldn't, but once you start . . ."

"Was it something I said?" Sabrina asked.

Sabrina's innocent question sent all of them into another round of laughter. This time, even Ryan cracked a smile.

"Sabrina, I think you may be the most refreshingly honest person I've ever met," Leigh said.

Sabrina frowned. "People say 'refreshingly honest' when what they mean is 'you said something wildly inappropriate.' I know. I do this a lot."

Behind Sabrina's back, Gabe shook with laughter.

Leigh tried not to look at him. "I don't need people in my life who tap-dance around me. I need people to shoot straight. And you aren't wrong. I will need therapy. I'd start tomorrow if I wasn't afraid of getting the therapist killed."

Ryan groaned.

Gabe raised a hand. When he had everyone's attention, he nodded toward Sabrina. "You, my dear, are a breath of fresh air, and I'm thrilled you are a part of our intrepid band of investigators." He chuckled as he said the words but still managed to convey them with sincerity and kindness. Sabrina's face flushed, but she was clearly pleased.

He pointed at Anissa next. "You, my captain, are a constant source of inspiration and insight."

Gabe's pronouncement shocked all of them, and based on the way her mouth fell open, Anissa most of all, but Gabe didn't elaborate.

He turned to Ryan. "You, my friend, have to keep your head in the game. We know you're smitten with the lovely Leigh." He nodded in her direction. "And who could blame you? She's a delight and a treasure. But if you want to keep her around so you can sweep her off her feet, you're going to have to focus. And, to be perfectly honest, you're going to have to quit worrying about protecting her feelings and worry more about protecting her life."

20

Thursday morning dawned dark and gloomy. The forecast called for five days of cooler temps and heavy rain.

But the sight of Leigh sipping her coffee warmed Ryan to his core. He'd sleep in her basement forever if he got this view every morning.

"Hi," she said. "How did you sleep?"

"Fine," he said. "You?"

A small shrug. When he got closer, he noticed the dark circles under her eyes. The even deeper bruising on her neck. He pulled her from her perch on the bar stool and she melted into his arms. "Bad dreams?"

"I'm not sure if they were bad dreams or panic attacks. Maybe both."

"I'm going to find him," he said. "And you won't have to be afraid."

He tipped her chin up and her arms slid around his neck without hesitation. His heart pounded in his chest as he pressed his lips to hers. He wanted to stay right here. Hold her until she fell asleep and be there if she woke in fear.

But Gabe had been right last night. He had to keep his head in the game, and hanging out with her wasn't going to solve her case.

"Parker?" The captain's voice echoed through the squad room, interrupting the memory of Leigh's kiss goodbye.

"Yes, sir!"

"My office."

"Yes, sir."

He glanced around the room. Anissa and Gabe both gave him small shrugs. They didn't know what was going on either.

He stepped into the captain's office.

"Close the door."

He did.

"Have a seat."

Not good.

"We have a situation."

Ryan waited.

"I got a call from downstairs. Mrs. Claussen is here."

"Okay." Not fun, but not what he would call a problem.

"But she's not the Mrs. Claussen I spoke to this morning."

Wait. What?

"Sir?"

"Yeah."

"With all due respect, sir—"

"How do I know? Because the woman I spoke to this morning is thirty-seven years old and according to her DMV records, she lives in Atlanta, where she works as an aerobics instructor. The woman downstairs, according to the driver's license she presented to the clerk, is fifty-nine and lives in Chicago. Just for fun, I called the Mrs. Claussen I spoke with this morning. She's still on her way. I talked to her while watching the Mrs. Claussen who is currently waiting downstairs. They are not the same woman."

"Two wives?"

"Wife #1, or my guess is she's wife #2, is already past Charlotte," the captain said. "She'll be here in the next hour. All either of them know is that there is a significant lead in their husband's disappearance."

Ryan put his head in his hands. Could this case get any weirder? "Any advice?"

The captain chuckled. "I've had them put Mrs. Claussen in the family interview room. I recommend you keep 'em in separate rooms and don't let them see each other, certainly not until we sort it all out. Get a couple of the white-collar investigators who specialize in identity theft on it and get them to figure out what's going on with these two. Treat them both like they are the wife. Do your interviews. Report back to me."

Ryan went into the observation room adjacent to the interview room first. He made sure everything was recording properly and paused to watch Mrs. Claussen #1 for a moment through the window. She wore a pair of slacks and a flowy shirt. Flat black shoes. She clutched a tissue in one hand and a large handbag in the other.

"Those shoes run about two-fifty a pair. And that bag is worth a week's salary," Anissa said.

Where had she come from? "How do you know?"

Anissa wasn't someone who struck him as a fashionista. She wore slacks and semi-dressy tops to work. Off hours, she usually had on gym clothes. He'd never seen her in anything else except a wet suit for diving.

"My roommate in college had about twenty of those bags," she said.

"Twenty?"

"Her dad bought her one every time he went away on business. Or, rather, his assistant bought one. She gave me a couple of them. I still have them."

"Thanks," he said. "But what are you doing down here?"

She laughed. "Are you kidding? Good news travels fast. I don't want to miss this. Can't wait for the wives to bump into each other."

"Captain wants me to keep them separated for now. He was quite clear on that. But depending on how things go, we may arrange for them to see each other. Look for any signs of recognition."

"You think our John Doe really had two wives?"

"I think the real question is whether the Mrs. Claussens know he had two wives."

"No way," she said.

"It happens," Ryan said.

"Not in North Carolina."

"It wasn't in North Carolina."

"What kind of guy keeps two completely separate families?"

"I don't know. I'm about to go find out. Want to join me?"

"You stepping out on me, man? How could you?" Gabe entered the room clutching his chest in mock agony.

"Since she's here, I was thinking that Anissa might have a better rapport with Mrs. Claussen #1. And if the captain is right, you might have a better rapport with Mrs. Claussen #2."

Anissa shrugged. "Why not? Besides, I'm curious to see if we can find any connection between our two bodies."

Gabe's only response was to step back for the two of them to leave the observation room.

"You got some 'splaining to do, buddy," Gabe said in a whisper as Ryan passed him.

"Trust me," Ryan said.

Ryan wasn't exactly sure why he'd asked Anissa to come in with him. It had seemed like a good idea in the moment, and the more he thought about it, the more he liked it.

He opened the door to the interview room and held it for Anissa to go in first. Mrs. Claussen #1 stood as they entered. "Can I see my husband? Where is he? Why won't anyone tell me anything?"

Ryan tried to keep his expression neutral. This was always tricky. On the one hand, he wanted to empathize with the victim's family. On the other hand, the spouse was always a suspect until proven otherwise. And with the addition of a second spouse, the chances of Mrs. Claussen #1 having a motive to kill Mr. Claussen skyrocketed.

"Mrs. Claussen—"

"Don't 'Mrs. Claussen' me, young man. I want an answer and if you can't give me one, then you turn your cute little self around and go find me someone who can."

He could almost hear Gabe laughing on the other side of the mirror.

Anissa didn't seem to be inclined to respond to Mrs. Claussen's comment. Some help she'd turned out to be.

"Mrs. Claussen," he tried again. "I'm Investigator Ryan Parker. This is Investigator Bell." He nodded in Anissa's direction.

"Lovely. I'm Muriel Claussen and I'm not going to ask you again, young man. You tell me where my husband is right now or my attorney will find ways to keep this little police station of yours in litigation for the next decade."

Oh, good grief. Ryan clenched his teeth together to keep himself from saying something he would regret. He had zero concerns about her lawyer or any litigation. He was just trying to give her time to talk herself into a nice deep hole.

Anissa gave the tiniest of shrugs. Seriously? That's all she could do?

"I'm very sorry to have to tell you this, ma'am, but I'm afraid your husband has passed away," Ryan said.

Mrs. Claussen #1's face paled beneath her makeup. She took a small step back, and for a moment he thought she was going to crumple.

He was wrong.

She caught herself and straightened. "I want to see him."

"I'm afraid I can't allow you to do that," Ryan said. "This is an active investigation, and there are some things about the nature of his passing we need to discuss with you first. Please, have a seat."

"I want to see him." Mrs. Claussen #1 articulated each word.

Anissa moved toward her. "Mrs. Claussen, could I please make a suggestion?"

Mrs. Claussen narrowed her eyes at her but gave a small nod of assent.

"I've been where you are. I've been in a room insisting that I see a friend who had passed. I understand how desperately you believe you must see him. But can I tell you how desperately wrong you are? There are things that can never be unseen. They can and will haunt you. I know you don't know us and you have no reason to trust us, but please. Let's talk for a little while."

Whoa.

Anissa wasn't one to lie in general, but was she telling the truth or was she just trying to establish rapport?

"Please, Mrs. Claussen. Please have a seat," she said.

This time, Mrs. Claussen #1 did crumple. "If you won't let me see him, how can you be sure it's him?"

"We're going to confirm it with a DNA analysis, but right now we are basing it on some other information. Including that the body we suspect is your husband has several things unique to it. The left femur and right ulna were broken at the same time while in his teens."

She blinked several times. "Yes," she said, her voice quavering. "We were in high school. He loved to ski, but he hit some ice and lost control. Cartwheeled down the slope. I saw it happen. It was brutal."

"And had he perhaps had some arthroscopic surgery on his knees?" Ryan asked.

"Yes," she said, narrowing her eyes at him. "But how . . . you cut him open? How could you do that without permission? What kind of monsters are you?" Her knuckles whitened around her purse.

"Mrs. Claussen, autopsies are standard procedure in cases of suspicious death."

Her mouth worked as she struggled to maintain her composure. "Suspicious? What happened to my husband? How did he die?"

Father, help me here.

"Mrs. Claussen, there's no easy way to tell you this. We believe your husband was murdered."

"Why?"

"We don't know," he said. Honesty was always the best policy.

"Was he robbed? Where did you find him?"

Oh boy. Ryan leaned toward her and tried to infuse his words with as much gentleness and sympathy as he could. "His body was found in Lake Porter."

Every part of her body registered shock. If she was behind this, she was a consummate liar. "In the lake?" The words caught in her throat and she tried to clear it. "Like, floating around in the water?"

"No, ma'am."

She looked relieved. That wouldn't last long.

"Our dive team located his body at the bottom. He had been wrapped up and weighted down. We don't think the killer intended for anyone to find him for quite some time."

He allowed silence to settle over the room, giving her time to process everything. If only the worst were over.

"Is that why you couldn't identify him from a picture? Had he been—" She shuddered. "Had he been eaten?"

"No, ma'am. I'm afraid the killer removed his head and hands and feet from his body. I'm very sorry. We've searched the lake, but we've been unable to find them."

"He . . . his head . . . what?"

Was he going to have to say it all again?

"Mrs. Claussen," Anissa said. "You have valid questions, and we will answer them as many times as you need us to. But right now, the best thing you can do to help us find your husband's killer is to tell us everything you can about him. His business, people he works with, what he was doing in North Carolina—"

"He wasn't in North Carolina." Mrs. Claussen looked confused. "He was going to Richmond on business. I have no idea how he got here."

"Okay." Anissa didn't indicate that this news was a revelation to them, but now they had both men in Richmond. That couldn't be a coincidence. "That's great. That's the kind of stuff we need to know. We're going to have officers who will need to have access to your house, his office, that kind of thing."

"Anything," she said. "Anything you need. I can instruct my staff to open everything on our property. You'll need to talk to his business partners, but I'm sure they'll cooperate."

"That's excellent."

The poor woman looked as though she was hanging on by a thread. She kept squeezing the tissue in her hand like it was one of those balls given to people to pump when they're giving blood.

Ryan's phone buzzed. Oh boy. Mrs. Claussen #2 had arrived. She must have broken every speed limit in three states to get here.

"I'm going to take a statement from you in a few minutes," Anissa said. "Could we get you some tea or coffee? Would you like to visit the restroom first?"

Gratitude flickered in Mrs. Claussen's eyes. "The restroom please. Then some water."

"Absolutely."

Ryan and Anissa left the room. Anissa grabbed a young female officer to escort Mrs. Claussen #1 to the restroom.

"You're going to take her statement?" Ryan asked.

"Don't you need to meet with the other Mrs. Claussen?"

"Yeah, but . . . why do you want to take the statement?"

Anissa didn't reply right away.

"Do you think she did it?"

Anissa shook her head. "Not personally. I think she was genuinely shocked about the manner of death. If she paid someone to do it, they took it in a direction she wasn't expecting. And right now I don't think she had anything to do with it, but it's early yet."

"Do you think she knows about the other wife?"

"No idea," Anissa said. "I think there's a good chance that as bad as things are now for her, they are going to get a lot worse. I wouldn't wish it on anyone."

Ryan waited. Maybe if he kept quiet she would elaborate.

"Look, I lost someone," Anissa said. "The cop who took my statement was a jerk and the experience haunted me for a long time. I don't want that to happen to her. And I'm not saying you would be mean, but I don't want some inexperienced rookie in there with her. I'll let you know what I find out. You go talk to the other wife."

Ryan didn't have any trouble distinguishing Mrs. Claussen #2 from the rest of the people waiting in the lobby. She stood as far away from everyone else as she could get and everything about her body language—the rigid posture, the angle of her chin, even the direction her feet were pointing—indicated that she did not wish to blend in.

"Mrs. Claussen?"

"Yes."

"I'm Investigator Ryan Parker."

Mrs. Claussen #2 extended a manicured hand. "Please, call me Melissa," she said with a drawl that hinted she'd spent most of her life in Georgia.

Really, Harold? Muriel and Melissa?

She tucked her long blonde hair behind her ear, flashing a diamond earring that would have been impressive had it not been in close proximity to the boulder-sized gem she was wearing on her hand.

"Could you come with me?" Ryan asked.

She picked up a bag the size of a small suitcase that rested at her feet. Same brand as Mrs. Claussen #1. Interesting.

"Certainly."

Her high heels clicked along beside him. She smelled of something floral and had on a sheath dress that clung to her as she walked. While Mrs. Claussen #1 looked like the sixty-year-old wife of a wealthy man, Mrs. Claussen #2 looked more like his thirty-year-old daughter.

He ushered her into a room on the opposite side of the station from Mrs. Claussen #1. "Could I get you some tea? Coffee? Water?"

"Water would be perfect," she said. "I'm parched."

"I'll be right back."

He left the room and put an officer outside the door. He had plenty to choose from. A small crowd had gathered. "Back to work," he said and they scattered. He texted Gabe as he went to the fridge to grab a water. By the time he got back to the room, Gabe was waiting on him.

"How's it going over there?" Ryan asked.

"Anissa's really good at this," Gabe said. "She's got Mrs. Claussen chatting like they were old friends. Not that there's been any surprising news. He traveled a lot. Worked a lot. Didn't go to church. She says they were happy."

Maybe *she* had been.

"Let's see what Mrs. Claussen #2 says," Ryan said as they entered the room.

He introduced Gabe and the two of them sat on the sofa across from Mrs. Claussen #2.

"Mrs. Claussen—" Gabe began.

"Melissa," she said with a coy smile and an appreciative look that didn't belong on the face of a married woman.

Gabe had noticed. Ryan could tell by the way he shifted in his chair, leaning toward her. This woman had no idea who she was flirting with.

Was she that callous? How could she behave in such a seductive way when her husband was missing? Or was this how she was with everyone?

Gabe broke the news to Mrs. Claussen #2, who received it with far less drama. And yet somehow, while she didn't react in anger, her sadness was more palpable. The coquettish woman disappeared and a heartbroken one took her place.

It was too soon to tell if the sorrow was genuine or a skillful facade.

"Mrs. Claussen, could you tell us about your husband? What he did? How you met? How long you've been married?"

She took a sip of her water. "He moved to Atlanta eleven years ago. His mother was dying and he wanted to be closer to her. She passed away two years later, but he'd fallen in love with Atlanta and didn't want to leave even after he went back to work full time. We met five years ago. Fell in love. Married three months later. I told him I'd move to Chicago with him, but he wouldn't hear of it. He's a good man. Goes to church when he's home. Spoils me with gifts. He travels a lot, so he's usually only home a couple of days a week."

"That must be hard," Gabe said, his brow furrowed in concern.

She gave a small shrug. "It's all we've ever known," she said. "I'm assuming you already know about his work."

Something about the way she said "his work" prickled Ryan's instincts. "We'd appreciate it if you could tell us what you know about it."

Her expression grew quite serious. "Don't worry. He never told me anything he wasn't supposed to."

What?

"I understood how things worked. His work was dangerous. He worried so much over me. Didn't want people to know we were married. We had a small civil ceremony. Never told anyone. He promised to retire in two more years. Then we were going to travel the world." She let a sob break free. "That isn't going to happen now, is it?"

"I'm very sorry, Mrs. Claussen," Ryan said.

She shook her head like she was trying to clear it. "Don't take this the wrong way, sir. But I don't care if you're sorry or not." She looked at Ryan with tear-filled eyes. "What I care about is what you're going to do to catch the evil person who did this. I know he had some fierce enemies, but you have to find his killer."

"We're doing everything we possibly can," Ryan said. "But we're going to need your help."

"Anything," she said as she dabbed at her eyes. "Whatever you need. Financial records. Calendars. Computers. Where we went out to eat and who our friends were. I'll tell you anything you want."

"That's a very specific list," he said.

She blew her nose before she spoke. "I was married to a spy, sir. And I watch a lot of cop shows. Between the two, I'm guessing that's most of what you'll need access to. Do you even need my permission for any of it?"

She thought she was married to a spy?

Maybe she had been. That was an interesting angle to pursue. But for now, he wanted to keep her talking.

"Under the circumstances, we'll get a warrant for most of what you offered, but it certainly is easier if you provide it willingly."

"Then you can have it. I'll call our attorney and accountant and instruct them to provide anything you need. Wills, trusts, insurance policies. Whatever."

"Would you be okay with us sending some officers to your home?"

After a slight pause, her shoulders sagged. "Why not? I have nothing to hide. And Harry never kept anything at the house. Said it wasn't safe. We don't even have family pictures or anything."

"Melissa," Gabe said in a soft voice, "this is important. We need to know if he ever told you who he worked for."

Her lips quivered. "Will he get in trouble?"

"No, ma'am. But we need to know so we can know how best to direct our investigation."

"Do you think something he was working on could have gotten him killed?"

"That's certainly a possibility we are considering."

She took several deep breaths. "The CIA," she whispered.

Ryan forced himself to look everywhere except at Gabe.

Wow.

He wasn't an expert, but there was absolutely no way Harold Claussen was a spy for the CIA. At least they now knew how he'd worked the scam. It was possible that neither of these women had any idea about the other wife. Claussen must have believed he'd fooled them both.

Or had he married two of the most convincing liars in history?

An hour later, Ryan joined Gabe and Anissa in a conference room. The captain walked in ten seconds later.

"Well?" he asked.

Anissa and Gabe stared at the table.

"It's a mess," Ryan said.

"I kind of guessed that."

"From what we've been able to put together, Harold Jackson Claussen married Mrs. Claussen #1 when they were both nineteen years old. He went by Jack and they settled outside of Chicago as he finished his studies in electrical engineering. He worked in an electronics firm for about ten years before joining a new venture providing computer networking support. That venture proved to be wildly successful. They expanded into some other Midwestern cities, then to the East Coast. DC, Atlanta, Tallahassee, Orlando. Claussen stayed fairly close to home in Chicago until his kids were in college. Traveled a lot but mostly in the Midwest. Then ten years ago, he took a position as the vice president in charge of East Coast operations."

The captain nodded. "I'm guessing that's how he met Melissa?"

"Seems like it. She claims he's a spy—for the CIA. She knows he has an office in Chicago but believes he travels all over the world when he's away from her. And here's the best part."

Ryan paused.

"Don't leave me in suspense," the captain said.

"Once we got a name and his other records, he wasn't that hard to track. And some of his travel doesn't match with what either wife accounted for."

"What do you mean?"

"It seems he spent a fair amount of time in the DC area and the Pittsburgh area."

"Your point?"

"Let's say we won't be surprised if a Mrs. Claussen #3 shows up."

21

Leigh hummed as she checked her makeup. It was ridiculous how the thought of Ryan walking through her door could make her forget—for a moment—that there was a maniac trying to kill her.

The doorbell rang and she adjusted the collar of her shirt one last time. The bruising had gone green and purple today, but this shirt covered up the worst of it.

She looked through the peephole and then opened the door to find Sabrina waiting, a tentative smile on her face.

"Could I come in?"

"Of course," she said. "I'm waiting for the invasion to begin. You're the first one to arrive."

Sabrina hung a garment bag on a doorknob and then unpacked a laptop. Then another one. She didn't say much, but Leigh didn't mind the quiet. It was nice to have someone else in the house.

"I can't stay long," Sabrina said. "I have a dinner engagement at eight."

Leigh glanced at her watch. Sabrina would need to leave in an hour. "You shouldn't have tried to come tonight. I don't want to mess up your date."

"Oh, it isn't a date," Sabrina said with an indelicate snort. "And what we found today can't wait."

Her tone pulled a veil over Leigh's earlier mood and the heaviness of her present reality settled around her.

Sabrina seemed oblivious to the effect her words had. "Are the others on their way?"

The knock on the door and the accompanying chatter behind it answered for her. Gabe, Anissa, and Adam spilled into the house, pulling off rain jackets and laughing at some joke. They each carried a bag from Luigi's and the smell of garlic permeated the air as they unloaded them on the counter.

Where was Ryan?

She peeked out the door and found him on the porch, out of the rain, leaning against the house, phone to his ear.

"Hey, buddy. I know. It's been ages. I'm going to come see you this weekend and we're going to play Trouble for an hour."

Ah. Caleb. Poor guy. He couldn't possibly understand why his uncle Ryan hadn't been by to see him. She'd picked up from previous conversations that Caleb didn't say much, but Ryan talked to him whenever he called Rebecca. Caleb's lack of response didn't seem to faze Ryan.

"Okay. Let me talk to your mom."

Leigh pulled her head back inside, but before she got away from the door, Ryan's hand closed around hers. He pulled her outside and into the protective shelter of his arms. She knew what he was doing. If someone was hoping to get to her, they'd have no shot with her back to the house and her face buried in Ryan's chest.

She could barely hear Ryan's words over the din of the rain pelting the porch roof, but she could feel the vibration in his chest as he spoke. His laughter at something his sister had said. Then the hand that had been holding the phone was on her face, and for the next few moments, nothing else mattered.

He was the one to break the kiss. Probably for the best. She would have been happy to stay here all night.

"Oh baby," he whispered into her ear. "You're killing me."

She kissed him again in response. Life was too short to play games. He clearly cared about her. Might even be on the way to being in love with her. And she wasn't going to leave any doubt in his mind about whether those feelings were reciprocal.

"If we don't go inside, they're going to be merciless." His breath tickled her ear.

She knew he was right, but she'd never cared less about anything in her life. Let them talk. Let Gabe make all manner of smart remarks. None of that mattered.

Ryan's growling stomach pulled her back to a state of reason. "When's the last time you ate?"

His arms tightened around her. "Who needs food?"

"You do, apparently." She pushed against his chest with both hands.

He regarded her with a look that sent butterflies cartwheeling through her. How could this be happening? How, in the middle of so much that was wrong, could she have been given this gift?

Ryan claimed her lips in one more fierce but brief kiss. Then he opened the door and she braced herself for the chorus of innuendo and teasing that would come.

Silence.

What had happened to the jovial group that had entered her home only moments, okay, minutes ago?

Ryan's gentle arm around her shoulder tensed and he pulled her in tight. "What's going on?" Leigh asked.

All eyes flicked to Sabrina, who hadn't looked up from her computer.

She was confused. "Sabrina?"

She bit her lip and shook her head back and forth.

Adam cleared his throat. "We may have another body."

Leigh's legs threatened to give out on her. Ryan's arm moved from her shoulders to her waist, and she leaned on him as he ushered her to a seat on the sofa.

"Where?" Gabe asked.

"Chatham County."

One county over. "The rain today," Sabrina said. "A car lost control and flipped into a ditch. When the crew pulled the car out, they found a bone sticking out of the muck. Didn't take long to uncover the rest of the body."

"What was left of it," Adam said.

Chills skittered across Leigh's skin.

"Male?" Ryan asked.

Nods around the room. "Their ME called our ME, who called the anthropologist again. She's coming out tomorrow. But based on initial examination, there's no way we aren't dealing with the same killer."

Sabrina finally looked up. "Which is why what we have to say is more important than ever." She nodded at Adam.

"Sabrina came up with a theo—"

"No, Adam. This was yours."

"Let's eat while we hear it," Gabe said. Everyone jumped to their feet and began piling plates high with lasagna and chicken parmigiana, salads, and garlic bread.

Leigh didn't move until Ryan laced his hand through hers and pulled her to her feet. "You need to eat too."

"I'm not hungry."

"At least come with me," he said.

That was a request she would never deny. Five minutes later, everyone was sitting around the coffee table, eyes focused on Adam. She really needed to replace the dining room table. Soon.

"I've been reading your notes from the interviews with the families," he said. "Both men were known to be in Richmond. Both men fell off the grid as soon as they arrived. I did some digging into their financials and discovered both men made significant cash withdrawals the day before they left."

"Define *significant*," Ryan said.

"Twenty thousand dollars."

Anissa whistled.

"That's pocket change for some people," Gabe said.

"Not really," Adam said.

Gabe started to argue, but Adam cut him off. "Come on, man. I know that much cash might be normal in the circles you're used to traveling in, but for a legit businessman? No. He might have several thousand dollars in cash, but he's going to use his card."

"Unless he doesn't want someone to know what he's doing," Anissa said.

"Exactly." Adam handed a tablet to Sabrina. She started working her magic, and once again, images appeared on the TV.

"As soon as we got a name for our John Doe #1, I got access to the video footage from the Richmond airport." Adam studied the screen, then tapped the tablet. The image stopped moving. "There."

"Harold Jackson Claussen," Ryan said.

They all stared at the grainy image. Was this the last footage anyone had of him alive?

Adam tapped the tablet again, and they followed Harold Claussen from the airport to a cell phone lot.

"We learned that the cameras in the cell phone lot had been malfunctioning when Calvin Staton came through Richmond, but they were working just fine last month."

As they watched, Harold Claussen climbed into the passenger seat of a white Cadillac Escalade. A nice car, to be sure, but not one that would generate any particular notice on the street.

The tag on the Escalade was partly obscured, but they were able to get four out of seven digits from it.

"We ran the plate and came up with a list of possible owners," Adam said. "Only one of the tags with these four digits is also supposed to be on a white Cadillac Escalade."

"The tag could be stolen," Ryan said.

"I agree, which is why I'm calling this a theory."

"Carry on," Ryan said.

"The car is registered to a company called PSA." Adam tapped the tablet again and the image on the screen changed. "It took some digging, but I found out the PSA stands for Plastic Surgery Associates." Leigh leaned closer to the screen. The website Adam had pulled up was for a plastic surgery center. "What's this?"

"This is where I think your guy might have been planning to spend that money." A few taps and everyone's phones buzzed. "I just sent the link to your phones."

"So these guys were planning on spending twenty grand on plastic surgery?" Gabe asked.

Leigh scanned the page from her phone. "Oh," she said.

"Sorry. I don't get it." Gabe took a bite out of a piece of garlic bread. "Plastic surgery gone wrong?"

"Leigh, what do you think?" Sabrina asked.

Leigh took a sip of her tea. "I've heard rumors of a place like this. It's a very posh plastic surgery center, by the looks of it." She scrolled through the pages. "Privacy is their biggest selling point. They don't take insurance. They check people in under false names. This may not even be legal. How did you find it?"

"Adam found it," Sabrina said.

"You mean to tell me that pretty face of yours isn't natural?" Gabe asked, directing his question to Adam.

"I haven't used them," Adam said. "But I know people who have. When I saw the Plastic Surgery Associates and connected it to the Richmond angle, I remembered my uncle had a friend who flew into Richmond and was whisked away for some sort of implants. My uncle went to see him while he was recovering. The place is about an hour from here. In between the state line and the Raleigh area."

"Then why not fly into Raleigh?" Anissa asked.

"The privacy." Adam said this like it explained everything.

"I don't get it," Gabe said.

Adam shifted in his seat and ran a hand through his hair.

"Uh-oh," Gabe said with a conspiratorial tone. "We must have ventured into the secret lives of the rich and famous. Is this information too precious to be shared with those in the lower classes?"

Leigh wanted to jump to Adam's defense, but before she could, he threw a piece of garlic bread at Gabe and then straightened his posture and adopted a haughty expression. "I wouldn't expect *you* to understand, my dear fellow, but I feel sure the ladies will follow along. Have one of them explain it to you later."

Gabe and Ryan laughed. Anissa rolled her eyes.

They must have teased Adam about his silver spoon upbringing a lot, because he didn't seem to be truly upset. He grinned at Leigh before he continued.

"Several of the women in my family have had plastic surgery," he said. "It's not a secret. They talk about their surgeons to their friends at lunch or at dinner parties. They brag about it. There's nothing taboo about it."

He stabbed some lasagna with his fork. "But several of the men in my family have also had plastic surgery. And they are not willing to talk about it. At all."

"Who?" Gabe asked.

Adam twisted an imaginary key in front of his mouth. "I'm sworn to secrecy. But I can tell you that while the women in my family don't mind disappearing from view for a few weeks, or even a few months, while they recover, the men handle it quite differently. In fact, one of my uncles had some work done and it was so skillfully handled that it was six months before any of us realized it. It wasn't so drastic that I noticed it when I saw him in person. Only when I looked at a family photo from a few years earlier did I realize it."

"These guys want plastic surgery done in complete privacy? They don't even want their wives to know?" Ryan asked.

"Not all men, but some. And this place"—he pointed to the tablet—"caters to those clients. The place is more like a spa than a hospital. Men go in for surgery, they get treated like kings while they recover, and then they go home. The family thinks they went on a business trip and never realizes they had butt implants or an eye lift or a tummy tuck."

"I would think the wives would notice," Anissa said.

"Depends on the wife," Gabe said.

"Or the procedure." Adam flipped to a page on the tablet. "The photos we have of Claussen and Staton are not of men who have let themselves go. In fact, I would argue they look quite young for their age. If we dig deeper—"

"Which we will," Sabrina said.

"I wouldn't be surprised if these men have been getting plastic surgery done for a while. And there's a good chance that when we ask the wives—"

"All three of them." Gabe chuckled.

"They may not know anything about it," Adam explained. "If you want to keep plastic surgery a secret, the best way to do it is to start young so the changes each time are quite minor."

"So you *have* gone under the knife," Gabe said.

"The point is, this facility has a whole procedure for the man who wants to keep his surgery a secret. The flight into Richmond, the walk to the cell phone lot. The unmarked car that whisks them away. It fits. And it explains why they both wound up in North Carolina when no one expected them to be."

"That's it," Leigh said.

"What's it?" five voices asked in unison.

"We need to find out who works there."

"What do you mean?" Ryan asked.

"Nurses, techs, even doctors who work during the week in a clinic will often moonlight at hospitals. They'll come pull a weekend shift in the ED or the recovery room or anywhere in the hospital to make extra money."

Gabe scooted his chair back. "So we've got a serial killer knocking off guys who are having plastic surgery? What's the motive?"

He disappeared into the kitchen and returned with the whiteboard they'd brought in a few days ago.

"Money?" Leigh asked

Gabe wrote it down, but Adam shook his head. "I don't think so. These guys made pretty significant withdrawals, that's true. But that's it. Their financials are in order."

"What if the killer is getting to them before they pay? A robbery/homicide."

"Seems risky. The clinic would have to know they've had multiple patients who have disappeared—"

"Unless they don't know," Anissa said.

"What do you mean?"

"Maybe they never got there. Maybe this person does work at the clinic and knows the people are coming in, but every so often he or she picks them up at the airport but never delivers them to the clinic. They tell the bosses the guy never showed up. The bosses assume he backed out. Maybe the guy had given them a burner phone or a false email or something and they don't have any way to track him. Maybe people back out from time to time. As long as it only happens every six months or so, no one would catch on."

"It's a theory," Ryan said

Gabe laughed. "Do you have a better one?"

Ryan shook his head. "I don't know. Revenge?"

"For what?" Gabe scrolled through some pages on his phone. "These guys don't seem to have any other connection other than the possibility that they both had plastic surgery."

"Maybe it's a woman and she hates men," Anissa said.

All three men moaned. Leigh chuckled. "That would have to be some serious hate."

Sabrina rose and leaned in near Leigh's ear. "Mind if I use your powder room?"

"Be my guest."

The conversation had continued for ten minutes with theories as varied as botched plastic surgery to love affairs gone wrong when Sabrina returned. “I’m sorry to have to cut out on you all tonight.”

Adam jumped to his feet. Ryan’s and Gabe’s mouths fell open. Anissa’s eyebrows rose. Leigh turned and blinked a couple of times.

Sabrina had transformed. The glasses were gone, as was the oversized sweatshirt. Her hair was piled on her head in an elegant twist. The black sheath she wore hugged her curves, and the black heels accentuated her legs.

“You’re stunning,” Leigh said.

Sabrina blushed. “Thank you. I feel like a freak.” She shifted uncomfortably. “This dress is ridiculous.”

“Oh, Sabrina. It’s fabulous,” Leigh said. “I don’t know where you’re headed, but you will be the belle of the ball.”

“You really think it’s okay?”

The guys all voiced hearty approval. Anissa gave her a thumbs-up. “Adam,” Leigh said, “I have a ginormous umbrella in that closet by the door. Why don’t you walk Sabrina out to her car?”

The poor boy fell over his chair trying to get to her.

When he returned a few minutes later, he still wore a dazed expression.

“Where was she going?” Gabe asked.

“Dinner,” Adam said.

“With who? The president?”

“Close,” he said. “The CEO of DOR International.”

Ryan whistled.

“Who?” Anissa asked.

“DOR International is a global supplier of medical supplies. The CEO is a guy named Darren Campbell.”

“Campbell? Any relation?” Leigh asked Adam.

“Cousin,” he said.

“What do they want with Sabrina?”

“This isn’t a business dinner,” Adam said. “Darren is recently divorced. He's only thirty-three. And Sabrina's work helped prove his innocence in a money laundering situation he ran into last year."

"She's dating Darren Campbell?" Gabe's remark earned him a nasty glare from Adam.

"Can we get back to figuring out who's got it out for a bunch of rich guys who want to have plastic surgery?" Adam asked.

"Worried you'll be next?"

Gabe's joke solidly moved the discussion back to the murder investigations and away from Adam's obvious despair over Sabrina's plans for the evening. It wasn't until several minutes later that Leigh realized he'd done it on purpose.

The group decided that Adam would get whatever warrants were necessary and compare the employment records from the plastic surgery center to those of the Carrington Memorial Hospital staff and see if he could find a match. Any matches would be investigated, but the jackpot would be any names that matched Leigh's list.

Ryan and Gabe once again elected to sleep in the guest rooms, and Leigh was fine with that. Even with the patrolling officers outside, she didn't like being alone in the house.

She knew it wasn't precisely protocol, but Ryan had assured her the sheriff and his captain both knew what he and the entire team were doing and had no problem with it. The sheriff had even encouraged it and said he slept better knowing there was a law enforcement presence with Leigh at almost all times.

She imagined her dad was nodding in approval, thankful for his friends who were still helping him protect his baby girl.

"We're closing in on him—or her," Ryan said as he told her good night. "It won't be much longer."

22

Ryan dodged puddles as he dashed into the office on Friday morning. He shook out his jacket and headed straight for the coffee pot.

He'd never tell Leigh, but he hadn't slept well in two weeks. He never slept great when investigating a homicide, but with the threats against Leigh, he found it almost impossible to shut down his brain.

Last night he'd turned over every piece of evidence in his mind. The dead bodies. The attacks on Leigh. The connection to the hospital and the plastic surgery clinic.

They were missing something.

"Earth to Ryan."

"Huh?"

Anissa stood beside him, coffee pot in hand. "I asked if you wanted a cup."

"Oh, yeah. Thanks."

Anissa filled his cup, then topped off her own. They walked to their desks together. He set his cup away from his case files and flopped into his seat.

Gabe was already at his desk talking to someone on the phone.

"You look awful," Anissa said. "Please tell me you aren't staying up all night talking to Leigh."

He glared at her through bleary eyes. "I am not."

She smirked at him. "What's on your agenda for the day, Romeo?"

"The detectives in Atlanta and Chicago sent me their reports from their searches. I'm going over them today to see if I can find anything, but . . ."

"But what?"

"What do you think about Adam's theory? About the plastic surgery?"

"Right now I think it's the best lead we have."

"I agree."

"But?"

"I still think we're missing something. Something big."

Adam burst into the room, tablet in hand. "Wyatt Jenkins."

"Who?"

"Wyatt Jenkins. Nurse anesthetist. He's on Leigh's list and has three known places of employment. Carrington Memorial, Carrington Technical College, and somewhere called Oraios."

"Oraios? What makes you think that's our clinic?" Gabe asked.

"*Oraios* is a Greek word for beautiful," Adam said.

Gabe threw a pen on the desk. "Of course it is. I was saying the other day how I needed to brush up on my Greek this weekend."

Adam rattled off something Ryan couldn't understand.

Gabe must not have either. "When I find someone to translate, I'll think of a crushing reply."

Adam turned to Ryan. "This is why I've had so much trouble finding more about Plastic Surgery Associates. That is the legal name of the company, but my guess is that was what they used when they were first starting out. Then they decided to specialize and change all their branding from PSA to Oraios. PSA is Oraios."

"Oraios isn't nearly as obvious as Plastic Surgery Associates when it shows up on your credit card statement," Ryan said. "It could be just about anything."

"Exactly." Adam pointed to his tablet. "This guy's banking

records indicate he works full-time for Oraios. He works one weekend a month at Carrington and teaches a class in the nursing program at the tech school. I think we need to check him out."

"I agree."

Ryan ran on pure adrenaline for the next five hours. The warrants came through and he, Gabe, and Anissa pored over everything they could find.

"We still don't have enough to charge him." Ryan stared at the whiteboard. "But I think we have enough to bring him in for questioning."

"Everything we have is circumstantial," Gabe said. "Yes, he works there. But we haven't even been able to confirm that either Claussen or Staton ever set foot on the grounds. And yes, he would have been able to get to Leigh's car the night her brakes were cut, and at five foot eleven, he fits Sabrina's profile, but he wasn't working that night and we have no evidence he was there."

"Maybe we should pay the clinic a visit before we try to talk to him. Ask around," Ryan said.

"I agree. Let's go." Gabe jumped to his feet.

"I was thinking Adam should go with me," Ryan said.

Gabe was not amused. "Are you saying you don't think I'm high class enough to handle myself with all those rich dudes? I'll have you know I've—"

"I have no doubt you would fit in fine," Ryan said. "But Adam's been the one looking at all the records and names. He's more likely to pick up on a connection than you are."

"I guess you want me to stay here and babysit your girlfriend," Gabe said.

"I don't want you anywhere near my girlfriend," Ryan said, only half joking. "But I would love it if you would interview the Mrs. Claussens again. Ask them about the plastic surgery. Anissa's going to ask Mrs. Staton about it as well."

"Fine."

Ryan turned to Adam. "What do you say?"

"I'm up for it. Give me fifteen minutes."

Ninety minutes later, Ryan and Adam pulled up to a gated road. Ryan flashed his badge. "Parker and Campbell, here to speak with Dr. Wooldridge," he said to the security guard.

The gates opened and he drove a full three minutes before the clinic appeared. It looked more like a resort than a hospital. Even through the rain, lush grounds, fountains, and a glittering swimming pool could be seen off to one side.

"I guess if you need to have some fat sucked out of your stomach, this would be a nice place to have it done."

"I guess." Adam looked over the facilities with a critical eye.

Ryan put the car in park. "Tell me what you see."

"What do you mean?"

"Oh, come on. I know where you grew up. I've been in your parents' house. And your grandparents' house."

Adam's features lit in surprise. "When?"

"I worked security a lot during my first couple of years in the uniformed division. You can make decent money working a swanky party. And your family throws some swanky parties." He waved a hand to indicate the property. "This place is big, but not as big as your grandparents' spread. Tell me, from that perspective, what do you see?"

Adam looked out the window. "It's nice."

Ryan waited.

"The landscaping is well done. That pool over there is impressive. It's hard to say for sure until I go inside, but my guess is they've done everything they need to do in order to appeal to the clientele they are targeting. But right now what I find most interesting is the privacy. That gate out there is no joke. If it's the kind I think it is, you'd need a tank to drive through it and even then it wouldn't be an easy job. There's no signage out front and a long driveway.

There are probably people who live out here who have no idea this place exists. My guess is there is a patrolling security staff along the perimeter of the property to keep people out."

"That's all well and good, but—"

"That's the key to the whole thing."

"I'm not following you."

"When we talk to Dr. Wooldridge, the privacy is what's going to matter most to him. If they lose their privacy—if the whole country finds out about this place in some tabloid and there are news vans and photographers outside of those gates? They lose everything."

"So the key to Dr. Wooldridge's cooperation—"

"Is focusing on what he has to lose."

And that was why Ryan had wanted Adam to come.

A leggy blonde with a tablet and headset met them at the door. "Right this way, officers."

She ushered them into a conference room and offered them everything from sparkling water to cappuccino, which they declined.

"Dr. Wooldridge will be with you in a moment." She indicated a button on the side of the wall. "If you need anything, press this." Her gaze lingered on Adam.

"Thank you," Adam said.

When the door closed, Ryan couldn't contain his amusement. "That girl would date you in half a second," he said.

"That girl isn't my type."

"Oh, right. You prefer women with bigger brains."

The door opened and a tall man in nice slacks and a polo shirt entered. The nametag dangling from his waist identified him as Dr. Wooldridge.

"Timothy Wooldridge," he said, extending his hand first to Ryan, then to Adam. "How can I help you gentlemen today? I confess our earlier conversation on the phone has left me quite intrigued." He poured himself a glass of cucumber water and settled into a seat.

Ryan slid a photo of Harold Claussen across the table. He caught a flicker of recognition on the doctor's face.

"Do you recognize this man?"

The doctor took a long drink. "Investigator Parker, you must be familiar with the laws of the land that prohibit me from sharing any sort of patient information with you."

"I am. But I never said he was a patient."

Dr. Wooldridge let out a huff. "What has he done?"

"He's dead."

Dr. Wooldridge removed his glasses. "Dead? Is this some sort of malpractice witch hunt? Do I need my attorney?"

"I can assure you it is not," Ryan said. Although, now that the good doctor had mentioned it . . .

He slid a picture of Staton across the table and rested it beside the picture of Claussen.

Dr. Wooldridge studied the photograph. "Is he dead too?"

Ryan nodded.

"I will tell you, off the record, that I recognize these men. But I cannot and will not discuss anything else with you."

"Dr. Wooldridge, we believe their killer is still out there. What we need to know is if these men were here for any length of time, if they left this facility in good health, and when they were released from your care."

"I'm very sorry, gentlemen. My hands are tied."

"We understand. And we're sure you'll understand that our next step will be to release these photographs to the public."

Dr. Wooldridge nodded his assent.

"Along with their last known whereabouts." Ryan let the threat hang in the air.

Dr. Wooldridge looked from him to Adam. Adam stared him down.

"Excuse me for a moment," he said.

When the door closed behind him, Adam punched a text into his phone.

"What are you doing?"

"Asking Sabrina to check this guy out for us. Looking for medical malpractice suits. If they had some surgeries go bad, maybe our nurse anesthetist was involved in covering them up."

"It's as good a motive as we've had so far," Ryan said.

Five minutes later, Dr. Wooldridge returned. "Are you, by any chance, in contact with either of these gentlemen's families?"

"We are."

"If they were willing to give consent, I would be able to legally speak to you about both of their cases."

"Oh really?"

"Yes. They listed emergency contacts on their privacy forms. It's something we require. We make no secret of the fact that privacy, while critical, is our number two priority. We will not compromise the health and safety our patients. We make this quite clear. If a patient refuses to give us permission to contact family members in case of emergency, we refuse to operate."

"How often do you have to contact someone?"

Dr. Wooldridge smiled. "We had to make a phone call earlier this week. One of our patients suffered a severe allergic reaction to an antibiotic. He was taken to the hospital in Raleigh and his wife was notified."

He walked to the door. "When you have those releases from the family members, feel free to return."

"Oh, we aren't going anywhere," Ryan said. "We'll wait."

Dr. Wooldridge's eyes bugged.

Adam waved his phone at him. "Already requested them. Both families have been exceptionally cooperative. I don't anticipate much of a delay."

"In fact," Ryan said, "if I were you, I'd go ahead and start pulling their files. It will save us some time later."

The requests for information came in less than fifteen minutes. Dr. Wooldridge handed the files over ten minutes later.

"In nonmedical terms," Ryan said, "what were they here for?"

"Mr. Claussen and Mr. Staton both came in for eye lifts."

Ryan picked up one of the three-inch files. "That's a lot of paperwork for an eye lift."

Dr. Wooldridge tilted his head and pursed his lips.

"Oh, for crying out loud," Adam said. "We aren't interested in putting you out of business. But if you can't fill us in on the specifics of what, when, and why these men were here, we'll bring in our forensic accountants and figure it out for ourselves."

The good doctor threw up his hands in disgust. "This is going to ruin me either way."

Wow. This guy was a real gem. Ryan didn't try to hide his disdain for the man. He gave him the coldest stare he could manage. It didn't take long before Wooldridge sighed in frustration.

"This was not their first visit. Mr. Staton has been here at least twice a year for a decade. Mr. Claussen even longer. Both of them insist on privacy. We pick them up from a spot in the cell phone lot at the airport. They stay with us a week or more. Long enough that any bruising or swelling has faded. We give them a ride back to the airport and they're on their way."

"When were they last here?"

The doctor checked the files. "Mr. Staton's last visit was a year ago." He frowned.

"What's wrong?"

"He should have been here a few months ago . . ." Dr. Wooldridge said.

Ryan watched as realization dawned.

"He wasn't killed recently, was he?"

"No."

He grabbed the file for Harold Claussen. "Mr. Claussen was

with us a month ago. He . . . he was planning to come back in three months . . ."

"Dr. Wooldridge, how do you keep track of your patients? Do you have any other patients that are regulars who've failed to schedule new procedures?"

"Let me talk to my office manager," he said.

"What about your privacy policy?"

Dr. Wooldridge's earlier attitude had evaporated. The man standing before them was rattled. "If someone is targeting my patients, what's to keep them from targeting me next?"

Still self-absorbed. But at least he was being more cooperative.

An hour later, they had sent three names to Sabrina for her to run against the missing persons cases and the new John Doe from Chatham County.

They also had confirmed that Wyatt Jenkins had been the nurse anesthetist for the final procedures for both Claussen and Staton. But that didn't necessarily mean anything. The surgical staff here was quite small. There were three surgeons on staff and they alternated procedure days. There was only one anesthesiologist, one nurse anesthetist, one surgical tech, one radiological tech, and twelve nurses who worked in the operating rooms or in pre-op and post-op.

"Is your surgical staff here today?"

"No. We generally do consultations on Mondays, procedures on Tuesday, Wednesday, and Thursday. Friday is for recovery."

"Okay. We're going to need to talk to them. All of them. Your cleaning staff, food service, maintenance. Everyone who works here."

"Of course. I can get phone numbers and addresses for you."

"That would be great."

When the doctor left the room, Ryan turned to Adam. "We need to focus on the employees here and also on these three patients."

Adam looked at his phone and his face paled. "Ryan, I sent the three names to Sabrina and she jumped on it."

"And?"

"All three of these men have been reported missing."

The next few hours were a blur of activity. Phone calls, records searches. Requests for warrants were submitted and the judge agreed they had probable cause to search the property of Wyatt Jenkins and bring him in for questioning.

But they were going to have to find him first.

They had officers waiting at his home and the Carrington hospital when they got a hit on a credit card.

He was in Raleigh.

The captain was good friends with a lieutenant in Raleigh. One quick phone call resulted in officers locating Jenkins at a restaurant. He ran through the kitchen, out the back door, and straight into an officer who had his weapon drawn.

Jenkins surrendered on the spot. Two uniformed officers were dispatched to pick him up and return him to Carrington for questioning.

Ryan would have gone to get him, but he knew his time would be better spent in the office. Especially since the Chatham County ME reported the body they'd recovered had had a knee replacement. The missing persons reports on the three plastic surgery patients indicated one of them had surgical scarring around the knee consistent with a knee replacement.

He'd even asked another homicide investigator to go with Dante and his forensics team to process Wyatt Jenkins's house. As much as Ryan wanted to see what sort of evidence they might find, he needed to talk to Wyatt Jenkins now.

Ryan had called Leigh with an update an hour ago. He knew she was sick of being stuck at home, and he hated to disappoint her by telling her he wouldn't be able to come over tonight. But if Wyatt Jenkins was their guy, losing one Friday evening together in exchange for getting her life back would be totally worth it.

23

Ryan took a seat across from Wyatt Jenkins in the small interrogation room.

"I don't know what you think I've done, but I can assure you I am innocent," Wyatt said. "I came willingly."

"After you ran from the police."

"A bunch of cops show up in the middle of my dinner. What was I supposed to do?"

"Oh, I don't know. Go with them?"

"It caught me off guard." Wyatt slouched further into the metal chair. "What do you want to talk to me about anyway?"

Ryan slid the picture of Harold Claussen across the table. "Recognize him?"

"Should I?"

"He was in your operating room a month ago."

Wyatt studied the photo. "What was he having done?"

"Does it matter?"

"Yeah, it matters. I do anesthesia, but the docs do a lot of work on faces. I'm close by, but half the time they've got pen marks all over them, not to mention the masks and oxygen I'm using to keep their airways open. You show me a photo of a guy in a suit and tie and ask me to match him with one of thirty faces I've seen on an operating table in the past month? Don't want much, do you?"

It annoyed him that the guy had a point.

He slid a picture of Leigh across the table. "Recognize her?"

Wyatt looked at the picture longer than Ryan would have liked. "She's pretty."

"That's not what I asked."

Wyatt frowned. "Wait a minute. She's not dead, is she?"

"Who said anything about anyone being dead?"

Wyatt tugged on his ears. "These babies work fine. I know you guys are working on a homicide case." He pointed to the photo of Leigh. "Seriously, has something happened to her? I know her from the Carrington hospital. Friendly. Good NP. The docs love her."

"But you don't know her?"

"Know her well enough to say hi in the hallway, chat about the rain in the break room when I stop in for coffee. But not like I'd strike up a conversation with her if I saw her at the movies or in a store."

"Where were you Saturday night, two weeks ago?"

Wyatt stared at the table. "I don't know. Probably at home?" Ryan waited while Wyatt counted back the days under his breath. "I was off that weekend," he said. "I stayed home."

"Can anyone confirm that you were home?"

Wyatt shook his head. "I live alone. My neighbors might have noticed? But no."

Ryan's phone buzzed. He glanced at it. "Sit tight for a moment."

He found Gabe and Anissa waiting for him in the hallway. "We've got some interesting banking activity for Mr. Jenkins," Anissa said.

"By *interesting*, she means since when does a nurse anesthetist deposit an extra two hundred thousand dollars over the past seventeen months?"

"Any idea where it came from?" Ryan asked.

Anissa pointed to the paper she was holding. "He had a cash deposit of ten grand a month ago."

"When Claussen was killed," Gabe added.

"You think he's taking the cash they don't use for their surgery? Pocketing it and killing them?" Ryan asked.

Anissa shrugged. "I don't know, but the cash deposits started smaller, around two thousand dollars for a couple of months. Nothing that would raise much suspicion. But they've grown over time, and for the past year he's been depositing anywhere from five to twenty grand—in cash—each month."

Gabe clapped his hands together. "Look, he isn't killing off one patient a month. But what if he's taking the cash off these guys and then depositing it slowly, trying not to grab anyone's attention?"

"It's possible," Ryan said.

"Is it enough to hold him?"

"His body size fits the statistics Sabrina gave us for our parking garage stalker."

Ryan's phone buzzed again. He showed the picture to Anissa, then Gabe.

A chain saw with a fresh blade but glowing luminescent from the spray the forensics techs had used to check for blood.

They hadn't told anyone that the ME and the anthropologist agreed the bodies had been dismembered with a chain saw.

"Time to crank things up with Mr. Jenkins," Ryan said. He whispered a prayer before he reentered the interrogation room. *Help me know if he's our guy*, he said. *Help us get the closure we need.*

The door to the interrogation room opened and the frantic face of the young officer he'd left inside poked out. "Somebody help me!"

Ryan rushed inside. Wyatt Jenkins lay on the floor. Ryan knelt beside him. No pulse.

"What happened?"

"I don't know! He was sitting there quietly. Then he reached into his pocket. I told him to keep his hands where I could see them. He . . . he said it was a mint."

The room's surveillance video would corroborate the young officer's story. The real question was how had Wyatt Jenkins been savvy enough to sneak in a poison capsule in his jacket? And what had he done that was bad enough he didn't want to risk going to jail?

Leigh hadn't seen Ryan in over twenty-four hours. The longest she'd gone since this drama began two weeks ago.

Two weeks. How crazy that two weeks ago today he'd knocked on her door, black hair glistening, smiling that smile that made her stomach clench and her palms sweat. That day had been warm for early spring. Sunny.

Today the sky was dark with heavy clouds. The lake had whitecaps as far as she could see. The rain wasn't supposed to stop for another forty-eight hours and the ground was saturated. Most of central North Carolina was under a flood warning.

The knock on the door sent her skipping through the house. She opened it, and once more, Ryan's smile made her stomach somersault.

But instead of standing there, awkward and embarrassed, she slid easily into his waiting arms, relishing the way he held her.

His hands tilted her face up and his lips found hers. Tender and gentle, more a brush than a kiss.

"Hi," he said, still cradling her face in his hands.

She didn't answer. As the rain pounded on the porch roof, she allowed her hands to explore his face, his chin, his hair before pulling him closer. "Hi," she whispered against his lips.

His response left her breathless.

"Let's get you inside," he said.

"Why? It's over."

"It's also raining and cold," he said.

"I'm not cold."

He groaned. "You are a dangerous woman, Leigh Weston." He laughed as he turned her around and prodded her inside the house.

Ryan pulled off his coat and draped it across the chair. He took her hand and drew her into the living room and settled them in the oversized chair. She listened as Ryan explained the events of the previous day, concluding with the dramatic death of Wyatt Jenkins.

"I can't believe he killed himself."

"Me neither. His mannerisms made me think he was too smooth to be innocent, but I wasn't convinced of his guilt either. I guess that's what made him good at it. He was able to fool people into believing he was harmless."

"Right up until the part where he cut their heads off," Leigh said.

"Exactly."

"So it was him?"

"It certainly looks like it."

"You don't sound sure."

"I don't like not being able to ask him what he was up to. Why he did it. How he did it. Where he did it. This case may be solved, but it is far from being resolved. We may have two more bodies out there somewhere. And who knows if they were the only other victims."

She tried to smooth the worried line in his forehead. "You'll find them," she said.

"I hope so."

She snuggled against him and he rested his cheek on her head. With his heartbeat in her ear and his arm around her shoulders, she rode the wave as his chest rose and fell in a sigh. She pulled back to look at his troubled face. "What's wrong?"

"Hmm? Oh, nothing. Thinking."

"About?"

He kissed her forehead. "You."

"Um, I'm not sure I like whatever you were thinking that generated that sigh."

"I'm waiting for you to come to your senses."

"There's nothing wrong with my senses."

"It's been a traumatic couple of weeks."

She pulled back further. "Are you trying to tell me that you've come to your senses?" She tried to brace herself for whatever was coming.

"Leigh. I've been in love with you since high school."

The pronouncement left her speechless.

"You really didn't know?" he asked.

She shook her head.

"You may be the only one. Rebecca knew. I suspect Kirk would have if he'd been willing to consider it. Which he wasn't."

"I'm going to kill him."

"He was trying to protect you."

"From you?"

He shrugged. "I'm not sure eighteen-year-old me was the best thing for fifteen-year-old you."

Leigh would have liked to have found out.

"For that matter, I'm not sure thirty-three-year-old me is right for thirty-year-old you."

Ice flowed through her veins. "What are you talking about?"

"You saw how things were over the past few weeks. An active investigation is all-consuming. How are you going to handle it when I work until midnight or don't come home to do anything other than take a shower and then turn around and go back out? And when I'm home but I'm not because my brain is somewhere else, trying to crawl inside the mind of a killer?"

He reached for her hair and twisted it around his fingers. "I don't want you to regret anything. And I don't want you to ever feel like you don't have a way out."

Why was he saying this? "You think I'm sitting here with you out of gratitude? That I don't . . . that I haven't . . ."

He really didn't know. She thought she'd been obvious, but now that she thought about it, she hadn't. Sure, she'd kissed him, but maybe he didn't realize how sacred that was to her.

He continued to play with her hair, but he was looking at the floor.

"I think I should tell you something."

He tensed.

"It isn't bad."

He looked at her then. "What don't I know?"

His phone buzzed between them. Leigh's phone buzzed on the table.

They both groaned and reached for their phones.

Leigh's eyes widened as she read the text. She looked at Ryan. "I have to go," she said.

"Leigh . . ."

"He's dead. I'm not in danger, and I'm not a danger to anyone else."

He glanced at his phone again. She knew they'd both received the same alert. The county had created a system a few years ago that included all the phone numbers for doctors, nurses, first responders, firefighters, and police officers. A text blast could be sent out in case of a catastrophic event that would call everyone in.

They'd tested it a couple of months ago and it had been a huge success.

This wasn't a test.

"I'll drive you to the hospital," he said. "Please don't leave the emergency department without me."

His worry was seriously misplaced, but she agreed. "I need three minutes." She raced to her room, pulled on scrubs, her jacket, and work shoes.

She was back downstairs in two minutes and found Ryan at the door. "Ready?"

"Let's go."

24

Leigh listened to the police chatter on Ryan's radio as they flew through Carrington's streets.

The details were murky, but the first reports indicated a minivan had hydroplaned on the interstate. It clipped a couple of cars before flipping in the median. On the rain-slicked highway, drivers in cars and trucks across all four lanes hit their brakes in an effort to avoid the disabled vehicles. It might have ended in a massive traffic jam if the eighteen-wheeler that was in the thick of it had been able to come to a stop.

Unfortunately, it had jackknifed across the highway and the number of vehicles involved in this secondary pileup continued to grow.

To make matters worse, there were already reports of three fatalities and every ambulance in the county was transporting the injured to Carrington's hospital. The trauma centers in the surrounding communities had been put on alert and at least three helicopters were trying to reach the victims, but the weather wasn't helping their efforts.

Ryan's job would be to help however he was needed—with

everything from traffic control to taking statements from the victims.

They rolled to a stop at the red light in front of the hospital. "Do you have a raincoat in here?" Leigh asked.

"Are you seriously worried about me getting wet?" His eyes lingered on her neck.

"I'll be safe and sound inside. You'll be outside in this monsoon, with traffic all around you. You'll be in way more danger than I am."

He pulled to a stop in front of the emergency department entrance. "I'll have my phone," he said. "Keep yours handy."

She reached for the handle, but he pulled her back and kissed her. Hungrily. Desperately. His fear bleeding through his touch.

"Please be careful. I can't live without you," he whispered.

His confession froze her in place, but only for a moment.

"You won't have to." She watched as a look of amazement spread across his face.

"Come pick me up when you're done," she said.

She got out of the car and ran inside. As soon as she swiped her badge to enter the department, all thoughts of kisses and love and the future she might have fled.

"Leigh!" Keri shouted from across the hall. "I need some help."

Leigh raced to her friend's side and pressed a compress against a gaping gash on the head of a teenager. "Glad you're here," Keri said. "I've got kids on this side—and their hysterical parents. There's a pregnant lady in four." Out of the patients' line of sight, Keri shook her head in sorrow.

Oh no. Keri was very sensitive to the pregnant mamas, and this one must be in bad shape.

"We've got everything from broken bones and head trauma to whiplash and abrasions."

Leigh looked at the teenager whose head continued to gush blood. "Do you know where your parents are?"

His face fell. "No," he said. "I . . . I don't know what happened."

"Okay," she said. "I'm going to get you patched up, and then I'll help you find them. You stick with me, okay?"

For the next three hours, Leigh didn't have time to think about anything except the patients in her care. The normal time for shift change came and went, but no one came or went. Everyone who could be there was already there and they weren't going anywhere. They'd figure out who was working through the night once things settled—which, based on the number of patients in the waiting room, might not be until tomorrow.

Leigh had never been so proud of the work she did or the people she did it with. Even in the midst of horror and trauma, their teamwork and skills were beautiful to behold. Tonight, the lines between physicians, nurse practitioners, registered nurses, and the various technicians had blurred as they had all done what needed to be done, regardless of whether it was generally in their job description.

She leaned against the wall and pulled her phone from her pocket. She'd send a text to Ryan. Something for him to see when he came up for air. The words poured from her heart and onto the screen.

"Leigh!" A voice called from the last room in the department. "Can you give me a hand?"

"Sure thing."

Love letters would have to wait. She slid the phone into her pocket and dodged people, stretchers, and wheelchairs as she maneuvered down the hall.

"What do you need?" she asked as she entered the room. She stopped inside the doorway. Where was the patient?

All her instincts screamed at her and she reversed her steps. She bumped into someone behind her. "Sorry," she said.

"No problem."

Leigh blinked a few times. Why was everything blurry?

"You don't look so hot," the voice said. "Why don't you have a seat?"

No. She didn't need to sit. She needed to get back to the nurses station. Miss Edna would know who had called her.

Why wouldn't her feet work?

She felt something slam into her. Oh wait. No. She'd run into the wall.

"Come on, now. No need to make this difficult."

Oh no. No. No.

She tried to pull away from the hands that pushed her into the room. At least, she thought it was the room. Was she lying down? Why was she on a bed? Or was she in a chair?

She fought to keep her eyes open. To stay aware of her surroundings. Was it possible Ryan had been wrong? Was the killer not really her stalker? Had it always been two people, not one?

Was she going to die?

25

Ryan pulled into the emergency department loop at two in the morning. He ran inside.

When he found Leigh, he was going to give her a piece of his mind for not answering his calls.

After he kissed her.

Priorities.

The waiting room teemed with people, all of whom looked worse for wear, but not like they were about to die. Based on the way the last eight hours had gone out on the interstate, he could only imagine how crazy things had been here.

The security guard waved him through and he made his way to the nurses station. He leaned over the desk and waited for Miss Edna to look up from the computer screen.

"I see you standing there dripping all over my floor, Investigator Parker," she said. "Do you need anything or are you looking for Leigh?"

He couldn't help but laugh. "I'm looking for Leigh and want to stay out of your way."

"Haven't seen her lately. Sure she's back there somewhere. Go find your girl, but take that soggy jacket off and hang it in the break room first."

"Yes, ma'am."

Ryan hung up the jacket and turned to leave as Keri slipped into the room and slid down the wall, tears streaming. "Keri, are you okay?"

"No." She didn't elaborate. "Please go away."

He was torn. He wanted to help, but he guessed Keri's tears were either a result of a specific patient or a buildup from the stress of the entire evening. She might need a few minutes alone to pull herself together.

Still, it rankled him to leave her there.

"I'm fine, Ryan. Go find Leigh. And no, I don't know where she is. It's been a crazy night."

She wiped her face and leaned her head against the wall.

"Okay," he said. He squeezed her shoulder and earned himself a weak smile.

He walked down one side of the hallway. No Leigh.

Fear twisted in his stomach, but he fought against it. Wyatt Jenkins was gone. His evil couldn't go any further. Leigh wasn't in danger, and overreacting wouldn't be good for their relationship.

Their relationship. He liked the sound of that.

His phone buzzed and his pulse quickened. Maybe—but no. Not Leigh. Gabe.

"Parker."

"Where's Leigh?"

"What do you mean where's Leigh?" Ryan asked.

"I mean have you seen her? Talked to her?"

"Not yet."

"I need you to find her now," Gabe said.

"You're freaking me out, man. What's going on?"

"Wyatt Jenkins wasn't the killer."

Ryan stopped in the middle of the hallway. "What?"

"Adam's been working all day on Wyatt's financials. Sabrina found some common IP address or something. I'm not sure how she did it, but somehow she figured out where the money came from. Wyatt's been selling drugs. Lots of them. And when they followed that trail, they found video footage of him in Raleigh the night Leigh's brakes were cut. He couldn't have done it."

"What about the blood on the chain saw?"

"Animal."

Ryan ran down the hall, bursting through each door. "Have you seen Leigh?" he asked whoever was inside.

Every time, his question was met with the same answer. "No."

"Get Adam to track Leigh's phone," he told Gabe. "I'm on my way to the security office here to see if we can find her in the building."

"On it. I'll call you back." The urgency in Gabe's voice scared him almost as much as anything else. Gabe was worried.

Gabe never worried. About anything.

Ryan ran to the nurses station and didn't bother with the niceties. "Miss Edna, we can't find Leigh. If you see her, please have her call me immediately."

Miss Edna's expression went from annoyed to worried as he spoke.

"You find our girl," she called to him as he ran back down the hall.

It took him two minutes to reach the security office for the hospital system. One of the guards was standing in the doorway. This guy had a deep tan. Must be the guy back from Hawaii. "Miss Edna called us," he said. "She says Leigh's missing. We're pulling up footage from the ED now."

Ryan's eyes burned at the sight of Leigh on the screen minutes after she arrived. She spoke to Miss Edna. Then raced down the hall. They traced her actions in high speed for six hours. At ten-thirteen she leaned against a wall for a moment, the expression on her face a mixture of fatigue and satisfaction.

How he wished he knew what she'd been thinking about.

She pulled her phone out of her pocket and it looked like she was texting someone.

Then she looked up like someone had called her name. She made her way down the hall and entered room 23. She backed out of it within five seconds and bumped into someone. Then she reentered the room.

Five minutes later, a scrub-clad person came out of the room with a stretcher. The body on the stretcher was covered with a blanket.

Leigh did not follow the stretcher.

And over the next thirty minutes, she did not leave that room.

"Go back and follow the stretcher." The security guard switched to a different camera and forwarded it to ten-fifteen.

"There." Ryan pointed to the monitor. Same person pushing the same stretcher.

They followed the stretcher down the hall and into a different room. Fifteen minutes later, the door opened and Leigh emerged in a wheelchair. The person pushing the wheelchair still had on scrubs and a mask, but Leigh appeared to be in street clothes. Her head was drooped, as if she were asleep.

More cameras and angles showed the trek through the hospital and out the opposite side.

"There are a lot of offices on this side of the building," the security guard said. "Not many people use these entrances on the weekends."

His phone buzzed.

"What is it, Gabe?"

"Adam says Leigh's phone last pinged in the area of the hospital, but it's been powered off. He can't find it."

Ryan filled him in on what he had seen on the video footage.

"I'm on my way," Gabe said.

Ryan didn't bother arguing with him. He was too busy watching the screen in silent horror as Leigh was rolled out into the pouring rain and loaded into the back of a minivan. The kidnapper—he refused to think of him as a murderer in this case—folded the wheelchair with quick movements and tossed it into the back of the minivan before running to the driver's side. Within seconds, the van disappeared from view.

"Can you get any sort of read on the license plate?" Ryan asked.

"It's obscured," the guard said. They tried to see it from several angles, but it was caked with dirt. Between the dirt and the heavy rain, they couldn't even tell what state had issued the tag.

The guard turned to him. "I'm sorry," he said. "With everything going on, we've been focused on the ED tonight."

"Yeah. Thanks. We, uh, we're gonna need that footage."

The guard who'd been finding all the correct cameras waved a hand at him. "Already on it. Probably take me an hour, but I'll have it on a flash drive ASAP. Or I can email it somewhere . . ."

"Dr. Sabrina Fleming." Ryan pulled her contact information up on his phone and read off the number. "Ask her how she wants it."

They were going to owe Sabrina a year's salary by the time this was over. He didn't care. He'd pay her out of his own pocket if she could find this van.

He stumbled out of the room.

How? What had they missed? Who was this mystery person in the mask?

He racewalked back to the ED. "Miss Edna, where's Keri?"

"Oh, hon, she went home a little while ago. Lost a patient." She clucked her tongue. "I told her to skedaddle. Things are busy, but not anything we can't handle."

His phone rang again. Sabrina. "Tell me you've got something good," he said.

"I'm sorry, Ryan. Truly. I was trying . . ."

"None of this is your fault. Don't go there." He gave her the description of the van and the time it left the hospital.

"We'll find it," she said.

He walked to room 23. A young patient sat there with his mom. He looked dazed. She looked exhausted. "I'm sorry, do you mind if I look around the room for a moment?"

The poor mom barely had the energy to lift one shoulder in assent. He walked around the room. Nothing obvious. He grabbed the trash cans and slid them out into the hallway. He dumped out the bag with the sheets and bedding. A thud grabbed his attention and he pawed through the pile with no regard to germs and bodily fluids.

Leigh's phone rested at the bottom.

He powered it on. Pulled up her text messages.

She'd been sending one to him . . .

Hey . . . You need to know that I had a crush on you in high school. I used to daydream about you asking me to the prom. Or asking me to the movies. Or dinner. Or even just to walk down to the dock and watch the stars. You may think I'm reacting to the trauma of the past few weeks, but if I had to go through it all again, as long as it brought you to me, it would be worth it. Be safe out there, and quit worrying about whether or not I can handle being with a cop. As long as you're the cop, I can handle it. I lo

The text ended there. Had she been going to say she loved him?

He didn't know how long he stood there, staring at her phone. At some point, he heard Gabe calling his name. When he looked up, Gabe came straight for him and pulled him into a bear hug. "We're gonna find her, man. I've got everyone on it. We'll get her back."

Leigh woke with a pounding headache and a kink in her neck that she worried might never be straightened out.

At least she was alive.

The relief lasted the three seconds it took her brain to remember what the killer had done to his victims.

Maybe she'd have been better off dead.

She blinked her eyes. Nothing. Either she'd gone blind or the room was black as pitch. At this point, it didn't matter. One way or the other, she couldn't see a thing.

She assessed her environment as much as she could. She was lying on her side on something hard. Probably the floor. She couldn't move her hands much. With every movement of her arms, the ties that bound her wrists dug further into her skin. Her ankles were bound as well, but she was able to swing them forward. Nothing that way either. At least she wasn't in danger of plunging to her death if she moved too far in one direction or the other.

It was chilly, but not frigid. A mustiness and earthiness permeated the air. Was she underground?

She gritted her teeth against the pain, stretched her hands out, and rolled back onto them. Wood. She might be underground, but she wasn't lying on dirt. Maybe a cellar of some kind?

She had no idea how long she'd been unconscious. She pulled at the threads of her memory, but all she could snatch was a masked face and flashes of the hospital hallways as she'd been pushed in a wheelchair. She strained to recall leaving the hospital but couldn't drag anything from her subconscious.

If it was still nighttime, that might explain the total darkness of her dungeon. And the silence. What she wouldn't give for the blissful white noise of her ceiling fan, the whir of the dishwasher, the hum of the furnace.

She couldn't think about heat. Or soft beds. Neither of those things would help her right now. Although if she survived to experience them again, she would never take them for granted.

She assessed her physical condition next. She would have welcomed a heated blanket, but she wasn't so cold she feared hypothermia. Yet. And while her body ached, no particular sensation made her suspect she had a broken bone.

She could breathe. Definitely a positive.

She could swallow. Wiggle her fingers. Toes. She could feel the surface underneath her, so she hadn't lost total feeling in any of her extremities. Although every one of her limbs felt like it weighed one hundred pounds each, she could move them if she concentrated. All good signs. And the heaviness should lift as the drug continued to wear off.

She was hungry, but not ravenous. That could be a leftover effect from whatever drug she'd been given to knock her out, but it could also mean it hadn't been that long since she'd been taken.

Had anyone even noticed her absence?

On a normal night they would. But tonight? Assuming it was still tonight. Regardless, this night hadn't been in the same hemisphere as normal. It had been without a doubt the worst night she'd ever had since going to work in the emergency department—and that was *before* some lunatic made off with her.

She'd held off as long as she could, but now she allowed Ryan's image to flood her mind. He'd been there all along, on the edge of every thought, but she'd refused to allow him to take his accustomed spot—front and center.

But he took it now. His strong chin. His five o'clock shadow that made an appearance by three every day. His black wavy hair. His dark brown eyes. Eyes she had hoped to be lost in for the rest of her life.

She allowed herself to venture into territory they hadn't explored yet. She knew he was the only one for her. He always had been. Every guy she'd ever dated had failed to measure up because each one had been in competition with the man of her dreams.

And when he moved from the dream world to reality, he'd been even better than she'd imagined.

He would be frantic when he realized what had happened.

And losing her . . . it would consume him. He would take responsibility for it. He would blame himself, and it would destroy him.

Oh, he would fight it. He would try. For Rebecca. For Caleb and Zoe. But his life would never be the same. He'd spend all his free time trying to find her body. A body that was probably going to lose its head, hands, and feet at any moment.

Father, please. Please help him. Help him know it wasn't his fault. That I don't blame him. That no one should blame him.

She lay there until the pain in her arms drove her to risk sitting. Her head continued to clear. The fog from whatever that drug was dissipated and with it went her acceptance of her impending doom.

"No." Her voice was rough and scratchy. The word came out more whisper than defiant battle cry.

But that's what it was.

She would not sit here and wait for this madman to take her. She had no idea what she'd ever done to make him come after her, but he was going to have to work a lot harder than this if he wanted to dump her body in an unmarked grave.

26

Ryan finally agreed to return to the sheriff's office after they'd interviewed everyone on the clock that night. All were accounted for. There was nothing left to do but look at the entire case in light of this new evidence.

Gabe followed him, headlights shimmering in the rain that continued to fall. He knew Gabe was following him to be sure he went straight to the office and didn't go do something rash.

But what else could he do?

Their only suspect was dead, and as it turned out, he wasn't their killer after all.

His windshield wipers slammed back and forth in a violent rhythm, struggling to keep the water off the glass. He pounded his hands on the steering wheel.

"Why?" he yelled as loud as he could. No one could hear him.

Maybe there was someone who could.

No. He knew he could. But would he listen? Would he act?

"Help me!" He screamed the words. "Please. Help me find her."

He knew other people were praying. Rebecca was praying. Half the church had probably already been pulled from their slumber with the call to storm heaven with prayers.

His prayers probably wouldn't make much difference. They were barely even prayers. More like the frantic cries of a desperate man.

Although the apostle Peter hadn't minced words. When he had gone walking on the water and then had started to drown, he'd called out, "Save me."

And what was it Jesus had said to him? "O ye of little faith."

"God," he whispered, "it's hard to have faith when people are so . . . so . . . bad."

Although Jesus did say he'd come to save the sick. That the well didn't need a physician. All those bad people . . . he'd come for them.

He'd come for the Clay Fowlers of the world. For the Wyatt Jenkinses.

And for the Ryan Parkers. The guys who didn't like the way God played the game, so they got mad, took their ball, and went home.

"I don't understand," he said. No yelling or screaming this time. A statement of fact. None of this made any sense.

He pulled into the parking garage beside the sheriff's office. Gabe parked beside him.

Help us. He put the prayer on repeat in his mind as he braced himself for what he would find when he got inside. *Help us.*

The homicide office had been turned into the command center for the search for Leigh Weston. Whiteboards, files, and laptops were everywhere. Sabrina had taken up three desks. Adam had moved to the desk beside her.

Like Cinderella after the clock struck twelve, Sabrina had returned to her typical attire of sweatshirts and skinny jeans. But it wasn't the attire that startled Ryan.

Sabrina was a mess. She looked up when he came in, swollen-eyed and shoving a collection of used tissues into a trash can.

"I'm sorry, Ryan." She tried, without success, to stifle a sob. "I missed something. But I'm going to find this beast." Her lips flattened into a tight line and she yanked a fresh tissue from the box with so much force the box flew across the desk.

Anissa wasn't in much better shape. No tears or sobbing, but her glacial demeanor was almost as terrifying as Sabrina's breakdown.

"We've called everyone in," she said. "The captain's approved all the overtime we need. I've got our best video guy combing all the security footage at the hospital. He's trying to find the masked person on the tape. Hasn't had any luck yet, but if anyone can find it, he will."

Best guy? The best person for the job was sitting in the room with them. Ryan cut his eyes over at Sabrina and Anissa shook her head.

"No." She waved him closer and whispered. "I'm not sure what she's doing over there. I'm not even completely sure it's legal. She said she had an idea and she's running with it. I'm not about to tell her no or try to divert her."

Ryan looked at Sabrina. If looks could kill, her computer screen would be going up in flames right now.

"Agreed."

The captain came in and took in the scene. "Parker, whatever you need, it's yours."

The captain had already filmed a spot that had aired in the wee hours of the morning and would re-air on all the local and regional news affiliates' morning shows. He'd explained about Leigh's disappearance and requested anyone who'd seen anything suspicious to call.

"We're already getting calls on the tip line," he said. "I'd say they are ninety-nine percent junk, but we're following up on everything."

"Thank you, sir."

"We'll find her," he said. He glanced around the room and his gaze lingered on Sabrina for an extra beat. He shook his head and held up his hands in a gesture that said, "I don't even want to know what you're doing, just do it."

He closed the door and the room went silent as all eyes turned to Ryan.

"All right, everyone," Ryan said. "Let's find her."

The longer she sat, the clearer things became. Leigh strained to hear anything beyond the thumping of her own heart or the whooshing of each breath.

What was that?

She held her breath as the sound grew from a few taps to a roar.

Rain.

Lots of rain.

Would the rain keep her captor away? Or bring him back sooner?

While she welcomed the distraction from the heavy silence, the downpour would keep her from hearing anyone approaching.

Not that she could do anything about it if they came. She needed to figure out the situation she was in. And she wasn't going to be able to do that tied up like this.

She tried to modulate her breathing. She knew the drug was fading from her system because as it went, it took the heaviness with it. But even as she could feel her strength returning, the throbbing misery the drugs had dampened now had full rein. With every movement of her wrists, pain ricocheted through her body. Every twitch of her ankles was agony.

Even when she didn't move, everything ached.

She had an idea. It would hurt. But it might work. All those years of gymnastics and yoga might come in handy after all.

She eased onto her back and whispered a prayer as pain splintered her focus. She would have to rest all her weight on her arms, but if she didn't pass out, she might be able to pull her legs through her bound arms. With her arms in front of her, she'd have a chance to break free. And even if she couldn't get loose, at least she could maneuver around. Maybe even find a way out.

She took a deep breath and let it out. As she did, she lowered her body onto her wrists and curled at the waist. Her shoulders screamed at the strain and there was the unmistakable sensation of skin shredding on her wrists as she forced her backside to the floor and her wrists up.

She cried out as she pulled her legs through, the tears she'd been fighting against spilling down her face.

She lay there, gasping.

Thank you, Lord.

The light came out of nowhere. She turned away and tried to shield her eyes with her arm.

"Oh. You're awake. Sorry about that. You shouldn't be."

Before she could find the source of the light or the voice, a prick of pain in her neck.

"Why?" she asked.

"I am sorry. But you know too much. I knew it the moment I saw you on the news, talking to that cop. It's really a shame they had to find him so close to your house. If I'd had any idea that's where you lived, I'd have dumped him somewhere else. We had just talked a few weeks earlier about my other job, and I knew you could tie me to that sorry piece of garbage."

So she'd talked to this person before now? How could she have been that close and not have realized she was in the presence of such evil?

"Don't worry. I won't make you suffer. Not like the others. You're innocent in all this, but my work is too important. I can't let you ruin it."

"What work?" Leigh asked. "I honestly have no idea what you're talking about. I have nothing to tell." Was her speech slurred? She fought to open her eyes, but she couldn't. It was as if she'd fallen into a black hole. The gravitational force that held her to the earth's surface had multiplied a hundredfold and threatened to flatten her.

"You had a pretty nice life, didn't you? Nice parents. Nice home.

I can assure you, it was nothing like mine. Dad found a younger woman and split. Mom and I had nothing, and did he care? Nope."

Something about the voice was familiar.

But Leigh was losing the fight with the drugs. She'd be out soon. This voice might be the last thing she heard.

"I know how these men are. Leaving their families to struggle as they go on and live the high life. They don't deserve to breathe. And their families are so much better off with them gone. These men don't even have the decency to be ashamed. They come in to the clinic and brag about their plans to bail on their families. Or about how many mistresses they have. Sometimes I'm able to take them out before they have a chance to hurt their children. Sometimes I'm too late, but I can stop them from making it worse. I do my best. It's my mission to keep them from doing the same things to their families that were done to mine.

"I'm not a killer, Leigh. I'm an avenging angel."

None of this made sense. Maybe it never would.

27

Ryan glanced at his watch—4 a.m.

Leigh had been gone almost six hours. Was she scared? Was she hurting?

He refused to allow himself to consider the possibility that she was already . . . no. He wouldn't even think the word.

He glanced around the homicide office. Everyone was focused on one goal.

Getting Leigh back.

Alive.

"Sabrina," he said.

"Yes, sir," she said, her voice wavering but determined.

"I'm not sure what you're up to over there, but I want images of every single employee Oraios has. From the grounds crew to the surgeons. We're missing something. There has to be someone else there who was behind this. Can you get those files to someone who can—"

"I can get it." Adam raised his hand. "Give me five minutes."

"Great."

"Anissa." He searched the room until he found her standing at her desk. Everything about her radiated fury. "This one may be trickier and I'm not sure how you could get this, but I'm thinking we should start with patients who have come through the emergency department but were admitted and won't be released for a few days."

"What are you looking for?"

"We know Mr. Staton was dumped while Mr. Cook was in the hospital. We know Mr. Claussen was dumped while Mr. Gordon was in the hospital. In both cases, they went to the emergency department and were then admitted. And in both cases, it would have been obvious to anyone working on them that they were going to be staying at the hospital for more than an overnight visit. Maybe talk to Miss Edna. We can't violate privacy laws, but we don't need to know their diagnosis or any details other than that they are in the hospital and won't be going home for a few days."

"On it."

"Oh," he said. "Check tonight's trauma victims first. We're looking for homes that will be vacant, so people who live alone will get our top priority."

Anissa already had the phone in one hand and her keys in the other. "I'm going to the hospital. I think things will go easier in person."

"Fine."

She paused as she walked past him. "We'll find her, Ryan." She patted his arm and then sprinted out the door.

"Gabe, get those guys"—he pointed to a group of volunteers standing in the corner, Pete Stanfield among them—"and have them pull death certificates. If someone died at the hospital and their place is empty, our killer may know. Have another group pull—"

Ryan's words froze on his tongue as the flat-screen TV at the end of the room filled with images. "Adam, do all these people work at Oraios?"

"Yep."

He walked to the screen. It couldn't be. "Who is this?" He

pointed to a large woman with the name "Vanessa Smith" underneath it.

When Adam didn't respond, he turned around. Adam had a confused look on his face. "Vanessa Smith? Let me do some checking."

Ryan had seen her before. Where, he couldn't be sure. But he'd seen her.

"Send her picture to Anissa's phone. Have her ask Miss Edna who she is."

Gabe joined him by the TV. "What is it?"

"Do you recognize her?"

"No. Should I?"

"I've seen her," Ryan said. "I think at the hospital. This says she's a surgical tech. Maybe I saw her when Leigh came in after her brake line was cut?"

"You could have seen her in the emergency department. Or the hospital halls. Pretty much anywhere," Gabe said.

"Adam—anything on Vanessa Smith?"

"Not yet," he said.

"Really?" Adam was a whiz at this stuff. What was taking so long?

"Yes, really." Adam lifted his head long enough to glare at them before he went back to the computer. "She exists. There's a driver's license and a social security number. And a surgical tech license. But I don't think they're real . . ."

His voice trailed off and Ryan bit back the urge to pester him for more. It was clear he was hunting something, and he'd be able to work faster if Ryan could wait.

But every second put Leigh in greater jeopardy.

Ten minutes later, Adam hadn't given him an answer on Vanessa Smith, but he kept typing and clicking and Ryan resisted the urge to stand behind him. That wouldn't help.

Ryan's phone rang. Anissa.

"Whatcha got?"

"That picture you sent. Miss Edna says that is Alice Grady."

Ryan groaned. There were about a million people with the name Grady in central North Carolina.

Anissa kept talking. "She's a surgical tech. Works one weekend a month. But Miss Edna says she has dark brown hair, not red, like in the picture."

"Adam," Ryan called across the room. "Vanessa Smith is Alice Grady. And Alice Grady has brown hair." Adam gave him a thumbs-up.

"Hey, Ryan," Anissa said. "Miss Edna says Alice worked last weekend. I'm going to try to find out who came in last weekend who might still be here."

"Great. Call me back."

He hit the end button as a new image popped up on the TV.

He knew where he'd seen her before. Random facts started to fall into place in his mind. He made his way through the crowded room to the desk Sabrina was sitting at. "Sabrina, this woman is at least five foot ten. She's not fat, but she's not a string bean either. Could she be the image on our parking garage footage?"

Gabe had followed him. "You think she's our killer? A female serial killer?"

The room went silent.

Sabrina bit her lip. "Her size works."

"What makes you think it's her?" Gabe said.

"Because she brought Leigh the tray of food that had the poisoned gelatin."

"The gelatin that got Pete?" one of the uniformed officers asked.

"Yes," Ryan said.

All eyes in the room flashed to Pete. Pete stared at the screen, mouth set. "That's her," he said.

Ryan pointed to the screen. "Everybody stop what you're doing. We need to find out everything we can about Alice Grady or Vanessa

Smith. Where was she born? Does she have family in the area? Does she work anywhere else? Where does she live? Nothing is too insignificant."

The room exploded in a frenzy of activity.

Father, help us. Help us see the clues we need to find Leigh. Alive.

28

Was she dead?

Leigh took a breath. So not dead . . . yet.

She tried to move, but for all the success she had she might as well have been encased in cement.

Had she been buried alive?

She forced her eyes open. Still dark. Had she been out an entire day and then into the night?

No. It wasn't quite as dark as before and the rain was still falling. The forecast had called for rain all weekend. Was it still Sunday?

She managed to get her fingers to twitch. They scraped across a wooden surface and she found it strangely comforting.

Not buried alive.

She was almost certain she hadn't been moved. Her arms were still in front of her and she was thankful for the small mercy of that.

She lay there as the drugs, once again, cleared her system. She was prepared for the pain to increase, even welcomed it in a perverse way. The more she hurt, the more she was regaining control over her extremities and the closer she came to being able to move.

Because she was going to move.

She counted to fifty in her head and tried to move her legs. Then to one hundred and tried again.

She got to seven hundred before she made any significant progress.

Somewhere around three thousand, she was able to sit up. Her head spun and her stomach twisted with nausea.

She closed her eyes and took deep breaths. She needed to keep moving. There'd been no warning at all when her captor had returned last time. She couldn't count on there being any warning this time.

Why she was still alive was a mystery. Maybe it had something to do with the fact that this crazy person was sorry for what was about to happen. She'd heard a hint of insanity in her captor's rambling before she passed out. And something about the voice teased a memory. She tried to pull it to the front of her thoughts, but it refused to cooperate.

She didn't have time to worry about why she was here. Not now. There'd be time enough for that when she was safe and sound in her own house.

Right now she needed to figure out how to get out of this place. She lifted her throbbing wrists to her lips and used her mouth to explore her bonds. Zip ties. Awesome.

She reached down to her ankles. More zip ties. Too snug for her to be able to walk.

She scooted forward like a caterpillar, stretching her legs out, then tightening her abs and pulling her body toward her feet. Each time shock waves raced through her arms. It took five scoots before her legs reached a vertical surface.

She reached forward with her hands. A wall of rough wood planks. Had she moved toward the back or the front of her dungeon? She despaired at the idea of going the long way, but she had no way to know until she tried. She twisted around until her right arm and leg were against the wall. This time it took twelve scoots to find a corner.

She took a moment to catch her breath, then stretched her back and shoulders as much as she could.

Something brushed against her hair and she choked back a scream. She reached up.

And touched more wood?

This didn't make sense. She rolled over to her knees and slammed her forehead into something very hard.

What was that? She reached again.

Shelves! She was probably in a cellar. Her grandparents had had one. By the time she came along, they no longer used it for food storage. Grandpa used it to store fertilizer and garden tools. But there had been shelves along three sides.

She gritted her teeth and scraped the zip tie that bound her wrists along the edge of the shelf. She didn't want to think about the damage she was doing to her arms, but then again, she didn't want to think about the damage her captor intended to do to her arms if she was still here when he returned.

Was she making any progress at all? She pulled her wrists back to her lips. Yes! She was close.

The hope of freedom spurred her on and she attacked the ties with renewed fervor.

They split apart with so much force she slammed her right hand into the shelf—but, oh, the bliss. She'd never take her arms and shoulders for granted again.

Now for the ankles. She sat on her backside and lifted her bound ankles to the shelf. It was much harder to keep them angled correctly, but she finally cut through the zip tie binding them too.

Her wrists and ankles oozed blood, but she could move them. She held on to the shelf for support, and stood. Then, still holding the shelf like a lifeline, she made her way around her cell.

When the shelf ended, she ran her hands along the walls, then traced the flooring with her foot.

Steps.

Thank you, Lord.

She crept up the stairs like a toddler, hands on the stairs ahead of her. Five steps up, her hands found the door.

Could she open it?

Was it locked? Was her captor waiting on the other side?

Did she have a choice? She had to try.

She reached for the door and pushed.

29

10 A.M.

Twelve hours and counting.

Everyone was working. Everyone was looking. The security office at the hospital had found footage of Alice Grady/Vanessa Smith entering a room and coming out two minutes later. Or they assumed it was her. The person who exited the room wore gloves and a protective gown and mask. The same garb Leigh's abductor had been wearing. They weren't surprised, but it did confirm what they had suspected.

That was about the only real information they had, unless you considered ruling things out progress. They'd sent patrol officers to five possible locations based on Anissa's findings at the hospital, but they'd come up empty.

Ryan's phone rang again. Anissa.

"What do you have?" He hated the defeat he heard in his own voice.

"A possibility. Did you ever meet Mrs. Claire Edwards?"

"The name is familiar. Can't place her. Who is she?"

"She taught half of Carrington County how to read. Retired from the school system in her seventies. Her husband died last year. Kids are local."

"I'm guessing she's in the hospital?"

"Hospice, actually."

"Oh. I'm sorry to hear that." He paused for what he hoped was an acceptable amount of time after hearing that someone was about to depart this world, and then he asked, "What's the connection to Alice Grady?"

"One of Mrs. Edwards's great-granddaughters came in last weekend. Appendectomy. The little girl's mom and grandmother were a wreck because Mrs. Edwards had taken a turn for the worse and they were trying to juggle being at the hospital with the girl and moving Mrs. Edwards into the hospice house."

"How'd you get all this?"

"Miss Edna. Poor woman hasn't gone home. She's been helping me run down leads. With this one, she said she didn't feel like it was a violation of privacy for her to tell me about it because everyone was talking about it in the waiting room last weekend.

"Half the town knows Mrs. Edwards and people were asking about her. Miss Edna made a call and found out Mrs. Edwards is still hanging on, but they've called the family in."

"I'm still not following you on this," Ryan said.

"Mrs. Edwards lives out near the old dairy," Anissa said. "On fifty acres in a 150-year-old house that has been empty since they moved her into the hospice house."

Now he was following her. "We'll check it out."

"I'm going to stay here and keep digging. I don't want to risk this being a rabbit trail."

"Agreed. Thank you."

Ryan explained Anissa's theory to the rest of the team.

Adam grabbed his phone. "I can get us permission to be on the property," he said. "Give me a minute."

They didn't necessarily need a warrant, given the circumstances, but it never hurt to get permission from the family.

Sabrina leaned back from her computer. "Gotcha."

The hair on Ryan's neck stood on end at the intensity of Sabrina's word.

"Sabrina?"

She held up a finger as Adam returned with a grim smile on his face. "Mrs. Edwards and my grandmother were friends," he said. "I talked to one of her sons. He said no one is out there and if we find anyone, to arrest them for trespassing."

He looked at Sabrina, then Ryan, then Gabe. "Did I miss something?"

Ryan nodded toward Sabrina.

"Vanessa Smith and Alice Grady are the same person," Sabrina said. "But neither of those are her real name. And they aren't the only fake names she's used. Her real name is Janine Liddle. Born in 1963 in Jackson, Mississippi."

Sabrina didn't even look at the screen as she spoke. "It will take me a while to be sure I've got it all figured out, but now that I know what I'm looking for, she's mine."

Sabrina wielded her laptop like a medieval knight wielded a sword. Fearless and deadly.

"Here's the part you need to know most. I've tracked her to three different locations so far."

She bit the side of her lip. "Normally I wouldn't share this information yet. I don't like to accuse anyone of something unless I'm one hundred percent sure. And I'm not sure. I might be wrong about this."

"I won't hold you to it. What are you thinking?" Ryan asked.

"I did some checking. Her previous employers have all been private plastic surgery clinics. Not all of them with the same level of security protocols Oraios has, but still the kinds of places people go who don't want to advertise they're having work done."

"Okay. So she specializes . . ."

"Yeah, but that's not what I'm getting at. I made a few calls, explaining the situation and asking if they could check their records for clients who had failed to show up for appointments. Particularly regular clients who they had an established relationship with."

"And?"

"The third one just called me back. All three of them have at least two. One location has four."

"You think . . . ?"

Sabrina pulled her glasses off and rubbed her eyes. "It's conceivable this is a coincidence, but the odds go down with each person. In my professional opinion, the data indicates that it's possible Janine Liddle has been killing for years."

Fresh terror swept through Ryan.

Leigh was in the hands of a true psychopath.

Gabe grabbed his keys and the rain jackets from their desks and brought one to Ryan. "Let's go check out Mrs. Edwards's place."

"Take backup," Sabrina said.

"I'll get it for you," Adam said. "Go."

Ryan couldn't seem to get his feet to move. Gabe grabbed his elbow and tugged. It snapped him into motion and they jogged for the car.

30

The door didn't budge.

Leigh tried again, pushing with all the strength she had left. It moved a few inches. Murky light filtered in, along with massive raindrops.

The door must be stuck in the mud. She shoved again and got a few more inches.

One more shove and the door moved enough that she thought she could slide through it.

"Help me, Lord," she whispered. Whatever was on the other side of this door couldn't be worse than what was coming for her.

As soon as she was through the door, she took off running. She could just make out a tree line through the deluge. Her legs quivered with exertion. She hadn't had food or water in who knew how long. She'd been drugged. Twice.

Her body wasn't going to be able to take much more.

With every step the trees seemed to move farther away. Was she hallucinating? Had all of it been a dream within a nightmare?

She pressed on. Slipped. She tried to brace herself as she fell, but her poor arms were no use. She crashed to the ground and the air whooshed from her lungs.

She lay there gasping.

And through the rain, flickers of light filtered toward her.

It took her exhausted brain longer than it should have to realize what she was seeing.

Headlights.

She lay in the weeds and the muck as the SUV came within fifty feet of her and continued toward the cellar. She tried to look behind her. She'd made more progress than she'd realized.

The rain increased in intensity and she lost sight of the SUV completely. Seizing her opportunity, she scrambled to her feet, and crouching low, fled toward the trees.

With every step she expected to hear a cry. Or a gunshot.

But nothing came. She reached the first tree and pressed her body against it, out of view of the cellar.

She counted to thirty and dashed to a tree twenty feet farther into the wooded area.

If her captor had any sense at all, he would look for her here. She had to keep moving.

This rain might be the only thing keeping her alive and she couldn't squander the opportunity. She dashed from tree to tree, farther and farther into the woods.

31

Gabe insisted on driving, which, Ryan had to admit, was for the best.

As they flew through the downpour to the outskirts of town, Adam emailed him the most recent tax assessment of the Edwardses' property. It showed the house, outbuildings, pasture, and wooded acreage.

"This place is huge." Ryan described it to Gabe. "It looks like there are two driveways, and the far side of the property borders Davis Road."

He glanced at Gabe. "How do you feel about hiking in the rain?"

Gabe didn't look in his direction, but his hands flexed on the wheel. "I thought you'd never ask."

"I'm afraid if we approach on either driveway, we may alert her. But if we park on Davis, we can hike through the woods and be on the side of the property where the barn and outbuildings are."

"And we know she has a fondness for outbuildings," Gabe said.

"Right."

He called Adam and passed along the plan. "We don't want people coming in here with sirens blaring," Ryan said. "I don't want to force her hand."

For a brief second, the thought of what they might find when they searched the property threatened to overcome him, but he forced it away. "We go in assuming Leigh is alive and in mortal danger."

It took another ten minutes, even with Gabe's lunatic driving, to reach the edge of the Edwardses' property. They had donned bulletproof vests and tactical gear before they left the sheriff's office. With the prospect of hiking through the woods ahead of them, they left their rain jackets in the SUV in favor of draping huge ponchos over themselves. Not so much to stay dry, but to protect their weapons.

"Ready?" Gabe had to yell to be heard over the rain.

They climbed from the SUV and moved into the woods.

With their eyes alert and searching always, they moved as quickly as they could. According to the map, they'd have to walk at least a half mile in the woods before they'd reach the barn and pasture.

Gabe led the way, compass in hand. Ryan followed. He wanted to focus more on their surroundings than on the direction they were headed.

It took fifteen interminable minutes before they could see an opening in the trees. He and Gabe slowed their approach and scanned the area.

"Is that an SUV?" He strained to see through the rain. He tapped Gabe on the shoulder and pointed to his right. "Over there? Near the barn?"

The last they'd seen of Janine Liddle, she'd been loading Leigh into a minivan. But a minivan might get stuck out here in these wet fields. Maybe she'd needed to go with something more robust.

The SUV continued toward them, then stopped near a low rise fifty feet from the house. From this distance, he couldn't tell what it was. A well house? Or maybe a cellar?

The driver, draped in a poncho that looked like the ones professional football players wear on the sidelines during games, jumped out of the car. It might be Janine Liddle, but he couldn't be sure.

If it was her and she was going into that little building, there was a good chance Leigh was in there. But they wouldn't be able to get to the building without being seen.

And when they did get there, they wouldn't be able to get inside without alerting Janine. In a tiny space like that, she'd have the advantage.

But what if she was going in there to kill Leigh now?

He leaned close to Gabe's ear. "I have to get over there," he said. "Cover me."

Gabe pulled out his service weapon in response.

But before Ryan could step from the cover of the trees, the hooded figure emerged from the building. She stopped a few feet from the SUV and turned in a circle before running straight toward them, brandishing a handgun.

They slid behind the trees.

"Let's see if we can come in behind her," Ryan said. Gabe nodded and they watched.

"Leigh! Where are you?" Janine's voice carried to them on the wind. "You can't have gone far. I promise I won't make you suffer, but I can't be stopped. My work is too important."

Leigh! She'd escaped! She might even be in the woods now. Ryan was thankful for the rain soaking his face as he processed the news.

Thank you. Thank you. Thank you. Help us end this. Help me find her.

Ryan recognized the voice even though he couldn't see her face. Definitely the same woman from the hospital. "That's her," he mouthed to Gabe.

Gabe showed him the text he was typing.

> Believe Leigh Weston alive. Escaped. Janine Liddle aka Alice Grady is abductor. Onsite. Send ambulance. Have backup surround property but do not approach.

Seeing the words *Leigh Weston alive* sent a chill down Ryan's spine. They were close.

A crack against Ryan's arm made him turn to the side. What was that? He tried to scan the area to his right while keeping Janine in his sights.

Then something hit him on the head.

He turned all the way around.

Leigh!

32

Leigh stood still, arms up, as Ryan turned toward her, his weapon drawn.

She hadn't known how else to get his attention without drawing unwanted attention to herself. When Kirk got home, she'd have to thank him for all those afternoons he'd begged her to play catch with him. It had been years since she'd tried to throw a baseball, but her acorn aim was on point.

She dropped the acorn from her hand and saw the recognition on Ryan's face. The joy. The relief. The love. All mingled together. He lowered his weapon and nudged Gabe, who turned.

Gabe winked at her but immediately turned back to where her abductor was lumbering around in the woods.

Ryan motioned for Leigh to get down, so she tried to hide herself behind some brush while still keeping an eye on Ryan and the dark figure stalking her.

She watched as Gabe pulled out his phone and sent someone a text. Then he and Ryan conferred in mouthed words and hand signals. Gabe moved to a position that would block the killer from returning to the SUV. Ryan moved to a position that would block the killer from her.

"Janine Liddle." Ryan's voice rang out in the lessening rain.

Janine Liddle? Who was that?

"Janine, we know what you've done," he continued. "We know you've used the name Alice Grady and many others over the years. We know you've killed many people. You won't get out of here, and you won't get away with this. It's over."

A maniacal laugh floated toward her. "No one can stop me."

Now Leigh recognized the voice. Alice Grady! How was this possible? But there was no question it was her. Leigh would have to blame the drug-induced haze for her inability to recognize Alice's voice before now. Alice spoke in a pitch low enough that she sounded more like a man than a woman.

So many things became clear. Alice had been the one who'd brought the poisoned gelatin. She hadn't recognized her that day and wouldn't have expected her to bring a meal tray anyway. Alice had probably been counting on that. And that's why she hadn't recognized her voice in the cellar—she was thinking her captor was a man and never imagined it could be the same surgical tech she'd chatted with briefly over coffee a few months ago. As far as she could remember, that was the only time they'd had any contact. Alice had been friendly enough. Maybe a little awkward, but Leigh still couldn't wrap her mind around how it was possible for Alice to be a serial killer.

And her name wasn't even Alice. What name had Ryan called her? Janine? Was that even her real name?

Leigh quit trying to figure it out and focused on praying. *Father, please help us all get out of this alive.*

When dealing with a sane woman, there'd be some hope they could get her to surrender, but this woman was crazy. Her responses couldn't be counted on to be logical or rational. Leigh hoped Ryan and Gabe understood that. The next sound that reached her through the rain was of crashing branches. Was she running away?

"Stop, Janine!"

Gabe and Ryan followed her as she ran. Leigh lost sight of them, but when she tried to follow, her legs buckled.

She waited. Listening. Straining to hear anything over the rain.

Three sharp cracks pierced the air.

Ryan ran toward the spot where Janine had fallen. They'd chased her out of the woods and right into the waiting line of officers. When she refused to stop, they'd stopped her.

Blood seeped into the ground beneath her. Her empty eyes stared into the rain.

No matter how many times he saw death up close and personal, he never got used to it. He prayed he never would.

Gabe clapped him on the shoulder. "I'll take care of this," he said. "Go get Leigh."

Ryan didn't argue. He ran back through the woods, retracing his steps.

She was sitting where he'd left her. Face ashen. Eyes closed.

"Leigh!"

Her eyes fluttered open and she smiled. Then her head dropped forward and she slid to the ground.

"Leigh!"

He grabbed his phone and called Gabe. "Send the ambulance around to the house."

He scooped her into his arms and carried her out of the woods. Her skin was cool, too cool. Dark circles ringed her eyes. Her wrists were shredded and bloodied, and his stomach heaved at the sight of her torn skin and the thought of the terror that had driven her to the desperate measures she'd taken to free herself.

The ambulance tires crackled over the gravel drive and a blonde EMT jumped from the still moving vehicle. She rushed toward him. "Is she okay?"

She studied Leigh with an experienced eye, but when her eyes landed on Leigh's wrists, she gasped.

"Please tell me you got the monster," she said as her partner opened the back of the ambulance.

"We did."

33

Ryan sat beside Leigh's hospital bed. Her bandaged wrists and the heavy layers of blankets a testament to her ordeal. She'd been conscious and demanding answers by the time they had made it to the hospital. He'd explained the Janine Liddle/Alice Grady connection. She'd filled him in on the bizarre comments Janine had made to her about being an avenging angel.

He'd passed the information along to Anissa. She could run with the case for now. He'd refused to leave Leigh's side in the emergency department and had set himself up as her personal guardian now that she was in a room. How else would she get any rest in this zoo?

Why wouldn't everyone leave them alone? Miss Edna had been one of the first to take the ride to the fourth floor to check on Leigh's progress.

"Young man, I expect her back at work and in top-notch condition as soon as possible. You hear me?" Miss Edna had peered at him over her reading glasses and he'd had no choice but to nod and stammer, "Yes, ma'am. I will, ma'am."

After Miss Edna had left, a steady stream of nurses, doctors, and random acquaintances had come by. All with a quick tap to the door, a head poked in, a whispered, "How's she doing?" and then a "Tell her I stopped by when she wakes up" before they disappeared.

He'd run Keri out of here twice in the past forty-five minutes with a solemn promise that he would text her as soon as Leigh woke and wanted company. She'd been on the verge of a panic attack when they brought Leigh in, and nothing he'd said had been able to convince her that Leigh's abduction wasn't somehow her fault.

He knew Leigh would appreciate the outpouring of affection when he told her about it. But he was counting the minutes until they were back at her house, cozy on the sofa, feet propped up on the coffee table, view of the lake in the distance.

Alone.

Another tap on the door. He bit back a growl as he pulled the silver handle toward him.

"Ryan!"

"Kirk!"

Kirk marched into the room like he belonged there. Which, of course, he did. He stood by Leigh's side, and a shudder rippled through him. "Thank you," he said. "Thank you for keeping her alive. I don't know what I would do without her."

What was the appropriate response to a comment like that? He couldn't say, "No big deal, man," because of course it had been a big deal. But "You're welcome" didn't seem right either. He went with a shrug.

They pulled two chairs close and caught up in whispers as Leigh slept on.

"Tell me everything," Kirk said.

Kirk already knew about the big events. Ryan understood what he really wanted to know was why Janine Liddle had targeted Leigh.

"Janine Liddle saw Leigh on the news when we found Harold

Claussen in the lake near the house," Ryan said. "She somehow got it in her head that Leigh had enough information to connect her to the murder."

"Did she?" Kirk asked.

"Theoretically, yes. But if Janine hadn't targeted her, Leigh wouldn't have ever put it together. If Janine had left town and started over, we never would have solved the case."

Kirk shook his head in disbelief. "What are the odds?"

"I know you don't want to hear this right now, but I know God used this to help us stop Janine. And she needed to be stopped. We have a computer forensics and cybersecurity professor from the university, Dr. Sabrina Fleming, who has already connected Janine to eight missing persons in three different states."

"Eight?" Kirk's eyes widened.

"And that's eight more than the five here in North Carolina that we know of. Janine was rambling a bunch of nonsense when she captured Leigh, and Sabrina is using it to try to follow her path from childhood to here. I have no idea how she's doing it. She starts talking about finding common IP addresses and then I can't follow it anymore. What I do know is that they're operating under the theory that there could be more murders in every city she's ever lived in."

Kirk ran his hands over his face. "How will you ever find all the bodies?"

"Honestly? We probably won't. But the information we pull together may be enough to help us narrow down some searches, maybe even give some closure to families whose loved ones disappeared one day."

They sat in silence for a while. The whir of the ventilation system provided the background music to their thoughts. Ryan watched Leigh sleep. Her chest rose and fell in a steady rhythm. Every now and then her hand twitched on the blanket. Was she dreaming?

Was it a nightmare?

How long would it be before she recovered? Not just physically, but mentally and emotionally?

He looked away and found Kirk staring at him.

"What aren't you telling me?" The way Kirk asked the question left no room for doubt. Ryan could tell Kirk was certain he was being kept in the dark about something.

"Did she do something horrible to Leigh? I mean more than you've already told me? You're keeping something from me, Ryan, and you've never done that before."

Well . . . that wasn't exactly true.

"She's fine," Ryan said in a hushed voice. "I mean, as fine as can be expected. I didn't leave anything out. The doctor said her wrists will have some scars, but they'll heal. She had some mild hypothermia, but she's warming up. The only reason she's asleep now is because they had to sedate her to clean her wrists. She was in a lot of pain."

Kirk didn't relax.

"Then what is it?"

"You know, you should have gone into law enforcement," Ryan said. "You'd have been great during interrogations."

Kirk leaned closer and crowded Ryan's personal space.

"I'm in no mood, Parker."

Ryan leaned away, arms raised in surrender. "Sorry."

Kirk quirked one eyebrow. "I'm waiting."

Here goes nothing. "I'm in love with Leigh."

Kirk pulled away so fast his back slammed into the chair. His eyes blinked a few times.

So Leigh hadn't told him.

"You're in love with my sister?" There was more than a hint of threat in the words.

"Yes."

"Are you going to try to explain yourself?"

"No. Love isn't something you explain, Kirk. When it's real, it's real. You of all people should know that."

Kirk ran his thumb across his wedding band. "I don't like it. She's off-limits. Always has been."

"She isn't a fifteen-year-old girl who needs protection from your friends," Ryan said. "In fact, maybe you need to quit seeing her as your little sister and start seeing her as who she is. A mature, intelligent, gifted woman who used everything in her arsenal to escape a serial killer this afternoon. I'm confident she will be more than capable of telling you off when she wakes up."

Kirk looked at Leigh, then back to him. "She knows?"

Heat crept up Ryan's neck. "I certainly hope so."

Kirk stood. "I should have known this would happen."

Ryan didn't respond as Kirk paced to the small window and stared outside.

"You haven't asked me for my approval," Kirk said.

"No, I haven't," Ryan said.

Kirk turned away from the window.

"Of course I want you to be happy for us, but the only approval I'm interested in is hers. And when you quit whining about your best friend falling in love with your sister, you'll realize you don't want her with a guy who cares more about your opinion than hers."

Kirk huffed.

"I realize this isn't what you were expecting to hear, but I have to be honest with you. I've cared about Leigh since before you told all of us to stay away from her."

Kirk rolled his eyes.

"Since she moved home, I've seen her at church and in the ED and around town, and every single time I've thought about what it would be like to get to know her better. To take her out for dinner or a twilight cruise on the boat."

"I do not want to hear about your dates with my sister." Kirk's lips twitched.

Ryan took advantage of Kirk's softened tone and grinned. "That won't be hard to manage since I still haven't taken her out on a real date, but now that we've put the danger behind us, I have a long list of things I cannot wait to share with her."

Kirk's face crinkled in disgust. "I guess I'll get used to it."

They both laughed, then Kirk grew serious again. "You do realize if you hurt her, it will destroy our friendship. I'll never forgive you."

Ryan felt the weight of Kirk's words. He understood the deep love Kirk held for both him and Leigh.

"I know. But I also know you don't have to worry about that. This is no casual fling, Kirk. I love her. With everything I am."

Leigh floated in and out of consciousness. Words filtered through the fog of pain medicine and fatigue.

Was that Kirk? Had he flown home?

Of course. They would have called him when she'd been abducted. And he would have jumped on a plane.

Was he talking to Ryan?

Ryan. Even in her fuzzy mental state, his voice sent tremors up her spine. She would never get over the fact that he loved her. Her muscles wouldn't cooperate right now with her desire to get lost in his eyes, to run her hand over his scruffy face, to pull his lips toward hers.

All she could manage was to listen.

The conversation was enlightening, infuriating, and ultimately exhilarating. She would strangle her big brother as soon as she finished hugging him. And then she would kick him out of her room so she could tell Ryan Parker exactly how she felt about him.

She had no idea how long it was before she managed to pry her eyes open. When she did, Ryan's face was the first thing she saw.

"Hey, beautiful." His smile could light up a room, but right now it was hers and hers alone.

"Hey." Her voice was still raspy, but her enforced silence had probably helped her vocal chords heal faster than they would have if she'd been her usual chatty self.

She reached for Ryan's shirt and pulled him toward her. His eyes registered surprise, then delight, then something else that sent shock waves through her. When his lips pressed against hers, she forgot where she was or why she was there. For this blissful moment, she was in heaven.

"Please don't make me watch this. I'm gonna be sick," Kirk said from somewhere behind Ryan.

They laughed and Ryan pulled back but didn't go far.

In his eyes she saw everything she had to live for.

The promise of a future where she loved and was loved well.

Where life was busy with hard, beautiful, meaningful work.

Where the days and nights would tumble after one another into a life that would make a difference, both in this world and the next.

"Oh, good grief. I can't take this," Kirk said. She heard the door open and then close seconds later.

"I didn't think he would ever leave," she said.

"He'll get used to it." Ryan brushed her cheek with his thumb. "He'll have to."

"You think?"

He pressed his lips to her forehead. Then her nose.

"I love you, Leigh."

"I love y—"

His lips claimed hers. Maybe someday she'd actually get the words all the way out.

Then again, maybe not . . .

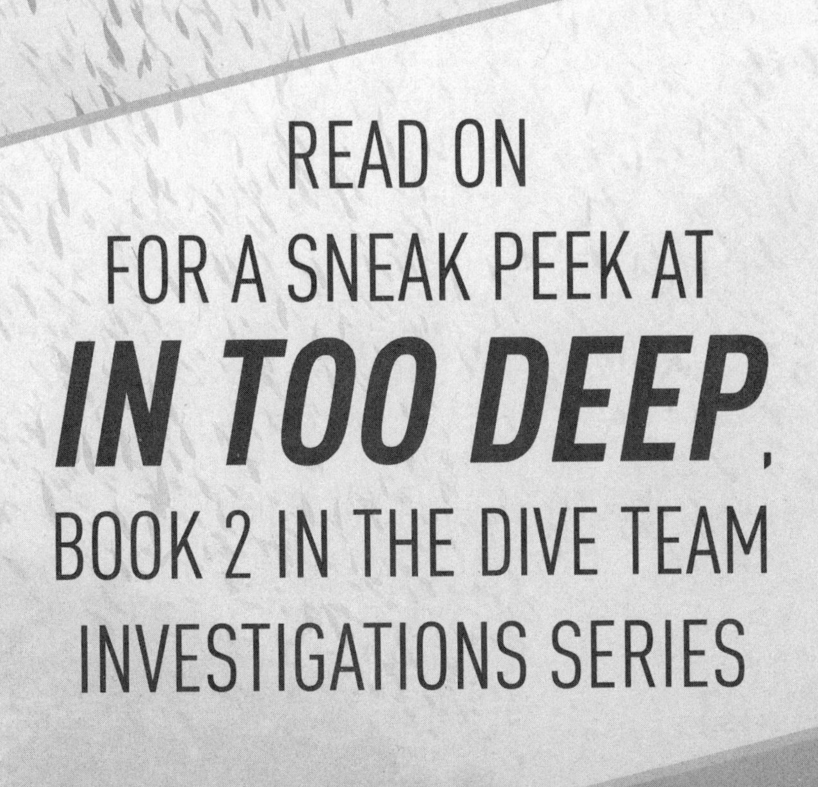

READ ON

FOR A SNEAK PEEK AT

***IN TOO DEEP*,**

BOOK 2 IN THE DIVE TEAM INVESTIGATIONS SERIES

1

The shrill ping of his cell phone earned white-collar crimes investigator Adam Campbell a vicious glare from his aunt Margaret. His cousins all dropped their gazes to their plates, several of them failing to suppress snickers, as Adam stood. He glanced around the table at the assembled family members, before focusing on the matriarch of the family. "Excuse me, Grandmother. Everyone. I'm on call."

Grandmother sniffed. "Very well."

Conversation resumed as Adam made his way around the perimeter of the oval dining room. He refused to look down or run like a frightened schoolboy. He maintained a measured pace and made eye contact with anyone who bothered to look in his direction. He had nothing to be ashamed of.

His parents were in Italy for the month, or his mother would have given him an encouraging smile. Oh well.

No one glared at his brother when he was on call. Grandmother never batted an eye when Alexander needed to miss Sunday lunch because he was in surgery. But heaven forbid Adam miss the monthly meal. Keeping the citizens of Carrington, North

Carolina, safe was a perfectly good job as far as Grandmother was concerned. But not for a Campbell.

Grandfather Campbell caught his eye.

And winked.

Adam didn't bother trying to hide his smile as he left the room. His grandfather was a rock. They met for breakfast at least once a week at the Pancake Hut and Adam regaled him with stories from the sheriff's office.

The restaurant was a favorite with the law enforcement and medical communities in Carrington, and Adam's standing breakfast date with his grandfather had gotten a lot of attention when he'd first joined the force.

The Pancake Hut wasn't the kind of place the Campbell family frequented.

As Charles Campbell made it a point to get to know Adam's coworkers by name, Adam's fellow officers soon realized that he might be worth several billion dollars, but he was no snob.

It was a poorly kept secret that Charles Campbell was in the habit of picking up the tab for every officer in the Pancake Hut whenever he was there—whether he was with Adam or not.

Grandmother wasn't exactly aware of that arrangement.

Before long, the other officers would come by Adam's desk and say, "Yo, Campbell. I've got one for your grandfather. He'll get a kick out of this." Or they'd stop by their booth and share something that had happened while they were on patrol.

Grandfather ate it up.

Over the last few years, Grandfather had managed to fund several scholarships for law enforcement officers, and he'd fallen completely under the spell of homicide investigator Anissa Bell, captain of the Carrington County Sheriff's Office dive team. All Anissa had to do was hint that she'd been eyeing some new piece of equipment for the team and Grandfather made it happen.

Grandmother wasn't exactly aware of that arrangement either.

Adam paused in the hallway and looked again at the text that had saved him from another hour of family politics.

Uh-oh. He walked briskly as he maneuvered his way through the library and music room, and then hit the marbled floor of the large foyer.

"Everything okay, Mr. Adam?" The concerned words from their longtime butler slowed his steps.

"Not really, Marcel. A car ran off the highway and over the embankment at the double bridges. Probably last night. A boater found the car this morning."

The double bridges spanned Lake Porter and connected the tourist side of the lake to the city of Carrington. The car would have gone several hundred yards over bumpy terrain before plunging into the water.

Failed brakes?

Road rage?

Suicide?

It had happened before.

"Oh no." Marcel shook his head in dismay as he handed Adam his coat. "You going to have to get in? It's cold."

"We have dry suits," Adam said. "We'll be okay."

"Be careful, sir." Marcel opened the door and Adam broke into a jog. "Thanks, Marcel. Hold the fort."

Marcel's low chuckle reached his ears as he slid behind the wheel and took the turns of the lengthy driveway at a speed that would have gotten him on Grandmother's bad list, if he hadn't already been there.

It took fifteen minutes to reach the double bridges. They had a formal name—after a local politician from the thirties—but no one used it.

He slowed as he approached the roadblock, then pulled in behind fellow dive team member and homicide investigator Gabe Chavez. Gabe climbed out first and met him at the door, giving a low whistle as he looked the Audi over. "When you gonna let me drive this baby?"

This was why he tried not to drive his personal vehicle to crime scenes, but sometimes he didn't have a choice. Grandmother had given him the car for his college graduation—even though he had told her he didn't need it—and she didn't approve of him arriving for Sunday lunch in the unmarked sedan he drove for work.

He held the keys out to Gabe. "Anytime."

Gabe eyed the keys, longing evident on his face. "One of these days I'm going to take you up on it."

Adam pulled his bag out of the back, locked the car, and pocketed the keys. He glanced at the line of cars on the side of the road. "Who else is here?"

"Ryan is hiking in the mountains with Leigh," Gabe said. Homicide investigator Ryan Parker was the second-in-command on the dive team. His girlfriend, Leigh Weston, had survived an attack by a serial killer last spring.

"Hiking? Or proposing?"

Gabe grinned. "I guess we'll find out when they get back. He got the text, but Anissa told him to disregard."

"You've talked to Anissa?" Gabe and Anissa hadn't gotten along well since she'd kicked him off the dive team a few years ago when his undercover work kept him from making it to training dives. But since he'd come back to homicide, and since two of their divers had left the team—one for medical reasons and another had retired—she'd been encouraged to allow him back. Their relationship remained strained, but since the serial killer case involving Leigh last spring, the tension between them had eased.

Slightly.

"Yeah. I talked to her. She bit my head off for being on the wrong side of town and told me to hurry up because she and Lane were already on scene."

"She didn't call me," Adam said.

Gabe smirked. "Man, it's the second Sunday of the month. We all knew where *you* were."

Adam bit back a retort. He loved his family. He really did. Some of them were awesome. Some of them weren't. Same as most families, he imagined. And a sight better than a lot of the families he'd seen while working in the uniformed division. Even Grandmother's disapproval, which irked him to no end, was part of her way of showing love.

At least Grandfather said it was. He said she worried about her grandson far more than her frosty demeanor indicated.

Gabe punched his arm. "Don't worry about it, man. This is an evidence recovery situation. Nothing we could have done for the victim even if we'd been sitting in the water waiting on the car."

"How do you know?"

"The guy who found her said she was dead in her seat belt. He was out here around lunchtime and saw the car. Dove in and pulled the body out. Probably destroyed a ton of evidence. His take on it was that her neck was broken."

Adam fought the image Gabe's words created. He was sorry for the victim. Horrified at the manner of death, regardless of whether it had been a dreadful accident or a successful suicide attempt. But he wasn't sorry he wouldn't have to be the one to pull her body from the water.

He scrambled down the incline to the waterline. There would be no need for any of their fancy sonar equipment on this case. He could see the car from the edge of the lake. Dive team captain and homicide investigator Anissa Bell and Officer Lane Edwards were in dry suits, checking tanks and gauges.

"'Bout time," Anissa said. "We're shorthanded. Chavez, sketch the scene. Campbell, get suited up for backup, but you're on topside evidence. Get the path of the car, etc. I want all of it documented before we pull the car out and contaminate the scene." Anissa pointed to a makeshift changing area—a couple of tarps tied up between a few trees. "And be quick. We're running out of daylight."

"Yes, ma'am," Adam said.

Gabe glared at Anissa for a second before grabbing a sketch pad and getting to work. "She thinks she's being mean, but I didn't want to get wet today anyway."

Adam didn't bother responding to Gabe's mutterings. Partly because he wasn't so sure Anissa had been trying to be mean. As far as he was concerned, she'd given the worst job to him. It took him ten minutes to change into the dry suit and prep everything he would need if Anissa or Lane required assistance.

He tried to ignore the shrouded body near the water's edge. They couldn't do anything about the evidence destroyed by the man who'd jumped in the lake and tried to save the victim. Even after he was sure she was dead, he'd gone down repeatedly until he freed her and pulled her body to the surface.

Adam focused on the work Anissa and Lane were doing in the water, prepping the car to be retrieved.

"Adam." Anissa's voice came through the earpiece he was wearing. "You might as well go ahead and call Sabrina."

Dr. Sabrina Fleming was a local professor of cybersecurity and computer forensics.

"What did you find?" Adam asked.

"A laptop."

The Carrington County Sheriff's Office had a wonderful forensics team and they did great work, but Sabrina had a lab filled with all the latest equipment, as well as everything that would be needed to attempt to pull any information from the waterlogged computer.

"I'll send her a text now." Adam retrieved his phone from his bag. He didn't need to look her up in his contacts. He had her number memorized.

She responded immediately.

"Anissa," Adam said, "she can come now. How long will it be before you bring it up?" Underwater criminal investigators never removed anything from the water. The laptop would need to be placed in a special box filled with lake water. Recovering anything from the hard drive was actually harder if it dried out improperly.

"Tell her to come on," Anissa said. "We'll have it ready."

Adam fought the grin that tried to cross his lips. This wasn't the time for it. Someone had died. But at least he'd get to see Sabrina this afternoon.

A shower of gravel drew his attention to the steep incline surrounding him. He gave Dr. Sharon Oliver, medical examiner, a nod as she inched her way down the embankment to the body. "Weren't you on call last weekend?" he asked her.

She let out a huff as she set her bag beside the body. "I was. And I will be on call for the next two weeks while Dr. Sherman enjoys his thirty-fifth anniversary by traipsing all over Europe."

Adam laughed. She sounded put out, but he knew she wasn't. "You're just jealous."

She flashed him a wicked grin. "You got that right."

"All right, honey," she said, addressing the victim. "Let's see what you can tell me and then let's get you away from prying eyes."

Gabe approached the body and snapped pictures as Dr. Oliver examined it. "I assume you're talking about our hovering friends." He glared at the heavens, where a news helicopter circled.

"Indeed," she said.

Adam studied the surface of the water, thankful he had an excuse to look away from the body.

"Um, Campbell?"

Adam tried to ignore Gabe, but he didn't want to be unprofessional. "What?" He didn't turn.

"You may want to see this."

Jerk. Gabe knew how he felt about dead bodies. "I'm watching Anissa and—"

"Adam." Gabe's tone was . . . off. What was going on?

He kept his eyes on the water but backed toward the body. "What is it?"

Gabe clapped a hand on his back. "I'll watch the water. You need to talk to the doc."

"Wha—"

Gabe nodded his head toward the body.

Adam made eye contact with the doctor. She pointed to the victim. Why were they so insistent that he look at a dead body?

Fine.

Lord, help me.

He glanced at the victim.

Then stared.

There, written in permanent marker on the victim's abdomen, were six words.

They killed me. Ask Adam Campbell.

Lynn H. Blackburn is the author of *Hidden Legacy* (Love Inspired, June 2017) and *Covert Justice*, winner of the 2016 Selah Award for Mystery and Suspense and the 2016 Carol Award for Short Novel. Blackburn believes in the power of stories, especially those that remind us that true love exists, a gift from the Truest Love. She's passionate about CrossFit, coffee, and chocolate (don't make her choose), as well as experimenting with recipes that feed both body and soul. She lives in Simpsonville, South Carolina, with her true love, Brian, and their three children.

MEET LYNN

WWW.LYNNHBLACKBURN.COM